High Time to Kill

Ian Fleming's JAMES BOND 007 in

HIGH TIME TO KILL

Raymond Benson

Thorndike Press • Chivers Press
Thorndike, Maine USA   Bath, England

This Large Print edition is published by Thorndike Press, USA and by Chivers Press, England.

Published in 2000 in the U.S. by arrangement with G. P. Putnam's Sons, a member of Penguin Putnam Inc.

Published in 2000 in the U.K. by arrangement with HarperCollins Publishers Ltd.

U.S. Hardcover 0-7862-2338-3 (Basic Series Edition)
U.K. Hardcover 0-7540-1389-8 (Windsor Large Print)
U.K. Softcover 0-7540-2293-5 (Paragon Large Print)

KENT
ARTS & LIBRARIES

The text of this Large Print edition is unabridged.
Other aspects of the book may vary from the original edition.

C040302 395

Set in 16 pt. Plantin.

Printed in the United States on permanent paper.

British Library Cataloguing in Publication Data available

Library of Congress Cataloging-in-Publication Data

Benson, Raymond, 1955–
    High time to kill / Raymond Benson.
        p.   cm.
    ISBN 0-7862-2338-3 (lg. print : hc : alk. paper)
    1. Bond, James (Fictitious character) — Fiction.
2. Secret service — Great Britain — Fiction.   3. Himalaya
Mountains — Fiction.   4. Large type books.   I. Title: Ian
Fleming's James Bond 007 in High time to kill.   II. Title.
PS3552.E547666 H54 2000
    813'.54—dc21   99-055205

For My Mentors

Francis Hodge
and
Peter Janson-Smith

ACKNOWLEDGMENTS

The author and publishers wish to thank the following individuals and organizations for their assistance in preparing this book:

Belgian Tourist Office (U.S.) —
  Liliane Opsomer
Carolyn Caughey
Tom Colgan
Dan Harvey
Hospital Erasme (Brussels) —
  Mrs. Laurence Taca
Captain Alexander Howard
Hôtel Métropole (Brussels) —
  Serge Schultz and Chafik Habib
Hotel Yak and Yeti (Kathmandu) —
  Richard Launay
Jaguar Cars (U.K.) — Fergus Pollock
Peter Janson-Smith
L'Alban Chambon restaurant (Brussels) — Dominique Michou
Madeline Neems
Roger Nowicke
Lucy Oliver
Louisa Parkinson

Police de Bruxelles (Brussels) —
   Lucien Vermeir
Doug Redenius
Dave Reinhardt
Moana Re Robertson
Dr. Patrick Sepulchre
Spymaster Inc. (U.K.) — Lee Marks
Stoke Poges Golf Club (U.K.) —
   Chester King, Ralph Pickering, and
   Nolan Edwards
Sulzer Intermedics Inc. (U.S.) —
   Julia Hsi Morris
Tor Imports (U.K.) — Mark Acton
Tourist Information Brussels —
   An Depraedere
Corinne B. Turner
Elaine Wiltshire
The heirs of Ian Lancaster Fleming
and, of course, Randi and Max, without
   whom, etc.

A special thank-you to the 1st Royal Gurkha Rifles for their invaluable assistance, and to Scott McKee, the first American to summit Kangchenjunga via the northface.

The Ian Fleming Foundation can be reached at P.O. Box 1850, Burbank, California 91507, or at the Web site Mr. Kiss Kiss Bang Bang at www.ianfleming.org

CONTENTS

ONE

Holidays Are Hell

The barracuda surprised them by opening its jaws to an angle of ninety degrees, revealing the sharp rows of teeth that were capable of tearing out chunks of flesh in an instant. It closed its snarling mouth just as quickly, leaving a half-inch gap.

Had it *yawned?*

It was easily a twenty-pound fish. One of the most dangerous predators in the sea, the barracuda is an eating machine that rivals the ferocity of a shark. This one swam lazily along beside them, watching. It was curious about the two strange larger fish that had invaded its habitat.

James Bond had never cared for barracudas. He'd rather be in a pit full of snakes than in proximity to one of them. It wasn't that he was afraid of them but merely that he found them mean, vicious, and unpredictable creatures. There was no such thing as a barracuda in a good mood. He had to be on his guard without showing fear, for the fish could sense apprehension and often acted on it.

Bond looked over at his companion. She was handling it well, watching the long, slender fish with fascination rather than trepidation.

He motioned for her to swim on, and she nodded. They decided to ignore the barracuda, which proved to be the best tactic. It lost interest after a few minutes and swam away into the misty blue.

Bond had always likened the undersea world to an alien landscape. It was silent and surreal, yet it was full of life. Some sea flowers shot down holes in the seabed as the two humans moved over them. A small octopus, or "pus-feller" (as Ramsey, his Jamaican housekeeper, called it), was propelling itself along the orange-and-brown-colored reef. Patches of sea grass hid the domains of the night-crawling lobsters and crabs.

They swam toward the beach, eventually reaching a spot where they could stand. Bond pulled off the face mask and snorkel. Helena Marksbury emerged from the water and stood beside him. She removed her own mask and snorkel and laughed.

"I do believe that fish wanted to take part of us home as a souvenir," she said.

"It wasn't interested in me," Bond said. "It was staring at you. Do you usually have that kind of effect on barracuda?"

"I attract all the meat eaters, James," she said with an inviting smile.

March in the Bahamas was quite pleasant at eighty degrees Fahrenheit. The hot summer was just around the corner, and Bond had decided to take a week's leave before then. It was the perfect time of year to be in the Caribbean. He had originally planned to spend the holiday at Shamelady, his private home on the north shore of Jamaica, but changed his mind when Helena Marksbury said that she had never been to Nassau. Bond offered to show her the islands.

"Where did everyone go?" she asked, looking around at the empty beach. Earlier, there had been a few other snorkelers and sunbathers in the area. Now it was deserted.

It was just after noon. Helena looked around for some shade and sat in the sand next to a large rock that provided some shelter from the fiercely bright sun. She knew she had to be careful not to get too much of it, as she had a light complexion and burned easily. Nevertheless, she had worn the skimpiest bikini she could find.

She was most likely the only person who might notice a flaw — that her left breast drooped slightly lower than her right — but Helena knew that she had a good body, and didn't mind showing it off. It just proved that nobody was perfect.

They were on the southwest side of New Providence Island, the most populous of all the Bahamas. Luckily, Bond had found a villa at Coral Harbour, somewhat removed from the hustle and bustle of metropolitan Nassau, which is the center of commerce, government, and transportation, on the northern side of the island. Here they were surrounded by beautiful beaches and reefs, country clubs and exclusive restaurants.

"What am I supposed to wear tonight?" she asked him as he sat down beside her in the sand.

"Helena, I shouldn't have to tell you how to dress," he said. "You look marvelous in anything."

They had a dinner invitation at the home of the former Governor of the Bahamas, a man Bond had known for many years. They had become friends after a dinner party at which the Governor had presented Bond with a theory concerning love, betrayal, and cruelty between marriage partners. Calling it the "quantum of solace," the Governor believed that the amount of comfort on which love and friendship is based could be measured. Unless there is a certain degree of humanity existing between two people, he maintained, there can be no love. It was an adage Bond had accepted as a universal truth.

The Governor had long since retired but had remained in Nassau with his wife. Bond had made it a point to stop in and see him every time he went through the Bahamas, which wasn't very often. When Bond went to the Caribbean, it was usually to his beloved Shamelady in Jamaica.

Helena reclined and looked at Bond with her bewitching, almond-shaped green eyes. She was beautiful — wet or dry — and could easily have been a fashion model. Unfortunately, she was Bond's personal assistant at SIS, where they both worked. So far they had kept their affair a secret. They both knew that if they carried on much longer, someone at the office would find out. Not that there was anything particularly wrong with it, but office romances in this day and age were frowned upon. Bond justified it to himself because there had been a precedent. Several years ago he had been romantically involved with another personal assistant, Mary Goodnight. How could he forget their time together in Jamaica during the Scaramanga case?

Helena was different from Mary Goodnight. A thoroughly modern woman of thirty-three, Helena Marksbury had none of Ms. Goodnight's charming yet scatter-brained personality. She was a serious girl, with weighty ideas about politics and current events. She loved poetry, Shakespeare, and fine food and drink. She appreciated and understood the work Bond did and considered her own job just as important in the scheme of things at SIS. She also possessed a stubborn moral conscience that had taken Bond several months to penetrate before she agreed to see him socially.

It had begun in the courtyard in the back of Sir Miles Messervy's house, Quarterdeck, near Great Windsor Park. The occasion was a dinner party held there a year earlier, and the mutual physical attraction between Bond and Helena had become too much for them to ignore. They had gone for a walk outside and ended up kissing behind the house in the rain. Now, after three months of false starts and two months of cautious experimentation, Bond and Helena were dating. While they both acknowledged that their jobs came first, they enjoyed each other's company enough to keep it going casually. Bond felt comfortable with Helena's level of commitment, and the sex was outstanding. He saw no reason to rock the boat.

There was no mistaking the invitation in her eyes, so Bond settled next to her wet body and kissed her. She wrapped one slinky leg around his thighs and pulled him closer.

"Do you think we're all alone?" she whispered.

"I hope so," he replied, "but I don't really care at this point, do you?" He slipped the straps off her shoulders as she tugged at his bathing trunks.

"Not at all, darling," she said breathlessly. She helped him remove her bikini, and then his strong, knowing hands were all over her. She arched her back and responded with soft moans of pleasure.

"Take me now, James," she said softly in his ear. "Here."

She didn't have to ask him twice.

The Governor greeted Bond with an enthusiastic warm, dry handshake.

"It's great to see you again, James," he said.

"Thank you, sir, you're looking well."

The Governor shook his head. "Lord, I'm an old man, and I look like one. But you haven't changed a bit. What do you do, take frequent trips to the Fountain of Youth? And who might this lovely lady be?"

"This is my assistant, Helena Marksbury," Bond said. She was dressed in a fashionable lightweight red cotton dress with a wrap covering her bare shoulders and ample cleavage. Bond was wearing a light blue cotton short-sleeve polo shirt and navy blue cotton twill trousers. His light, gray silk basketweave jacket covered the Walther PPK that he still kept in a chamois shoulder holster.

"Do you remember my wife, Marion?" the Governor asked, gesturing to a handsome woman with white hair and sparkling blue eyes.

"Of course, how are you?"

"Fine, James," the woman said. "Come on in, both of you, please."

The dinner party was in a century-old colonial-style mansion off Thompson Boulevard, near the College of the Bahamas. The former Governor was obviously wealthy, as there seemed to be no end to the line of servants waiting to attend to

Bond and his date. More than two dozen guests were already in the drawing room, which was next to a large living room with an open bay window overlooking expansive gardens. There were people outside as well, standing in clusters with drinks in hand. Ceiling fans leisurely provided a breeze.

For the first time since he had been visiting the Governor, Bond also noticed an undeniable presence of security. Large men dressed in white sport coats were positioned at various entrances, suspiciously eyeing everyone who walked past. He wondered if there was perhaps some VIP present who would require such protection.

As they were uncomfortable socializing with people they didn't know, Bond and Helena kept to themselves and went outside to the gardens. It was still bright, and night wouldn't fall for another two hours.

They approached the outdoor bar. "Vodka martini, please," Bond said, "shaken, not stirred, with a twist of lemon."

"I'll have the same," Helena said. She had actually grown to like the way Bond ordered his martini.

"This is lovely," Helena said.

"It's lovely as long as we're alone," Bond

replied. "I don't relish making small talk with the Mr. and Mrs. Harvey Millers of the world," he said, indicating the other people milling around.

"Who are Mr. and Mrs. Harvey Miller?"

"Just a couple I met at a previous dinner party here."

"Ah, there you are," the Governor declared. "I see you've got yourselves something to drink, good, good. . . . How's Sir Miles doing, by the way?" He was referring to Bond's old chief, the former M, Sir Miles Messervy.

"He's fine," Bond was happy to report. "His health improved rapidly after he retired. Getting out of the job was the best thing for him really. He seems ten years younger."

"That's good to hear. Tell him hello for me the next time you see him, would you?"

"Certainly."

"How do you get on with the new M?" the Governor asked with a twinkle in his eye.

"We have a sterling relationship," Bond said.

"No problems accepting orders from a woman? I'm surprised, James! You're the one who once told me that you could marry only an air hostess or a Japanese woman."

Bond grinned wryly at the memory. "She runs a tight ship and runs it well."

"Well, that's great! I'm glad to hear it," the Governor said with a little too much enthusiasm. Bond thought he might be a bit drunk. "Listen, I'm so glad you came, really, James, because I want to —"

The Governor's attention was distracted by the head servant, a black man with gray hair and glasses, whispering to one of the security guards some fifteen feet away. The guard, a Caucasian who might have been a professional wrestler, nodded and left the scene.

"Everything all right, Albert?" the Governor called.

"Yessuh," Albert said. "I sent Frank to take a look at someone's motor scooter parked outside the fence."

"Ahhh," the Governor said. For a moment Bond thought he appeared nervous and perhaps a little frightened.

Bond asked, "You were saying?"

"Right. I was saying there was something I'd like you to take a look at. Privately. In my office. Would you mind?"

Bond looked at Helena. She shrugged. "I'm fine," she said, eyeing a large tray of peeled shrimp. "Go ahead. I'll be somewhere around here."

Bond squeezed her arm and then followed the Governor back into the house. They went up an elegant winding staircase to the second floor and into the Governor's study. Once they were inside, the Governor closed the door.

"You're being very mysterious," Bond said. "I'm intrigued."

The Governor moved around his desk and unlocked a drawer. "I think I'm in a bit of trouble, James," he said. "And I'd like your advice."

The man was genuinely concerned. The levity in Bond's voice immediately vanished. "Of course," he said.

"Ever heard of these people?" his friend asked, handing over a letter in a transparent plastic sleeve.

Bond looked at the piece of paper. It was an 8½-by-11-inch piece of typing paper with the words "Time Is Up" centered in the middle of the page. At the bottom it was signed "The Union."

Bond nodded. "The Union. Interesting. Yes, we know about the Union."

"Can you tell me about them?" the Governor asked. "I haven't gone to the local police here, but I've already sent a query to

London. I haven't heard anything yet."

"Is this message, 'time is up,' meant for you?" Bond asked.

The Governor nodded. "I'm heavily in debt to a man in Spain. It was a real estate transaction that wasn't particularly . . . honest, I'm sorry to say. Anyway, I received one letter from this Union, or whatever they are, two months ago. In that one it said that I had two months to pay up. I don't want to do that because the man in Spain is a crook. I got this letter four days ago. Who are they, James? Are they some kind of Mafia?"

"They're not unlike the Mafia, but they are much more international. SIS only recently became aware of their activities. What we do know is that they are a group of serious mercenaries out for hire by any individual or government that will employ them."

"How long have they been around?"

"Not long. Three years, maybe."

"I've never heard of them. Are they really dangerous?"

Bond handed the letter back to the Governor. "As a work-for-hire outfit, they have to be experts at anything from petty street crime to sophisticated and elaborate espionage schemes. They are reportedly responsible for the theft of military maps from the Pentagon in the United States. The maps disappeared from right under the noses of highly trained security personnel. A well-protected Mafia don was murdered about a year ago in Sicily. The Union supposedly supplied the hit man for that job. They recently blackmailed a French politician for fifty million francs. The Deuxième got wind of it and passed the information on to us. One of the most recent reports that went through my office stated that the Union were beginning to specialize in military espionage and selling the fruits of their findings to other nations. Apparently they have no loyalty to any one nation. Their primary motive is greed, and they can be quite ruthless. If that letter was meant for you, then, yes, I would have to say that they are indeed quite dangerous."

The Governor sat. He looked worried. "But who's behind them? Where are they based?"

"We don't know," Bond said. "Despite all the intelligence we've gathered on them thus far, SIS have no clues as to who they are or where they make their home."

The Governor swallowed. "What should I do?"

"I can see you already have extra protection around the house. That's good for a start."

The Governor nodded. "There are so many guards around here, I can't keep track of them all."

"I'll alert Interpol and see if the letters can be traced. It's a difficult thing, though. Tomorrow I'll make a report to London and see what we can do about surveillance. It's highly likely that you're being watched. Your phones may even be tapped."

"Good Lord."

"The local police know nothing about this?"

"No."

"I wouldn't involve them just yet. The Union have an uncanny ability to infiltrate law enforcement organizations. Tomorrow let's go to Government House and file an official report. I'm glad you told me about this. We have orders to gather as much information about the Union as we can."

"Thank you, James. I knew I could count on you." He stood up, but the blood had drained from his face. He was clearly frightened. "I think we should rejoin the party."

"Try not to worry," Bond said.

They left the study and went back outside. Helena was sitting on a stone bench alone, gazing across the gardens at the house. She gave Bond a warm smile.

"Working, James? I thought we were on holiday," she said when he joined her.

"We are. Just giving a little professional advice," he said.

"Really, James, a *Japanese woman* or a *flight hostess?*"

Bond laughed. "Don't believe everything you hear."

Dinner was a magnificent feast consisting of traditional conch chowder, peas 'n' rice, Bahamian lobster, Dover sole fillets simmered in white wine, cream, and mustard sauce and topped with shrimp, and pineapple spring rolls with rum crème anglaise for dessert. Helena was in heaven and Bond enjoyed watching her eat. She savored each bite, squeezing out the juices with her cheeks and tongue before chewing and swallowing. She had one of the most sensual mouths Bond had ever kissed.

Afterward they retired to the gardens to enjoy the star-filled night sky along with several other couples. Some of the men were smoking the cigars that one of the servants had passed around. To get away from the crowd, Bond and Helena walked along a dimly lit path that circled the garden and ran around the perimeter of the grounds.

Helena sighed heavily and said, "I don't want to go back to London."

"All good things come to an end," Bond replied.

"Does that mean us, James?"

"Of course not," he said, "unless you would prefer that. I don't want to lose the best assistant I've ever had."

"Do you mean that?"

"Look, Helena, you're a wonderful girl, but you should know me by now. Entanglements can get messy, and I don't like them. I think while we're in London we need to tone it down. Being the sensible girl you are, I know that you'll agree."

They found themselves at the far end of the expansive lawn, some fifty yards from the house. A ten-foot-high stone fence separated the grounds from the street. They stood beside a toolshed and held each other.

"You're right, James," she said. "It's just that sometimes I dream of a different sort of life. One that borders on the edge of fantasy. My sister in America seems to live a fairy tale existence. She has a husband who adores her and two lovely children, and they live in an area of southern California where the weather is always perfect. She's always so incredibly happy when I speak to her that I get a little jealous." She smiled and took his arm. "But you're right, James. Let's not get morose. I want to enjoy every last minute of our time here."

He pulled her chin toward him so that he could kiss her, but her eyes widened and she gasped. "James!"

Bond whipped around to see what had startled her. A body was lying just off the path. The shadows would have completely hidden it had it not been for the moonlight reflecting off pale skin. Bond moved quickly to the corpse and saw that it was Frank, the security guard. He had been stripped of his shirt and white jacket; his throat had been cut, ear to ear. He was lying in a pool of fresh blood.

"Wait here!" he commanded. He turned and sprinted across the lawn toward the house. He heard her call behind him, "James! I'm coming with you!" as he took a shortcut over a set of stone benches surrounding a stone fountain. He ran through the gardens toward the back of the house, searching frantically for the Governor. He found the man's wife beside some guests.

"Where's your husband?" Bond asked.

Startled, the woman replied, "Why . . . I

believe I saw him go upstairs to the office with one of those security men."

Bond left abruptly, entered the house, bolted up the stairs three at a time, and ran to the open doorway. The former Governor was lying on the floor in a ghastly pool of red. Like the guard, his throat had been slit so fiercely that his head lopped at a grotesque angle. There was no one else in the room, but two distinct footprints in blood led from the body toward the door to another bloody patch on the carpet. The killer had wiped his shoes clean before leaving the office.

Others had made their way up the stairs by this time. Bond was unable to stop the Governor's wife from glimpsing the horrid sight. She screamed loudly just as Bond pulled her away and slammed the door shut. He told one of the men to call the police and look after her, then he rushed down to the first floor. The bewildered head servant was at the foot of the stairs.

"Did you see a guard come down the stairs?" he barked.

"Yessuh!" Albert said. "He went through the kitchen."

"Would that lead to the motor scooter you saw earlier?"

Albert nodded furiously. He ushered

Bond into the kitchen, where several servants were cleaning up after the huge meal. He then led him into a corridor and pointed to a door at the end.

"That's the servants' entrance," he said. "Go out of the gate and turn left. It was just down the street a bit."

"Tell the girl I came with to wait for me," Bond said as he went outside.

He found himself in a small parking area reserved for the servants. He ran to the open gate and peered carefully around to look at the street. Sure enough, a black man dressed in a guard's white jacket was on an old Vespa motor scooter. He was just beginning to pull away.

"Stop!" Bond shouted. The man looked back at Bond before accelerating down the street. Bond drew his Walther PPK and fired at him but missed. His last chance was to give chase on foot.

The man was a quarter-mile ahead of him. He had turned onto Thompson Boulevard and was headed north through busy traffic. Bond ran into the street in front of a bus traveling in the same direction. The bus driver slammed on his brakes, throwing several passengers to the floor. The bus still hit Bond hard enough to knock him to the pavement, stunning him slightly. He got up quickly, shook his body, and continued the pursuit.

The Vespa crossed Meadow Street and zipped into the entrance of St. Bernard's Park, circling around St. Joseph's Baptist Church. Bond jumped on the hood of a BMW and scrambled over it just in time to see the assassin slam into a street vendor's kiosk that had been set up at the corner of the park. T-shirts and souvenirs went flying, and the angry proprietor shouted and shook his fist at the driver. The scooter then disappeared into the park.

It was darker off the main road. Bond kept running, panting heavily. Should he risk firing a shot? He could just see the taillight of the scooter some thirty feet ahead. He didn't want to kill the man. If he had ties to the Union, it was imperative that he be taken alive. The Vespa rounded a turn and was traveling on relatively straight pavement. It could easily speed away if he didn't stop it now. Carefully aiming the handgun at the scooter's taillight, he fired once.

The bullet hit the back tire, sending the scooter skidding across the pavement on its side. The killer landed hard, but immediately got up and started to run with a limp. Bond pursued him across the lawn.

The assassin was holding his leg as he ran — he wouldn't go far.

He did, however, make it to the western edge of the park and ran across the road and into a residential street. Bond followed him, almost collided with a taxi, spun around, and fell. Not wasting a second, he leaped to his feet and continued the chase. He could see the killer hobbling along about thirty feet ahead.

"Stop!" Bond shouted again.

The man turned. Bond could see him holding something in his hand. A flash of light and the unmistakable sound of a shot forced Bond to roll to the ground. His hope of taking the armed man alive had diminished greatly.

When he got to his feet, Bond saw that his prey had disappeared. There were a couple of alleys, either of which he could have run into. Bond sprinted to the corner and peered down one of them. Sure enough, he heard the sound of running feet. Bond hugged the wall and crept quickly toward the noise. He could see the man at the end of the alley, trapped in a dead end. Bond took cover behind some rubbish barrels.

"Give up!" Bond shouted. "You're caught. Throw down your gun."

The man turned and looked toward the voice. His eyes were wide. He fired blindly, unable to see his target. The bullet ricocheted off the alley wall.

It was now clear to Bond what had happened. The assassin had jumped the fence, killed the guard Frank, and taken his shirt and jacket. Impersonating a security man, he then persuaded the Governor to follow him inside the house. The Governor certainly wouldn't have known all the security guards by sight.

"I'm counting to three," Bond shouted. "Throw down your gun and raise your hands. I have a clear shot at your head. I assure you that I'll blow a hole in it."

The man pointed his gun in the direction of the voice. From Bond's distance it appeared to be a revolver of some kind. Another shot went off, this time piercing the garbage can next to him.

"One . . ."

The man hesitated, not sure what to do. He knew he couldn't escape.

"Two . . ."

Then the killer did a curious thing — he smiled. There was only one thing to do that made sense to him.

"You won't take *me* alive, man," the man said in a heavy West Indian accent. Then he pointed the gun at his temple.

"No!" Bond shouted. "Don't —"

The man pulled the trigger. The noise reverberated like a thunderclap in the close confines of the alley.

TWO

Old Rivals

"The trick is not in the amount of force you use when you hit the ball, Mr. Bond, but in the *negative* force," said Nolan Edwards, the starter at Stoke Poges Golf Club.

"Well then, it's perfectly clear," Bond replied with sarcasm. The ball he had just knocked ninety yards onto the putting green overshot the hole and continued to roll into the rough.

He was frustrated by his lack of progress in mastering a difficult shot. It was called "backing the ball on the green." Pro golfers perform it successfully most of the time; formidable amateurs such as Bond found the shot elusive. He was determined to get it right, for he had always played golf with the attitude that one should incorporate new techniques and strategies to keep the game alive. This particular shot would be useful should he ever need to hit the ball into a tough pin placement. If he overshot the hole, it would roll off the green (as he had just so aptly demonstrated). However, if he could successfully put a backspin on the ball, it would roll *back* toward the hole and be in a perfect position for him to sink the putt.

Bond had been on the practice green in front of the club for half an hour. He hadn't got it right once.

Edwards, an American from Illinois and longtime Stoke Poges employee, shook his head and wrinkled his brow. "It's a tough one, Mr. Bond. I've seen very few amateurs do it. To spin the ball with some kind of accuracy, what you need to do is combine swing speed, impact position, hand action, and acceleration into one smooth swing."

"What I need is a stiff drink," Bond said, picking up his wound three-piece Titleist ball and pocketing it.

"Any sign of Bill?" he asked.

"I believe that's his Alfa now," Edwards said, nodding in the direction of the starter shed, where Bill Tanner, the Chief of Staff at SIS, had just parked his red Alfa Romeo.

"Hello, James," he said, getting out of the car and opening the trunk. "How are you, Edwards?"

"Fine, Mr. Tanner," the starter said.

Tanner pulled out the clubs and handed them to Edwards. "Mr. Bond was just practicing a very difficult shot."

"You still trying to put a backspin on the ball, James?"

Bond nodded, unsnapping the glove from his left hand. "I'm close, Bill. Damn close."

Tanner chuckled. "You're taking this *much* too seriously, James. Come on, let's go and get a drink. The others will be here soon."

Bond left his bag of Callaway clubs with Edwards and walked with Tanner to the front of the clubhouse, an impressive grade-one Palladian mansion. He had joined the club in 1993. The dues were sizable, but the splendid public and private rooms of the clubhouse, the elegant dining room and fine cuisine, the attentive staff, and the golf course itself made membership a cherished luxury. Founded in 1908, the Stoke Poges Golf Club is one of the finest in England. Located in Buckinghamshire in the south of England near Eton and Windsor, the thousand-year history of the estate is just as colorful as its surroundings. Decades of established traditions complement the clubhouse, its ancient gardens and parkland, and its world-famous course created by Harry Shapland Colt.

Bond and Tanner entered the lobby and walked past the grand staircase, which, at the time it was built, was the largest cantilever staircase in the UK. They went through the bright and cheery Orangery and into the more subdued President's Bar. Bond preferred the bar, as it was a room that was both elegant and masculine. There was a yellow marble fireplace, a well-stocked oak bar, and comfortable furniture with cream-colored upholstery. Trophies and wood plaques adorned the yellow walls, proclaiming the names of past captains and other vital historical facts about the park.

Bond ordered a bourbon and Tanner asked for a Black Label whisky. Tanner looked at his watch. It was still early in the day. "They should be here soon. Do you think it will rain?"

English weather in April is unpredictable. So far, the sun had managed to skirt around the hovering dark clouds.

"Probably on the back nine," Bond prophesied. "It never fails."

Bond had been home for two weeks. The Governor's murder had spoiled what had begun as a delightful holiday in the Bahamas with Helena. Now that they were back at the job, their relationship was a masquerade. They tried to put the romance behind them and, as much as possible, pretend that it never occurred. So far it wasn't working. The situation was further complicated by the fact that their affair had been a secret before the incidents in Nassau, but now a number of people at SIS knew that he had been there with his personal assistant. Bond could feel Helena's tension when he was at the office, so he made excuses to leave or work at home. He was extremely grateful when Tanner had suggested that he take Thursday off and play a round of golf with two other SIS civil servants.

"How is your research on the Union coming?" Tanner asked.

"Must we talk shop?" Bond snapped.

"Sorry," Tanner said. "You really do want to master that shot!"

"No, I'm sorry, Bill," Bond said. "I've been on edge lately. That business with the Governor in Nassau, and the killer who blew his own brains out . . . it's all a big mystery that I'm still trying to sort out."

"Never mind, James, it's all right." He tapped his glass against Bond's. "Cheers." Tanner knew damn well what was really on Bond's mind, but he had the tact not to mention it.

Two men entered the bar. Bond glanced up and grimaced. The taller of the men spotted Bond and Tanner and waved.

"Well, well!" he said. "If it isn't James Bond and Billy Tanner!"

"Roland Marquis," Bond said with feigned enthusiasm. "Long time."

Group Captain Roland Marquis was blond, broad-shouldered, and very handsome. A neatly trimmed blond mustache covered his upper lip. His eyes were a cold blue. He had the kind of weather-beaten face that suggested years of outdoor activity, and the square jaw of a matinee idol. He was the same age as Bond and just as fit.

He held out his hand as he approached their table. Marquis squeezed Bond's hand roughly, reminding 007 of their lifelong rivalry.

"How are you, Bond?" Marquis asked.

"Fine. Keeping busy."

"Really? I would have thought there's not a lot to do over at SIS these days, eh?" Marquis sniffed.

"We have plenty to do," Bond said with little humor. "Mostly cleaning up messes left by others. How about you? The RAF still treating you better than you deserve?"

Marquis laughed. "The RAF treats *me* like a bloody king."

The other man stepped up to the table. A man in his late thirties, he was smaller in stature, thin, and had glasses, a long nose, and bushy eyebrows, all of which gave him a birdlike appearance.

"This is my partner, Dr. Steven Harding," Marquis said. "He's with the Defence Evaluation and Research Agency. Dr. Harding, I present you James Bond and Bill Tanner. They work for the Ministry of Defence, in that gaudy building next to the Thames."

"SIS? Really? How do you do!" Harding held out his hand. Both men shook hands with him.

"Join us for a drink?" Tanner asked. "We're just waiting for our friends to make up the fourball."

Marquis and Harding pulled up chairs. "Bill, I haven't met your new chief," Marquis said. "What's she like?"

"She runs a very tight ship," Tanner replied. "Things are not that different since Sir Miles retired. What about you? I think the last time we spoke you were working at Oakhanger?"

"I've moved," Marquis said. "They've got me liaising with the DERA now. Dr.

Harding here is one of their top engineers in the aeronautics division. Almost everything he does is classified."

"Well, you can tell *us*. We won't say a word," Bond said.

"You'll hear about it soon enough, I should think. Won't they, doctor?"

Harding was in the middle of taking a sip from a gin and tonic. "Hmmm? Oh, quite right. I must be sure to phone Tom after we play the front nine. We're almost there."

"Almost where? Marquis, what are you up to that you haven't told us?" Tanner asked.

"Actually we have told you," Marquis said with a broad grin. "Your chief knows all about it. Ever heard of Thomas Wood?"

"Sure," Bond said. "He's Britain's top aeronautics physicist."

At the mention of Wood's name, Tanner nodded his head. "You're right, I do know all about it, Marquis. I just didn't know that you were involved."

"It's my pet project, Tanner," he said smugly.

"Dr. Wood is my boss," Harding said.

Bond was impressed. To be working with a man of Wood's stature would require a considerable amount of gray matter. Harding must be smarter than he looked. In contrast, Bond had never thought much of Roland Marquis's brain or any other part of him. His great-grandfather, a Frenchman, had married into a wealthy English military family. The Marquis name was passed down from son to son, every one of them becoming a distinguished and decorated officer. Roland Marquis inherited his family's snobbishness and was, in Bond's estimation, an egotistical overachiever.

Ralph Pickering, the club's general manager, looked in the bar and spotted Bond. "Ah, there you are, Mr. Bond," he said. He stepped over to them and gave Bond and Tanner a message that their other two partners would not be joining them. "They said they had to go away on business unexpectedly and that you would understand. They send their apologies," he said.

"Thank you, Ralph," Bond said. He wasn't as annoyed with them for not showing up as he was with the fact that they had received orders and had probably left the country. Even after two weeks Bond was restless. He was ready to do anything to get out of London and away from Helena for a while.

After Pickering left the room, Bond looked at Tanner and asked, "What do you want to do now? Play by ourselves?"

"Why not play with us?" Marquis asked. "I'm sure we could make it interesting. Dr. Harding and I against the two of you? Straight Stableford level handicaps?"

Bond looked at Tanner. Tanner nodded in approval.

"I assume you're talking money?" Bond asked.

"You'd better believe it. How about two hundred and fifty pounds per man for every point by which the winners beat the losers?" Marquis suggested with a sly grin.

Tanner's eyes widened. That could be a lot of money. He didn't like gambling.

Nevertheless, the glove had been thrown. Bond took challenges *very* seriously and couldn't resist accepting it.

"All right, Roland," Bond said. "Let's meet at the starter's shed in, say, half an hour?"

"Splendid!" Marquis said, grinning widely. His straight white teeth sparkled. "We'll see you on the course, then! Come along, Dr. Harding." Harding smiled sheepishly, downed the rest of his drink, and got up with Marquis.

After they had left the bar, Tanner said, "My God, James, are you mad? Two hundred and fifty pounds a point?"

"I had to accept, Bill," Bond said. "Roland and I go way back."

"I knew that. You were at Eton together, right?"

"Yes, for the two years I was there we were bitter rivals. We often competed in the same athletic arenas. Whereas I left Eton and went to Fettes, Marquis went through Eton and Cranwell. As you know, he distinguished himself in the RAF and was rapidly promoted to his present rank."

"Didn't I read somewhere that he's a mountaineer?"

"That's right," Bond said. "He's actually quite famous in the world of mountain climbing. He made international headlines a few years ago after climbing the 'Seven Summits' in record time."

" 'Seven Summits'?"

"The highest peaks on each of the seven continents."

"Ah, right. So he's been up Everest, then?"

"More than once, I believe," Bond said. "I've run into him from time to time over the years. We still regard each other as rivals. I don't know why. It's extraordinary, really."

Tanner frowned and shook his head. "We're not going to have a boxing match out on the course, are we?"

"I'm afraid that whenever I'm thrust into a situation with Roland Marquis, it ends up that way. Cheers." Bond finished his bourbon and asked the bartender to put the drinks on his tab.

They went downstairs to the changing room. Bond put on a Mulberry golf shirt, gray sweater, and pleated navy slacks — his preferred attire for the golf course. He hung his Sea Island short-sleeve cotton shirt and khaki trousers inside a polished wooden locker and shut the door. Even the changing room was opulent, with paintings of Sir Edward Coke and Elizabeth I on the walls. Coke, one of the estate's more famous tenants, was the man who sentenced Guy Fawkes to death and often entertained the queen when she stayed at the manor house in 1601. Bond never took the splendor of Stoke Poges for granted.

"Do we want caddies?" Tanner asked.

Bond shook his head. "I don't. Do you?"

"I can use the exercise."

They walked through the corridors and an outdoor tunnel that smelled faintly of fertilizer. This led to the Pro Shop. Bond paused there long enough to purchase another set of Titleist balls with the number 3 imprinted on them, then followed Tanner outside to the beautiful course. Large, gnarled cedar redwood trees adorned the edges of the fairways. The freshly cut green grass was once prime grazing for deer, so the turf was very fine. It could hardly have been better for golf.

"They've really changed things in the past year," Tanner observed. "The fifteenth hole used to cross the main road here, didn't it?"

Nolan Edwards, who was standing nearby, answered, "That's right, sir. We actually had a couple of broken windscreens in the parking lot. We redesigned a few holes. It keeps the players on their toes."

Roland Marquis and Steven Harding were on the putting green. Bond and Tanner retrieved their clubs and put them on trolleys. Bond had recently purchased the Callaways, which he felt were the most advanced golf clubs on the market. The set included BBX-12 regular flex graphite irons, which he had chosen because he could swing through the shot more easily with the regular flex than with the stiff-shafted clubs.

They all met at the first tee, and the game began at precisely 10:45 A.M. The sun was shining brightly behind them, although several dark clouds were moving around the sky. It was breezy and cool, which invigorated Bond. He took a moment to take in his surroundings, for he believed that in golf his human opponents were not his only adversaries. The course itself was the real enemy, and the only way to conquer it was to treat it with respect.

"Bond, I hope you brought your checkbook," Marquis said, sauntering up to the tee. Harding trailed behind him, struggling with his own trolley.

"I'm ready if you are, Roland," Bond said. He looked over at Tanner, who held two golf balls in his hand. Bond picked his Titleist 3, leaving Tanner with a Slazenger. Marquis and Harding were also using Titleist balls, with the numbers 5 and 1, respectively, marked on them.

After winning the toss, Bond was the first to tee off. He was currently delighted with the results he was getting off the tee with the Callaway firm-shafted War Bird driver. He found that a firm-shafted driver allowed him the maximum distance and, unlike many good players using firm-shafted equipment, Bond avoided hooking his drives with it.

The first hole was a gentle opening to a test of skill laid out by an acknowledged master of golf course design. It was a par 5 with a long fairway of 502 yards. Tricky cross bunkers lay 100 yards short of the green. Bond placed his ball on the tee, took his stance, concentrated, swung, and achieved an even follow-through. The ball sailed a good 225 yards to an impressive position just past the first tree on the right side of the fairway.

"Nice one, James," Tanner said.

Marquis was next. His drive didn't send the ball as far as Bond's, but it landed square in the center of the fairway. It gave him a slight advantage in that all he had to do from then on was hit the next shot to an easy lie around 100 yards out.

Tanner's drive was terrible. The ball overshot the fairway and flew into the trees on the right.

"Oh, damn," he muttered.

"Bad luck, Bill," Marquis said, obviously enjoying himself.

Harding was not much better. At least he hit the ball on the fairway, not much farther than 150 yards from the tee.

As Bond and Tanner walked together toward their balls, Tanner said, "I think the prospect of losing hundreds of pounds has got me a little edgy, James."

"Don't worry about it, Bill," Bond said. "The man's an insufferable boor. I shouldn't have accepted his wager, but it's done. If we lose, I'll take care of it."

"I can't let you do that."

"Just play your best, and we'll see what happens."

The par for the course was 72. Using the Stableford system, players received one point for a bogey, or one over par; two points for par; three points for a birdie, or one under par; four points for an eagle, or two under par; and five points for the rare albatross, which was three under par.

Bond put the ball on the green on his third stroke. If he could sink the putt in one more, then he'd have a birdie. Unfortunately, Marquis did the same and managed to put his ball three yards from the flag. Tanner's bad luck continued: On his third stroke he landed in one of the bunkers. Harding made it on to the green in four.

Marquis sunk his putt to get it out of Bond's way. Bond took the Odyssey putter from the bag and stood over his ball. It was 25 feet to the pin, so he had to give the ball a good, firm tap. His stroke sent the ball across the green, where it spun around the lip of the cup and stopped a foot away from the hole.

"Oh, bad luck, Bond," Marquis said.

At the end of the first hole Marquis had three points, Bond two, Harding two and Tanner one. At the end of the game Bond and Tanner would combine their scores, as would Marquis and Harding. The team with the most points would, of course, win.

After the disastrous first hole, Tanner calmed down and began to play evenly. He made par on the next hole, as did the other three.

The third hole was a par 3 that Bond made in two. The other players all made par. As the four men walked over to the fourth tee, Marquis said, "Bond, do you remember the fight we had?"

Bond had never forgotten it. It had been at Eton after a grueling wrestling match in the gymnasium. The instructor, a friend of Marquis's parents, had pitted Bond against Marquis because it was well known that the two boys couldn't stand each other. Bond was obviously the better wrestler, but Marquis had surprised Bond with an illegal blow to the jaw. The instructor turned a blind eye, ultimately declaring Marquis the winner. After that a fistfight broke out.

"That was a long time ago," Bond said.

"Still smarting from that, eh?" Marquis taunted. "Just be thankful the headmaster came in to save your arse."

"I seem to remember that it was you he rescued," Bond replied.

"Isn't it funny how two grown men remember the same event differently?" Marquis slapped Bond on the back and gave a hearty laugh.

By the time they had played through five holes, the score was twenty-one to nineteen in favor of Marquis and Harding.

The sixth hole was a straight 412-yard par 4 with bunkers right and left at 195 and 225 yards from the tee. The green was uphill, small, and difficult to putt on because of its varied slopes.

Bond drove the ball 200 yards off the tee. Tanner followed suit, putting both balls in position for a straight shot over the bunkers and onto the green. When Bond made his second shot, he put the ball just in front of a center bunker about 100 yards from the green. It would be a perfect opportunity to try to back up the ball. He could hit it over the bunker, onto the green behind the pin, and hopefully put enough of a backspin on the ball to make it roll near the hole. He had to try it; otherwise making par would be extremely difficult.

When Bond's turn came, he removed the Lyconite 56-degree wedge from the bag and took a couple of practice swings.

"Come on, Bond," Marquis said patronizingly. "All you have to do is hit it over the bunker."

"Shhh, Roland," said Tanner. Marquis just grinned. He was getting cocky. Even Harding grimaced.

Bond swung and chopped the ball up and over the bunker. It fell just behind the pin but failed to roll toward the hole. Instead, it bounced forward off the green and into the rough.

"Oh, bad luck!" Marquis said with glee. Bond eventually took a bogey on the hole, while the others made par. Marquis and Harding maintained their lead.

While walking up the seventh fairway together, Tanner said to Bond, "Nice try."

"Bollocks," Bond said. "You know, I think it's taken me all these years to realize how intensely I dislike that man."

"Try not to let it affect your game, James," Tanner advised. "I agree with you, he's as obnoxious as hell."

"I can't hate him too much, though."

"Why not?"

Bond thought a moment before answering. "He's made of the same stuff as me," he said. "Roland Marquis, his personality faults notwithstanding, is good at what he does. You have to admit that he's a bloody fine player, and he's one hell of an athlete. His accomplishments in the RAF and in the mountains are impressive. He could just use some lessons in humility."

"I understand he's quite a ladies' man as well," Tanner mused.

"That's right. England's most eligible bachelor."

"Besides you."

Bond disregarded the quip. "He flaunts his dates with supermodels, actresses, very wealthy widows, and divorcees. He's the sort of celebrity that bores me to tears."

"I'll bet you were rivals over a girl when you were younger," Tanner said perceptively.

"As a matter of fact, we were," Bond admitted. "He stole her right from under my nose. He engineered the entire seduction to get the better of me."

"What was her name?" Tanner said, smiling.

Bond looked at him and said with a straight face, "Felicity Mountjoy."

The chief of staff pursed his lips and nodded, as if that explained everything.

Bond got lucky on the ninth hole and made a birdie, while the other three all made par. Bond was one under par on the front nine and Tanner was two over. Marquis, however, was two under par and his partner was two over. The Stableford score was Marquis and Harding thirty-six, Bond and Tanner thirty-five.

They sat outside in back of the clubhouse to have a drink before playing the back nine. Bond ordered vodka, on the rocks, and set his gunmetal cigarette case on the table beside the glass. Tanner had a Guinness. The sound of bagpipes and drums was coming faintly over the trees from outside the chapel on the estate grounds.

"The Gurkhas are here," Tanner observed.

The Pipes and Drums marching band of the Royal Gurkha Rifles often played at Stoke Poges, for the Gurkha Memorial Garden was located near the course. Elite fighting men recruited from Nepal to serve with the British army since 1815, Gurkhas are considered to be among the fiercest and bravest soldiers on the planet.

"We're not far from Church Crookham," Bond said, referring to the regiment's home base.

Marquis and Harding joined them, each carrying a pint.

"Vodka, Bond?" Marquis pointed.

"That's right, I remember now. You're a vodka man. You like *martinis*." He pronounced the word with exaggerated erudition. "Vodka will dull your senses, my boy."

"Not at all," Bond said. "I find it sharpens them." He opened the gunmetal case and removed one of the specially made cigarettes with the three distinctive gold bands.

"What kind of cigarettes are *those?*" Marquis asked.

"I have them custom made," Bond explained. Morland's and H. Simmons had gone out of business, so he now ordered his cigarettes directly from a company called Tor Importers, which specialized in Turkish and Balkan tobacco. His was a blend with low tar that he liked.

Marquis chuckled, "Well, let's try one then!"

Bond offered the case to him, and then the other men. Harding took one, but Tanner refused.

Marquis lit the cigarette and inhaled. He rolled the smoke around inside his mouth as if he were tasting wine. He exhaled and said, "Can't say I care for it much, Bond."

"It's probably too strong for your taste," Bond replied.

Marquis smiled and shook his head. "You always have a comeback, don't you, Bond?"

Bond ignored him and finished his drink, then put out the cigarette. He glanced up at the sky and said, "Those clouds don't look friendly. We had better get started."

The sun had completely vanished. Thunder rumbled lightly in the distance.

As Bond predicted, it started to rain on the thirteenth hole, but it wasn't heavy, and they continued to play. Apart from Marquis's birdie on the eleventh, everyone had made par on the first three holes of the back nine. With Marquis and Harding still in the lead, the game had become a contest of machismo between Bond and Marquis. The tension between them was palpable; it even made Tanner and Harding uncomfortable. The rain didn't help matters. Everyone but Marquis was in a foul mood when they approached the fourteenth tee.

The score remained constant after the fourteenth and fifteenth holes. Bond had to do something to better theirs. Hole sixteen had recently been redesigned. It was a par 4 at 320 yards. The old green had been tree-lined on both sides and protected by a bunker in front and a greenside bunker to the left. Now the green was farther back, closer to the small pond, so that an overshot would be a disaster.

It was another opportunity for Bond to try his backspin.

His tee-off sent the ball 210 yards straight down the fairway, where it landed in an excellent position. Marquis performed an equally impressive shot, dropping a mere six feet away from Bond's ball. Tanner and Harding did well enough, both driving their balls 175 yards onto the fairway.

Bond approached the ball with the Lyconite wedge once again. If he could make this shot, he would narrow the gap between the scores.

The rain had subsided, so now the grass was wet and heavy. It made the task even more difficult.

"That little backspin might work for you this time, Bond," Marquis said. He perceived that Bond was about to try it again and simply wanted to rattle his nerves.

Bond paid no attention and concentrated on the ball. He shook his shoulders, rotated his head, and felt his neck crack, then took his stance over the ball. He was ready.

Tanner watched, biting his lower lip. Harding, who hadn't said more than twenty-five words all day, nervously chewed on a scoring pencil. Marquis stood with casual indifference, expecting Bond to muck it up.

Bond swung, snapped the ball into the air, and watched as it fell neatly on the back of the green. Would it roll off, away from the hole and into the pond? He held his breath.

The ball, propelled by a perfect backspin, rolled toward the hole and stopped an inch from the pin. If it weren't for the moisture on the green, the ball would have dropped in the cup.

Tanner and Harding both cheered. Marquis didn't say a word. His feathers ruffled, he knocked his ball straight into the bunker on the side of the green.

As they approached the eighteenth tee, the score was 70 to 69 in favor of Marquis and Harding. It was a par 4 at 406 yards. With a magnificent view of the mansion, the hole was uphill with bunkers on the right at 184 yards and out of bounds on the left from the tee. What made the hole extra difficult was the second shot, which had to go over a hollow just short of the green. The green was slightly elevated and bunkered on both sides, and it sloped from left to right.

Bond knocked the ball to a position nearly 180 yards from the green. Marquis made an identical shot, knocking his ball into Bond's and causing it to roll a few feet forward.

"Thanks, that's where I really wanted to be," Bond said.

"As the song goes, Bond, 'anything you can do, I can do better,' " Marquis said. He had meant to hit Bond's ball just to prove something.

All four men made par on the hole. After Harding sank the last putt of the game, Tanner sighed heavily and looked at Bond. They had lost the game with the score at 74 to 73. Now they had to come up with five hundred pounds.

"Bad luck, Bond," Marquis said, holding out his hand.

Bond shook it and said, "You played a fine game."

Marquis shook Tanner's hand and said, "Bill, your game has improved a great deal. I think you ought to have your handicap updated."

Tanner grunted and shook Harding's hand.

"Shall we meet back on the patio for drinks after changing?" Marquis suggested.

"Fine," Bond said. He and Tanner left their clubs at the starter shed, went to the dressing room to shower and change clothes, and emerged feeling fresher, if not altogether happy. Tanner hadn't said a word to Bond since the game had ended.

"Bill, I know you're terribly upset with me. I'm sorry. I'll pay for it all," Bond said as they took a seat at a table. The sun had, in inimitable English-weather fashion, re-appeared.

"Don't be silly, James," Tanner said. "I'll pay my share. Don't worry about it. I'll write you a check now and you can pay them in one lump sum."

Tanner began writing the check and murmured, "Why the hell does Marquis always call me by my Christian name, but he always addresses you as Bond?"

"Because the man is a complete bastard who thinks he's a superior being. I'm doing my best to swallow my pride and put this behind me, but if he says 'bad luck' one more time, I'm going to punch him in the nose."

Tanner nodded in agreement. "Too bad he's working with us, or I'd kick him in the arse myself!"

"What is this top secret project, anyway?"

"James, it's classified. M and I are privy to it, but it's something that the DERA have been working on for quite some time. I can tell you more later, at the office. I had no idea Marquis was the RAF liaison with the project."

"You've aroused my interest. Can you give me a hint?"

"Let's just say that when the project is completed, it will change the way wars are fought."

Right on cue, Marquis and Harding joined them.

"Excellent game, gentlemen," Marquis said. "I'm so glad we ran into you. It made the day so much more interesting."

Bond took out his checkbook. "Shall I make it out to you or to Dr. Harding?"

"Oh, to me, by all means. I want to watch you write my name on that check," said Marquis. He turned to Harding and said, "Don't worry, doctor, I'll give you your share."

Harding smiled complacently. He gazed at Bond's check as a sparrow might eye a worm.

Bond tore out the check and handed it to Marquis. "Here you are, sir."

"Thank you, Bond," Marquis said, pocketing it. "You played admirably. Someday you just might be able to beat me."

Bond stood up and said, "That might give you an inferiority complex, Roland, and that would be so unlike you."

Marquis glared at Bond.

"Bill and I must be going," Bond said quickly. "It was good to see you again, Roland. Nice meeting you, Dr. Harding." He held out his hand to both of them. "Take care."

"Rushing off so soon?" Harding asked.

Tanner stood up, following Bond's lead. "Yes, I'm afraid he's right. We have to be back at Vauxhall before the end of the workday."

"Well, by all means, you've got to keep our precious country safe and sound," Marquis said with mock sincerity. "I'll sleep better tonight knowing you boys are on the watch."

After they said their good-byes, Bond and Tanner walked around the clubhouse to pick up their bags. As men who were quite used to winning or losing, they quickly put the loss of money and the game behind them.

Bond drove the old Aston Martin DB5 back to London, and instead of heading straight for Chelsea, went into West

Kensington. The car had been kept in excellent condition, but Bond wanted something new. What he really had his eye on was the company's Jaguar XK8 that he had recently used in Greece. Sadly, it would probably be a while before Q Branch removed the "extras" and sold it as an ordinary secondhand car, as they had done with the DB5. He kept the Aston Martin in a garage in Chelsea along with the other dinosaur he owned, the Bentley Turbo R. His friend and American mechanic, Melvin Heckman, made sure that both cars were always in prime condition.

Helena Marksbury lived on the third floor of a block of flats near the Barons Court underground station. All day he had been glad to be away from her. Oddly, now he was starving for her.

Bond parked the car in front of her building, got out, and buzzed the intercom. It was just after four. He knew that she had been planning to leave the office early that day.

"Yes? Who is it?" Her voice, usually soft and seductive, sounded odd and metallic through the small speaker.

"It's me," he said.

There was a moment's hesitation, then the buzzer sounded.

Bond took the stairs two at a time and found her waiting in the doorway of her flat. Her hair was wet, and she was wearing one of his shirts and nothing else.

"I just got out of the shower," she said.

"Perfect," he said. "I'll dry you off."

"How did you know I left the office early today?"

"It was a hunch. I had a feeling that you were thinking about me," he said.

"Oh, really? Awfully sure of yourself, aren't you?"

"And I have a tension headache that needs some tender loving care."

She made a face, whispered "Tsk, tsk, tsk," and ran her fingers through his hair.

He took her by the waist and pulled her inside, closing the door behind them. Their mouths met as she hopped up and wrapped her smooth, bare legs around his waist. He carried her into the bedroom, where they spent the next two hours releasing the stress that had been dogging them both for the past two weeks.

THREE

Skin 17

The Defence Evaluation and Research Agency runs, on a commercial basis, the research establishments that were formerly part of the Ministry of Defence Procurement Executive. With locations scattered around the UK — both public and private — the DERA is, in part, responsible for research in aerodynamics and materials used to build aircraft for the RAF. One of their larger facilities is located in Farnborough, southwest of London, at the former Royal Aircraft Establishment and home of the Farnborough air show. While most of the DERA's work is done at such official sites, which are guarded by heavy security, a few laboratories and offices are located in seemingly innocuous, unmarked buildings. Some of the agency's most sensitive and classified secrets are generated at these locations as a preventive measure, should there ever be any industrial espionage attempts against the DERA.

Not far from Farnborough is the small village of Fleet, a quiet residential community surrounded by warehouses and industrial complexes of neighboring towns. It has a railway station used daily by commuters to and from London. Its convenience to both London and Farnborough was one of the reasons the DERA hid their most secret and important project in a warehouse that appeared to be unused.

The exterior had been treated to look old. Windows were boarded and posted signs read NO TRESPASSING. All doors were locked. It was always dark and quiet. As the warehouse was off one of the main roads, the residents of Fleet took no notice of a building that one day looked much older and decrepit than it really was. In actuality, the building contained a secret entrance, a 20-foot-by-500-foot wind tunnel, foundry equipment, a sealed pressure vessel called an autoclave, and the offices and laboratory of a small research team headed by the noted aeronautics physicist and engineer Dr. Thomas Wood.

Two years previously, the DERA had hired Dr. Wood away from Oxford to work on a classified assignment. He was an expert in ceramics, especially when it came to designing "smart skins" for aircraft fuselages.

Wood was fifty-three, a warm and intelligent man with a family. He loved his new job, for he found "government work" exciting. He had missed out on military service because of a heart murmur and other indications of an unstable condition. An insensitive army doctor had told him that he wouldn't live to see forty. He had fooled them all. Even though he was overweight, he felt great and was enthusiastic about the project. If tonight's tests on the $1/8$-scale prototype were positive, and Skin 17 was indeed a success, he might be on his way to a Nobel Prize.

Skin 15 had almost worked. There were some minor flaws. The scalable autoclaved material showed possible defects in the built-in photo electrolysis that served to change the skin's resistance to abuse. The impedance sensitivity was weak. When his assistant, Dr. Steven Harding, suggested that they keep trying, Wood concurred. That had been three months ago. What they thought would be a week's tinkering resulted in a major overhaul, and out of the ashes rose Skin 16.

Wood considered that particular version of the formula to be his most brilliant creation. The team had almost declared themselves victorious; but the prototype skin failed one of several key tests. Despite the material's radio frequency transparency, one sensor was unable to transmit and receive through an aperture. There were glitches, but they were closer than ever to the goal. The biggest hurdle was always how scalable the material could be so that prototype models might be built and tested in extreme conditions. Another month's work perfected Skin 16 to Dr. Wood's satisfaction. Today he was to see the results of the tests conducted on Skin 17's prototype. If it worked, the carbon-fiber and silica ceramic that he and his small team had developed could change the world of aviation forever.

An admitted eccentric, Wood gave his team the day off so that he could work alone. He had, however, asked his second in command, Dr. Harding, to come in that evening.

Wood sat at a computer terminal, punching in data at a furious speed. Harding watched him from across the room near the autoclave, which contained a prototype of Skin 17.

"You didn't say how your golf game was," Wood remarked, still typing.

"It was lovely. We won," Harding said. "I actually made a little money."

"Splendid!" Wood said. "I hope you didn't mind me kicking you out today. I just needed to work on these figures alone. You understand, don't you, Steven?"

"Of course, Tom," Harding said. "Don't worry about it. I thoroughly enjoyed myself! Except for the bit of rain we got, it was a lovely day. I must admit that I found it difficult to concentrate on the golf. I kept thinking that you might finish it today."

"Well, Steven," Wood said as he clicked a button to execute a program that he had written himself, then sat back with his arms folded. "We'll know in a few minutes, won't we?"

Harding nervously tapped his fingers on the oval-shaped autoclave that looked like a pressure chamber used by divers. "The waiting is dreadful! I must say, this is very exciting." He looked at his watch intently. The physicist's birdlike qualities always seemed more pronounced when he was agitated or tense. His hair tended to stand up, and he involuntarily made jerking movements with his head. Wood presumed that Harding had some kind of tic.

"Staring at the minute hand on your

watch will only make the time seem slower," Wood said, laughing. "It's hard to believe it's been two years since we started."

Harding got out of his seat, stepped over to Wood, and looked over his shoulder. They watched the figures appear on the monitor at an alarming rate.

"Steven, go over to the Mac and punch up the juice," Wood ordered.

Harding adjusted the level of temperature in the autoclave's chamber.

No one said anything for ten minutes as the printer began spewing out a long stream of perforated paper. It was filled with equations, letters, numbers, and symbols.

Skin 17.

When it was done, Wood peered at his monitor and a smile played on his lips. He took a deep breath, then swiveled around and faced his assistant.

"Dr. Harding, Skin 17 is a success. It's passed every test."

Harding beamed and said, "Congratulations! My God, this is bloody marvelous! I knew it, Tom, I knew you'd do it." He clasped Wood's shoulder.

"Oh, come now," Wood said. "You and the others were a tremendous help, and so were the boys at Farnborough. I didn't do it all alone."

"But it's in your contract that you get the credit," Harding reminded him.

"Well, there *is* that!" Wood laughed. "Shall we have some wine? I think there's still some in the refrigerator. Now I'm sorry I sent everyone home today. I feel our entire team should have been here."

"We were all grateful for the holiday, Tom. Jenny and Carol were both going away for the weekend, and Spencer and John had family coming to London. But they'll hear about it soon enough."

Wood got up from the desk and started to walk toward the kitchen.

"Shouldn't we save it to disk?" Harding asked.

"You're right," Wood said. "I'll burn a disk. It'll be the gold master."

Wood placed a blank compact disk into the recorder and punched the computer keypad. The entire Skin 17 formula was saved on the disk. He removed the disk and placed it in an unmarked jewel box. Wood found a red marker on the desk and wrote "Skin 17 Gold Master" on the cover.

"I better put this in the safe so it won't get lost," Wood said. "I'll make some more copies later."

"Nonsense, Tom, go and get the wine!" Harding said, laughing. "There's no one else here! Put it in the safe later."

Wood felt foolish for a few seconds, then his better judgment took over. "No, I'll just put it in quickly," he said.

He walked to a twenty-four-inch safe embedded in a wall and carefully turned the combination knob. The door swung open and Wood placed the jewel box inside.

"Now, about that wine," Wood said, closing the safe and starting to move toward the kitchen again. He was stopped by the front office buzzer. Wood looked at Harding with a furrowed brow.

"Who in hell could that be?"

Harding punched the intercom and said, "Yes?"

A voice announced, "It's Marquis. Code Clearance 1999 Skin."

Wood was surprised. "He didn't say he was coming by tonight. What does he want?"

"Shall I not let him in?" Harding asked.

"No, no, let him in. He's the messenger boy from our employers, you know," Wood said. "I just didn't want to have to share our victory with him tonight, that's all. I find him rather rude."

Harding pushed the button and a portion of the building's back wall opened just enough for a man to slip through. A passage led through a vacant ground floor that had been treated with dust and cobwebs, then up a flight of stairs to a false wall. By slightly rotating an electrical fixture hung there, a visitor could open the wall and get inside the DERA laboratory. Marquis had been there several times, so he knew the way. In a few moments Harding got up and went to the lab door to let their visitor in.

Group Captain Marquis was dressed in full uniform and was carrying a small black box. He was a physically imposing man in his own right — but when he wore his RAF uniform, he always commanded attention. The epitome of a disciplined British officer, he looked sharp, stern, and efficient.

"Good evening, gentlemen," he said. "Sorry to barge in on you like this, but I have new orders. I'll explain after you tell me about your test results, Dr. Wood."

"New orders?" Wood asked. "What do you mean? How did you know we were testing tonight?" He looked at Harding.

Harding's beady eyes widened as he shook his head.

"Dr. Harding didn't tell me," Marquis

said. "I knew. It's my job." He placed the black box on a counter.

Wood looked uncertain. Marquis had visited the office a few times over the last year, but it was always during the day and with a specific administrative agenda.

"All right," he said, "but I find this highly irregular."

"Dr. Wood, you're among friends," Marquis said. "I, too, have an emotional investment in the success of your project — *our* project."

"You're right," Wood said, relaxing a little. "Steven, why don't you tell our friend what we've just learned."

Marquis looked at Harding, who grinned and said, "We did it. Tom did it. Skin 17 is a success."

"Unbelievable!" Marquis said. "Well done, Dr. Wood! This calls for a celebration," Marquis said. "Where's that wine you said you had?"

Wood pointed to the kitchen. "It's in the —" He stopped abruptly and looked at Marquis. "How did you know I said anything about wine?"

Marquis reached into his jacket with his right hand and pulled out a 9mm Browning Hi-Power pistol. He revealed a small black rectangular object with a short antenna in his left hand.

"I heard you, of course," he said. "This is a two-channel UHF receiver. And the transmitter is over there in Dr. Harding's wristwatch. I was right outside the building all the time, listening to your conversation. I only had to wait for my cue. Dr. Harding was certain you would strike gold tonight, and you did."

Wood looked at Harding, but the traitor couldn't look his colleague in the eyes.

"I don't understand," Wood said. "What's going on? Steven?"

"I'm sorry, Tom," Harding said.

Before Wood could move, Marquis shot him in the right thigh. Wood screamed and fell to the ground. Howling in pain, he writhed and squirmed on the wood floor. Blood poured from a huge hole in his leg.

Marquis calmly stood over Wood and said, "Mmmm, bad luck, eh, doctor? Now, about those new orders. Dr. Harding is to take the formula for Skin 17 and see that there are no copies left. I'm to make sure he does." He handed the gun to Harding. "He's all yours."

Harding squatted down to Wood. He waved the gun barrel at his colleague's head and said, "I'm sorry, Tom, but you have to give me the combination to the safe. I need that disk."

Wood was in agony, but he managed to spit out, "You . . . traitor!"

"Come, come," Harding said. "Let's not be like that. I'll make sure you still get the credit for developing Skin 17. It's just not going to be Great Britain that uses it first."

"Go to hell," Wood cried.

Harding sighed, then stood up. He held on to the edge of a counter for leverage, then placed his shoe on Wood's wounded thigh.

"The combination, Tom?" he asked one more time.

Wood glared at Harding but said nothing. Harding thrust all his weight onto the physicist's leg. Wood screamed horribly.

"Yes, yes, go ahead and scream," Harding said. "No one can hear you. The warehouse is closed, it's night, the street is deserted. We can go on for hours like this, but I'm sure you'd rather not." He continued to apply pressure to the wound.

Marquis stood idly by, examining the computer monitor and trying to make sense of the hieroglyphics displayed on the screen.

Two minutes later Harding had the answer he wanted. Wood curled up in the fetal position on the floor, sobbing. Harding wiped the blood from his shoe on Wood's trousers, then went to the safe. Using the combination Wood had given him, Harding had it open in seconds. He removed the Skin 17 master disk and all the backup copies of the previous versions of the specification. He placed everything except the master disk into a plastic bag, then went to the physicist's desk and rummaged for specific file folders. He found what he was looking for, took the new printout, and stuffed all of it into the bag as well.

"Make sure there are no copies of *anything*," Marquis said.

Harding went back to Wood and knelt beside him. "Tom, we have to make sure there are no traces of the formula left. Now, tell me. Do you have any copies at home? Where are the backups?"

"All the backups . . . are with the DERA . . ." Wood gasped.

Harding looked at Marquis. Marquis nodded and said, "Yes, I already got those. They've been destroyed."

"Nothing at your house?" Harding asked again.

Wood shook his head. "Please . . ." he muttered. "I need a doctor. . . ."

"I'm afraid it's too late for that, Tom,"

Harding said. He stood up and walked away to his own desk. He began to pack, placing personal items and other file folders that he might need in a brown attaché case. Wood began to moan loudly.

After a few minutes Marquis said, "Oh, for God's sake, Harding! Don't leave him like that!"

Harding stopped what he was doing and looked at Wood. The traitor nodded grimly, then stepped over to Wood and pointed the gun at his head.

"Thanks for all your hard work, Dr. Wood," Harding said. He fired once, and the moaning ceased. He then set down the gun on a counter and extracted a long, thin dagger from his attaché case. Harding squatted down, trying his best not to get blood on his clothes, grabbed Wood's hair, and pulled back his head to expose his neck. Harding positioned the blade against the dead man's skin as Marquis said, "Oh, *must* you do that?"

Harding replied, "It's our way. I know it seems rather superfluous at this point, but I have my orders, too." He swiftly slit Wood's throat from ear to ear. The deed done, he dropped the man's head and stepped away with a disgusted look on his face. Harding wiped the dagger on Wood's trousers and put it away, then picked up Marquis's gun and gave it back to him.

Marquis holstered the pistol and said, "Doctor, make sure you delete all the files from that hard drive. Give me the master disk."

Harding handed him the disk and began to work on the computer. Marquis opened the black box he had brought with him. It was a peculiar but efficient device with a laptop computer, CD-ROM drive, micro-dot camera, and developer. He inserted the disk into the machine, adjusted tiny knobs, and closed the cover. He pressed a button and copied the disk's files onto the hard drive. Marquis punched in more commands, then carefully removed a glass slide from the edge of the developer. He placed it in a tray and maneuvered a magnifier over the slide. A tiny microdot, produced on positive-type film and practically invisible to the naked eye, was now on the glass. Marquis took a piece of thin, transparent film from the black box and pressed it smoothly over the glass slide. The microdot was transferred from the slide to the film. Marquis placed the film in a small plastic envelope and sealed it. He then removed the Skin 17 master disk from the machine, dropped it on the floor, and crushed it with his heel.

The next thing Marquis did struck Harding as strange. He opened the autoclave and removed the Skin 17 prototype — a small piece of rubberlike material stretched on a specimen tray. He placed it inside the jacket pocket on Wood's body.

"There," Marquis said. "The only existing record of Skin 17 is now on this microdot. Take good care of it."

He handed the envelope to Harding, who took it and said, "Right, this hard drive is blank." Harding put the envelope in his attaché case. "I'll get the petrol." He went out of the lab, down the stairs, and into a storage closet in back of the office space, where he had left two five-gallon cans of petrol. He carried them back up to the lab, opened one, and began pouring the petrol all over the floor and furniture. Marquis had placed the plastic bag full of the backup copies and printouts on the floor next to Wood.

"Make sure you get the computers and the autoclave," Marquis said, taking the other can, and he poured petrol over the other side of the room. He made sure the body and the prototype were completely covered. The smell was overpowering, but the traitors continued until the containers were almost empty.

Marquis grabbed the black box and Harding took the attaché case. They backed down the stairs, pouring petrol as they went. They made their way to the lower, vacant level, through the darkness to the exit, where they dropped the empty cans. Harding punched in the code that opened the trick door and held it open. Marquis paused long enough to remove a handkerchief from his pocket and set it on fire with a lighter. He calmly tossed it onto the floor behind him. The petrol immediately ignited and the flames spread quickly.

The two men shut the door behind them and walked to a BMW 750 that was parked twenty yards away from the building. Marquis got behind the wheel and they drove toward London. No one saw them.

Firefighters were alerted to the emergency within five minutes, but by then it was too late. The flames had spread into the laboratory, where the concentration of petrol was most intense. The building became a fireball. The firefighters did everything they could, but it was no use. Within fifteen minutes the secret DERA facility in Fleet was completely destroyed.

In the BMW, Harding reached for a mobile phone. "I need to call my headquarters," he said.

Marquis put a hand on his arm. "Not on my mobile. Use a pay phone at the station."

Marquis dropped Harding off in front of Waterloo Station. Harding took the attaché case and a bag that was already in the trunk. He had already purchased a ticket on the last Eurostar of the day to Brussels. Before boarding the train, he entered a phone booth and called a number in Morocco.

As he waited for someone to pick up, he thought about how much money Skin 17 was going to make for him. The plan had gone smoothly so far.

After several pips, a man finally answered. "Yes?"

"Mongoose calling from London. Phase One complete. I have it. Commencing Phase Two."

"Very good. I'll relay the message. You have a reservation at the Hôtel Métropole in the name of Donald Peters."

"Right."

The man hung up. Harding sat for a few seconds, tapping his fingers on the attaché case. Then he picked up the phone again, put in some coins, and made one more call before getting on the train.

The number he dialed was a private line at SIS headquarters.

FOUR

Emergency

James Bond walked briskly past Helena Marksbury's desk on the way to his office. Usually she greeted him with a warm smile in the mornings, but today she swiveled her chair around so that her back was to him. He was sure she had heard him coming. Bond thought that their unscheduled coupling yesterday after the golf game had perhaps confused and upset her.

"It was my understanding that we were supposed to 'cool it' while we're in London," she had said. He reiterated that indeed they should do so, but he also convinced her that she was just as hungry for him as he was for her. In the privacy of her flat, what harm could be done? They had thrown caution to the wind and allowed their passion to overwhelm them.

Afterward, however, Bond brought up the subject of their relationship again. Feelings were hurt, emotions were frayed, and this time it ended in a terrible fight.

Helena accused him of "taking what he wanted, when he wanted," and he admitted that there was some truth to that. She called him a "selfish bastard."

He knew then that their affair had to end, especially if he wanted to keep her in place as his personal assistant at MI6.

"Do you want to continue working for me?" he had asked her.

"Yes, of course," she replied.

"Then you know as well as I that we can't keep doing this."

"You're the one who surprised me at my door."

He couldn't argue with that. He had been a bloody fool. He had let his loins do his thinking for him once again.

They had agreed to end their romantic involvement — again — and, with tears in her eyes, she had sent him packing. Now he only hoped that they could get past it and that things at the office would be normal again, if such a thing was possible, without anyone losing their job.

He closed the door to his office and found a notice from Records indicating that the updated file on the Union was ready for his review. It was the information he had been waiting for. At least that would kill some time.

Bond sat down at his desk, took a cigarette from his gunmetal case, and lit it. Dammit all, he thought. How could he have been so bloody stupid? He should have realized that she was becoming more emotionally involved in the relationship than he wanted her to be. She would just have to get over it.

Lost in thought, he sat in the quiet solitude of his office and finished his cigarette.

One of the many improvements M made after she took charge was in the area of information technology. Old Sir Miles Messervy had been completely computer illiterate and hardly ever approved funding to update technology at MI6. Barbara Mawdsley, the new M, was all for it. The most controversial thing she did during her first year in office was to spend nearly a half million pounds to upgrade the computer equipment and network systems. Part of this money went to Records, where a state-of-the-art multimedia center was developed and built. The "Visual Library," as it was called, was a computerized encyclopedia on a grand scale. One merely had to punch in a topic and the Visual Library would find every file available on the subject and organize it into a cohesive multimedia presentation. A full-time staff maintained the various sound, photo, video, and music files so that information was constantly kept up-to-date. Hard copies of the text could be printed and distributed as well, but it was infinitely more instructive when one could sit and view information in much the same way as one watched television.

Bond thought it would be appalling, until he saw the Library in action. It was an impressive feat of design and engineering. Now he enjoyed locking himself in one of the cubicles, putting on the headset, and watching the large wall-sized monitor in front of him. All he had to do was type the commands on a keypad and watch. He didn't have to take notes; a "memo" button on the keypad automatically saved any particular segment and printed it.

After getting a cup of SIS's mediocre coffee, he made himself comfortable in one of the Visual Library booths and punched in the code for the new file on the Union. The lights dimmed as he put on the headset.

Using a mouse, Bond clicked on the "intro" main menu button. The presentation began much like a newsreel of old. There was a bit of military music, a quick series of logos and credits, and the show began.

A familiar male narrator from the BBC began to speak over a montage of famous terrorist scenes from history: Nazis with concentration camp prisoners; the American embassy crisis in Iran; a hooded man holding a gun to an airline pilot's head; the Ku Klux Klan; and Ernst Stavro Blofeld.

"Terrorists have been with us since the dawn of man. When we think of terrorists, we imagine groups of men and women who will do anything for a cause. They almost always have a political agenda and perform acts of violence to further their aims. But there is another kind of terrorist that has been cropping up more and more in the past thirty years. We have seen the rise of nonpolitical, commercial terrorists, or, to put it another way, terrorists who are in it only for the money. The difference between a political terrorist and a commercial one is important in our analysis, for the reasons that motivate these individuals are the keys to understanding them. Whereas a political terrorist may be willing to lie for what he believes, a commercial one may not be so inclined. Usually very intelligent, the commercial terrorist will weigh situations as they occur and decide whether it's worth continuing in his present course of action.

Shots of large amounts of money; hunters in the wild; a soldier walking alone in a jungle . . .

"However, the lure of big money is a powerful enough temptation for the commercial terrorist to take a risk. If this enticement is combined with certain psychological factors in specific individuals, they may be persuaded to do *anything*. We believe these people possess an inherent desire for high adventure, danger, and excitement. Profit is the primary reason for their actions, but they also have a strong desire to do something that 'normal' people don't do. This makes the commercial terrorist totally unpredictable, and, therefore, extremely dangerous. The Union are the most recent group of commercial terrorists to come to the attention of SIS and other law enforcement agencies around the world. They are not the first, nor will they be the last. But at the moment they could very well be the most influential."

Bond stifled a laugh. The report had been rushed. The narration was terribly clichéd, but it was the truth. He clicked on the "history" button.

"They began innocently enough." A *Hired Gun* magazine appeared on the monitor. Inside was an advertisement showing a smiling man dressed in fatigues and holding a rifle. " 'Come join the Union and be a mercenary! See the world! Earn top dollar!' These words appeared three years ago in magazines such as this one. The advertisements were printed in publications in the United States, most western European countries, the former Soviet Union, and throughout the Middle East. The Union were the brainchild of an American named Taylor Michael Harris, an ex-Marine who worked as a security guard in the state of Oregon."

Taylor Harris's mug shot filled the screen. He had a shaved head and a swastika tattooed on his forehead. "In early 1995, at age thirty-six, Harris founded a small militia group who proclaimed themselves white supremacists. After the local authorities arrested several of his members during a rally that turned violent, he was run out of the state. Harris traveled to Europe and the Middle East, then came back to Oregon with a large amount of capital six months later. He had apparently gone into business with foreign investors located either in the Middle East or North Africa. With this funding, he created the Union, which certain specialist magazines touted to be a freelance mercenary outfit. Qualified men with proper military training could get a high-paying job with the Union — as long as they were willing to travel, be discreet, and show that they had the stuff. The 'stuff,' it turned out, was having the ability to commit murder, arson, burglary, kidnapping, and other serious crimes."

The visuals changed to a grainy black and white film of men in fatigues doing push-ups on a field, running around a track, shadow boxing. . . . "The ad campaign lasted six months, and men from all over the world joined the Union. This film of early trainees was confiscated during a raid on the Union's Oregon headquarters in December 1996. The American authorities became aware of their activities after Taylor Harris was gunned down in a restaurant in Portland, Oregon, a month earlier."

The screens filled with police photographs of Taylor Harris, lying on the floor in a pool of blood and spaghetti.

"It is believed that Harris was murdered by his lieutenants, all of whom fled the country. Prior to this incident, no Union 'jobs' had ever been reported. Recruiting advertisements disappeared after the raid, and it appeared that the Union had been only a crazy whim of a deranged ex-Marine."

Maps of the world popped up on the screen. "The truth became clear in 1997 as evidence began to surface that former Union members were involved in terrorist-style operations. It is believed that unknown foreigners now control the Union, and that they are managed as an underground, networked organization. Recruitment occurs only by word of mouth. SIS is convinced that the Union already have a strong base of tough, talented men. To date, this group of criminals and mercenaries have struck around the world half a dozen times. Besides hiring themselves out to countries and governments, members often initiate their own projects in the hope that they might prove to be profitable later."

The camera focused on the Mediterranean. "The Union are a rapidly growing network of tough professionals, and it is believed that they are coordinated from somewhere in the Mediterranean region. It is estimated that there may be as many as

93

three hundred Union members world-wide."

A man's silhouette was superimposed over the map, and a big question mark hung over his head. "The Union boss is thought to be a businessman, very wealthy and very powerful. Likely suspects are Taylor Harris's three lieutenants, all of whom fled the United States after his murder and are wanted for that crime. They are" — the monitor lingered on mug shots of the three men — "Samuel Loggins Anderson, age thirty-five, ex-Marine and former insurance salesman." He was bald, had long sideburns and crooked teeth.

"James 'Jimmy' Wayne Powers, age thirty-three, former National Guardsman who spent time in jail for armed robbery." He was thin, and had large dark eyes and black hair.

"And Julius Stanley Wilcox, age thirty-six, another ex-Marine and former forest ranger." Wilcox was the ugliest and mean-est-looking, with a scar above his right eye, a hawk nose, and greasy, slicked-back gray hair.

"None of these three men has been seen since they left the United States."

A flowchart appeared on the monitor. "Like the Mafia, the Union are run by a manager or president whom they call *Le Gérant.* Beneath him are three or four trusted lieutenants — all men high in hierarchy who each control a vast worldwide network of murderers, arsonists, safecrackers, loan sharks, prostitutes, mercenaries, and blackmailers."

Bond clicked on the "projects" button.

Another mug shot flashed on the screen. He was a small man with fear in his eyes. "This is Abraham Charles Duvall. He was arrested in Washington, D.C., after the armed robbery of the Georgetown Savings and Loan in April 1997. He kept telling authorities that he was 'Union,' and that he would never go to jail. An 'uncle' posted bail, and Duvall was never seen again. Washington, D.C., police later received a notice from individuals claiming responsibility for the robbery. They called themselves the Union.' "

The image on the monitor changed to that of a newspaper front page. The photograph below the headline featured American soldiers carrying a wounded man on a stretcher. "Rumors that the Union was a real organization were not taken seriously by Interpol until a car bomb killed several American soldiers in Saudi Arabia in mid-1997. What was first dismissed as a political attack on the West was later revealed to be the work of a group of individuals hired by the Libyan government. Four suspects were killed when authorities attempted to arrest them. They put up a fierce fight, and one of the dying men had this to say —"

Low-quality video footage showed an Arab in fatigues lying in the dusty street of a North African village. A medic was tending to his wounds, which appeared to be massive. The cameraman asked the man something unintelligible, but the Arab's answer was quite clear: "I am proud to die for the Union."

"Even though some members have been arrested, thus far the Union have been successful at every crime they have committed and claimed responsibility for. The world's law enforcement agencies now take the Union very seriously. It appears that they have an uncanny ability to infiltrate legitimate intelligence organizations. One of the Union's most notorious achievements was recruiting a mole in the Central Intelligence Agency."

A mug shot of a man with glasses and a pockmarked face flashed on the screen. "Norman Nicholas Kalway, a midlevel official at the CIA, was caught red-handed with classified documents. It was learned that he had provided over ten million dollars' worth of data to the Union. His story was that he had been blackmailed by the organization with evidence of unusual and felonious sexual practices (all of which came out publicly after Kalway was caught). Whether the CIA agent was a victim or not, his case is indicative of the lengths that the Union will go to in order to ensnare workers."

Another mug shot replaced Kalway's, an attractive woman in her twenties, except that she had bruises on her face and hate in her eyes.

"The Mossad experienced a similar scandal when one of their agents, Katherine Laven, was found to be Union after she had poisoned her lover, Israeli cabinet member Eliahu Digar. Digar had a number of enemies, any one of whom might have tempted agent Laven with a large payoff to get rid of him. It was this case that alerted authorities to what has been called the Union's 'signature' when it comes to assassinations. Apparently poisoning Mr. Digar wasn't enough. After he had died, Miss Laven slit the man's throat from ear to ear with an extremely sharp instrument. Other murders in which the victims' throats were cut in this manner have been reported as being Union-related."

Bond was familiar with all of the Union's alleged cases. He clicked back to the "projects" menu and clicked on the most recent addition. The picture changed again to that of Bond's friend.

"The latest notch on the Union's board is the March 1999 assassination of the former governor of the Bahamas."

The photo was replaced by one of the Bahamian man who had cut the governor's throat. "Lawrence Littleby, aged twenty-seven, was responsible for the murder. He was a troublemaker who had been in and out of the local jails on various misdemeanors. He had most likely been approached with the lure of a sizable amount of money. Investigators found ten thousand U.S. dollars hidden in the man's bedroom."

Bond clicked out of "projects" and clicked on the "exit" button.

The visuals became a full-motion montage of newspaper headlines, news photos, and newsreel footage of soldiers in various forms of combat. "We believe that the Union have become more powerful in the last year. When they cannot buy someone's services, they find other, less pleasant means to persuade them to work. They are experts at everything from petty street crime to elaborate espionage schemes. It cannot be stressed enough that the Union should never be underestimated and that they should always be considered extremely dangerous."

The presentation ended. Bond thought of his old enemies, SPECTRE. They were a lot like the Union. They had been interested only in making money, and Ernst Stavro Blofeld had run the cabal with the efficiency of a corporation. The Union were different in that their tactics were more guerrilla oriented. SPECTRE had gone for grand, world-shaking events. The Union weren't particular in the jobs they performed. There was no social status or class prejudices in the Union. It was one of the keys to their success in recruiting members.

The phone by the keypad buzzed. Bond picked it up. "Yes?"

It was Miss Moneypenny. "James, I thought you were in there. You're wanted in the Briefing Room at eleven hundred sharp." Bond glanced at his watch. It was 10:50.

"Nothing like twenty-four hours' notice, Penny," he said.

"Never mind that. This is serious. Some big brass will be sitting in. See you there." She rang off and left Bond to ponder the empty, dark monitor in front of him. He sighed heavily, gathered his materials, punched the keypad so that a complete printout of the Union presentation would be delivered to his office, then left the Visual Library and took the lift to the top floor.

The place was buzzing with activity. Secretaries were rushing back and forth and phones were ringing. Bond caught up with Miss Moneypenny, who was walking fast and carrying a stack of folders toward the briefing room.

"What the hell is going on?" Bond asked.

"M declared a Code Three a few minutes ago, James. You had better get in there. The Minister of Defence and a lot of military brass are here."

"Someone probably lost a contact lens," Bond muttered, and went into the room.

The Briefing Room could easily sit a hundred people or more. Similar to the Situation Room, it contained large screens on the walls for multimedia presentations, rows of school-type chairs with attached desktops arranged in a semicircle facing the podium, and an abundance of electronic equipment. Bond eased into the room and found a place near the end of a row of chairs. Looking around, he was surprised to see some of the people there.

M was quietly conversing with the Minister of Defence near the podium. Bill Tanner was standing by, awaiting instructions. Occupying the other chairs were various top staff members such as Head of S., Head of Records, and Head of Counterintelligence. There were several visitors next to them, including Air Marshal Whipple, the head of MI5, and none other than Group Captain Roland Marquis.

Tanner called the meeting to order. "Ladies and gentlemen, the Minister of Defence wishes to address you first."

The Minister took the stand and cleared his throat. "Last night an act of industrial espionage and terrorism was committed against our country. A top secret formula for a hot plasma bonding process known as Skin 17 was stolen from one of the DERA's secret research facilities in Fleet. It is of vital importance to Great Britain that we track down the individuals responsible for this and retrieve the formula. Christopher Drake, a director of the DERA, will explain further."

The Minister relinquished the floor to Mr. Drake, a tall, distinguished man of fifty.

"Good morning. I've been asked to explain in layman's terms what we at the DERA were developing for the RAF. It has been a longtime goal for the UK to be the first country in the world to develop an aircraft material that could withstand a speed of Mach 7. An as-yet-unattainable speed, Mach 7 is the Holy Grail in the aerospace industry. Now, we all know that the technology has existed for years to create the power to push a plane to that speed, and the materials exist to build an airframe. Think of it. The benefits to both civil and especially military aviation are self-evident. One could fly from London to New York in forty minutes — or bomb three countries in a half hour. Two years ago the Minister of Defence ordered us, along with the RAF, to develop a material that could stand up to the wear and tear that would occur at a speed of Mach 7.

"The problem has always been that at such a high speed, mere atmospheric dust is sufficient to dent and tear the skin off the plane. The way around this dilemma is found in the science of fluid dynamics. An object traveling through a fluid creates

102

around itself a boundary layer which essentially pushes the elements of the fluid out of the way, creating a 'tunnel effect.' It's through this tunnel that the object travels relatively unimpeded. Turbulence issues abound in this science; the mathematics are extremely complicated; the engineering problems are bigger. The trick is to create 'Smart Skin' materials for the plane that would expand and alter this boundary layer, essentially forming the optimal aerodynamic configuration through which the plane would fly. This material would be a carbon-fiber and silica ceramic. But because carbon-fiber and silica do not easily bond, the DERA spent two years developing a hot plasma bonding process."

Slides began to appear on the large screens. The first was a photo of Dr. Wood.

"Yesterday Dr. Thomas Wood, whom we hired to work on the project at our secret warehouse in Fleet, successfully completed the formula — or so we believe. The DERA and the British military establishment have kept this project top secret and we were quite eager to unveil the results — giving the UK a much-needed leg up, strategically speaking, over our allies and enemies. Commercially, it is worth billions."

The slide changed to an exterior shot of the Fleet warehouse.

"Shortly after twenty-one hundred hours last night, someone infiltrated the lab in Fleet. The entire facility was burned to the ground. Records were destroyed and there was virtually nothing salvageable. We did unfortunately find the remains of Dr. Wood, who had been shot in the leg and in the head. All traces of Skin 17, the specification he created, have disappeared. The thieves were also successful in stealing backup copies of previous versions of the formula that were kept at the DERA facility in Farnborough, indicating that, I'm sorry to say, a DERA employee may have been involved in the crime. Unfortunately, there are no other copies of this important work, which represents two years of intensive research and development. Needless to say, it is vital that no copies of the Skin 17 specification fall into the wrong hands."

Tanner had inched along the wall and was now standing next to Bond's seat.

"I assume this was the project you were referring to yesterday," Bond whispered.

Tanner whispered back, "Uh-huh."

The slide changed to a picture of Steven Harding.

"This is Dr. Steven Harding, who was serving as Dr. Wood's right-hand man. The rest of his team have been summoned back from various parts of the country and are here in this room. Dr. Wood had given them the day off yesterday because he wanted to make the final tests on the scalable prototype alone. We know that Wood left instructions for Dr. Harding to come to the lab at nine o'clock last night. Whether or not he did this is unknown, but we find it disturbing that Dr. Harding is missing. He is simply nowhere to be found."

Bond whispered to Tanner, "Christ, we just played golf with him yesterday!"

"I know," Tanner replied. "This is all very bizarre."

Mr. Drake said, "I'd like to call to the stand Group Captain Roland Marquis, who was the RAF liaison to the 'Smart Skin' project."

Marquis stood up and stiffly walked to the front of the room. "Before I field questions," he said, "I want to say that I am extremely proud of the work Dr. Wood and his team did on this project. Great Britain has lost a national treasure in him. Now, Minister, M, distinguished colleagues, I am at your disposal."

The Minister spoke first. "Group Captain, we understand that you saw Dr. Harding yesterday."

"Yes, sir," Marquis replied. "I played golf with him at Stoke Poges. It was around seventeen hundred hours when we said good-bye and parted company."

"Did he indicate to you what his plans were?"

"No, sir, I knew that Dr. Wood had given the team the day off, and that he was close to finishing Skin 17. Dr. Harding was quite eager to hear news from Dr. Wood. He made at least two phone calls from the club to find out what was going on. I knew that Dr. Harding would be visiting the lab later that evening, that is, last night. Other than that, he didn't say much. He's a professional and would never talk about the work outside the DERA complex, even with me."

M asked, "How well do you know this Dr. Harding?"

"Not very well. I got to know him over the last two years during the normal day-to-day administrative work I did in supervising Skin 17. One day we discovered a mutual interest in golf. That's all. Yesterday was the third time we had played together."

"How close to the project were you?" she asked.

"I had no idea what they were actually doing, technically. I mean, I knew what their goal was and I knew generally how they were going about it. But I'm no physicist, ma'am. My job was to control the budget, make sure they had what they needed, and make monthly reports to my superiors in the RAF."

"And you have no idea where Dr. Harding is now?"

"None, ma'am."

"Do you think he is capable of doing something like this?"

Marquis paused a moment before answering. Finally, he said, "I don't think so, ma'am. Dr. Harding always struck me as an introvert, a quiet type with a high intellect. I never once saw him get angry. I can't imagine that he'd have a violent bone in his body, much less be a traitor to his country. He has no criminal record. I know that stranger things have happened in our government's history with regard to spies and counterspies. Nevertheless, it is my opinion that Dr. Harding may have come to an untimely end, along with Dr. Wood."

After a moment's silence, Bond raised his hand. Marquis raised his eyebrows when he saw who it was. "Yes, uhm, Mr. Bond?"

"Have there been any communications at all claiming responsibility for this act?"

"No, not yet."

"In your opinion, do you think it's the work of a foreign power?"

"At this point, I'm not ruling out anything. MI5 is handling the investigation. However, as you will see in your briefing packet, there is a copy of a fax that was received at the DERA Fleet facility exactly nine and one half months ago. Dr. Wood had shown it to me, thinking it was some kind of prank. I kept the note since the fax number at the facility had always been classified. Can we show that slide, please?"

The slide on the wall changed again to reveal a blurry copy of a faxed piece of paper. There was no mistaking the wording, however.

GOOD LUCK WITH THE SKIN PROJECT. WE ARE VERY INTERESTED IN YOUR PROGRESS.
                                    THE UNION

Bond felt a chill slither down his spine.

Marquis continued. "I don't know a lot about this Union, but I was briefed this morning on the group's recent activities. It sounds to me like the kind of job they would pull off. Any other questions?"

When there were none, M stood up. "Thank you, Group Captain. We'll start the debriefing with you and the rest of Dr. Wood's team after lunch."

Bond stepped into M's office to find her alone with Bill Tanner.

"Come in, Double-O Seven," she said. "Sit down."

He sat across from the woman whom he had grown to admire more and more during the past two years. There had been a considerable amount of friction between them when she first took over MI6, but now they had mutual respect. Bond had especially proved his value to her during her personal crisis during the Decada affair a year earlier.

"I understand you and the Chief of Staff played golf with Group Captain Marquis and Dr. Harding yesterday," she said.

"Yes, ma'am."

"I want to hear what you think."

Bond shrugged. "I'm just as puzzled as anyone. I agree with Marquis's assessment of Harding — that he really didn't seem the type to do something like this. My suspicions would be directed more toward Marquis."

M's eyebrows rose. "Really? Why?"

"Because he's an arrogant son of a bitch."

Bond's outspokenness didn't faze her. "I know all about your history together," she said. "Please don't carry schoolboy prejudices into this, Double-O Seven."

"Nevertheless, ma'am," Bond said, "I don't think too highly of him."

"Group Captain Marquis is a distinguished officer and a national hero of sorts. You're aware of his mountaineering achievements?"

"Yes, ma'am. You're absolutely right, I'm allowing my personal feelings about the man to influence my opinion of him. And my opinion is that he is an ass."

"Your opinion is noted," M said, "but I'm afraid you'll need more than professional jealousy as evidence of Group Captain Marquis's guilt."

That stung.

She nodded to Tanner. He handed an eight-by-ten glossy black-and-white photograph to Bond. It was taken by a security camera and revealed a fuzzy shot of Steven Harding in a line of people. He was carrying an attaché case and a travel bag.

"We just got this," Tanner said. "It was taken last night around ten-thirty by one of the customs security cameras at Waterloo Station — at the Eurostar terminal. Dr. Steven Harding boarded the last train to Brussels."

"Why Belgium?" Bond asked.

"Who knows? We've contacted Station B to see if we can have his movements traced. MI5 have turned the investigation over to us. We believe that Skin 17 is no longer in the UK."

M spoke up. "Double-O Seven, I want you to go to Brussels and rendezvous with Station B. Your job is to track down Dr. Harding. If he has Skin 17, you're to do everything in your power to get it back. The Minister of Defence is obsessed with this Mach 7 business and with Great Britain being the first to achieve this goal. He's told me in no uncertain terms that the formula must be recovered. I'm afraid I agree with him that it would be disastrous should Skin 17 get into the hands of a country like, say, Iraq or Iran . . . or Red China. I wouldn't want the Russian Mafia to get hold of it. I wouldn't want *Japan* to have it. Double-O Seven, it's also a matter of principle. We developed it. Here in Britain. Dr. Wood was a brilliant British physicist. We *want* the credit for developing the process. Do I make myself clear?"

"Yes, ma am."

"Good luck, then."

Bond stopped by his office to gather his things, then paused by Helena Marksbury's desk.

"I, uhm, have to go to Brussels," he said.

Helena was typing furiously and didn't stop to look at him. "I know. You're to pick up the Jaguar from Q Branch before you leave today. I'm making arrangements for you to use the channel tunnel so you can drive across. I thought you'd prefer that."

"Thank you."

"Station B is handling your hotel. The contact's name is Gina Hollander. She'll meet you at the Manneken-Pis at fourteen hundred hours tomorrow."

"All right."

"Good luck."

Bond placed his hand over hers to stop her typing. "Helena . . ."

"Please, James," she said softly. "Just go. I'll be fine. When you get back, everything will be . . . as before."

Bond removed his hand and nodded. Without saying another word, he turned and walked toward the elevator.

FIVE

The Golden Pacemaker

Approximately twelve hours before James Bond received his assignment to track Dr. Steven Harding to Belgium, the physicist arrived at the Midi station in Brussels and took a taxi to the Métropole, the only nineteenth-century hotel in the famed city. Located in the heart of Brussels in the Place de Brouckère, the historical center, the Hôtel Métropole is more like a palace than a hotel. French architect Alban Chambon brought a mixture of styles to the interior by infusing it with an air of luxury and richness of materials — paneling, polished teak, Numidian marble, gilded bronze, and forged iron.

Most visitors find the French Renaissance main entrance and the Empire-style reception hall breathtaking, but Harding wasn't interested in the historical or aesthetic qualities of the hotel. He was tired and frightened, and he wanted to get Phase Two out of the way as soon as possible so that he could collect his money and flee to some island in the South Pacific.

"*Oui, monsieur?*" the receptionist asked.

Harding stammered, "Uhm, sorry, I only speak English."

The receptionist, used to foreign visitors, smoothly switched languages. "What can I do for you, sir?"

"I have a reservation. Peters. Donald Peters."

The young woman looked it up on the computer. "Yes, Mr. Peters. Your room has been paid for. How many nights will you be staying?"

"I'm not sure. Possibly three?"

"That's fine, just let us know. Do you have bags?"

"Just what I'm carrying."

He wrote false information on the registration card, then took the key.

"You're in the Sarah Bernhardt Room, Number 1919 on the third floor."

"Thank you," Harding said. He took the key and carried his luggage to the elevator, waving away the porter. The elevator was an old-fashioned cagelike contraption with impressive metallic beams rising up through the ceiling.

Sarah Bernhardt's autograph was engraved on a gold plaque on the door of his room. Apparently the famous actress had once lived in the suite. The hotel was indeed *the* spot for the rich and famous throughout the last century.

Harding locked the door behind him and breathed a sigh of relief. So far, so good. He hadn't noticed anyone tailing him. There were no suspicious characters lurking about. Perhaps he was really going to get away with it.

Feeling more confident than he had in weeks, Harding went straight to the minibar in the sitting room, unlocked it, and found a small bottle of vodka. He opened it and drank it straight, out of the bottle. Only then did he begin to appreciate the splendor of the hotel.

The suite was divided into two large rooms. The sitting room was equipped with a large wood desk, the minibar, a television, a glass-top coffee table, green chairs and a sofa, a closet with a full-length mirror, potted plants, and a large window that opened onto a terrace. The walls were yellow with white molding. The bedroom was just as spacious, with a king-sized bed, another glass-top table, chairs with the same green upholstery, a second television, oak dresser and cabinet, and small tables by the bed. Another large window opened to the terrace. The bathroom was in brown tile and contained all the amenities one could ask for. A frosted-glass panel covered half the area above the bathtub for showering.

"This is *great!*" Harding said aloud, rubbing his hands with glee. He was not accustomed to such luxury. Working for the Union certainly had its perks.

The taxi driver was curious as to why Harding wanted to go to a doctor's surgery after midnight.

"They closed, they closed," the driver said in imperfect English.

"He's expecting me," Harding insisted. He handed the man one thousand Belgian francs. "Here, I'll pay you the fare when we get there. And I'll need you to wait for me."

The driver shrugged and took the money. The cab took Harding to Avenue Franklin-Roosevelt, located in an elegant area of the city near the Hippodrome. It is full of lush green parks and expensive town homes, but in the dark it looked like anywhere else.

The driver let him out at Dr. Hendrik Lindenbeek's residence. As in most European countries, doctors in Belgium usually carried on their practice from their homes.

Harding rang the bell, and Lindenbeek answered the door after a few seconds. He was a young Flemish cardiologist.

"Come in," he said in English. Harding noted that Dr. Lindenbeek's hand shook as he gestured him inside.

Lindenbeek led him through the patient waiting area, which consisted of wicker furniture in a white room, and into the large examination room. Besides the examining table, there was a large wooden desk, bookshelves, trays with equipment, and an X-ray machine with lead wall partitions.

"Is our patient ready to go?" Harding asked.

Dr. Lindenbeek nodded. "The surgery is scheduled for eight o'clock tomorrow morning. I need to get some sleep so I don't make any mistakes!" He laughed nervously.

"You had better not make any mistakes. Now, tell me exactly what you're going to do."

Dr. Lindenbeek took some stationery from his desk and drew a sketch of a man's torso. He made a small square on the figure's upper left breast. "The pacemaker will be inserted here. It's a routine operation. Takes about three to four hours, maybe less."

"Does the patient go home the same day?"

"He can, but I prefer him to remain in the hospital overnight. He can go home the following day."

Harding didn't like that. He was on a tight schedule.

"What about traveling? Will he be able to fly?"

"Sure," Lindenbeek said. "He just needs to take it easy for a few days to make sure the skin heals. The pocket of skin where we put the pacemaker might open up. It could get infected. We wouldn't want that to happen."

"No, we wouldn't," Harding agreed. "But could he handle a long aeroplane flight?"

"I don't see why not."

"Good." Harding took the sketch and opened the attaché case. He dropped it inside, then removed the envelope containing the Skin 17 microdot. "This is it. It's attached to a piece of film. Whatever you do, don't lose it. It'll be *your* neck. Remember what the Union have on you."

Lindenbeek swallowed hard. "How can I forget?" He gingerly took the envelope from Harding.

Hospital Erasme, located on Route de

Lennik south of Brussels, is one of the most modern and largest facilities in all of Belgium. As it is also a university hospital, Erasme is considered to have the best equipment and technology in the country, as well as the most sophisticated and professional staff.

At exactly 7:55 A.M., a few hours before Bond would attend the Skin 17 emergency briefing, Dr. Lindenbeek walked into surgery on the second floor wearing greens, mask, and a cap. He scrubbed his hands and allowed a nurse to fit rubber gloves over them. The patient, a fifty-eight-year-old Chinese man named Lee Ming, was already on the table and was groggy from the drugs he had been given. Preparing the patient for surgery had taken nearly an hour.

A local anesthetic was applied to Lee's left side, under the collarbone. Lindenbeek examined his equipment while he waited for the drugs to work. The pacemaker was a top-line "demand" model made by Sulzer Intermedics Inc., which meant that the device sensed the heart's activity and stimulated it only when the natural rate fell below a certain level. Lindenbeek preferred Sulzer Intermedics, an American company, not only because they had a convenient office in Belgium, but because he considered them the best.

"He's ready, doctor," the anesthetist said in Flemish.

Dr. Lindenbeek inserted a needle to find the subclavian vein under the left collarbone. After he found it, he made a subcutaneous incision to one side of the needle. He then slid an introducer over the needle, which looked like a big syringe with no plunger. The next step was to insert the pacemaker leads through the introducer down the vein into the heart. Fluoroscopy was used to visualize the lead in the patient.

"I think I'll need a stylet," Lindenbeek said. He removed the lead and placed a wire stylet on it so that it would be a little stiffer. This would aid in positioning the lead.

It was a tedious process but one that had to be performed with precision and care. The first lead took nearly an hour to position, and there was still a second one to insert. Ninety minutes into the operation, Lindenbeek was ready to go on to the next step.

The electrical status of the leads was checked to see how much energy was actually needed to pace the heart. Lindenbeek cautiously adjusted the electricity, then took the gold-colored pacemaker from the tray. He attached the leads to the pacemaker, then gave the order to check everything on the EKG.

"Looks good, doctor," the nurse said.

He nodded, then proceeded to carry on with the final phase of the operation. He carefully made a "pocket" under the incision by blunt dissection between the pectoral muscle and the skin. Once that was done, Lindenbeek inserted the sealed pacer into the pocket and closed the incision.

"Right," Lindenbeek said. "You're all finished, Mr. Lee."

Lee blinked. "I think I fell asleep."

"You did fine. We're going to take you to the recovery room now. I'll see you in a little bit. Try not to move too much."

Lee was wheeled out of surgery and Lindenbeek removed his gloves and mask. He went to the waiting room, where he found Steven Harding reading a magazine. Harding saw him and stood up.

"Well?" he asked.

"Everything's fine," Lindenbeek said. "He can go home tonight if you really want, but I recommend he stay until tomorrow morning."

Harding considered this and said, "All right. I'd rather be safe than sorry." He then lowered his voice and asked, "So . . . where exactly is it?"

Lindenbeek whispered, "The microdot is attached to the battery inside the pacemaker. I had to do it that way in order to seal the pacemaker and sterilize it."

Harding nodded. "Good. That's fine, then. Well done."

"I'm glad you are pleased. Now, will this nightmare finally end?"

Harding smiled, his beady, birdlike eyes sparkling. "I will speak to my superiors this afternoon. I'm sure they will be in touch. Thank you, doctor."

As Harding left the waiting room, Dr. Lindenbeek stood and watched him. He didn't like that man. He didn't like anyone associated with the so-called Union. At least he had done what they wanted. Now he prayed that he could get on with his life in peace.

Harding took a taxi back to the hotel and indulged himself in a fine lunch at the Métropole café. It consisted of creamed potato soup with smoked eel, salmon in flaky pastry with sevruga caviar, asparagus, and a bottle of Duvel beer. After lunch he went to the Rue d'Aerschot, Brussels's meager red light district, where he spent several thousand Belgian francs in the company of a plump but serviceable prostitute.

When he got back to his room that evening, the message light on his phone was blinking. He retrieved the message, frowned, and returned the call.

It was not good news.

"Damn," he muttered to himself. He hung up the phone, then dialed a local contact in Brussels.

"Hello?" he muttered to the Frenchman who answered. "I don't speak French. Listen, this is Mongoose, right? I've just learned that a British secret service agent is driving here tomorrow in a blue Jaguar XK8. He's on to us. He'll be on the E19, coming into Brussels, between noon and two o'clock. Is there something you can do about him?"

SIX

The Road to Brussels

James Bond picked up the Jaguar XK8 from Q Branch after receiving a brief admonition from Major Boothroyd concerning a couple of new features he had added since Bond had used the car last. One of these was a supercharger, an Eaton M112, which normally delivered 370 bhp and 387-pound-foot torque. Bond had insisted on a modification to increase the boost to give 500 bhp, which Boothroyd had reluctantly made.

He took the M20 motorway to the Channel Tunnel Terminal between Dover and Folkestone and boarded Le Shuttle auto-transporter, which, in thirty-five minutes, unloaded cars at Calais. Bond skirted south toward Lille, then got on the E19, the Paris to Brussels autoroute. Recent rains and sunny weather made the landscape rich with green, yellow, and orange brushstrokes. The countryside whipped past Bond as he tested the new supercharger on the open road. It felt great to get away from England and finally make headway on the case.

The Jaguar was twenty miles from "the Ring," the busy roadway that encircled the main city, when Bond noticed two high-speed motorcycles gaining on him. They appeared to be identical dark green Kawasaki ZZ-R1100 superbikes. Bond was familiar with the vehicles and knew them to be powerful, heavy, and very fast. Obtaining an extra boost from a ram-air system that ducted cool air from a slot in the fairing nose to a pressurized air box, they could easily keep up with the Jaguar.

A third ZZ-R1100 pulled out onto the highway from an entrance ramp in front of him just as the other two reached a point fifty yards behind Bond's car. He was certain that they were performing rehearsed maneuvers — the timing was just too skillful. Bond sat straight in the seat, gripped the wheel, and increased his speed to ninety in order to overtake the motorcycle in the right lane in front of him. It didn't help that traffic was moderately heavy.

Bond veered into the center lane so that he could pass the rider and get a good look at him. At that angle he appeared to be dressed in army fatigues and an olive green crash helmet, neatly color coordinated with the bike. Was it a costume? Perhaps the three riders were part of some kind of auto show and weren't dangerous at all?

The motorcycle suddenly swerved into Bond's lane, preventing him from passing. Bond was forced to ease his speed down to seventy, which gave the two men behind him an opportunity to close the gap.

Now at a distance of thirty feet, the two pursuers were side by side in the same lane behind Bond. Bond swerved into the far left lane, but all three motorcycles followed suit as if they were operating by remote control.

There was no doubt now, Bond thought, these men had to be professionals. He changed lanes again, back to the center, and then to the far right, as the super-bikes immediately adjusted to pin him in again.

Bond was peering at the riders behind him in the rearview mirror when he noticed a sudden puff of black smoke just below one of the windshields. He felt a series of fast, hard jolts in the back of the Jaguar.

Bond set his jaw. The bastard had fired a volley of machine gun bullets at his petrol tank.

The two riders looked at each other as if to ask "Why didn't the car explode?" Bond allowed himself a smile. The body's chobam armor was impenetrable and had reactive skins that exploded when hit, thereby deflecting the bullets. The metal was self-healing by virtue of viscous fluid.

Apparently able to communicate with each other via headsets, the riders prepared a new strategy. One of the men behind Bond pulled into the right-hand lane and sped up so that he was parallel to the Jaguar. The rider looked at Bond and mouthed what must have been an unsavory epithet.

Bond pulled the wheel sharply to the right, ramming into the motorcycle. The Kawasaki was knocked off the road and onto the shoulder, where it fell on its side and skidded for a hundred feet before stopping. Bond had hoped the cycle would be completely wrecked, but the rider apparently wasn't harmed and would be back on the road in a minute or two. He moved the J mechanism into manual mode and floored the accelerator. The Jaguar shot ahead of the front cycle, then maneuvered around slower civilian vehicles to put some distance between him and the green bikers. Bond hoped that he wouldn't have to use deadly force against these men on such a busy highway, and wondered if he should telephone the Belgian police on his mobile phone.

The remaining two cyclists darted in and out of the traffic to catch up with Bond. Road repairs had caused the far left lane to be closed at one point. Now relegated to only two lanes, the traffic was thicker. Bond sped up and soon found himself tailgating two ten-wheel lorries that were blocking both lanes. They were both traveling at unsafe speeds, attempting to outrace each other. Bond honked the horn, hoping that one would pull into the other's lane. The driver in the lorry in front of him blasted his own horn, challenging Bond to do something about it.

"Defense systems on," Bond said aloud. One of the new features that Q Branch had put in the car was voice activation for all systems — phone, audio, lighting, and, of course, weaponry. An icon flashed on the telematics screen on the dashboard, indicating that Bond's command had been executed.

"Activate flying scout," he said. An outline of the scout, a device the size of a small model airplane, appeared on the screen. It was stored underneath the chassis until it was activated from inside the car. The scout could fly out from under the vehicle and reach an altitude of Bond's choosing. It was steerable by joystick or satellite navigation.

The display changed to read SCOUT READY.

"Launch scout," he commanded. He felt a sudden whoosh behind the Jaguar as the scout ejected from its bay. The batlike vehicle soared out and up into the air, then turned so that it was traveling thirty feet above and parallel with the Jaguar. The two motorcyclists couldn't believe their eyes. One of them pointed to the scout and shouted something.

Keeping one hand on the wheel, Bond used his left hand to manipulate the joystick. He sent the scout forward and increased its speed so that it would move up beside the lorries, which were still barreling down the road neck and neck.

Bond lowered the scout slowly without decreasing its speed. Like a hummingbird, the aircraft gently positioned itself so that it was flying at door level in between the two lorries. The driver of the lorry on the right looked to his left and saw the strange contraption flying just outside his window. He gasped and almost ran off the road, but he managed to straighten the wheel in time.

The chobam armor, which also coated the scout, was quite effective for battering purposes. Bond moved the joystick so that the plane swung to the right with great force, shattering the driver's window with its wing. He pulled the scout up and out of the way as the driver then completely lost control of the lorry. It careened off the road, over the shoulder, then turned over and crashed into the ditch.

That should get the attention of the police, Bond thought. He increased the speed and shot past the other lorry, whose frightened driver had dropped his speed to forty. The scout, meanwhile, returned to its place above the Jaguar.

Surprisingly, a stretch of road ahead of Bond was relatively traffic free. He opened up, hoping that the two pursuers would follow him into the clear area. In a moment he saw them zoom past the lorry that he had left behind. One Kawasaki was gaining fast, the other dropping back a bit.

"Prepare silicon fluid bomb," Bond said. Another new feature on the car, the oil or silicon fluid explosives could be dropped from the rear bumper into the path of a pursuing vehicle. They were more direct and caused "cleaner" damage than the Jaguar's heat-seeking rockets, which were meant for heavier targets.

The Kawasaki moved into position behind Bond, and the rider fired its machine gun again. Bond felt the impact ricochet off the back of the car, then said, "Launch bomb."

A device the size of a compact disc dropped out of the bumper and rolled out onto the road. The rider on the motorcycle saw it and attempted to swerve around it, but it was too late. The device exploded with a tremendous blast, sending pieces of the Kawasaki and its rider into the air. The highway was soon littered with black smoke, burnt metal, and seared body parts.

The other rider pulled into the left lane and zigzagged around the debris, staying on Bond's tail. When he was in range, he fired his guns at the Jaguar, too.

"Ready rear laser," Bond said. The icon appeared on the screen.

The cycle moved closer, the bullets still flying. One of the back tires burst, but the car was engineered so that it could run on flats.

"Count of three for one-second laser flash," Bond said. "One . . . two . . . *three*."

The sudden bright light confused the rider behind him. At first he thought it was glare from the sun, bouncing off a piece of reflective metal on the back of the Jaguar. Momentarily blinded, he kept the handlebars straight, hoping that his sight would clear in a few seconds — but then the pain began. His eyes felt as if they were being burned with hot pokers, and then there was nothing but darkness. The laser flash had permanently seared his retinas.

Bond watched in the rearview mirror as the Kawasaki wobbled and veered to the left. It crashed through the repair lane and guardrail, then slid into the oncoming traffic on the other side of the road. Horns blared and drivers slammed on their brakes. Several cars crashed into one another in an effort to avoid hitting the motorcycle, but the Kawasaki was run over by a van and dragged at least two hundred yards before both hunks of metal came to a stop.

Bond could hear sirens in the distance. They were coming from the city, the opposite direction from which he was traveling. He looked in the rearview mirror and saw that the third motorcycle, the one he had bumped off the road earlier, had rejoined the chase. Bond presumed correctly that this rider was unaware of the flying scout soaring above the Jaguar at a safe distance. He gently pushed the joystick so that the scout decreased speed, then made an about-face. Bond brought the scout down to a level equal to that of the cyclist, then pushed the throttle. It shot back toward the cycle at full speed.

The rider gasped when he saw the strange, birdlike thing headed straight for him. He barely had time to scream.

The scout met the cycle head-on, knocking the rider off the bike. Bond pulled the scout up and away as the motorcycle skidded on its side and eventually came to rest in the ditch.

"Prepare to dock scout," Bond said as he maneuvered the remarkable device back behind the Jaguar.

He gave the command, and the bird pulled underneath the chassis and locked into place just as Bond entered "the Ring." Blending in with heavy traffic, the Jaguar safely drove past the power plants, car dealerships, and business parks that dotted the landscape.

Bond activated the mobile speaker phone, then called out the speed dial code for headquarters in London. After the normal security checks, he was put through to Bill Tanner's office. His secretary answered and told Bond that M and the Chief of Staff were off-site at a meeting.

"Damn," he said. "Put me through to Helena Marksbury, please."

In a moment he heard his personal assistant's lilting voice.

"James?" she answered. Bond could hear her apprehension. She probably had looked forward to a few days of his absence.

"Helena, we have a problem," he said. "Someone knew I was on my way to Brussels, and three men on motorcycles tried to kill me."

"My God, James, are you all right?" she asked with concern.

"Yes. I need you to get this message to the Chief of Staff immediately. He and M are at a meeting off-site." He gave her the details. "Find them and tell them that a Code Eighty is in effect." This meant that a security breach had occurred.

"Right," she said. "I'm on it now, James. Are you in Brussels?"

"Almost. I'll talk to you later."

"Be careful," she said, then rang off. Despite the awkward situation that existed between them, Bond was thankful that Helena was capable of carrying on in a professional manner.

He soon got off the Ring road and onto Industrial Boulevard, which led toward the center of Brussels, and once again offered a silent thanks to Major Boothroyd and the rest of Q Branch.

It was a beautiful, sunny, spring day. Bond parked the car in a garage near the Grand Place, the magnificent square that is considered the centerpiece of Brussels. Bordered on all four sides by icons of Belgium's royal history, the Grand Place is a dazzling display of ornamental gables, gilded facades, medieval banners, and gold-filigreed rooftop sculptures. The Gothic Town Hall, dating back to the early 1400s, remains intact; the other buildings, the neo-Gothic King's House and the Brewers Guild House, date from the late 1600s. The Brussels aldermen continue to meet in the Town Hall, the exterior of which is decorated in part by fifteenth- and sixteenth-century insider's jokes. The sculptures include a group of drinking monks, a sleeping Moor and his harem, a heap of chairs resembling the medieval torture called strappado, and St. Michael slaying a female-breasted devil. Bond had once heard a story that the architect, Jan van Ruysbroeck, committed suicide by leaping from the belfry when he realized that it is off center and has an off-center entrance.

It was nearly two o'clock. Bond put on a pair of Ray-Ban Wayfarers sunglasses that would identify him to his contact, then walked southwest through the colorful and narrow cobblestoned streets to the intersection of Rue du Chêne and Rue de l'Étuve. There, surrounded by camera-snapping tourists, was the famous statue of the urinating little boy known as Manneken-Pis. Although not the original statue (which was subject to vandalism and was removed), the current idol is an exact replica and is perhaps the most well known symbol of Brussels. Bond didn't know what its origins were, but he knew that it dated from the early 1400s and was perhaps the effigy of a patriotic Belgian lad who sprinkled a hated Spanish sentry who had passed beneath his window. Another story was that he had saved the Town Hall from a small fire by extinguishing it using the only means available. Today, "Little Julian," as he is called, was dressed in a strange red cloak with a white fur collar. Louis XV of France began the tradition of presenting colorful costumes to the little boy and since then he has acquired hundreds of outfits.

"He must have a very large bladder to keep peeing like that," a female voice said in English, but with a thick European accent.

Bond glanced to his left and saw an attractive woman dressed in a smart beige trouser suit and a light jacket. She was wearing Ray-Bans; had strawberry-blond, short, curly hair; a light cream complexion; and her sensual lips were painted with light red lipstick. A toothpick lodged at the corner of her mouth. She appeared to be around thirty, and she had the figure of a fashion model.

"I'm just glad this isn't considered a drinking fountain," Bond replied.

She removed the sunglasses to reveal bright blue eyes that sparkled in the sunlight. She held out her hand and said, "Gina Hollander. Station B."

Bond took her hand, which felt smooth and warm. "Bond. James Bond."

"Come on," she said, gesturing with her head, "let's go to the station house, then we'll get your car and take it to your hotel." Her English was good, but Bond could tell she wasn't terribly comfortable with it.

"*Parlez-vous français?*" he asked.

"*Oui,*" she said, then switched back to English, "but my first language is Dutch, Flemish. You speak Dutch?"

"Not nearly as well as you speak English," he replied.

"Then let's stick to English, I need the practice."

She was not beautiful, but Bond found her very appealing. The short, curly hairstyle gave her a pixielike quality that most people would describe as cute, an adjective Bond always avoided. She was petite, but she walked with confidence and grace, as if she were six feet tall.

"Which is my hotel, by the way?" he asked.

"The Métropole. It's one of the best in town."

"I know it. I've stayed there before."

"Our target is staying there, too."

"Oh?"

"I'll tell you all about it when we get to the station house. It's just over here."

She led him into a very narrow street off Petite Rue des Bouchers, near the famous folk puppet showcase Théâtre Toone, and into a pastry shop. The smell of baked goods was overpowering.

"Care for a cream puff?" she asked.

He smiled and said, "Later, perhaps."

Gina said something in Flemish to the woman behind the counter, then led Bond through a door, into the kitchen, where a large, sweating man was loading a tray of rolls into an oven. She went through another door to a staircase that led to a second-floor loft: the headquarters of Station B.

It was a comfortable one room/one bathroom flat that had been transformed into an office, just barely large enough for an operative and some equipment. Besides the usual computer gear, file cabinets, fax machine, and copier, there was a sofa bed, a television, and kitchenette. It was decorated with a decidedly feminine touch, and there was an abundance of Belgian lace draped over the furniture.

"I don't live here, but the sofa bed is handy if I ever have to stay late," she said as they entered. "Have a seat anywhere. You want something to drink?"

"Vodka with ice, please. Before we do anything, though, I have to call London. We have a little problem."

"What's that?"

"We have a security leak. Someone knew I was coming. I was attacked on the E19."

"Really? That was *you?* I *heard* about the

accidents on the road! Are you all right?"

Bond removed his gunmetal case and took out a cigarette. He offered one to her, but she shook her head.

"I'm fine, but they're not," he said. "Three men on motorcycles. Came from nowhere, tried to kill me. I'm afraid a lorry was smashed, and a few passenger cars, too. I tried to call London earlier, but everyone was in a bloody meeting."

She pointed to the desk. "I assure you there's been no security breach here. The phone is there. Please."

Bond reached for the phone and removed from the inside pocket of his jacket a device that looked like a small black light meter. He pulled out a three-inch antenna and flicked a switch. He scanned the phone with the detector.

"I do that every morning, Mr. Bond," Gina said. "With more sophisticated equipment."

"I doubt it could do much better than this little toy," Bond said, satisfied with the reading he got. The CSS 8700V Bug Alert was usually accurate. "Sorry, I had to check."

"That's all right." She went to the kitchenette to get the drinks.

Bond picked up the phone and called

the secure line again. This time Tanner picked up.

"Hello, James, sorry I was away earlier. M wanted me to —"

"Never mind, did Helena give you the message?"

"Yes, she did. We're looking into it now. How many people knew you were on the way to Brussels?"

"Just you and M. Moneypenny and Helena, of course. Major Boothroyd, Head of S., Records . . . well, I suppose there could be quite a few people, Bill."

"No one outside the firm?"

"No, not even my housekeeper. She never knows where I am."

"Right," Tanner said. "Look, don't worry, we'll see if we can find the hole and plug it. In the meantime, M has new orders for you."

"Oh?"

"Since Agent Hollander has tracked down Harding, you are to observe him. Repeat, *observe* him. We want to find out who he's working for or dealing with. He must have Skin 17 or he wouldn't have fled the UK."

"Understood. You do realize that there is the possibility that he doesn't have it any-more. . . . What would you like me to do when he makes a move?"

"Use your judgment. We'd like him brought back to the UK, certainly. We're already making arrangements for extradition. If it looks like we might lose Skin 17, do whatever it takes to retrieve it."

Bond signed off and stretched back in the large reclining leather armchair behind the desk. Right on cue, Gina brought Bond's vodka and a bottle of Orval beer for herself. She sat on the sofa bed and put her feet up.

He held up his glass and said, "Cheers." He took a sip of the ice cold vodka and was pleasantly surprised. "Wolfschmidt from Riga. Well done. I think you and I will get along splendidly."

"Thanks. I save it for special occasions," she said. "I heard that Brits are hard to impress." She laughed.

"Quite the opposite. England is such a bore most of the time, so we're really quite easy. Anyway, you impressed this one. Is that the stuff made by Trappist monks?" he asked, indicating her beer.

She nodded, taking a long drink from the bottle. She managed to keep the toothpick sticking out of her mouth as she swallowed. For the first time, Bond noticed how fit she really was. Her shapely, strong leg muscles could be traced through her clothing. Her arms were also well toned. Although she was dressed as if she might be the manager of an upmarket women's department store, the toothpick in her mouth gave her an impish, mischievous quality. There was no mistaking that this woman was streetwise. She was a mature little Peter Pan with breasts, which also happened to be quite shapely.

"So, tell me about Dr. Harding," Bond said.

"When I got the alert on him from London, I ran a routine check with immigration at the Midi terminal. They caught him on camera, coming through as Donald Peters. Once I knew that, it was a matter of finding the right hotel with a Donald Peters registered there. He was at the Métropole. I waited at the café just outside. I drank a hell of a lot of coffee! He finally came out last night after dinner." She giggled slightly and said, "He went to the street where women . . . where women sell sexual favors."

Bond smiled with her. "Did he have a good time?"

She blushed. "Don't ask me," she said. "Afterward he went back to the hotel. I tipped a bellhop to phone my pager if he left. He was there all night. This morning he took a taxi somewhere . . . and I lost him. He hasn't checked out of the hotel, though."

"So there was nearly a complete period of twenty-four hours when he could have done anything."

"I'm afraid so."

"And he could be making a deal right now."

"It's possible."

"We had better go," he said, sitting up. "I want to get into his room."

SEVEN

Bitter Suite

Bond left Gina, drove the Jaguar to the hotel, and left it with the valet. She followed him and sat in her usual seat in the sidewalk café outside the building. The plan was that she would watch the front while Bond was inside.

As he checked in, he was reminded of the time he had stayed at the Métropole when he was a young man. He had become involved with a French film star who had a husband in Paris and a career in London. They would meet in Brussels to escape the press. It was a stormy, passionate affair that went on for several months before she landed a role in a picture being shot in the Far East. He never saw her again.

As a hotel catering to the rich and famous, the Métropole's staff respected the guests' privacy. It was everything Bond expected from a good hotel with tasteful luxury and unique personal character. Full of gilded coffers, Italian stucco, modern wrought iron, Renaissance-style blue stained-glass windows, and glittering chandeliers, it was a true palace.

Bond was given a room on the fifth floor that he thought would do nicely. He unpacked his bag and removed an electric toothbrush. He snapped off the brush and unscrewed the bottom of the device. Next to the three C-cell batteries was a set of thin, stiff wires. Old-fashioned skeleton keys were still being used at the hotel, so Q Branch's electric pick gun would be the best tool for the job. Made of aluminum, it could pick pin tumbler locks much faster and easier than hand picks and could even open some of the pick-resistant locks that other tools wouldn't.

Bond slipped it into the pocket of his jacket, then reached for the phone. He called the front desk and asked to be connected to Donald Peters's room. There was no answer. Good. That was what Bond wanted.

He checked the magazine in his Walther PPK and slipped the gun in the custom-made Berns chamois shoulder holster, then left the room. He descended the grand staircase two floors and peered down the corridor. There was no one around. He moved quickly to Room 1919 and knocked. When there was no answer, he took out the pick gun, selected an attachment, and had the door unlocked in three seconds.

Closing the door behind him, he moved from the entry hall to the sitting room, where Harding had deposited his attaché case and other personal items. Harding had written "Hospital Erasme" on a notepad next to the phone. Bond tried the briefcase, but it was locked. He selected another attachment for the pick gun and inserted the wires into the keyholes. The snaps flipped open.

There wasn't much there. A map of Brussels, rail timetables, calculator, paper, pens . . . and a strange sketch on a piece of physician's stationery.

It was the torso of a man with a small rectangle drawn over his left breast. Bond noted the name and address on the stationery and replaced everything.

He quickly went through the cupboard and found nothing of interest, then went into the bedroom. Harding's suitcase was in the wardrobe, along with a few items of clothing he had hung up. Bond reached for the suitcase but stopped cold when he heard a rattling of keys outside the door.

He bolted forward and slipped into the

small bathroom. He quickly closed the door, leaving it slightly ajar, then stepped behind the frosted glass panel over the bathtub. Bond heard the suite door open, and the approaching voices of three men.

"You have to take it easy, Mr. Lee," one of them said. Bond recognized Harding's voice. "Basil here will make sure you get on the flight. How do you feel now?"

The door closed and the men went into the sitting room.

"It's not too sore," another man said with an Asian accent. "Except when I laugh." Mr. Lee . . . Chinese, perhaps?

"Basil," Harding said, "I'm leaving Brussels now. My job is done. You follow Mr. Lee and make damn sure he gets on that flight without any problems. Understand?"

"Yeah," came a deep voice.

"Sit down, Mr. Lee, while I pack," Harding said. "You want something out of the minibar?"

"No, thank you. I'll just watch TV." Bond heard the television in the sitting room switch on. A newscaster spoke in French.

"I want a beer after I go piss," Basil said. He had a pronounced French accent, but Bond thought he might be Senegalese.

"Go ahead, it's right in there," Harding said.

Christ! There was nowhere to hide. Bond's shape could easily be seen through the frosted glass. He squatted in the tub and drew the gun.

The door swung open. Through the foggy glass Bond could see a huge bulk of a man. He was black, and was dressed in a dark T-shirt and trousers. Although the image was distorted through the glass, his shoulders looked as wide as a dam's.

Basil stood in front of the toilet and started to urinate. Bond couldn't help but think that he was looking at the evil counterpart to Manneken-Pis.

"Basil?" Harding called from the other room.

"One minute, monsieur!" he yelled.

Bond didn't wait for him to finish. He stood up slowly and stepped out from behind the glass. Basil was so busy watching his stream that he didn't notice. When he felt the nuzzle of the gun in his back, he didn't stop urinating.

"Don't say a word," said Bond. "Just finish up."

The man nodded. After a few seconds, his bladder was empty.

"Go on, give it a good shake and zip up."

149

The man did as he was told.

"Better flush. Someone else may want to use it."

Basil reached out and pulled the steel bulb on top of the commode. The toilet flush was loud. Bond took the opportunity to cold-cock the man on the back of the head.

Unfortunately, it was like hitting an anvil. This took Bond by surprise, and Basil took advantage of the hesitation. He swung around, using his huge girth to slam Bond against the frosted glass panel, shattering it. The Walther PPK fell to the floor of the bathroom, discharging a round.

Basil grabbed Bond by his jacket collar and lifted him as if he were paper. Now that he was face-to-face with the thug, Bond could see that he was well over six feet tall and probably weighed in the neighborhood of three hundred pounds. His upper arms had a circumference of at least twenty inches.

Like a cat with a mouse, the big man slammed Bond back and forth against the walls around the bathtub. The tiles broke off in chunks.

"What the hell?" Harding looked in the bathroom. He stood in horror for a second, then turned to Lee, who was behind him.

"Come on, let's get out of here!"

Bond caught a glimpse of Harding and the Chinese man before Basil grabbed hold of his hair with one hand, then punched him in the face with the other. It might as well have been a wrecking ball. Once again Bond crashed back into the tub on top of shards of broken glass. Basil then raised his left leg and stomped on Bond's chest with his heavy boot, over and over.

Harding ran into the sitting room, gathered his attaché case and a couple of items from the bedroom, and pulled Lee out of the room. "Leave them, come on!" he shouted.

Bond was stunned, nearly unconscious. He could feel the boot slamming down on his rib cage and felt a terrible sharp pain. If he didn't get out of that tub fast, the man would kick him so hard that his chest cavity would collapse.

Blinded and in agony, Bond groped beside him and felt pieces of broken glass. His fingers wrapped around a long one with a sharp point. When the boot came down again, Bond thrust the weapon as hard as he could into Basil's calf.

The thug yelled so loudly that it snapped Bond out of the fog. He clutched the boot with both hands and shoved upward, throwing the big man off balance so that he toppled to the bathroom floor.

Bond jackknifed to his feet and leaped over the edge of the tub. He saw the Walther lying in the opposite corner, near the door. He tried to jump over Basil's body, but the brute managed to trip him and shove him against the toilet. Bond landed hard against the porcelain, striking his lower back. He felt the edge of the toilet dig into his kidneys, sending jolts of anguish up his spine.

Basil rose and put his hands around Bond's throat. He began to tighten his viselike grip. The man was so strong that he wouldn't merely choke Bond to death. The man was about to crush his windpipe, and possibly his neck.

Bond's eyes rolled into the back of his head as the pressure on his neck increased. Instinctively, he reached up to the counter by the sink to his left to feel for a weapon — anything that might give him an advantage. He found it in a can of spray deodorant. With the thumb and fingers of one hand, Bond flicked the top off and positioned his index finger on the button. He aimed it in front of him and sprayed.

Basil screamed again and let go of Bond's neck.

Bond immediately brought his legs up to his chest and kicked forward, knocking Basil off him and back against the bathroom wall.

There was barely enough room for one person in the bathroom, let alone two grown men, one of whom was a giant. Bond struggled to get to his feet, gasping for air as the black man bounced off the wall. The glass shard was still in his leg. Bond scooped the rest of Harding's toiletries off the counter into Basil's face. It gave Bond just enough time to get up and leap for the gun. The black man was just as fast, though. He tackled Bond and the two of them burst out of the bathroom into the entry hall. The gun was still in the bathroom.

They had a little more room here. Bond rolled backward so that he could get to his feet in the bedroom. Basil thundered after him. Bond picked up one of the chairs and threw it at the black man, who brushed it away as if he were swatting a mosquito. The chair smashed against the full-length mirror, breaking it into a hundred pieces.

"Now look what you went and did," Bond said, completely out of breath. "Your seven years of bad luck is just beginning."

Basil made a grotesque sound that resembled the roar of a lion, then charged Bond. They both fell back onto the king-sized bed, then rolled off the other side onto the floor. Bond got in two good punches, but the man was so strong, they didn't seem to bother him at all. Bond twisted out from under him and got to his feet. He performed a neat back kick and struck Basil in the face. Basil, in retaliation, simply lifted the huge mattress off the bed as if it were a pillow. He threw it at Bond with the strength of a rhinoceros. The mattress knocked Bond into the dresser. Bond grabbed a lamp and clubbed the black man with it, smashing the lamp shade and bulb.

The fight moved into the sitting room, where they had even more space in which to move. There was an open bottle of wine on top of the wet bar. Bond took it by the neck and broke it against the wall, splashing bloodred liquid all over the place. Now he had a jagged weapon. The two men faced and circled each other slowly. Bond kept Basil at a distance with the sharp edge of the bottle.

Basil smiled, then lunged at Bond. Bond swung. The razor-edged broken bottle scraped across the black man's face, creating five even tracks of blood on his skin.

Whereas any other man would have been blinded by the attack, Basil merely seemed annoyed.

Bond swiped the bottle at him again, but this time Basil caught Bond's arm and squeezed it. In pain, Bond dropped his weapon. Basil flung Bond over the writing desk and into the window. Like everything else in the beautiful hotel suite, it shattered on impact.

The desk was between him and the black man. Bond kicked and toppled it over, but Basil easily brushed it aside. Before the man could catch him, Bond spun around and dived between Basil's legs for a space on the floor behind him. This maneuver gave Bond the two seconds he needed to get back on his feet.

Just as his sense of balance returned, his opponent got up and lunged. With split-second timing, Bond grabbed the man's head and used the momentum to pull him hard and fast to his side.

Basil's head crashed into the television set that Lee had left on. It exploded with great force. There was a cloud of sparks and gray smoke as the black man suddenly tensed, then started shaking violently. After a few seconds he went limp. With the television still fitted around his head he slumped to the carpet. It was over.

Bond took stock of the damage to his body. His lower back was screaming in pain, and his ribs hurt like hell. One or two might be broken. His kidneys might be damaged. He was bleeding from several contusions on his face and hands.

But he was alive.

He found the phone on the floor and called Gina's mobile.

When she answered, he said, "Harding and a Chinese man just left the hotel. Did you see them?"

"No. When did they leave?"

"Just a few minutes ago."

"Damn. They must have gone out the back."

"Try to find them. Call me in my room in ten minutes."

"Are you coming down?" she asked.

The pain in Bond's back was making him dizzy. "In a while" was all he could manage to say. He hung up, then opened the minibar and removed a bottle of bourbon. He unscrewed the top and took a long swig. The liquor made him cough once, but the warmth felt great.

He limped to the bathroom and picked up his gun, then left the suite. Surprisingly, no one had heard the commotion. The corridor was empty.

Bond climbed the stairs to his own floor and the sanctity of his room. He went into the bathroom and looked at himself in the mirror. There was a nasty gash above his right eyebrow, and there was a darkening bruise on his left cheekbone. He washed his hands and saw that the cuts on his knuckles were superficial. His lower back and ribs were the main problems.

He plugged the drain in his own bathtub and ran the hot water until it was steaming. He undressed, gingerly pulling off his shirt and trousers. By the time he was naked, the tub was full.

Wincing, Bond lowered his bruised and battered body into the near-scalding water and fell asleep within two minutes.

EIGHT

A Taste of Belgium

The next morning, Bond allowed Gina to take him to a private infirmary, where he submitted to an examination. Sore and stiff from the ordeal in the hotel suite, he felt particularly irritable. His conversation with M on the phone the night before hadn't helped.

"So you let Dr. Harding get away?" she had asked.

"Ma'am, I didn't *let* him do anything," Bond had replied. "He escaped while I was fighting for my life."

"Hmpfh." She was beginning to sound more and more like her predecessor.

"And where was Ms. Hollander at the time?" she asked.

"Doing her job. Harding and the Chinese man slipped out by a back exit. We know they haven't left Brussels."

"How can you be sure? You seem to have butterfingers lately, Double-O Seven."

Bond wanted to snap at her but took a

deep breath instead. "Ma'am, Ms. Hollander has unshakable connections with immigration here. We would know if they had left by plane or train."

"What about by car?" she asked. "They could get in a car and drive right out of Belgium and no one would know."

The conversation ended badly. Bond promised to do his best to find Harding, and M said something to the effect that his best wasn't enough. After he rang off, he threw a glass of whisky against the wall.

Things hadn't improved in the morning. He got up feeling as if his body had been the target of a battering ram.

The doctor spoke in French to Gina. Bond understood him perfectly. He had a cracked rib.

"I see no damage to your kidneys other than bruising," the doctor told him in English. "If you notice blood in your urine, then of course you must come in for more tests."

The doctor wrapped Bond's chest in a tight harness and told him to wear it for at least a week. It had Velcro straps, so he could take it on and off for bathing, but he should certainly wear it to bed.

As they left the clinic, Gina led him to her own car, a red Citroën ZX. "We'll go and see that doctor now," she said. She moved the ever-present toothpick from one side of her mouth to the other. "I checked him out. Dr. Hendrik Lindenbeek is a cardiologist, and from what I gather, a good one."

Bond was silent in the car as they drove southeast. Away from the central historical section, Brussels became like any other modern European city. Vestiges of the old world disappeared and were replaced by late-twentieth-century architecture, shopping malls, office buildings, and elegant town homes. Franklin Roosevelt Avenue might have been Park Lane in London.

"Don't worry," Gina said, uncomfortable with Bond's sullen mood. "We'll find him. My gut tells me he hasn't left Brussels."

"My gut tells me that I should leave this ghastly business and take early retirement," Bond said bitterly.

"Come now. Surely this isn't the first time something has gone wrong for you?"

"No, it isn't. It's just that sometimes I wonder why I bother. In the old days, the enemy was clear cut. Communism was a worldwide threat and we were motivated by ideology. Today it's different. I feel as if I've become a glorified policeman. There must be a better way to die."

"Stop it," she said, her voice stern. "You do your best. What else is there? Everyone has his or her limit."

"I've been to my limit. Many times."

"James," she said. "There will come a time, probably very soon, when you will push yourself *past* your limit. When that happens, you will come to terms with your life and this job of yours."

Bond was too weary to argue.

"What you need is an evening out," she said brightly. "A good Belgian dinner, some drinks . . . How about it?"

Bond looked sideways at her. "Are you asking me for a date?"

She grinned in her pixielike way. "Is that all right? Providing we are free tonight, of course."

Bond allowed himself a smile. "Sure."

They arrived at their destination and she parked in front of Dr. Lindenbeek's building. They got out, pressed the intercom button, and explained that they were "police." A nurse met them at the door and said that Dr. Lindenbeek was with a patient.

"We'll wait," Gina said in Flemish. She showed the woman her credentials and they were led into the austere waiting room.

"It shouldn't be long," the nurse said, then left them alone. They could hear a man's voice speaking softly through the wall. After a few minutes, an elderly woman emerged, followed by the doctor. He said good-bye to her in French, then turned to Gina and Bond.

Gina spoke in Flemish, explaining that they were from the government and wanted to ask him some questions. Immediately, Bond knew that the man was involved. Lindenbeek's eyes widened and he swallowed hard.

"Come in," he said in English, gesturing toward his office.

Bond asked, "Dr. Lindenbeek, do you recall making a sketch that looks like this?" He took a pen from the doctor's desk and drew a torso on the prescription pad. When he outlined the pacemaker position, Dr. Lindenbeek slumped back in his chair and held his head in his hands.

"Well?" Bond asked.

"Am I under arrest?" he asked.

"Not yet. But it will help if you tell us everything."

"I must keep my patient's confidentiality . . ." he muttered.

Bond perceived that this man was merely a pawn. Perhaps if he scared him a bit, he would open up.

"Dr. Lindenbeek," Bond said. "We're here on a serious matter of espionage. I can assure you that if you don't cooperate with us, then you *will* be under arrest. Espionage is a major crime. It can carry the death penalty. At the very least, you would lose your licence to practice medicine. Now, are you going to talk to us, or are we going to have to take you to the police?"

The doctor almost whimpered. "Yes, I performed the operation. I was forced to."

"Why don't you start at the beginning," Gina suggested. The toothpick went from one side of her mouth to the other.

Again Lindenbeek hesitated.

Bond added, "Dr. Lindenbeek, you could also be in serious danger. The people you're dealing with are quite ruthless. They're killers."

Lindenbeek poured a glass of water from a pitcher on his desk. He offered some to his visitors, but they shook their heads.

"If I tell you everything, can you guarantee me protection?" he asked.

"Perhaps," Bond said. "It depends on how much you tell us and how helpful it is."

The doctor nodded and began to speak. "Five . . . no, six months ago, I got into a little trouble. There was a patient, a woman. I'm not married, and sometimes it is difficult for me to meet women. I was attracted to a patient and I may have gone too far. She certainly encouraged me, though. It was, how do you say, mutual?"

"Consensual," Bond said.

"Yes. But somehow photographs were taken of us, here in this examination room. I had been set up. Afterward, this woman filed charges against me for rape and malpractice. The truth is that she is a member of something called the Union."

He looked at Bond and Gina for a sign of recognition when he mentioned the name.

Bond nodded and said, "Go on."

"You know of them?"

"Yes. Please continue, doctor."

The doctor seemed relieved. "Thank God. I was afraid you would think I was crazy. This Union, they contacted me and said they could make this malpractice suit go away if I did something for them. At the time, I was defiant and thought I could prove in court that the woman wasn't raped. Then they did something horrible. I began to receive photographs in the mail — child pornography. The packets would come two or three times a week. I burned them, but the Union got in touch with me again and said that I was now on some kind of 'list' of child molesters. If I didn't help them with a service, they would make sure that I was arrested and charged with dealing in that filth."

"How did they contact you?" Bond asked.

"Always by phone. Some Frenchman. It was a local exchange, I'm pretty sure."

"Then what happened?" Gina asked.

"What could I do? I agreed to help them," he said. Lindenbeek was sweating and his hands were shaking as he poured himself another glass of water.

"What did they want you to do?"

"I was told that a Chinese man, Mr. Lee Ming, would come to see me. He was in his late fifties and actually needed the pacemaker. His heart rhythm went up and down. I was told to schedule an operation at Erasme for this man. I was to obtain a pacemaker and have everything ready. The night before the operation, I was told that an Englishman would visit me and deliver what they called a microdot. It would be on a piece of film. I was to put this microdot inside the pacemaker before performing the operation. As it seemed harmless, I did it."

"When was this?"

"The operation was two days ago."

"Can we see Mr. Lee's file?" Gina asked.

At first Lindenbeek hesitated, but then he nodded. "It's right here." He handed it over. Bond examined it, but there wasn't much there. "Lee Ming" could very well be an alias. The patient's address was listed as the Pullman Astoria Hotel.

"Did they ever tell you what was on the microdot?"

Lindenbeek shook his head. "I didn't want to know."

Bond believed him. The man was too scared to lie.

"Do you know where Mr. Lee is now?" Bond asked.

Lindenbeek shrugged his shoulders. "I don't know. He's a Chinese citizen visiting this country. The Englishman asked how soon Mr. Lee would be able to travel. I assumed that he was going back to China."

"And you're sure that the people who wanted this done called themselves the Union?"

"Yes."

Bond stood up. "Right. Dr. Lindenbeek, I think it would be best if you come with us. We'll want to interrogate you in more detail and show you some mug shots. This is for your own safety. If the Union are indeed behind this, and they learn that you've talked, you could be a dead man."

"I'm under arrest?"

Gina nodded. "It's better that way, doctor. You'll be safer. We'll take you to the police station downtown. Once we get this sorted out, we can move you somewhere else. We will need you for a trial if and when we catch the people responsible for this."

"You mean . . . testify?"

Bond nodded. "You're the only one who can prove that our man, Harding, gave you this microdot."

"He told me his name was Donald Peters."

"He lied. Come on, doctor. Better cancel the rest of your appointments today. Let's go."

Hendrik Lindenbeek was taken to the police station at Rue Marché au Charbon, a more than fifty-year-old dark brown brick building. The Brussels authorities had been contacted by the Ministry of Defence and were now aware of the situation. Lindenbeek would be held pending a hearing that would take place the next day at the Palais de Justice. A public prosecutor had been assigned to consider espionage charges against Steven Harding and Lee Ming, and an all-points alert had been issued for their arrest. Extraditing the suspects would be another matter altogether, as Belgium would hold its own hearings on whether or not they could indeed be sent to England. Bond figured that they would hold on to Lindenbeek, as he was a Belgian citizen. A Chinese national would probably be sent back home. Harding, however, was English, and belonged back in the UK.

Bond and Gina spent the afternoon at the police station and saw that Lindenbeek was put in a cell alone. Inspector Opsomer assured them that they would be contacted as soon as he heard something. Belgium's state security force, the Securité d'État, was taking charge of the investigation. From then on, there was nothing more that could be done.

Before leaving the station, Gina phoned the Pullman Astoria Hotel and learned that Lee Ming had checked out.

Although they had caught a big fish, Bond felt frustrated. He knew M wouldn't be completely happy, either.

They went back to the Métropole. Gina collapsed in an armchair while Bond sat at the desk to phone London. After the ritualistic security checks, he was put through to his chief.

"Double-O Seven?"

"Yes, ma'am."

"How are you feeling? I heard about your injuries," she said. Her concern sounded genuine.

"I'll live, ma'am. Just a cracked rib and some bruises."

"I dare say you've survived much worse."

"I'm afraid I don't have much to report. Dr. Lindenbeek is in custody and the matter is being handled by the Securité d'état. We're out of the loop as far as he is concerned."

"That's all right, as long as the Belgians hold on to him. For the time being anyway. No leads regarding Harding or this Chinese man?"

"None. They could very well still be in Brussels. Then again . . ."

"I understand. Double-O Seven, I want you to continue your work with Station B for at least another day. If nothing turns up, come back to England. I'm afraid I'll have to give the Minister news he's not going to like."

Bond could hear the disappointment in

her voice. He had let her down. "Ms. Hollander and I are going to go through Interpol files tomorrow and try to determine who Lee Ming really is. He looked familiar somehow."

"Fine. We'll talk tomorrow."

Bond hung up and said nothing. Gina picked up on Bond's gloom and said, "Hey, remember what I said you needed tonight? Come on, let's go have dinner. The restaurant downstairs is fabulous. Change your clothes or do whatever it is you Brits do to get ready for an evening out with a gorgeous, fun-loving Belgian girl."

They met again in the hotel's luxurious bar, Le 19ème, which was laid out in the style of a gentleman's club, with Corinthian columns and deep leather chairs.

She was dressed in a low-cut, short black cocktail dress that revealed more of her legs than Bond had previously seen. The single pearl on her necklace dangled teasingly at the top of her pronounced cleavage. Her eyes sparkled.

"You look good enough to eat," Bond said.

"So do you," she said, taking his arm. He was dressed in a tailor-made Brioni dinner suit.

L'Alban Chambon is considered one of Belgium's finest restaurants. It is tastefully designed with wood floors, white walls, and intricately carved blue molding. There are mirrors on two sides of the room, creating the illusion that the room is much larger than it really is. The headwaiter showed Bond and Gina to a small round table covered by a white tablecloth on top of a blue one.

As they sat, a tall man wearing a chef's hat approached them.

"Monsieur Bond?" he asked.

"Dominique!" Bond said. He shook hands with the *chef de cuisine*. "How good to see you again. This is my colleague, Gina Hollander. Gina, this is one of Europe's best chefs, Dominique Michou."

She spoke to him in French. "Pleased to meet you." Mr. Michou kissed her hand, then said, "I would like you to try our featured special tonight."

"We'd be delighted."

"Splendid. I'll turn you over to Frederick, then. Enjoy your meal." Michou bowed and returned to the kitchen. Frederick, the headwaiter, presented them with menus and a wine list. Bond ordered a full-bodied red wine, Château Magdaleine Bouhou.

New Age solo piano music was playing softly over the sound system. A plaintive, high-pitched male voice began to improvise lyrics over the music. Gina closed her eyes and smiled.

"You know this music?" Bond asked.

She nodded. "It's a Belgian composer named Wim Mertens. He's contemporary and does some beautiful things. I find his music very sad at times."

Bond shrugged. "If I have any taste in music at all, it's for jazz and big hand. Ever hear of the Ink Spots?"

"I don't think so."

When the wine came, Bond toasted Gina and they drank together. Then he asked, "Gina, what is your cover?"

"I beg your pardon?"

"Do you use a cover? In the old days when MI6 was known as Universal Exports, and later Transworld Consortium, I traveled the world as an importer/exporter. What do you tell people when they ask you what you do?"

"My *memoir* in college was in fashion design," she said. "I really am a designer, so that's what I say. I'm partners with a friend of mine from school. She owns a dress shop in Brussels. We design things together."

"You look the part, then."

"Thank you. And what do you tell people now that MI6 is no longer an 'importer/exporter'?"

Bond smiled wryly. "Usually I say I'm a civil servant. That tends to shut them up right away."

A waiter brought them *salade d'asperges à l'oeuf sur le plat et crème d'estragon,* which was made of tender white and green Belgian asparagus with a poached egg on top and creamy tarragon sauce on the side.

"You're not like other grits," she said after a while.

"Oh?"

"We have always seen Brits as very serious and easily shocked. Except for the ones who come over and booze it up for a weekend."

"I am neither," Bond said.

"No! You like your alcohol, but it does not seem like you would be easily shocked. Another way I've always thought of British men is that they are 'real' gentlemen. You are a gentleman."

"Flattery will get you everywhere."

"What do you think of Belgian women?" she asked, licking a bit of sauce from the corner of her mouth. Bond realized that this was the first time he had seen her

173

without a toothpick in her mouth.

"Are you a typical Belgian woman?"

She laughed. "I don't think so. I'm not sure we can be classified, since Belgium is such a multilingual country. The French girls in the south are a little different from the Flemish girls in the north, and so on. We are perhaps not as wild and sexy as Dutch girls."

"You're not? Bloody hell . . ."

That made her laugh. "I mean, we're as sexually open as any other European girls, I suppose, we just don't talk about it. It depends on the level of education, I think. Am I making sense?"

"You're saying that actions speak louder than words?"

She knew he was teasing her. "I had better be careful," she said, wagging her finger at him. "My English is not so good. You will twist my words and make me say something I'll be sorry for later!"

The main courses came. She was having *filet de boeuf poêlé, légumes de saison frits, et sauce choron* — sauteed fillet of beef with fried vegetables and choron sauce. He tried the chef's special, *médaillon de veau de lait et risotto aux légumes et parmesan* — fillet of milk-fed veal and rice with vegetables and Parmesan cheese. The rice was packed in the shape of a hockey puck with potatoes mixed in.

"This is delicious," she said, taking a dainty bite of beef.

"Monsieur Michou does it again," Bond said. The veal was light and tender, cooked a perfect medium so that the pink center was juicy and succulent.

"How important is this formula that was stolen?" she asked.

"Quite, although I think it's more important to Britain for political reasons than for scientific ones."

"Why?"

"Britain is no longer the empire it once was. My superiors believe that this process will give us more face, I suppose, and it's worth a fortune. Our Ministry of Defence have visions of profits dancing before their eyes, but it's more about proving to the world that we can still come up with technological advances."

Dessert was a Belgian specialty, one of Bond's favorites — *véritable "Café Liègeois"* — a cold, creamy coffee milk shake that left white mustaches on their upper lips. Gina gently scraped hers clean with her index finger and then licked off the excess cream. Bond found the sight incredibly erotic.

When Bond and Gina finished, it was nearly eleven o'clock.

"It is said that in Belgium, dinner *is* the evening's entertainment," Gina said. "Usually, a night out might consist of the theater or a show, or perhaps a dinner — but not both. Dinner in Belgium is a ritual to be savored and never rushed. It sometimes lasts hours. The time flew by, didn't it?" Bond could see that she was slightly nervous about how the rest of the evening might go. After they had drunk two bottles of the wine between them, she was more relaxed and flirtatious.

As they left the restaurant, he asked, "What now? Shall we take a walk?"

She wrapped her arm in his and pulled him down closer to her lips, then whispered, "No. Take me to your room."

"Why, I'm shocked! Positively shocked!"

A dim golden light seeped in from the bedroom window and splashed across the bed. She let the cocktail dress slip off her shoulders to reveal a pink, scalloped daisy lace underwired bra and thong. She gingerly undressed him and removed the rib harness, and gently pushed him back on the bed. She straddled him, then leaned over to kiss him.

Her agile tongue darted around inside his mouth. Considering that she was able to perform tricks with a toothpick, Bond wasn't surprised. He sucked it and probed her mouth with his own.

She sat back up and slipped the bra off. Her breasts were full and firm, the nipples erect and hard. He reached up and touched them, rubbing the tips lightly in the palms of his hands. She moaned softly and closed her eyes. She moved back a little so that she could touch him. Bond let her manipulate him until he was as hard as stone. Gina removed her thong and slid her wetness down over him. She rocked back and forth on his body, slowly and purposefully at first, then faster and faster in wild abandon as their passion increased. Her tight, compact body writhed and wiggled over him, sending spasms of pleasure to the very depths of their souls.

"Oh, James," she cried as she approached climax. "It's perfect . . . perfect . . ."

He could feel her spasms around him, triggering his own release. For those few moments, they were both lost in each other, melding into one living being with fire for a heart and electricity for a soul.

Perfect indeed.

NINE

Covering Tracks

At precisely eight-thirty A.M., the Belgian police removed Hendrik Lindenbeek from his cell in Police Headquarters and prepared to take him to the Palais de Justice for a preliminary hearing. It was standard operating procedure for the police to transfer all the prisoners who were arrested during the night to the massive ornate building dating from 1883.

Bond had suggested that they transport Lindenbeek under cover, for the Union might very well attempt to assassinate him if they could get a clean shot. Inspector Opsomer, an efficient but impetuous officer, humored the British agent and assured him that they would take every precaution.

Nevertheless, Opsomer was not present in the morning. He was called away on another matter and left the transfer of prisoners to his assistant, Sergeant Poelaert.

Poelaert, who hadn't been apprised of the seriousness of Lindenbeek's crime and his importance to an ongoing investigation, put the doctor and two other prisoners in an ordinary police van. Under special circumstances, armored cars were used, but this didn't seem necessary to Poelaert, as it would have required more time and manpower.

Lindenbeek, handcuffed and in leg chains, was escorted to the garage by two gendarmes. The two other prisoners had been arrested for mugging a tourist and were already inside the olive green Mercedes van. Lindenbeek climbed in the back and sat down, nervous and frightened since his arrest. He wasn't accustomed to this kind of treatment. He was a medical doctor! He had a respectable list of patients! He hoped that all this could be sorted out quickly and that he would be sent to a safe hiding place. His lawyer was confident that everything would turn out for the best, but Lindenbeek wondered if he would ever practice medicine again.

Sergeant Poelaert locked the back of the van and got in the passenger side. He gave the signal to open the garage door.

A small seventy-year-old chapel stood less than a half block away from the police station. A window in the steeple was conveniently placed so that anyone crouched inside could see the entire street.

Dr. Steven Harding sat at the window, his eyes locked on police headquarters. He held a CSS 300 VHF/UHF radio transceiver to his face.

"Stand by," he said.

The garage door opened.

"Okay, they're coming out," he said. "Send in the bird."

"Roger that," came a voice at the other end.

The van pulled out of the garage to begin its ten-minute journey to the Justice Palace.

"It's a green van," Harding reported. "Two men in the front. Looks like there are others in the back with Lindenbeek. I can't tell how many."

"Does it matter?" came the other voice.

Harding snickered. "Not at all. A prisoner is a prisoner, right?"

The van inched along the narrow road in traffic. Aside from the normal rush hour congestion, the transfer was on schedule. Poelaert saw nothing out of the ordinary on the streets. It was going to be an easy delivery.

As Brussels is a large metropolitan city, the presence of helicopters in the air is never a cause for alarm. The Soviet-made

Mi-24 Hind assault chopper had been painted white so that it wouldn't be conspicuous; in fact, it was completely ignored when it appeared in the sky over the heart of the city.

The van turned down Rue des Minimes, a wider artery, and headed southwest toward the Palace.

Harding said, "I see the bird. It's all yours now. Over and out." He pushed in the antenna and got up from his cramped position in the steeple. He quickly climbed down the steps and slipped out the back, where he had left a rented dark blue Mercedes 500 SEL. Lee Ming was in the passenger seat, his eyes closed.

Harding got in the car and pulled away from the chapel. Lee woke up and asked, "How did it go?"

"We'll know in a few minutes. Let's get out of here," Harding said.

The van progressed slowly down the large, crowded street. The helicopter hovered overhead. Armed with thirty-two 57mm projectiles in rocket pods located on the stub wings, the Hind is particularly adept at hitting small targets with precision.

When the van stopped at a red light, the driver heard the chopper and looked out the window. He pointed it out to Poelaert.

The sergeant peered at the sky, but the sun was in his eyes. All he could see was the silhouette of the helicopter and that it was white.

"It's from a TV news channel," he said. "Don't worry about it."

The driver laughed. " 'Don't worry about it' is at the top of the list of best famous last words."

The light turned green and the van moved out into the intersection.

Up above, the Union member with his hand on the trigger saw that the van was clear of most of the other traffic. The timing was perfect.

Two rockets shot out from underneath the helicopter and zoomed down to the van so quickly that witnesses were not sure what had really happened. All they knew was that the van exploded with powerful force. Pedestrians screamed. Other vehicles skidded and slammed into each other in an effort to avoid the blast. For several minutes there was utter chaos on the street. When the smoke finally cleared, the only thing left of the van was a burning chassis with five charred corpses.

The Hind pulled away and sped to the south. By the time the authorities determined that the van had been shot at from the sky, the helicopter was long gone.

Meanwhile, the Mercedes SEL made it to "the Ring," and headed toward the E19 exit.

"How long to Paris?" Lee asked.

"I don't know," Harding said. "Just sit back and enjoy the scenery. I'll get you to your plane on time."

"My superiors are not happy with the change of plans." Over the past couple of days, Harding had been holed up with the Chinese man and found him to be cantankerous and annoying.

"Look, we can't help it if Lindenbeek got caught. I had to see that he was eliminated. We couldn't have him identifying us. The Union had to make last-minute changes, all right? The original plan with you flying out of Brussels to Beijing just wouldn't have worked. They've probably got both of our faces plastered on every Immigration desk in Belgium. You would have been arrested before stepping on the plane."

Harding sounded more sure of himself than he felt. Ever since the encounter in the Métropole, he had been a nervous wreck. Everything had begun to fall apart. Basil had been hired to guard Lee, but instead had fouled up. The Chinese thought that Lee was going to be on a plane to

Beijing, but that plan had to be changed at the last minute.

"I would have you know," Harding said, "that the Union fulfilled their end of the deal. We got the formula on a microdot, and we got that microdot inside of you. It was your problem to get back to China with it."

"No," Lee said. "It was part of the Union's bargain with my people that you would see me safely into China."

"We were going to do that, weren't we? All right, so we changed the original plan. The new plan is more complicated and will take more time but it will get you to China. Relax."

"I don't particularly want to go to India," Lee said.

"I can't do anything about it," Harding said. "These are the orders from *my* superiors. I am to take you to the Paris airport, and there you'll get on a flight to Delhi. You'll be there only a short while. Then you'll get on a plane to Kathmandu. That's in Nepal."

"I'm not stupid."

Harding shrugged. "You will be contacted by someone in Kathmandu. They'll find you at your hotel. All of that information is in the packet I gave you. Arrangements are being made to smuggle you across the border into Tibet. From there, you're home free. But you'll have to make your way to Beijing from Tibet."

"It sounds very tiresome. Don't forget I just underwent surgery."

"You could be a little more grateful, you know," Harding said. "The Union are going to all this trouble to get you to Tibet as a *favor*. We don't *have* to do this. Like I said, our obligation stopped with getting you the formula. The Union simply want our clients to be happy, so we're taking this extra step to see that you get home safely. After all, we don't get the other half of our money until you're back in Beijing."

"What about you?" Lee asked. "You are a traitor to your country. Where will you go? How much of the fifty million dollars is your percentage?"

"I can't go back to England, that's certain. Don't worry about my percentage. I am being paid enough to make all this worthwhile. I have to leave my home, my country, my job . . . I plan on retiring on an island somewhere in the South Pacific."

"Stay away from the Philippines," Lee said. "That place is no fun."

As they drove out of Belgium and into France, Harding worried about the next phase of the plan once Lee got to Nepal. At least he would be through with his end of the operation after he dropped Lee off at the Paris airport. What happened next was out of his hands, although he had helped plan it. If only that damned secret service agent hadn't poked his nose into it. What was his name? Bond? That's right . . . the golfer.

Keeping track of him would be easy enough.

James Bond and Gina Hollander sat in her office, staring at the computer monitor. Her spare laptop had been set up next to it so that they could work simultaneously. They had patched into Interpol's database using Gina's authorized password. The mug shots of Asians had been flashing on the screens for three hours and they had yet to make a match to Lee Ming.

"They're all too young," Bond said. "Is there any way we can narrow our parameters?"

"Not really," she said. "Not from here. You ask for active Chinese agents, you get active Chinese agents."

"This is getting us nowhere. We must have looked at hundreds of faces, and frankly, they really *are* starting to look alike. I don't mean that derogatorily."

"Perhaps he's not a criminal. Maybe he's an ordinary Chinese citizen. Maybe he's not from China at all," she suggested.

"Look up *inactive* Chinese agents. He's in his late fifties. He could be retired."

Gina typed on the keypad until a different set of screens appeared. As expected, the faces looked older, more seasoned.

"This is more like it," Bond said.

She typed on the laptop and brought up the same database there. "I'll take N through Z, all right?"

They worked for the next hour.

"At least there are not as many inactive agents," she said.

Bond was coming to the end of his half, when a face popped on the screen that looked familiar. He stopped and studied it closely. The man was identified as Ming Chow, a former member of China's dreaded secret police. He had retired in 1988 due to a heart problem.

"This is him," Bond whispered.

"Really?"

The photo was twenty years old, so the man appeared much younger than Bond recalled. He clicked on the "details" button and more biographical information flashed onto the screen.

Gina read aloud: "Ming Chow worked in counterintelligence through the seventies and later became an officer in the People's External Security Force. He distinguished himself with the investigation and arrest of a British spy stationed in Shanghai. MI6 agent Martin Dudley was caught red-handed with Chinese military secrets being smuggled in antiquities. Before Dudley could stand trial, he was found dead in a jail cell. Ming Chow was promoted shortly afterward."

"Of course! Now I remember why this man looked so familiar. Martin Dudley was providing intelligence to MI6 for years when they finally caught up with him. There was quite a stink between Britain and China at the time. I was sent to China with a delegation of diplomats to testify at his trial. He was found dead the morning his trial was supposed to have begun. We were convinced he had been murdered, but the Chinese claimed he hanged himself. Ming Chow — how could I forget him? — he was the man in charge. When we suggested that perhaps Mr. Dudley had been killed, Ming Chow just grinned. 'So sorry,' he said, 'accidents happen.' I knew the bastard was lying. I could see it in his eyes."

Bond tapped the monitor with the back of his index finger. "He's older now, but our Lee Ming is Ming Chow."

"So he's not inactive at all?"

"Not necessarily. He may not be officially working for China's secret service. Many times, as you know, former agents hire themselves out for 'freelance' work."

"The Union, perhaps?"

"I smell them in this, all right. Their fingerprints are all over this case."

"We had better get this mug shot out to all the Immigration stations in Belgium."

"We'll do better than that. This fellow's face is going out all over the world," he said.

Lee Ming, alias Ming Chow, had just checked in for his flight to Delhi when his mug shot was transmitted by Interpol to all Western immigration authorities. Unfortunately, he had already cleared Customs and Immigration and was waiting at the gate for boarding to begin. As it was, he probably would not have been caught. The Interpol information accompanying the photo of the Chinese man failed to mention that the man being sought was at least twenty years older than he was in the photo.

A young British Airlines customer service representative named George Almond happened to be on break and was sitting with a sketch pad in a café across from Lee's gate. George considered himself a fairly good artist, and he especially enjoyed drawing people. The Chinese man sitting across the way was a good subject. He had a lot of character and there was a timeless expression of world-weariness about him that George was determined to capture on paper.

It wasn't long before he had quite a decent drawing of Lee Ming.

Thirty minutes later, as Lee Ming was flying toward Asia, George Almond went back to his post in customer service. One way that he amused himself between customers (who invariably wanted to complain about the airline's food or lost luggage) was to look at Interpol's broadcasts. He liked to get ideas for sketches by viewing the mug shots. The criminals always had character.

When he saw Lee Ming's photo, his heart started to pound. He opened his sketchbook to the drawing he had done less than an hour earlier and compared the two faces.

"My God," he said aloud, then picked

up the phone to call security.

The scratchy substance he had used to age and wrinkle the skin on his face had worked beautifully. Steven Harding looked at himself in the mirror and was pleased. He now had crow's-feet at the corners of his eyes and droopy bags beneath them.

For the second time, he applied spirit gum to the false mustache. He hated the smell of the stuff, and it was awfully tacky. His first attempt to disguise himself with it had failed miserably. He had used too much and it got all over his fingers. It took him a half hour to clean them with nail polish remover.

He nervously looked at the clock. He had a little less than an hour before he had to go to the Paris airport and catch his own flight.

Harding carefully pressed the mustache on his upper lip. He held it in place with the dry sponge for thirty seconds, then examined his handiwork. The mustache was straight, symmetrical, and looked great. He was pleased. Now the hair.

It was an ingenious device that the Union had given him. It looked like a small harmonica, but in reality it was hair whitener. By removing the metal comb hidden inside and running it through one's hair a few times, a person could age himself considerably. Harding did as he had been instructed to do, and within minutes he was a graying man of sixty.

After Bond and Gina had found Lee's face, both the Chinese man's and Steven Harding's mug shots were broadcast simultaneously to law enforcement agencies all over the world once again.

When the gray-haired man with a mustache and glasses approached Immigration and presented a British passport, the officer had no reason to connect him with any of the most-wanted faces that continually flashed across his screen.

"May I see your ticket, please?" the man asked. Harding complied. "Morocco, eh? It will be hot there."

"It's good for my asthma," Harding said.

"Be careful with the water." The officer, who had no idea that the passenger was wanted for international espionage, stamped the passport and handed everything back.

No one paid further attention to the small man who breezed through security, checked in at the gate with no problems, and then boarded a flight to Casablanca.

TEN

Flight into Oblivion

"It's *out* of your hands, Double-O Seven," M said sharply.

"All I need to do is catch a flight to Delhi and —"

"That is all, Double-O Seven." The finality in her voice shut him up.

"Yes, ma'am," Bond said after a pause.

They stood in her office at the end of the day. He had just returned from Belgium and made his report. The meeting did not go well. Steven Harding was missing, presumably out of Europe. Lee Ming, thanks to the astute airline representative in Paris, was traced to Delhi and then Nepal.

Bill Tanner had received a report from the Delhi authorities saying that Lee Ming had come through the airport and had boarded a flight to Kathmandu. As requested, the Immigration officers in Delhi had stopped Lee before he got on the plane. They had orders to search him, but due to some unforseen bureaucratic foul-up, they had no idea what they were looking for. They searched Lee's luggage and forced him to strip anyway, hoping they would find something incriminating. They failed. Noting that the Chinese gentleman had a recent implant scar, they became confused. Had they grabbed the wrong man? He certainly seemed perfectly innocent. What should they do now?

They had let him go. Lee got on the flight and was now somewhere in Nepal. It had never occurred to the Indian authorities to hold Lee until they received further instructions.

Tanner had said, "You can't win them all, James," but it hadn't helped. Now Bond felt frustrated and angry that Steven Harding had slipped through his fingers. He was particularly sensitive about traitors. Bond had encountered his fair share of betrayal in his lifetime.

"Station I is in charge now," M said. "By the time you could get to Nepal, Lee Ming or Ming Chow — whatever the hell his name is — would be in China. We'll keep our fingers crossed that Station I is successful in stopping him from leaving Nepal. As I understand it, they've traced him to a hotel in Kathmandu. We've been told that an arrest is imminent. You're to go back to regular duty until further notice. Of much further concern, I think, is the leak from our office here. There's been a breach of security at home, and I don't like that. I don't like it one bit, do I make myself clear?"

She seemed to think that it was his fault somehow. "Ma'am, I assure you, I've treated this assignment with the same discretion that I've afforded every other one," Bond said.

"Stop it, I'm not blaming you," she said. There were times when she really did sound like a mother hen. It was as if she were upset with her eldest son and, although she still loved him, held him more accountable than her "other" children.

"It's a short list of people who knew you were going to Brussels," she said. "Do we have a traitor here at SIS? The thought is horrifying to me."

"I agree, ma'am. It's been a long time since something like that's happened."

"I don't want it happening on my watch. Mr. Tanner, tell him what we've learned."

Tanner cleared his throat and said, "An autopsy was performed on the remains of Dr. Thomas Wood. Besides being shot in the head and leg, it appeared that his throat had been cut. From ear to ear."

"That's the Union's signature," Bond said.

"Could be," Tanner agreed. "The slugs recovered from the body were nine millimeter, but they were too badly damaged to indicate what gun fired them."

M said, "Our analysts believe that Union involvement is entirely possible, especially considering that strange fax that Dr. Wood received. You know that they have recently gained a reputation for being quite good at infiltrating intelligence organizations."

"So, it's possible," Bond said, "that the Union are responsible for the breach of security."

M looked hard at him. "I'm afraid you have to play plumber for a while, Double-O Seven, and plug that leak."

Zakir Bedi, an Indian national based in Delhi, had been employed by the British Secret Service for nearly three decades. Over the years he had assisted in arresting terrorists, spied on Pakistan, smuggled Russian military secrets out of Afghanistan, and served as bodyguard and guide to visiting dignitaries. Now approaching retirement, Bedi wanted to perform one last exciting assignment for the firm before hanging up his hat. He would then go out with a nice pension and perhaps a service medal that he could display with pride.

It looked as if he might realize his goal that afternoon in Kathmandu.

It was just after lunch and he was sitting in a blue Tata jeep, one of the many used by the Nepalese police. Across the road was the famed Hotel Everest, isolated out on the Ring Road away from the central city in the section known as Baneshwar. One of the top hotels in Nepal, it was formerly the Everest Sheraton and it still maintained a very high standard with a bar, restaurants, sports facilities, disco, casino, and mountain views from upper floors.

The sergeant to his left was speaking Nepali into a walkie-talkie. Three policemen were ready to enter the hotel, burst into the room occupied by a Chinese man, Mr. Lee Ming, and arrest him for international espionage. Extradition papers had been filed in a hurry, and after intense negotiations between Britain, India, and Nepal, it was agreed that Zakir Bedi, in representing Britain, could enter the country, observe the arrest, and take charge of the prisoner.

Inside his air-conditioned room, Lee Ming lay on his bed, fighting the stomach cramps that had held him in a viselike grip since the night before. As he had become older and developed heart problems, he didn't travel well. He realized that he never should have volunteered for this assignment. Still, the money would be good if he ever made it back to Beijing.

He had been in Kathmandu a little over twenty-four hours and had slept very little. His body wasn't adjusting to the time change. After all, he had been in Belgium for three weeks and had undergone exhausting surgery. Now he was very tired and wished he could just sleep for a few hours. The problem was the edginess he felt because he didn't know when he would be contacted for the surreptitious escape into Tibet. He had to be ready at a moment's notice, which meant he couldn't leave the hotel — not that he felt like doing so.

He was just beginning to doze, when there was a loud knock at the door. Lee groaned, then pulled himself out of bed to answer it. When he opened the door, three rough-looking Nepalese men rushed inside.

"Shhh," one said, holding his finger to his lips. All three were short and stocky, and one had a black mustache. Obviously the leader of the group, he went to a window and pulled back the shades an inch. He gestured for Lee to come and look.

The blue jeep and two men were down below. One was dressed in the traditional dark blue trousers, light blue shirt, and V-necked woolen sweater with badges of rank and medals attached. He wore a faded maroon beret and black combat boots.

"Police?" Lee asked.

The man nodded. "Come with us now. We get you out of Nepal," he said in hesitant English.

Lee said, "Okay. Let me grab my —"

"No. Just come." The man spoke a stream of Nepali to his companions. One of them opened the door and looked in the hallway. He waved, indicating that it was all clear.

The men ushered Lee out of the room and to the fire escape stairs. Lee, unable to move quickly, was immediately a burden. Two of the men locked arms, picked him up, and allowed him to sit on them as they carried him down the stairs.

The Nepalese policemen entered the hotel and took the lift to Lee's floor. They arrived just as Lee and his rescuers came out of the stairwell on the ground floor and made their way toward one of the restaurants.

They pushed around a group of tourists, then went through the restaurant and into the kitchen. There, the leader spoke Nepali to one of the chefs, who gave him a large burlap bag normally used to sack potatoes.

"Put this on," the man said to Lee.

"What?"

Without wasting any more time, the man threw the bag over Lee's head. Lee began to protest, and the man said, "Shut up! Don't make a sound!"

Lee quieted down and allowed himself to go through this humiliation. The burlap bag completely covered him. Since he was a small, lightweight man, it was easy for one of the men to pick up the bag and haul it over his shoulder — like a sack of potatoes.

The three men hurried out into an alley with the bundle. There they loaded Lee into the back of a pickup that was full of real sacks of potatoes. He grunted loudly as they dropped the bag on top.

"Quiet!" the leader said again. "You are in truck. We drive to airport. Silence!"

The men got into the truck, backed out of its space, and took off down Arniko

Rajmarg toward the Kathmandu airport.

Zakir Bedi noticed the potato truck pulling out from behind the hotel and heading southeast, but there were dozens of such trucks making deliveries to hotels in the area. He turned his gaze back to the front of the hotel, awaiting word from the men inside.

Upstairs, one of the Nepalese policemen raised his hand to knock on Lee's door but realized that it was ajar. He kicked it open to find the room empty. He swung the walkie-talkie to his mouth and shouted.

Bedi, who understood Nepali, heard the report and cursed.

"We have to find him!" he said to the sergeant. They got out of the jeep and ran inside the hotel. The two policemen met them in the lobby. They agreed to spread out and cover every conceivable exit.

Bedi was running toward the casino when he passed the restaurant. Going on a gut feeling, he asked the maître d' if he had seen a Chinese man come through there. He flashed a photo of Lee. The maître d' made an affirmative noise and pointed to the kitchen. Bedi shouted into his own walkie-talkie and ran through the restaurant.

The other policemen met him in the

kitchen, where the leader questioned the chefs. Finally, one of them admitted being paid to hide the Chinese man in a potato sack.

"Potatoes?" Bedi asked. "I just saw a potato truck leave the hotel. They're headed for the airport! Let's go!"

The policemen and Bedi rushed outside to the jeep and took off in pursuit.

Tribhuvan International Airport is located four kilometers southeast of Kathmandu and is the country's single international air entry point. Built in 1989, it handles over a thousand passengers per hour, quite an improvement over the old terminal with lines trailing out the doorway and an open-air waiting lounge. Among the international and domestic flights that operated out of Tribhuvan, several private tourist agencies offered sightseeing trips from the airport.

The potato truck sped into the airport, jostling Lee Ming and the potato sacks with every bump in the road. They passed the main terminal and drove around to the private hangars. One sight-seeing operation, a British-run company called Above the Earth Flights, was preparing to send a twin-propeller plane around the Himalayas with a group of ten to fourteen British and

American passengers. The truck, however, shot past the line of tourists and headed for another hangar, where a single-prop plane was fueled and waiting with the pilot on board.

The truck halted with a screech and the men poured out. They quickly pulled the burlap bag out of the back and freed their Chinese client.

"You fools!" Lee cried. "All that bumping could have opened up my chest!"

"Shut up and get in the plane," the leader ordered. "Do as we say or you'll be arrested. The police are right behind us!"

Lee grumbled and walked toward the plane. "Is this thing safe?" he asked.

Behind Lee's back, the leader looked at his other two companions and gave the signal they were waiting for.

The jeep, meanwhile, drove into the airport complex at a high speed. The sergeant contacted airport security and was told that a potato truck had been seen near the private hangars. He directed the driver to pull around the terminal. They also passed Above the Earth Flights, and then saw the single-engined four-man plane taxiing, ready to move toward the runway.

"Stop that plane!" Bedi shouted.

The jeep swerved in front of the aircraft.

The three policemen jumped out and aimed FN 7.62mm self-loading rifles at the cockpit. The sergeant grabbed a bull-horn and ordered the pilot to stop.

The plane came to a halt as the officers approached it. Bedi got out of the jeep and went to the side of the aircraft. As the door opened, he leaped up the steps and stuck his head in the cabin.

It was completely empty.

Confounded, he turned to the pilot and asked where his Chinese passenger was. The pilot shook his head as if he didn't understand. Bedi drew a Browning Hi-Power 9mm handgun, the same pistol used by the Nepalese police.

"Tell me where he is or your brains will be all over your nice, clean windscreen," he said. Although Bedi had been raised a Hindu and still believed that the taking of human life was a grave sin, he had never hesitated doing so in the line of duty. As he had grown older, religion became less and less important to him. He figured that Shiva the Destroyer was on his side since he worked for law and order.

The pilot pointed to a hangar some two hundred yards away. It was the tourist company's outfit.

Bedi jumped out of the plane and

shouted for the policemen to get into the jeep.

"He's over there!" he yelled, pointing to the twin prop that was just leaving the hangar.

The words ABOVE THE EARTH FLIGHTS were painted on the sides of the plane. It was beginning to pick up speed on the runway. The jeep sped after it, and the sergeant blasted orders with the bullhorn. The pilot refused to stop. The sergeant contacted the control tower and ordered them to halt the takeoff. He was told that the pilot was not responding.

Had they been able to see inside the cockpit, they would have understood why the pilot was incommunicado. The leader of the three Nepalese men was holding a pistol to his head.

"Just take off and get in the air," he commanded.

The other two hijackers were holding guns on the eleven frightened passengers, all British or American adults of both sexes. Lee Ming was sitting among them, next to a window. He didn't know what the hell was going on. Was this the Union's plan? Hijack a tourist plane? Where did they think they were going to go? Surely they couldn't cross the border into Tibet in a tourist plane!

Zakir Bedi ordered the jeep's driver to speed up, although the plane was now gaining momentum and would soon be off the ground.

"Shoot at them!" he ordered. One of the policemen aimed his SLR and fired. A bullet pinged off the tail, damaging it slightly, but it didn't slow the plane.

The aircraft reached its top speed and lifted off. It sailed neatly over the terminal and into the sky.

"Call your air force! We have to stop that plane!" Bedi shouted at the sergeant.

"Air force? We don't *have* an air force!"

Zakir Bedi put his head in his hands. After taking ten seconds to count to himself, he said, "Tell the control tower to keep track of that plane. I want to know where it goes."

Passengers were beginning to panic inside the aircraft. One of the Nepalese men told them to shut up.

The leader told the other man to keep the gun on the pilot, then went into the small, cramped cabin to address the people.

"Please remain calm," he said. "This plane is not going to look at Mount Everest as originally scheduled. We're taking a little side trip to Darjeeling. No one will be harmed if you stay quiet and cooperate. You'll be back in Kathmandu in a few hours."

Darjeeling? Lee Ming thought. Why Darjeeling? They were supposed to be going to Tibet! Was this a new, roundabout way of getting there?

One of the passengers, a man in his fifties, said, "Excuse me, I'm Senator Mitchell from the United States, and this is my wife." He indicated a man and a woman across the aisle. "That's Mr. Roth and his wife. He's a Member of Parliament in Britain. I'll have you know that both our governments will not tolerate —"

"Shut up!" the leader said, pointing the gun at him. The senator complied.

Lee gestured for the leader. "What is going on? Since this is all about me, I demand you tell me what is happening."

The leader smiled and said, "I'm sorry I could not say before. We're taking you to a safe place in Darjeeling. What becomes of you there is not our responsibility."

"What do you mean? I thought I was going to Tibet."

"Plans change" was all the man said.

Smelling a rat, Lee Ming suddenly became very agitated. He felt his heart start to pound, but the pacemaker kicked in after a few seconds. Still, he felt very anxious. Something was very wrong. These men weren't Union.

Relying on old skills and the experience of a man who was, in his prime, a formidable secret service agent, Lee Ming jumped out of his seat and attacked the leader. They struggled in the aisle as passengers screamed. The Browning went off accidentally. The hijacker holding a gun to the pilot's head was hit in the throat. He fell back against the controls, gagging.

The plane swerved dangerously before the pilot was able to level it and set a course for east Nepal.

The leader punched Lee hard in the face. The Chinese man fell back into his seat, unconscious. The leader told the woman next to him, "Fasten his seat belt."

He went back to the cockpit and pulled his companion out and laid him in the aisle. He was dead. The other conspirator looked frightened. Now what would they do? In answer to the unstated question, the leader said, "We continue as planned. It just means more money for the two of us, right?"

The other man hadn't thought of that. He grinned nervously and nodded.

"Keep an eye on the passengers, and especially that Chinese piece of dirt," the leader said, then went back to the cockpit.

The pilot said, "There's a storm over east Nepal. Looks like a bad one. We should not fly that way."

"Just get us to Darjeeling," the leader said.

"I can't without going through the storm. We don't have enough fuel to skirt around it. We'll have to go back to Kathmandu."

"No! Fly into the storm. We'll take our chances."

"Are you mad? We could crash into one of the mountains!"

The leader shoved the barrel into the pilot's temple, hurting him. "Get us to Darjeeling, or you're dead."

"If you shoot me," the pilot stammered, "then you will die, too."

"So be it. You want me to shoot you now and get it over with?"

The pilot hesitated, then turned the plane eastward.

A half hour later, they felt the effects of the storm. High winds, sleet, and snow battered the little plane. The turbulence bounced it up and down, frightening the passengers even more. Some of them were praying aloud, others were sobbing and holding on to their loved ones, and a few were sitting silently, staring ahead in horror. The senator from America was sweating profusely. The Member of Parliament was biting his lower lip.

They were over Taplejung when visibility became impossible. Now even the leader was concerned.

"Do you know where we are?" he asked.

The pilot shrugged. "Somewhere over east Nepal. The navigation isn't working. They shot at our tail earlier, on the ground. There's something wrong with it. I can't maneuver the plane very well. We should turn back."

"Keep going."

The pilot, who was not accustomed to anything more complicated than sightseeing flights over the Himalayas, didn't know how to handle the situation. He was lost, and he had no clue as to which way was north or south. For all he knew, he could be flying completely off course.

The storm assaulted the plane with intensity. At one point the aircraft dipped so abruptly that the pilot thought for certain that it was all over. He managed to pull the aircraft back up into the thick white wall of horror and kept going. He didn't know that the plane was now headed northeast into the Himalayas.

"She's not responding!" he cried. "I can't get a decent reading on where we are! For the love of God, we must turn back!"

For once the leader was quiet, staring out the windshield at the whiteness. His eyes widened when he saw the summit of a large mountain materialize out of the milk-colored curtain.

"Look out!" he yelled, but it was too late.

The plane scraped the edge of the mountain and went careening off into oblivion. This time the pilot screamed as he fought for control of the little plane. He pulled the stick back as far as he could so that the aircraft would climb as high as possible. Miraculously, it worked. After a minute of sheer terror, the plane leveled.

"What kind of damage did that do?" the pilot asked the leader. The man peered out the windshield but couldn't see a thing.

"I think we hit a wing, but we're still flying," he said. Then he noticed that the right propeller was behaving erratically. "That propeller — is it all right?"

The pilot looked at his controls. "No,

we're losing it. We're going to crash. There's no way we can get back to Kathmandu now."

"What about Darjeeling?"

"Forget it," the pilot said. "We're in the Himalayas. I don't know how to get there. We can try to save ourselves by turning back."

The leader thought a minute, then said, "Okay, let's try. Turn her around."

The pilot couldn't see a thing. He punched in new navigation coordinates, but something wasn't right. The controls weren't responding.

"Navigation is completely out," he said quietly.

"What do we do now?" the leader asked. His abrupt, authoritarian manner had completely vanished.

"Pray."

Through the ice and snow that was assaulting the windshield, the two men saw a dark shape getting closer. Given the conditions, it was impossible to determine how far away the peak was, but they could see that it was a monster.

The pilot reacted and tried to turn away from it. The dark shape loomed even nearer until it filled the entire windshield.

"Pull up! Pull up!" the leader shouted.

"I can't!" was the last thing the pilot yelled.

The plane hit a relatively flat ledge not far from the summit of Kangchenjunga, the third tallest mountain in the world. The wings were snapped off immediately and the fuselage slid along the rocky ice and caught fire. It smashed against a wall of rock and ice, rolled over twice, and finally settled on a slanting but near-level patch of glacier.

The impact, the freezing cold, and the lack of oxygen at such a high altitude were immediately fatal to nearly everyone aboard. Three people, however, extraordinarily survived the ordeal but were knocked unconscious. Their hell would begin shortly.

ELEVEN

The Green Light

The Walther P99 roared with a barrage of amplified noise.

The walls of the underground room bounced the crashing sound back and forth until he had emptied the magazine. James Bond remained with his arms outstretched and his grip firm, then slowly relaxed and ejected the magazine and placed the pistol on the counter. He pushed the button on the wall to his right to move the target.

The silhouette of a "bad man" slid forward on the track so that Bond could examine how well he had done. Each bullet had hit the bull's-eye inside the outlined heart.

"Not bad, Double-O Seven," the instructor said. Reinhardt was a veteran of the service, a man in his sixties who had refused early retirement and still worked part-time in the firing range in the basement of SIS headquarters. A Canadian of

German ancestry, the instructor had come to England and joined the secret service during its glory days after the Second World War. Bond thought he was an excellent tutor, and at times felt that he owed his life to the man who had taught him a thing or two about weaponry.

"Not bad?" Bond exclaimed. "I blew his heart to bits, Dave."

"Not bad" in Reinhardt's book was to be interpreted as "excellent," for Bond had never received higher praise from him. Reinhardt never handed out compliments. In fact, the instructor considered 007 the best shot in the entire building, but he believed that too much praise was anathema to the soul.

"But what did *he* do to *you?* He could very well have blown your head off," Reinhardt said. He punched a button on the machine behind them. A computerized image of Bond appeared on the attached television monitor. The instructor pushed another button; the tape rewound to the beginning. Bond's silhouette could be seen drawing his pistol, taking a stance, and aiming at the camera. Flashes of white light swarmed around the gun as he fired, but at the same time, red pinpoints began to dot his torso. The instructor pressed button and froze the image.

"There, you see?" Reinhardt said. "He got you in the . . . shoulder, the right lung, and just below the neck. Not fatal, but enough to spoil your aim on your last few rounds. You'd have to go to hospital in a hurry, or you'd be dead within the hour."

"My first shot would have killed him," Bond countered.

"Perhaps," the instructor acknowledged. He knew full well that Bond was right; he just didn't want to give him the satisfaction of a pat on the back. It was his way, and he was aware that Bond knew it.

Bond removed the Zeiss Scopz shooting glasses and Aearo Peltor Tactical 7 ear defenders, and wiped the beads of sweat off his brow. "I think that's all for today, Dave, I need to get back upstairs," he said.

"Fine, Double-O Seven. It's good to see you haven't lost your edge."

"But you're saying there's room for improvement?"

"There's *always* room for improvement, Double-O Seven. Never get it in your head that you're the best shot on the planet. Look what happened to Billy the Kid."

"What happened to Billy the Kid other than that he was shot by Pat Garrett?" Bond asked.

"He got careless and cocky. It was his downfall. That's how Garrett got to him. Never think that you're better than the other guy, or you won't try as hard. You'll let down your guard. Remember that."

"Thanks, Dave. But isn't it also psychologically helpful to have the self-confidence to believe you're going to win, no matter what?"

"Of course! I don't claim to make perfect sense when I tell you these things!" He chuckled. "You're supposed to assimilate everything I say, even if it's contradictory!"

Bond holstered his gun and said goodbye. He normally kept the old PPK in his shoulder holster and used the newer P99 for backup. The trouble was that the P99 was slightly bulkier and was less easily concealed beneath a jacket. A lot of men used the P99 in a shoulder holster, but Bond's habits died hard. He loved the old PPK as much as he had once adored the Beretta. He would never be able to make a permanent switch.

He took the elevator to his floor and walked into the reception area. Using his key card to gain access to the work space, Bond said hello to one of the newer secretaries and made his way down the aisle toward Helena Marksbury's desk.

Her back was to him as she typed; a phone receiver was cradled between her left shoulder and her ear. As he walked past, he lightly squeezed her other shoulder. She looked up at him, forced a grin, and waved slightly. Bond walked on into his private office.

It was an awkward situation. Obviously everything wasn't back to normal. At least he felt better physically. His body had healed quickly. He didn't have to wear the harness around his torso any longer, and the cracked rib was a vague memory.

The in tray held a report from Foreign Intelligence regarding the search for Steven Harding. It was inconclusive, but preliminary findings indicated that he might have left Europe for North Africa or the Middle East. Bond thought that this wasn't much of a leap in logic. The Union's headquarters was rumored to be located in either of those two places. As for Lee Ming, the last word received at SIS was that Station I's attempt to arrest him had failed. Word on his whereabouts was expected at any time.

Helena, now off the phone, stuck her head in the door and said, "I'm glad you're back. M wants to see you in ten minutes."

She started to leave, but Bond stopped her.

"Helena."

She paused and looked at him.

"Come in here," he said.

She swallowed, made a face of resignation, then stepped inside the office.

"Are you handling this all right? You're not thinking of transferring to another department, are you?"

She shook her head. "I'm fine. How are you handling it?" She said it with a touch of sarcasm.

The inflection in her voice was just enough to make Bond's blood rise. He hated it when relationships broke down into pettiness.

"Helena, sit down." She sat in the leather chair across from his desk and looked at him as if he were a headmaster and she, the naughty girl, had received a summons.

"Now, look. We've had a fine time, you and I. We both agreed that it was not the best idea for us to continue this affair while we're here in London. Am I right?"

"You're right."

"But you seem to be having a problem with it."

She bit her lower lip to keep from saying

something she might regret, then said instead, "James, I will be fine. Don't worry about me. Now I must get back to work."

"Wait," he said. "Let's leave us for a moment. I have to ask you about the leak."

Helena regained her composure. At least she could display the facade of professionalism when she had to, even when she was suffering inside.

"They questioned me for two hours," she said. "I had nothing to tell them, of course. There is no way that the information could have been leaked out of my office."

Bond didn't say anything.

"You believe me, don't you?"

He did. "Helena, I trust you implicitly. It's just bloody disconcerting that someone knew my movements in Belgium before I made them. Do you have any idea who could have done this?"

She shook her head. "I answered that question at least twenty times, James. No. Now, can I go back to work? I have to get out a report."

He nodded, giving her permission to stand and leave the room. Her manner was cold and abrupt. It was to be expected, Bond thought, considering the nature of their relationship now.

Why did his love affairs, whenever they became somewhat serious, always end up so messy? Salvaging them was always a problem, which is why he rarely remained friends with former lovers. It was a pattern that he had long ago resigned himself to, even though he would never grow accustomed to it. He had met few women who were able to distinguish the difference between sex and a relationship, or who could have one without the other. In his own perfect world, men would be completely happy going through life from partner to partner, loving their mates equally but not exclusively. Cynically, Bond liked to think that women invented the concept of relationships and marriage in an effort to exert control over their male counterparts.

She would get over it. It would take some time, and then perhaps they could renew their passion on another extended holiday away from England. In the meantime, though, Bond decided he must keep Helena Marksbury at arm's length until things cooled down — or warmed up, as the case might be.

"Something's up, James," Moneypenny said as he stood beside her desk, waiting to be buzzed into M's inner sanctum.

"News on Skin 17?"

"I think so. She's been with the Minister of Defence most of the day and just got back."

"That sounds interesting."

The green light flashed above the door.

"In you go," she said, giving Bond the warm smile he knew so well.

M was sitting in her black leather swivel armchair, studying images on the monitors behind her desk. Bill Tanner was standing next to her, pointing out some detail in a picture. If Bond wasn't mistaken, they were photographs of Himalayan peaks.

"Sit down, Double-O Seven," M said without looking at him. Then, to Tanner, "How can we be sure there are bodies intact inside the fuselage? It looks to me as if it was burned badly."

"Yes, ma'am, but as you can see from this shot" — Tanner pressed a button and zoomed in on what appeared to be the wreckage of an aircraft — "the entire fuselage is intact. The burn marks are back here, all over the tail end. The front is relatively damage free. The wings are gone, of course."

"You don't suppose anyone could have survived that crash?" she asked.

"Highly doubtful," Tanner answered. "If

anyone did, they would certainly be dead by now. The abrupt change in altitude from a pressurized cabin to twenty-six thousand feet above sea level would kill a man quite quickly. Not to mention the freezing temperatures and the fact that it was unlikely that any of the passengers were dressed for exposure of that kind."

M swiveled her chair to face Bond. "Double-O Seven, you're an experienced mountaineer, aren't you?" she asked.

Not sure how to reply, Bond said, "Well, yes, I used to take great pleasure in the sport, but I haven't done it in a while."

"Haven't you climbed Everest?"

"Yes, ma'am, and Elbrus, too. Most of my experience has been in the Alps and Austrian Tyrol. Why?"

With pen in hand she pointed to the image of the plane wreckage on the monitor. "Skin 17 is here, in this airplane, high on one of the Himalayas' tallest peaks."

Bond raised his eyebrows. "What?"

Tanner filled him in on what they had learned that morning from Station I. Lee Ming had boarded a sight-seeing flight that had apparently been hijacked. Its final destination was unknown, but the plane was tracked eastward, into a bad storm. The aircraft went down less than two thousand feet from the summit of Kangchenjunga, located in the northeast corner of Nepal on the border with Sikkim.

"We now have a very good excuse to go up there and find Mr. Lee's body," M said. "Because the travel agency that owned the plane is British, we have a compelling reason for the Nepalese government to give us a permit to climb the mountain. There were American and British citizens aboard the flight, and their families want to salvage the bodies and see what personal belongings can be found. More significantly, the plane was carrying an MP and an American senator and their wives."

"That's normally not done, ma'am," Bond said. "Hundreds of people have died in climbing accidents over the years. Everest has claimed the lives of at least a hundred and fifty people, and their bodies have remained on the mountain to this day — no matter who they were. I'm sure there are many such corpses on Kangchenjunga."

"I understand that, Double-O Seven, but we have to tell the Nepalese something reasonable. We can tell them that we want to perform a salvage operation for humanitarian reasons so that the victims' loved ones can give their family members a proper burial. And there's the matter with the government officials being aboard. What we're really going to do is find that bloody pacemaker."

Bond's heart started to race. He knew what was coming, and he was already well aware that it would be a difficult and challenging assignment.

"The Ministry of Defence is organizing an expedition. They're arranging with the government of Nepal for permission to climb the mountain, which I understand is sacred to the people there."

"Kangchenjunga is a special case, ma'am," Bond said. "It is indeed sacred, and as I understand it, people are allowed to climb it as long as they don't summit. Many do anyway. I've always heard the mountain referred to as 'Kangch.' "

"Whatever. As I was saying, the Ministry are organizing an expedition to climb the north face, as this is a route that has proven successful in the past, and it's the best way to the plane. I think you should tag along and pick up that pacemaker for us."

Bond thought for a moment before replying carefully, "Ma'am, Kangchenjunga is the third tallest mountain in the world. What is it, Bill, twenty-eight thousand feet?"

"Twenty-eight thousand two hundred and eight feet, to be exact," Tanner said. "Or eight-thousand five hundred and ninety-eight meters."

Bond continued. "Any peak over eight thousand meters is considered *extremely* formidable. Everest isn't that much taller, and it's a hell of a lot easier. Not that Everest is a piece of cake, either. Kangchenjunga is one of the most difficult climbs anywhere."

"What's your point, Double-O Seven?" M asked.

"That it's not a walk in the park. I hope the Ministry are gathering very experienced people for this job."

"They are. You're going to have some help, too. I've arranged with the First Royal Gurkha Rifles to lend you a man who is an experienced mountaineer. You're to go meet him down at Church Crookham, near Aldershot, this afternoon."

"A Gurkha, ma'am?"

"That's right. A sergeant, I believe. Comes from Nepal, of course, and happens to be an expert climber. Gets along well with Sherpas. I thought you should have Nepalese backup."

Although he preferred to work alone, Bond didn't protest. If this mission was going to be as dangerous as he thought it might be, he could use the extra help.

"Now," she said. "It's vitally important that you retrieve what is left of Lee Ming. You're to get the pacemaker with the microdot — before anyone else does. It's in the interest of Britain's national security. Not only that, the Minister has told me that my job is on the line with this one. He wants that formula and wants it bad. Do I make myself clear?"

"Yes, ma'am."

"We believe that whoever arranged to have it stolen in the first place will send their own expedition to retrieve it. If the Union are involved, our analysts believe that they will mount an expedition as well. Your job will be performed with the utmost discretion. No one on the team will know of your mission except for your Gurkha companion and the expedition leader."

"Who is . . . ?"

M leaned over to her intercom and pressed a button. "Miss Moneypenny?"

"Yes?" came the voice.

"Send in our guest, please."

Bond looked at Tanner questioningly. The Chief of Staff averted his eyes, warning him that he wasn't going to be pleased

with what was coming. M watched Bond
closely to evaluate his reaction.

The door opened, and Group Captain
Roland Marquis entered the room.

TWELVE

Not Quite Impossible

"Group Captain Marquis? Commander Bond?" M said. "I understand you already know each other. And you know my Chief of Staff."

"Right, how are you, Bond — er, James?" Marquis said a bit too warmly. "Colonel Tanner."

Bond stood halfway up, shook hands, and retook his seat. "Fine, Roland. You?"

"Good." Marquis sat in the other chair facing M, next to Bond, and placed the briefcase he was carrying on the carpet.

"Group Captain Marquis," M said, "Mr. Bond is one of our Double-O operatives. He will be accompanying you on the expedition, as we discussed. His mission to retrieve the specification for Skin 17 is classified. Double-O Seven, your cover is that of a Foreign Office liaison."

"What about the Gurkha?" Bond asked.

"Gurkha?" Marquis furrowed his brow.

"I'm assigning a man from the Royal

Gurkha Rifles to accompany Double-O Seven. He's an experienced mountaineer and knows the area. He'll take his orders from Double-O Seven. Aside from you, he's the only other person on the team who will know of Mr. Bond's assignment."

Marquis flashed his white teeth and said, "The more the merrier."

Not impressed by Marquis's levity, M said, "I must emphasize that SIS would greatly appreciate any help that you can provide Double-O Seven so that he can accomplish his mission."

"Certainly, ma'am," Marquis said. "However, when I lead a team, I must insist that safety take precedence over everything else. If I'm asked to do something that might endanger the lives of any other team members, I will refuse. An authority figure is important in an expedition of this magnitude. As team leader, we must agree that my word is final."

M looked at Bond for approval. He shrugged. "I would expect nothing less if I were leading," he said.

Marquis seemed happy with the response. "Right. I'm sure we'll get along splendidly. Bond and I are old schoolmates, isn't that right, Bond?"

Before Bond could answer, M jumped in

with "Tell us about the other team members, please."

"Of course. I've managed to snare some very good people at such short notice. The team's doctor will be Hope Kendall, an experienced mountaineer from New Zealand. I've climbed with her before. She's thirty-two and very fit. Our communications officer is a Dutchman named Paul Baack. He was recommended to me by the ministry. I met him this morning and I'm confident that he will be more than adequate. He comes with some sophisticated equipment that the ministry is lending us. Two mountaineers who have worked with me before, Thomas Barlow and Carl Glass, will be my immediate lieutenants. The American State Department are sending over three well-known climbers. They'll be looking after the American interests in the expedition." He went on to name a man to be in charge of Nepalese relations and hiring the Sherpa porters and cooks in Taplejung, a famed French climber to be the equipment manager, and explained that the rest of the team would be filled out with dozens of Sherpa porters and other climbers who will assist in hauling down whatever might be left of the plane's passengers and their belongings.

"SIS will be conducting security checks on everyone, of course," Tanner interjected.

"Now, I've drawn up a preliminary schedule," Marquis continued. He pulled some notes out of the briefcase.

"Beginning tomorrow there will be three days of intense physical exercise and training, followed by a medical examination."

"Most people train for months for an expedition like this," Bond said.

"You're right," Marquis said. "But the Ministry wants this job done as soon as possible. We need to get to that plane before the monsoon season starts in June. It's already the twenty-third of April. We can't afford the luxury of a long training period. We don't want to be caught on that mountain when the storms come in."

Bond understood and nodded. "Go on."

"We'll fly to Delhi, spend the night, then go on to Kathmandu, where we'll rendezvous with the Americans and the others. We'll spend three days there acclimatizing and making further preparations for the expedition."

He unfolded a large trekking map of Nepal. A route was highlighted in yellow. "We'll fly in a chartered aircraft to Taplejung, here." He pointed to a dot in eastern Nepal. "It's normally an eight-day trek to the Kanchenjunga Base Camp from there, but we're going to cut it down to six. We'll have to push extra hard to do it, but the more time we save, the better. Base Camp is here, at 5,140 meters." He indicated an X on the north side of a triangle marked "Kanchenjunga," which straddled the border between Nepal and Sikkim.

"We'll have to spend a week there acclimatizing. No getting around that."

"Why?" M asked.

"A human being's body adjusts slowly to the change in altitude," Bond explained. "Ascent has to be taken in stages, or one can become extremely ill."

"We don't want any altitude sickness on this expedition," Marquis said. "After the week at Base Camp, we'll slowly lay siege to the mountain within three weeks." Marquis opened a detailed map of the side of the mountain. "We'll set up five camps on the north face. Camp One will be here at 5,500 meters. Camp Two is at 6,000 meters. When we get to Camp Three at 6,600 meters, we'll need to spend another week acclimatizing. I'm hoping that's all the time we'll need. There may be some of us who can't ascend as quickly to Camp

Four, which will be set up here at 7,300 meters. Camp Five will be at 7,900 meters, right next to the site of the plane wreckage. We're extremely fortunate that the aircraft is on this relatively level plain. It's called the Great Scree Terrace. It's less than 2,000 feet from the summit."

Marquis sat back and looked at Bond.

Bond frowned. "It's an extremely ambitious schedule."

Marquis replied, "I agree. I'm not saying it will be a picnic. We'll have to push ourselves to the limit, but we can do it."

There was that word again, Bond thought.

"We *will* do it," Marquis continued. "I've been asked to get us up, the mountain in the safest but quickest amount of time possible. I aim to do that. This schedule gives us just a little over a month. The weather will be unpredictable toward the end of May. We're sure to encounter storms as it is, being that near the monsoon season. We have to race against time."

Bond had no choice but to go along with the plan. Nevertheless, he foresaw possible personality conflicts with the expedition leader.

M looked at Bond. "Well, Double-O Seven?"

"As he said, it won't be easy. But I think I'm up to it, ma'am."

"Fine. Moneypenny will draw up the details for you to attend the training sessions. Thank you, gentlemen. That will be all, Group Captain."

Marquis started to get up, then asked, "So, Bond, do you think this Chinaman, Lee Ming — or whoever he is — still has the specification?"

"We have every indication that he does," Bond replied.

"Where would he have hidden it?" Marquis asked. "Do you know?"

"That's classified," M said. "Even to you. I'm sorry."

Marquis nodded and said, "Of course. I meant only that if it had been placed somewhere in his clothing or hand luggage, the crash could very well have —"

"We know exactly where the formula is hidden," M repeated. "Let Double-O Seven handle that end of things. You just get him up and down that mountain in one piece, all right?"

Marquis stood and bowed slightly. "Yes, ma'am." He turned to Bond and said, "We'll see you tomorrow, eh, Bond? Bright and early?"

"I wouldn't miss it," Bond said dryly.

* * *

The drive in the DB5 was extremely pleasant. It was a beautiful April day without a cloud in the sky. Bond almost wished he were driving a convertible, but he could never own one. They were enjoyable as a novelty every once in a while, but Bond preferred hardtops.

Church Crookham is a quiet village not far, coincidentally, from Fleet, and is the home of the 1st Battalion of the Royal Gurkha Rifles. Bond had never known any Gurkhas personally, but he had a great deal of respect for them. When M had mentioned that he would be working with a partner, Bond had momentarily stiffened. He relaxed when she told him that his companion would be a Gurkha. Bond was intrigued with the prospect of working with a member of what he considered to be the world's fiercest and bravest fighting force.

Made up of hardy hillmen from Nepal, the Gurkhas have been a part of British military history since the Anglo-Nepali conflict of 1814. Bond thought wryly of the British army at that time. He admired the tenacity with which his country had attempted to expand the empire. Britain, already in control of India and hoping to extend the border, pushed northward into Nepal. They were met with such determined, independent, and resourceful soldiers, many not more than five feet four inches tall, the British army was surprised and impressed. Britain eventually won the war, but a friendly, long-lasting relationship was created with the Nepalese government. It was agreed that the British army could recruit soldiers, and being selected became an honor to the Nepalese people. The pay a Gurkha received from the British army was considerable when compared to that of his countrymen, and he could look after his entire family with it.

The Gurkhas were later incorporated into the Indian Army, and when India became independent after the Second World War, the Gurkhas were split between the two countries. Several regiments remained in the Indian Army. Britain retained four — the 2, 6, 7, and 10 Gurkha Rifles. In July 1994, due to "options for change," the regiments were amalgamated into one regiment — the Royal Gurkha Rifles, consisting of two battalions, the 1 RGR based in the UK and the 2 RGR based in Brunei. The Gurkhas stationed in England were originally the 2 and 6 Gurkha Rifles.

As he had reviewed this history before driving out from London, Bond couldn't help but visualize the stereotypical Gurkha: a short, stocky man with legs the size of tree trunks, running through the jungle after an enemy, wearing the traditional Nepalese *topi,* a white cotton cap that was decorated with colored designs (although in battle they would wear a camouflaged jungle hat or helmet) and waving the deadly *khukri* knife. They were known to behead their opponents during hand-to-hand combat. Such was their fierce reputation that during the Falklands conflict, Argentine forces supposedly fled when they heard that the Gurkhas were coming. *"Ayo Gurkhali!"* — the famous Gurkha war cry meaning "The Gurkhas are upon you!" — was intended to strike terror in the heart of the enemy.

Bond pulled into the compound after showing his credentials to the sentry, then drove past the barracks, which were painted black with white trim. When he presented himself at the officers' mess, he was greeted by a tall young Englishman in civilian clothes.

"Mr. Bond?" he asked.

"Yes."

"I'm Captain Alexander Howard." They

shook hands briefly. "Come this way."

He led Bond into a magnificent room that could have served as a museum for the entire history of the Royal Gurkha Rifles. The lounge was decorated with a blend of British colonialism and Nepalese culture. Along with the more westernized brown vinyl-covered chairs and green carpet, there were real ivory tusks mounted on a nonworking black wooden fireplace with a grand carving of the Hindu god Ganesh in the front. A tiger skin covered the carpet, and there were silver trophies and ornaments all over the room. Bond took a moment to admire the famous paintings portraying the Battle for Sari Bair, Gallipoli, August 9, 1915, and the Battle of Kandahar on September 1, 1880. A portrait of Prince Charles, who serves as colonel in chief of the regiment, hung over an impressive display of *khukris*, medals, and awards. A painting of Field Marshal the Viscount Slim, the most famous Gurkha officer, was also on display. Bond greatly admired his book about the Gurkhas' exploits during World War II, which is now required reading at Sandhurst.

Captain Howard said, "Have a seat and Sergeant Chandra will be with you soon."

"I thought his name was Gurung," Bond said.

"The Nepalese automatically adopt their tribal name at birth, like you and I would adopt our parents' surname. Because there are only a handful of the main tribes, there are an awful lot of people with the same surname," Howard said. "Hence, we have several men whose last name is Gurung. A lot of Gurkhas are Gurungs. They're mostly either Gurungs or Magars, from the western part of Nepal, and there are subtribes within those. There are a few from the eastern tribes, the Rais and Limbus. We refer to the men around here either by their first names or by their numbers. It's much less formal here than in other regiments."

"I see."

"Can I get you something to drink?"

"Vodka martini, please."

Howard smiled with approval. "Excellent choice." He moved to fetch the drink, but Bond stopped him.

"Could you please shake it? Don't stir it."

Howard looked at Bond curiously, then said, "Yes, sir." He left Bond alone in the room that contained so much history: monuments and memorials to the ghosts of foreign men who had died for Britain, as well as the proudly displayed commendations and trophies for those who had survived.

The captain returned with the drink and said, "I understand that what you have to discuss with the sergeant is classified, so I will take my leave."

"Thank you, captain," Bond said. He sipped the drink and said, "You make a fine martini."

Howard gave a slight bow and left the room.

After a few moments, Sergeant Chandra came into the room. He, too, was dressed in civilian clothes consisting of dark trousers and a green pullover sweater. He was a stocky five feet two inches tall and weighed roughly one hundred and fifty pounds. He had shiny black hair slicked back on his head, and his skin was the olive brown color prevalent among the middle-Asian races who appeared to be mixtures of Indian and Chinese. What was immediately striking about the man was his huge, warm smile, which seemed to transform his entire face into a pleasant configuration of dimples and lines, especially around his sparkling, friendly eyes.

"*Namaste.* I am Sergeant Chandra Bahadur Gurung," he said in good English. *Namaste* is the traditional Nepali greeting. Gurkhas are required to learn English, just as British officers serving in the regiment are required to learn Nepali, or Gurkhali, as the military calls it. The reason for this is that many words used are specific to the army and wouldn't necessarily be part of normal conversation in Nepal.

Bond stood up and shook the man's hand. He noted that it was a firm, dry handclasp, one that was full of strength and confidence. Chandra looked to be in his thirties, and there was experience and intelligence in his eyes. Bond knew from his record that the sergeant had been in the army since he was eighteen years old.

"James Bond," he said. "It's a pleasure."

"Please, sit down." Chandra gestured to the chair and waited until Bond had sat before taking the chair across from him.

"Sergeant, I understand you've been briefed on all aspects of the mission."

"Yes, sir."

Bond put up his hand. "Let's forget the sir, all right? This isn't a military operation, and I'm not your commanding officer. As far as I'm concerned, we're equals."

Chandra smiled again. "My orders are to follow *your* orders."

"Well, yes, unless they are totally without merit. In the Himalayas, they might often be."

Chandra laughed. "You have climbed before?"

Bond nodded. "Oh, yes, but I'm no expert. I've been to the top of Everest and several big peaks in Switzerland and the Austrian Tyrol."

"Never on Kangchenjunga?"

"Never. What about you?"

"I went halfway up Kangchenjunga once. I was forced down by an avalanche and then a bad storm. I am eager to try again."

"How did you get to be such a climber?" Bond asked.

"We live our entire lives going up and down hills and mountains," Chandra said. "That's why the muscles in our legs are so big. When I was a boy I went on a climbing expedition with my father, who was friends with some Sherpas in Kathmandu. They operated one of the first trekking services there. As I grew older, I made frequent trips to the Himalayas and climbed. I guess I just like it."

"You get on well with the Sherpas?" Bond asked. Sherpas are the tribe of Nepalese hill people more prominent in eastern and northern Nepal who are expert climbers and are almost always hired to haul equipment and luggage for western tourists wishing to trek across the country or up into the mountains.

"Yes, absolutely. Although Nepal has many dialects and tribes, Nepali is understood by everyone. Sherpas have called me their 'climbing cousin' because not many Gurungs have shown much interest in mountain climbing. I am an exception. Every time I go home to Nepal, my wife gets angry with me because I take some time to go climbing!"

"She's in Nepal?"

"Yes," Chandra said. He smiled broadly, obviously pleased with the thought of his mate. "Our wives remain in Nepal. They are not allowed to visit very often. Every three years we can go home for six months. That is in addition to our normal block leave of one month and the family leave in which she was with me for two years in the Far East. So I see her every now and then."

"What do you think of Group Captain Marquis's schedule for getting up Kangch?"

Chandra shook his head. "Not quite impossible."

"But almost."

Chandra's smile said a thousand words.

Then he added, "We must beat the monsoon. It's the only way."

"What do you think our chances for success are?"

Chandra looked hard at Bond. "Sixty-five percent."

Bond leaned forward and lowered his voice. "What do you know about the Union?"

Chandra frowned. "Not much. I spent most of last night reading the file your people gave me. Very interesting group of people. I am interested in their psychology."

"I beg your pardon?"

"I mean, I am interested in how their minds work," Chandra clarified. "I don't understand men who will do that sort of thing for money. I come from one of the poorest countries on earth. The concept of working hard for a living is an accepted way of life for us. To turn to crime, especially betraying one's country, is confounding to me."

"They are very dangerous," Bond said. "We'll have to have eyes in the backs of our heads."

"If they are responsible for the theft of Skin 17, then I'm sure we will encounter them along the way," Chandra surmised.

"They will try to sabotage the mission."

Bond sat back in his chair and raised his martini glass to his new companion. "Oh, of that I am sure, sergeant. You can count on it."

THIRTEEN

Le Gérant

Steven Harding hated North Africa. It smelled, the vast culture shock frightened him, he was suspicious of everyone he met, and it was hot. It was so hot that he was afraid the sweat would ruin the carefully applied makeup that had enabled him to get to Morocco as Randall Rice.

At least Casablanca was a bit more westernized than other places Harding had been to. By far Morocco's largest city with a population of three million, it is the country's industrial center and port, and the most attractive tourist stop in western North Africa. The famed Humphrey Bogart and Ingrid Bergman film is, in part, responsible for the attention that Casablanca receives. As it is the place to go when Moroccans aspire to fame and fortune, Casablanca has all the trappings of a western metropolis, with a hint of the decadent ambience of southern European cities. Alongside the business suits, long legs, high heels, and designer sunglasses are the willowy robes of *djellabas* and burnooses of traditional Morocco.

Wearing a suit much too heavy for the climate, Harding stepped out into the bright sunlight and donned his sunglasses. The heat was barely tolerable, and it was only midmorning. Frowning, he walked away from the Sheraton and went south on Rue Chaoui, ignoring the cluster of beggars, old and young, who reached out to people entering and exiting the hotel.

He walked along what seemed to be a fairly modern street with western architecture. The atmosphere completely changed two blocks away, when Harding entered the Central Market bazaar. Here he felt as if he'd walked into another century. As colorful and noisy as any Hollywood film depiction, the market was an overwhelming assault on the senses. Harding focused straight ahead, walking quickly through the mass of veils, fezes, turbans, and fedoras. The visual display of the distinctive customs and clothing of local tribespeople who had come to buy and sell didn't excite him. He didn't want to buy fruits, vegetables, or spices.

No, thank you, he thought as he rudely brushed past a vendor. He was not interested in the "special" on rich, golden argan oil. There was another one tugging on his sleeve. Sorry, he hadn't any money today. That flatwoven carpet is indeed a beauty, but he didn't want to buy one, thank you anyway.

Harding was drenched with sweat by the time he got all the way across the bazaar to its southeast corner, where a dilapidated shanty was built against a larger stone building. A beggar, who seemed at least ninety years old, sat cross-legged on the dirt in front of the door, which was simply an open space in the wood covered by a cloth hanging from an eave. There was a bent metal dish next to the beggar.

Harding knew he had to do something specific. He reached into his pocket and found ten dirhams in coins and dropped them into the tin. The old man mumbled something and gestured to the cloth. Harding turned to make sure no one was watching, then he ducked under the drape and went inside the shack.

It stank like a toilet. Harding was forced to take a handkerchief from his jacket pocket and hold it over his mouth. Other than the rancid smell, the room was empty. Harding immediately went to the stone wall and put his hand out to touch it. He felt the ridges along a crack, searching for a catch that couldn't be seen. He found it, then pushed it with the requisite force. The secret door slid open, revealing a passage lined in steel. Harding stepped through, and the door closed behind him.

At last! Air-conditioning! And his ticket out of this dreary place. The hard work was over. He had come to claim his reward and move on to the next phase of his life, which would resemble nothing of what he had left behind in England. He hoped that *Le Gérant* wouldn't create a problem about Lee Ming's plane being hijacked. He had done his job and that part of the operation was completely out of his hands. Harding had delivered Skin 17 in precisely the manner that the Union wanted him to. They had better not renege on the five million U.S. dollars he was being paid!

Harding knew, however, that *Le Gérant* was capable of anything. He would consider himself lucky to get out of Morocco alive.

An Arab dressed in fatigues appeared and gestured for Harding to follow him. It was unnerving, especially when the clank-clank of the man's boots on the metal floor echoed throughout the tunnel. The corridor took a right turn, and they went down eight steps to a wider, open area with a table, computer terminals, banks of video surveillance screens, and other sophisticated, high-tech equipment. Two more guards were waiting there.

"Spread your legs and arms," one of them said.

Harding did so while the other one ran a metal detector around his body.

"Look into here," the first man said. He pointed to a device that resembled a microscope. Harding stepped to it and looked in. He knew that this would identify the tattoo that had been burned into the back of his retina when he initially joined the Union. He often wondered what an optometrist might say about the tattoo during an examination. Luckily, it looked more like scar tissue than any recognizable symbol.

It was discernible only to members of the Union.

Harding felt the beam of light pass over his eye. He straightened up and looked at the guards, one of whom studied a computer terminal on the table. The other one stared at him with a look of distaste.

"All right, he checks," said the man at the computer. Harding's escort tapped his shoulder and led him around the table to a

door. The guards pressed a button and re-
leased a lock. The escort pushed the door
open and held it for Harding.

"*Le Gérant* is waiting," he said.

Harding nodded and grinned nervously,
then went through the door.

The room was dark, long, and had a very
low ceiling. The only illumination was provided by lamps hung over the seven men
and three women who sat at a conference
table, each with a legal pad in front of
them. However, there was no light hanging
over the man at the head of the table, the
one sitting in shadow.

Le Gérant. The Manager.

Harding had never met him face-to-face.
Very few Union members had. The inner
circle, those sitting around this table, were
the only individuals who were so entitled.
Nevertheless, it was still difficult to discern
what *Le Gérant* looked like. His silhouette
disclosed that he was tall and broad-
shouldered, but thin and fit. The face and
hands were in shadow, but there was just
enough illumination to reveal him to be
Caucasian. He was more likely a Berber, a
descendant of an ancient race that has
inhabited Morocco since Neolithic times.
Berbers characteristically had light skin,
blue eyes, and often blond or red hair.

Harding knew that they were famous throughout history as warriors and notoriously resistant to being controlled by any system beyond the tribe.

Le Gérant wore a beret and was dressed in dark clothing. His face was further shielded by dark glasses that completely hid his eyes. Harding had once heard a rumor that *Le Gérant* was blind. Perhaps he really was. . . .

As the doctor stepped into the room, conversation halted abruptly and everyone turned to look at him.

"Come in, Dr. Harding," *Le Gérant* said. His voice was educated and smooth, and its deep timbre sounded vaguely French. If the man was indeed a Berber, he didn't sound like one. "Sit down there at the end of the table. We have saved a seat for you."

Harding took the chair and swallowed. Now he was nervous as hell.

"It is good to meet you at last, doctor," the leader said. "We have been following your progress on the Skin 17 project with great interest. I must congratulate you on everything you've done on behalf of the Union. It must not have been easy to find the courage to betray your country and steal the specification right out from under the noses of the DERA."

"Thank you, sir," Harding said.

"You also did a splendid job getting the formula to Belgium and into our client's pacemaker. Was that your idea, planting it there?"

"Yes, sir," Harding said. He felt a thrill that perhaps the meeting was going to go well after all.

"You also acted responsibly with regard to the physician who was caught in Brussels. Having him eliminated was the right thing to do. I'm still a little confused as to how he was caught in the first place, but nothing ever goes perfectly, does it?"

"No, sir," Harding said, swallowing and managing a smile.

Le Gérant took a moment to extract a cigarette from a gunmetal case that he removed from the inside of his jacket. He kept his head straight, staring ahead at a spot on the wall just behind Harding. The man *was* blind! the doctor thought. How extraordinary! The head of the Union couldn't see a damn thing.

Le Gérant lit the cigarette with a gold-plated Dunhill lighter, took a deep drag, exhaled, and spoke again.

"That brings us to the problem of what

has happened to Skin 17."

Harding involuntarily closed his eyes with dread.

Le Gérant continued. "As I understand it, Lee Ming was in Kathmandu, awaiting instructions for his transfer to Tibet. However, precisely one day earlier than scheduled, he was kidnapped from his hotel and taken to the airport. There, he was shoved aboard a tourist Himalayan sight-seeing flight that was hijacked by his kidnappers and flown into the mountains, where a storm knocked it down. Do I have the facts right?"

Harding cleared his throat. "That's what I understand happened, sir, yes, I think that's what happened."

Le Gérant took another drag on the cigarette and shifted slightly in his chair.

"This is highly embarrassing for the Union, you understand that, Dr. Harding? We've let down our Chinese clients. They want their money back. After all, the Skin 17 specification wasn't delivered as promised."

"We did our part, sir," Harding protested. "Our obligation was to get him to Kathmandu. We did that. Our people in Nepal didn't keep a close watch on Lee. Apparently the Union weren't the only ones that wanted that spec. Someone got to him first."

"But how did anyone else know he had it?"

"Perhaps the British agent who tracked me to Belgium . . . ?" Harding mused.

"Oh, yes. The British agent. What's his name? Oh, I remember now. Bond. James Bond. I think you were a bit careless leaving England, Dr. Harding. One of our first rules is to cover your tracks in such a way that no one can follow you. Unfortunately, this man did."

"It was unavoidable, sir," Harding said. He was beginning to sweat despite the cool temperature in the room. His heart was pounding and his stomach cramped.

"What about the RAF officer who helped you steal the formula? Could he have betrayed you?"

"I don't think so," Harding said. How did *Le Gérant* know about Roland Marquis? Harding had been given free rein to pick and choose his team. No one was privy to the information.

"How much was he paid?" the leader asked.

"Fifteen thousand pounds sterling," Harding replied.

"Do you believe that's enough to persuade him to keep his mouth shut?"

"Yes."

For the first time, *Le Gérant* raised his voice. There was such internal animosity in it that everyone in the room felt a chill run down their spine. "Then *who* hijacked that plane and took potentially one of the Union's biggest moneymaking ventures away from us?"

Harding was speechless. The meeting had taken a turn for the worse.

"Well, Dr. Harding?"

"I . . . I have no idea. Sir." Harding was shaking now.

"Shall I tell you, Dr. Harding?"

"Sir?"

The leader took another drag on the cigarette, then snuffed it out in an ashtray attached to the arm of his chair. He had lowered his voice and appeared to be calm once again. "Shall I tell you who foiled our plans to sell Skin 17 to the Chinese?"

"Please do, sir," Harding stammered.

"It was someone trying to double-cross the Union. Someone on the inside. Someone who thought they were smarter than we. Not delivering Skin 17 as promised makes us look bad and damages our reputation. That makes me extremely unhappy. We may be losing two other prospective deals because of this mess. Do you know anyone in the Union who may be trying to outsmart us and get away with something, Dr. Harding?"

Now there was a ringing in Harding's ears. Had he been caught? "N-no, sir. How do you know? I mean, how do you know it's someone on the inside?"

"I know much more than anyone in this room could ever dream," *Le Gérant* said. "I believe that whoever is responsible for kidnapping Lee Ming was planning to take Skin 17 for their own. Perhaps they were going to try to sell it *back* to us for a higher price. After all, we're not the only ones in the extortion business. But no one can treat the *Union* that way."

Le Gérant flicked a switch on the control panel in front of him and a bright photograph appeared on the back wall. It was a picture of the three Nepalese men who had abducted Lee Ming from the Everest Hotel and whisked him away in a potato sack.

"These are the three men who are responsible," *Le Gérant* said. "They are Nepalese, but they do not reside in Nepal."

He *knows!* Harding thought. *My God, he knows!*

"Now, help me understand something, Dr. Harding," the boss said. "We know that Dr. Lindenbeek was caught in Brussels, and he probably talked a little before he was . . . uhm, put out of action. Right?"

"Possibly," Harding said.

"How much did he know about the Union?"

"Virtually nothing. He knew that we were going to expose him if he didn't perform the surgical procedure. He was killed so that he couldn't identify me and Mr. Lee. I covered my tracks there."

"Yes, you did," *Le Gérant* said. "What about our operative inside SIS?"

"In London?"

"Where else?"

"The operative there knows very little about the Union. We receive reports on the movements SIS are making to track down Skin 17. We stay one step ahead of them, so to speak."

"And this Bond fellow. He's the one they've sent?"

Harding nodded. "He was in Belgium. I have no idea if they're sending him to Nepal. I've been traveling."

Le Gérant withdrew another cigarette from his case and lit it. "I have news for you, Dr. Harding. They are indeed sending him to Nepal to join a little expedition that the Ministry of Defence is organizing. They're going to climb that mountain and retrieve the specification."

"Well," Harding said, faking a laugh. "That gives us another opportunity, then, doesn't it? We can get it back!"

"Perhaps," the leader said. He took another moment to relish his tobacco. "Dr. Harding, do you know these men on the screen behind me?"

He shook his head. "I've never seen them before!"

"Never?"

"No, sir."

Le Gérant flicked another switch on the control panel and the slide changed. This time it was a shot at a pub, one that Harding recognized. When he saw who was in the picture, his heart skipped a beat.

The three Nepalese men were sitting with pints of beer talking to none other than himself.

"This photograph was taken three days before the Skin 17 operation went down," *Le Gérant* said. "In the Lake and Goose public house, not far from Aldershot. You know it well, don't you, doctor?"

Harding closed his eyes. It was all over.

"You hired these men to steal the specification, didn't you, Harding?" This time the voice was menacing, trembling with anger.

"No — I — it's that I . . ." Harding was blubbering.

"Shut up!" *Le Gérant* pushed another switch on the panel and the door behind Harding opened. One of the guards came in and stood behind him. Terribly frightened now, Harding glanced over his shoulder and back at the rest of the people at the table. They were all staring at him, expressionless.

"Le Gérant," Harding said. "Please, I didn't know . . . I was going to —"

"You were *going* to betray the Union, divert the formula, and make more money than we were paying you by selling it to someone else. You got greedy. Isn't that right, doctor?"

"No, sir. I mean yes, sir, it was! I didn't do this! Honest to God I —"

"You're a fool," *Le Gérant* said. "And I do not suffer fools." He gave an imperceptible nod to the guard behind Harding.

The guard roughly grabbed Harding's hair with his left hand and pulled back his head. The man produced a long, thin dagger in his right hand and with one smooth, swift stroke, slit Harding's throat from ear to ear. Blood splattered the table in front of him as he gurgled horribly. He writhed and struggled for a grip on life for a full minute before he finally slid out of the chair and onto the floor. The other Union members at the table were shocked, frightened, and speechless. None of the blood had splattered on them, but the memory of what they had just witnessed would stay with them for the rest of their lives.

The guard behind Harding lowered his dagger, stooped to the body, and wiped it clean on the dead man's clothes.

"Thank you, sergeant," *Le Gérant* said. "You can go. Have the cleanup crew come in five minutes. We'll be finished then."

"Yes, sir," the sergeant said, saluting. He turned and left the room.

The others couldn't tear their eyes away from Harding's body and the mess on the table. One woman involuntarily heaved. After a moment, though, they regained their composure and looked at the man in shadow. If there had been any doubt, he was now unquestionably their leader.

"I want Skin 17 before anyone else gets it," he said. Now his voice was controlled and even, but it was laced with venom. "We have learned that there are at least three expeditions being organized to climb Kangchenjunga and retrieve that specification. One is from England and is, of course, the one that is our most formidable adversary. Another is from Russia, manned by our friends in the Russian Mafia. The Chinese are mounting an expedition as well, with the hopes of retrieving the formula before we do — thereby giving them a reason to never pay us for the work we've already done for them. There may be more."

Le Gérant pulled another cigarette from his case and lit it. He inhaled, pausing for calculated dramatic effect. "Plans are now under way for the Union to accompany one of these expeditions to the great mountain. We *will* be the first to retrieve Skin 17. It could be the most important venture we undertake this year. Many of you will be called on to help arrange this. There will be no failure. Is that clear?"

Everyone nodded, but *Le Gérant* couldn't see them. Several of them turned back to look at the disgusting pool of red liquid dripping off the end of the table. A few felt physically ill.

"IS THAT CLEAR?" he shouted.

They quickly turned back to him and cried, "Yes, *Le Gérant!*"

Le Gérant smiled. "Good. Then let's have lunch. Is everybody hungry?"

FOURTEEN

Welcoming Reception

After spending all day climbing up and down staircases while wearing heavy backpacks with Marquis and other members of the team on an officer's training course near Oakhanger, James Bond drove to SIS headquarters for a late meeting with Major Boothroyd in Q Branch.

"I want you to know that I postponed a very important dinner date to be here this evening," Boothroyd said, punching in the security code to let Bond into the laboratory. "With a very beautiful woman, I might add."

"Really?"

"Don't act so surprised, Double-O Seven. I may be an old man, but I'm still very healthy in that regard."

"I didn't say a word, Major," Bond said, smiling. "She is a very lucky woman."

"I should say so," Boothroyd replied. "We've been married twenty-eight years. It's our anniversary, and here I am, spending the evening with you."

"Well, let's make it brief, shall we?"

"Quite. Now, pay attention, Double-O Seven." He led Bond to a metal table that was covered with various items. "I pulled these out of storage this afternoon after I learned the nature of your assignment. We're also working with the Ministry in supplying some sophisticated communications equipment to the expedition. The Dutchman, what's-his-name, he'll have all that."

"Paul Baack?"

"That's right."

Boothroyd went on, handing him a small tube with a mouthpiece on it. "This is similar to our underwater emergency breather, except it's for use at high altitudes. It holds about fifteen minutes of oxygen and fits into a pocket of your parka. Again, it's only for emergencies."

The major indicated a pair of boots. "These are the best One Sport 'Everest' boots with alveolite liners and built-in supergaiters. They're ultra light, and I think you'll find them quite comfortable. The unique thing about them is that they've been designed with our special field compartments in the heels. In the right boot you'll find medical and first aid equipment. In the left one you'll find a set of small tools. Screwdriver, pliers, wrench . . . they might come in useful."

Bond examined the bivouac sack made by North Face. "Ah, that," the major said. "It's a bivouac sack for when you're caught outside of camp at night. We've installed a special battery-operated power pack that will heat it up like an electric blanket. It also expands to allow room for a second person."

"How convenient," Bond said.

"You have your P99 on you?"

"Yes."

"Let me have it."

Bond handed him the Walther P99 and Boothroyd put it in what Bond hadn't realized was a fur-lined holster.

"I could just imagine you attempting to draw your gun out from under all those layers of clothing and the down parka you'll most likely be wearing. By the time you got it out, you'd be a dead man. I think this outer holster should solve that little problem. It can be worn on top of your parka, but it's still disguised to look like another pocket."

Boothroyd removed the gun and handed it back to Bond. "We'll have your own gear sent to you in Kathmandu. We've ordered

266

all the clothing and tools you'll need, and we've spared no expense. Apparently M feels that this mission is important enough to spend a few hundred pounds on a sleeping bag. If you have any questions regarding any of it when you get there, send me a fax."

"What if I have a question in the middle of the Himalayas?"

"You can still send a fax. Paul Baack will have direct satellite linkup to the Internet, fax, and telephone. You can send me a digital snapshot from the summit of Mount Everest if you'd like."

"I'm not climbing Everest."

Boothroyd shrugged. "It's much the same thing, isn't it?"

Finally, the major opened a box and pulled out a package of plastic. "Inside this is an inflatable, portable seven-kilogram Gamow Bag. As you know, a Gamow Bag is a hyperbaric chamber used in an emergency to treat altitude sickness. This one is special because it's got its own air pump and generator, eliminating the need for another person to use bellows on it."

Bond picked up a strange contraption that looked like an oxygen regulator, but it had two mouthpieces on it.

Boothroyd smiled. "Ah, it figures that

you would be attracted to that particular item."

"What is it?"

"It's an oxygen regulator, of course."

"Why two mouthpieces?"

Boothroyd shook his head. "I know you all too well, Double-O Seven. It's a two-person regulator. You both can share the same oxygen at a pinch."

"Seeing that most of the other members of the team are men, I resent that remark," Bond said.

The flight to Delhi was horrendous, and the overnight stay in the hotel closest to the airport was even worse. Even though the team arrived in the city at nearly midnight, the streets were heavily congested with traffic, pedestrians, and cows.

Symbols of India's religions were everywhere — Hindu images of Shiva, Ganesh, and Krishna, Buddhist statues, Sikh turbans, and even crucifixes. Nepal, though, would be completely Hindu and Buddhist. In fact, Nepal officially designated itself as the "only Hindu country in the world."

Not normally a religious person, Bond respected Eastern beliefs. Even so, he had fitful dreams of these various religious icons and woke up irritable and stiff. Sergeant Chandra, with whom he shared a room, seemed to take it all in his stride. Gurkhas are typically good-natured, no matter how unpleasant conditions may be, and Chandra was no exception. When Bond awoke, the Gurkha was humming to himself, standing at the counter dressed only in boxer shorts, making coffee with a ten-year-old Mr. Coffee machine that, surprisingly, came with the room.

"Good morning, sir," Chandra said, a large grin spread over his face. "Coffee?"

Bond groaned and pulled himself out of bed. "Please. Black. Strong. Hot. I'm going to take a cold shower."

"That's all there is," Chandra said. "Apparently the hotel lost its hot water last night."

Bond told himself that he must get used to these little inconveniences. Once they had embarked on the trek to the Himalayas and set about ascending Kangch, all remnants of a civilized world would be long gone.

Shortly before lunch the party met back at the airport to catch an Indian Airlines flight to Kathmandu.

Because they were officials representing the British government, the team passed quickly through Immigration. They were met by the Nepalese Liaison Officer, an official who is always assigned to climbing expeditions. His duties include making sure proper permits and paperwork are submitted, and seeing that the expedition doesn't stray from its allotted peak.

The team piled into a rickety bus that must have been at least thirty years old. Bond gazed out the window at the streets, finally taking in that he was truly in the third world. It was such a contrast, even from Delhi. The blending of cultures in Kathmandu was striking. The traffic snaked around water buffalo pulling wagons carrying rice. There were open sewers along the sides of the roads. The people were dressed in an odd mixture of western fashions (T-shirts, blue jeans) and Nepalese and Tibetan dress. Barefoot, skinny children ran up to the bus when it stopped at a traffic light, holding out their hands and calling out, "Bonbon! Rupees! Iskul pens!" Apparently the universal English word for "sweets" in Nepal was "bonbon," and as some tourists were prone to hand out pencils and pens, the children often asked for "iskul pens," claiming that they needed them for "school."

The Yak and Yeti is one of the few luxury hotels in Kathmandu. Located on

Durbar Marg, built around a wing of an old Rana palace, the lavishly decorated 270-room building is "modern" in every sense of the word, yet its history is thoroughly integrated in the design. Bond noticed that the architecture was both westernized and Nepali-Victorian.

"This hotel is a beautiful one," Chandra said as they got out of the bus. "For many centuries Nepal was cut off from the outside world. Initially it was ruled by the Mallas, but Prithivi Narayan Shah established a kingdom in Kathmandu. During his tenure, a young army general, Jung Bahadur Rana, usurped power from the monarchy and established himself as the Prime Minister, with the title of maharaja and powers superior to those of the sovereign."

Bond and the others walked into the lobby through double glass doors and onto sparkling granite flooring. To the left was a large gazebo with huge French windows. The reception desk, built with a black granite top, was to the right. A magnificent and traditional Newari wooden window, exquisitely hand-carved by local artisans, stood above Reception, where a smiling Guest Relations Officer gracefully draped in a sari sat. Beyond the reception area was a lounge furnished with yellow and green upholstered chairs. The lounge overlooked the hotel's lovely, well-manicured and landscaped lawns through picture windows.

Chandra continued. "The Rana regime lasted for a hundred and four years, until 1951, and contributed to the country's ornate neoclassical palaces. One of the reminders of this Rana period is the Red Palace, or Lal Durbar. It was built, oh, I think it was around 1855. This reconstructed palace now houses two fine restaurants — the Naachghar and the Chimney, as well as the Yak and Yeti Bar — all under one roof. Did you know that the Chimney owns the original copper fireplace from Boris Lissanevitch's famous Royal Hotel? The bar there was called the Yak and Yeti, which is how this hotel got its name. Boris Lissanevitch opened the first western hotel in Nepal."

"Fascinating," Bond said.

The strong smells from the streets were not present inside the hotel. Instead, there was the pungent aroma of curry coming from one of the restaurants.

Bond and Chandra were put in what was called a Tibetan suite. Rich silk was used to cover the walls of the room with typical Tibetan motifs in green and blue. The living room had a comfortable seating area containing furnishings of intricately carved wood. The walls and ceiling were adorned with brass and copper work. A private terrace offered a spectacular view of the Himalayan range and the Kathmandu valley. The master bedroom contained two queen-sized beds covered in silk in the same rich Tibetan colors. The bathroom was in marble with an oval-shaped bathtub and a separate shower.

"Enjoy the luxury while you can!" Chandra said, dropping his bags on the floor. "In three days we leave all of this behind!"

"Indeed. However, we're supposed to meet our man from Station I at the hotel bar in an hour. What time is our orientation with the team?"

Chandra looked at his itinerary. "Tonight, before dinner. We have the rest of the afternoon free."

"Good," Bond said. "We'll want to go to the temporary station house in Kathmandu and see what our man has for us."

Bond changed into lightweight khaki trousers and a Sea Island cotton navy shirt, while Chandra wore fatigues from his regiment. They went down to the Piano Lounge, just off the lobby, where the Mixture Trio Band were playing standards from the fifties, sixties, and seventies. Bond ordered a double vodka with ice. Chandra ordered Iceberg, the local Nepalese beer.

"Are you going to see your wife?" Bond asked.

"She is coming to Kathmandu and we'll meet before we leave for the mountain. It's a long journey for her. Most of the way has to be on foot."

"What's her name?"

"Manmeya."

"That's a pretty name."

"She's a pretty woman," Chandra said, his grin stretching across his face.

They finished their drinks just as Zakir Bedi came into the bar. He spotted Bond and Chandra and approached their table.

"Mr. Bond?" he asked.

"Yes?"

"The tour you arranged is ready. Would you like to come with me?"

"Certainly." Bond charged the bill to his room, and he and Chandra followed Bedi outside.

The midday sun was strong. The dust and heat and smell of the street assaulted Bond as they walked a mile to Durbar Square, the heart of old Kathmandu city.

Clustered around the central square are the old Royal Palace and several temples designed with the multiroof Nepali pagoda style of architecture that spread to China and East Asia. Many of the temples are oddly adorned with erotic art on the roof struts. Unlike those in India, where the erotic carvings are sometimes sensuous, these are smaller, cruder, and even cartoonlike. Chandra told Bond a legend suggesting that the goddess of lightning was a shy virgin and wouldn't dare strike a temple with such "goings-on."

The square was noisy and full of life. Taxis and cows shared the same roads. Street vendors huddled around their wares, barking for attention. At least three *sadhus*, or holy men, sat on blankets in the dirt, half naked, smeared in dust, their hair and beard matted. Several women carried *dokos* on their backs. These large wicker baskets were filled with a variety of items from vegetables to firewood, and were fixed to the body by means of a *namlo*, a strap around the forehead.

The three of them walked behind the Shiva temple known as the Maju Deval, one of the larger temples in the square, and into a quieter side street. Bedi led them to an antiques shop that still bore the name Universal Exports Ltd.

"We never changed to Transworld Consortium," Bedi explained. "I rarely had to open the Nepal office, so we kept it the same. It's normally unmanned. Saves money."

Bedi unlocked the door and ushered Bond and Chandra inside. The place was musty and filled with bric-a-brac, some of which might have been worth something in the tourist trade. Most of it, however, was junk that was in place to create the illusion that the shop was legitimate.

"Please excuse the dust," Bedi said. "I had not been here for months until we tried to arrest Lee Ming. Come over here, I have something to show you."

They went through hanging drapes and into a passage leading to a door with a padlock on it. Bedi unlocked it, saying, "We're not so sophisticated in Nepal, Mr. Bond. No keycards, no electronic steel doors, nothing like that. Just an ordinary key gets you into the Nepalese branch of the British secret service!" He laughed heartily.

The "office" was a very small room containing a computer and monitor, file cabinets, a small refrigerator, a desk, and four chairs.

They had worked up a sweat simply walking across town, so Bedi opened the refrigerator and took out three bottles of Iceberg beer. The beer was refreshing, but Bond didn't care much for it. It had a curiously sweet taste, unlike some Indian beers that he enjoyed, such as Cobra.

"I've learned something about the three hijackers," Bedi said. He removed some eight-by-ten glossy photographs from an envelope on the desk. "They were Nepalese nationals who escaped from prison five years ago and were believed to be dead. They were identified by two workers at the hangar where the tourist plane was kept."

"Do we know if they're Union?" Bond asked.

"We've been unable to determine that. It's possible, I suppose, but they've been living in Nepal for the last five years. If they were Union, it seems that we would have had more evidence of their activities. We think they were living in the hills somewhere. What we did learn is that they were part of the old Thuggee cult that originated in India in the 1800s."

The "Thugs" were a religious organization that murdered and robbed in the service of a goddess.

"If I remember correctly, the British government supposedly hanged the last Thug in 1882," Bond said.

"Mostly true," replied Bedi. "But remnants of their group exist. I would think present-day Thugs would be prime recruitment candidates for the Union. You want to know the most interesting thing?"

"What?"

"They were in England briefly, shortly before the Skin 17 formula was stolen. Flew in one day, flew out the next."

"How did they get in?"

"The visas were issued for 'family reasons.' We have since discovered that their so-called families in England never existed."

Bond studied the photographs, then turned his attention to three more pictures that Bedi laid on the table. They were aerial views of the crash site on Kangchenjunga. The fuselage was plainly visible, surprisingly intact.

"Reconnaissance photos reveal that the plane is quite accessible once you get up to the Great Scree Terrace," Bedi said. "But look at this detail." He showed them another photo that magnified one of the aerial shots.

Footprints were evident around the open

door of the aircraft.

"Someone survived the crash," Bond observed.

"They couldn't have survived the altitude," Chandra remarked. "They may have gotten out of the wreckage, but they wouldn't have lived long at that height. None of those people was prepared for those conditions."

"Do you have any other pictures? Where do the footprints lead?"

Bedi shrugged. "We tried to take more shots, but the winds and snow had covered the tracks by the time we went back. You can see that they went off in this direction, toward the south, but beyond that we don't know. He's right, they couldn't have survived at that altitude for very long. They hadn't acclimatized themselves at all. Whoever it was, you'll probably find their frozen body in a crevasse somewhere."

The men went through various other documents and reports. Zakir Bedi had no solid evidence that the Union were involved in the plane hijacking. To his knowledge, the Union had not operated on the Indian subcontinent at all.

By late afternoon they were finished. Bedi offered to walk them back to the hotel and led them out of the makeshift intelligence office.

The streets were still crowded, but the heat was beginning to subside as dusk approached and they walked into Durbar Square.

High above them, inside the Maju Deval temple, a Nepalese man held a Galil Sniping Rifle, a 7.62mm semiautomatic weapon that is manufactured in Israel. Designed with battlefield reliability in mind, the Galil could score head shots at 300 meters, half-body hits at 600 meters, and full-figure hits at 800 to 900 meters. The man was a good shot, but he wasn't an expert. A sniper must have special training and technique, for bullets don't fly in a completely straight line. Gravity and friction pull on a flight path; snipers must allow for "rise and drop" conditions. Some telescopic sights incorporate range finders to help the marksman in calculations, but intense practice is necessary to get it right.

It was this factor that saved James Bond's life.

The first bullet hit the dirt at Bond's feet. All three men dropped to the ground, then attempted to determine where the sniper was located. Bond squinted into the sun, almost certain that the shot had been fired from the large triple-roofed temple in front of him.

"He's up there!" Bond pointed. He got to his feet and started to run toward the building. The other two followed him, but a passing rickshaw momentarily blocked their passage. When the man pulled the contraption away, Bedi was in front of Bond, peering at the temple.

"Is he still there?" he asked.

Up above, the sniper took a bead on Bond's head. He didn't know who the other two were. His orders were to kill the Englishman. The crosshairs centered neatly on Bond's nose, then the man squeezed the trigger. Somehow, though, the Indian man got in the way.

The bullet struck Zakir Bedi on the side of the face, knocking him back into Bond.

"I see him!" Chandra shouted, running toward the temple. Bond dropped Bedi's corpse on the ground, drew his Walther, and ran after Chandra.

The Gurkha stopped Bond at the door. "You can't come in," he said. "It's forbidden to non-Hindus."

"To hell with that!" Bond spat out.

"I'm sorry, James," Chandra insisted. "Let me go. You wait here."

"No, I'm coming with you."

Chandra made a face, then went into the

temple. In Nepal, there was a fine line between Hinduism and Buddhism. A well-known Shiva lingam was inside, but the roof was topped by a pinnacle shaped like a Buddhist stupa. It was dark, and Bond almost choked from the thick incense smoke. Worshippers looked up in horror at the westerner who had run inside the sacred place with a gun.

Bond followed Chandra to a set of stairs in the back that led to the layered roof. Another shot rang out, this time inside the building. Women screamed, got up, and ran out of the temple. The men who were there didn't move, but instead watched with interest. They hadn't seen this much excitement in a long time.

Chandra and Bond saw the sniper attempting to climb onto the sloping roof so that he could jump down to the ground below. Chandra was remarkably fast, scuttling out on the roof just in time to catch the man's leg. The rifle fell as the two men struggled. Bond rolled out on the roof, halting his descent by lodging the heels of his boots in the shingles. Before he could lend the Gurkha a hand, the sniper twisted away and slipped off the edge of the roof. The man screamed as he fell, but the sound was abruptly cut short as he hit the hard ground.

Bond and Chandra climbed back into the temple and ran down the stairs. Chandra spoke Nepali to the spectators, explaining that they were policemen. Outside, they found the sniper had fallen on his head. His neck was broken.

Chandra examined him and said, "He's a local man. I can't believe that he would have had much experience in shooting people."

"That fits with Union recruiting practices, doesn't it?" Bond asked.

"In Nepal, I would say, yes. Those bullets were meant for you."

"Obviously," said Bond. "That bloody leak at SIS is getting worse. There is no way that anyone in Nepal could have known of my presence. Bedi was the only one."

They heard police sirens approaching. "Come on," Chandra said. "We don't want to get involved in this."

They ran through the crowd and lost themselves before the police arrived.

FIFTEEN

Teamwork

The team met in one of the Yak and Yeti's impressive meeting rooms normally used for business functions. It was seven-thirty, and dinner was scheduled for eight o'clock in the fabulous Chimney Restaurant. Everyone was tired and hungry, but there was still excitement and anticipation in the air.

Marquis sat beside Bond and Chandra while waiting for two late arrivals. He leaned over and whispered, "I hear there was an Indian found shot to death today in Durbar Square. A Nepalese, it appears, was the killer. He's dead, too. I was questioned this afternoon by police. Apparently, a Caucasian man and another Nepalese were observed fleeing the scene of the crime. Do you know anything about this?"

"Lord, no," Bond lied. "Who was it that was killed?"

"Some Indian businessman. Sorry, Bond, I had to ask. You two are the only

Caucasian/Nepalese combination I know at the moment. Never mind, it's time to start."

Marquis got up as the two missing stragglers came into the room, and from the podium said, "May I have your attention, please?"

Many of the eighteen people who had assembled in the room were old acquaintances from previous expeditions and were therefore embroiled in lively conversation. There was one Nepalese Liaison Officer, sixteen male team members, and one female.

"Please, let's get on with this, so we can eat!" Marquis said even louder.

Finally everyone stopped talking and focused their attention on the leader.

"I have to keep reminding myself that I'm not addressing members of the air force," Marquis muttered, but loud enough for everyone to hear. They laughed. "Well. It's good to see old friends and nice to meet new ones. Welcome. I'm glad you all could make it. You're probably wondering why I asked you here. . . ."

There were more chuckles in the room, but less enthusiastic. Bond was put off by Marquis's manner. He projected unquestionable authority over the team, but he also tried too hard to entertain them.

"Seriously, we're on a very important mission for the governments of Great Britain and the United States," Marquis said with thin sincerity. "I'm sure we all want to get to know each other well over the next few days, but tonight we want to eat and go to bed! This is a very nice hotel, and I for one want to take advantage of it while I'm here! So, let's get on with the introductions. I'm Group Captain Roland Marquis, RAF, and something of a mountain climber in my spare time. . . ."

There was some applause from two or three members of the audience, including the girl.

"Thank you." Marquis beamed. He indicated two Nepalese men standing near the wall, apart from the others. "You all met Mr. Chitrakar at the airport this afternoon. He's our Liaison Officer. He is our contact here in Kathmandu." The man on the right smiled and gave a little bow. "Mr. Chitrakar needs to say a few words. Mr. Chitrakar?"

"Thank you," he said. His accent was thick. He proceeded to rattle off the various governmental rules and regulations the team should abide by when trekking across the countryside and when ascending the mountain.

"Of most importance," he said, "is that you do not summit Kangchenjunga. This is a very sacred mountain to our people. You may go as high as you need in order to perform salvage operations, but no higher." He smiled, and said, "You might anger the goddess who lives there."

Indeed, Kangchenjunga means "Five Treasures of the Great Snows," and is thought to be the home of Nepalese gods, as are other Himalayan peaks.

"Thank you, Mr. Chitrakar. I can assure you that none of us has any intention of summiting the mountain. Now, next to Mr. Chitrakar is Ang Tshering, a splendid *sirdar,* with whom I've worked before," Marquis said.

The man on the left smiled and waved. The same two or three people who applauded before did so again. Bond thought that Tshering looked competent. The role of a *sirdar,* or Sherpa trekking leader, was important. He would run the Base Camp while everyone else climbed.

"Now I'd like to introduce the most beautiful person in the room! She comes from New Zealand, so those of us who know her sometimes call her Kiwi Kendall. Meet our team doctor, Hope Kendall."

Red-faced, Dr. Kendall stood to the

loudest applause anyone had received thus far. Bond thought that Marquis was right in one respect — she was stunningly beautiful. Hope Kendall had blond hair, green eyes, and a wide smile. She was in her early thirties and was obviously fit and healthy. She was over six feet tall, with long legs that were hidden by khaki trousers. Due to social customs in Nepal, Bond knew that he might never get a glimpse of those legs, since women revealing bare legs in shorts or miniskirts were frowned upon.

"Hello, everybody," she said. "I just have a few words to say because I'm your doctor for the next few weeks. I know you are all fit as buck rats, and you know everything I'm going to tell you now, but I'm actually required by law to give you the 'talk.'"

She managed to exert a great deal of authority over the men, and not just because of her physical beauty. Even Marquis sat down and gave her his undivided attention.

"We're going to be climbing much more quickly than any of us have ever done before. The schedule is extremely tight, and I know we all want to be off the mountain before the monsoons hit. Nevertheless, we must be conscious of any symptoms of acute mountain sickness. It can strike anyone at any time. It is each and everyone's job to recognize the symptoms in your teammates, because many times an individual cannot recognize them in himself. You must understand that the atmospheric condition at high altitude is the same as at sea level, with twenty percent oxygen, but a reduction in atmospheric pressure reduces the amount of oxygen you can take in with each breath. You're really breathing roughly half the oxygen you're accustomed to when you're above five thousand meters. The first signs are a general malaise, loss of appetite, then headache. This is followed by increasing weakness and a loss of interest in the climb. If you start to experience apathy, nausea, dizziness, or sleepiness, there's a good chance you've got AMS."

Bond knew all of this, but Dr. Kendall had such powerful charisma that he hung on every word.

"Note that these symptoms can occur at relatively low altitudes. So make sure you use what we call 'rest steps' to give your leg muscles little rests all the way up and help you maintain measured, methodical breathing. Take occasional full rest stops with forced deep breathing. Drink *lots* of water, and I mean it. Eat frequently to keep your nourishment up. Now, you should be aware of the two severe types of AMS, and these are High Altitude Pulmonary Edema, or HAPE, and High Altitude Cerebral Edema, or HACE. HAPE is when there is leakage of blood and other fluids into the lungs, restricting the air sacs in exchanging oxygen and carbon dioxide in the blood. The symptoms are similar to pneumonia. HAPE can kill you and kill you fast. Fortunately, it rarely occurs in healthy people below nine thousand feet or so. HACE, the other one, is worse. That's when there is accumulation of fluid in the brain, and symptoms begin with a severe, relentless headache that is a result of pressure due to the swelling of brain tissue. You'll soon have difficulties with physical coordination, slurred speech, irrational behavior, collapse, and eventually you die. Descent is the only treatment for these things. Forget drugs like Diamox and dexamethasone. Although they might treat the symptoms of AMS, they don't make the damaging effects go away. As your doctor, here and now I forbid the use of these drugs, got it?"

Several people in the room mumbled, "Uh-huh."

"Finally, be aware of what we call retinal hemorrhaging. This is very serious, and it's caused by damage to the retina due to pressure changes and the tiny bundles of arteries in your eyes rupturing. If you contract it up on that mountain, you're in deep trouble. You may not regain your eyesight until weeks after descending, if you're able to descend safely at all! I'm not trying to scare you, I just want you to be aware of all this. I'll be performing routine examinations on every member of the team, so get used to it."

"I'm looking forward to that!" Marquis said with a laugh. Some of the others chuckled.

She glared at him but smiled. "Roland has told me that I have the authority to send anyone down the mountain who I think is unfit to continue the climb. That goes for you, too, Mr. Marquis!"

Bond wondered if there was something romantic between the two of them.

"Finally, I just want to say that although we're about to embark on a seemingly insurmountable task, there's an old Maori proverb that says *He nui maunga e kore e taea te whakaneke, he nui ngaru moana mā te ihu o te waka e wāhi.* 'A great mountain cannot be moved, but a giant wave can be broken by the prow of a canoe.' In plain English, that means 'Do not give up too easily — some things are possible.' That's all I've got," she said, and sat down.

Marquis took the floor again and said, "Thank you, Dr. Kendall. I'm sure we'll all put ourselves in your capable hands."

She smirked and turned red again as the others laughed.

"Right," Marquis said. He then introduced the man who was in charge of Nepalese relations. He would be working with the *sirdar* to hire the Sherpa porters once they reached Taplejung. Other climbers would be hired there to assist in the hauling once the team reached Camp Five and the aircraft.

The equipment manager was a renowned French mountaineer. Bond was aware of his talents. He was probably the only mountaineer on the team who was as experienced as Roland Marquis. He was a small man but had extremely broad shoulders and a big, bald head.

"My lieutenants on the team are my friends Tom Barlow and Carl Glass, there in the second row."

Barlow was tall, lanky, and hirsute with thick glasses, while Glass was stocky, clean shaven, and expressionless.

Marquis then introduced three men representing the Americans, who stood and said hello. One of them seemed very young, probably in his early twenties, and looked even younger. Bond had already heard one of the others refer to him as "the kid."

Three other men were presented as "haulers." Two were known British mountaineers. The third, introduced as Otto Schrenk, was a last-minute replacement.

Marquis explained. "Apparently Jack Kubrick was involved in a terrible accident the night before our departure from London. We had to scramble for someone else, and Mr. Schrenk here, from Berlin, volunteered to step in."

This news took Bond by surprise. He had spent quite some time studying the backgrounds of each and every team member. SIS had done a complete security check on all of them. Bond wasn't comfortable with an unknown. If the Union were going to infiltrate the team, they would do it at the last minute. Bond made a note to put in a call to SIS and have Schrenk scrutinized.

He leaned over to Chandra and whispered, "Keep an eye on that one."

Chandra nodded imperceptibly.

Marquis then gestured to them. "Over here are representatives from the Foreign

Office, Mr. James Bond and Sergeant Chandra Bahadur Gurung, his assistant. The sergeant is on loan to us from the army. He's with the Royal Gurkha Rifles, isn't that right?"

Chandra grinned and nodded. His eyes wrinkled when he smiled, giving the impression that every line in his face was smiling.

Bond nodded at the others, then sat down. He caught Hope Kendall's eye, and lingered there a moment. She was studying him, attempting to figure him out with a spontaneous first impression.

"Last but not least is Paul Baack, our communications officer," Marquis said, gesturing to a tall, large man with a neat goatee and deep brown eyes. Baack stood up, immediately dispelling the notion that anyone else might be bigger than he.

"Thank you," he said with a pronounced Dutch accent. "I am happy to be here." He smiled broadly, then sat down.

In Bond's opinion, it was Baack who had the most impressive credentials. Not only was the man a top-notch mountaineer, his work in communications was widely respected in intelligence circles. Q Branch routinely consulted the Dutch engineer, but Marquis hadn't known that. Bond had never met him and looked forward to doing so.

The girl was a big question mark, Bond thought. Was she Marquis's girlfriend? They certainly flirted with each other a lot in public. She seemed capable, but in Bond's opinion, bringing a girl along with a team of men was just asking for trouble. She might insist that more effort be expended on providing her with a certain amount of privacy. On the other hand, she might be a distraction if she simply tried to be "one of the boys."

"One other thing I need to mention," Marquis said. "There are three other expeditions climbing Kangch."

Bond knew that there were two. Another must have appeared in the last day or two.

"Permits for a Chinese expedition were applied for on the same day as ours. A Russian expedition was mounted just a few days later. The Chinese are climbing the north face as well, but slightly south of us. If you ask me, they're doing it the hard way. The Russians are also coming up the north face, and at this point we don't know what route they're taking. Just a few days ago a Belgian team applied for permits. I understand that they were granted today."

Bond raised his hand and was acknowledged by Marquis.

"What do we know about them?"

"Not much. They're all experienced climbers. They came up with the money, and that's all Nepal cares about. They don't represent any specific groups. As far as we know, they're in it only for the sport."

Bond frowned.

"Right," said Marquis. "Are there any other questions?"

Otto Schrenk, the newcomer, raised his hand.

"Yes, Mr. Schrenk?"

"Why are we climbing the north face? That is very difficult." He had a thick German accent.

"It happens to be the most direct route to the aircraft. Also, the politics involved with obtaining permission to climb from the Sikkim side were too complicated. The north, west, and southwest sides of the mountain are in Nepalese territory. Of these, the north face is the safest. There have been deaths there over the years, to be sure, but several people have made it to the top."

That seemed to satisfy Schrenk. He nodded and folded his arms.

"Anyone else?"

No one said anything.

"Fine, then," Marquis said, slapping his stomach. "I'm ready to eat!"

The group stood up and stretched, picking up the conversations they had halted a half hour ago.

Bond looked at Hope Kendall, who was gathering her things. Could she really take the next seven or eight weeks being the only woman among such testosterone-heavy human beings as Roland Marquis . . . and himself?

"Just a second," Bond said to Chandra. "If I'm not back in sixty seconds, you'll have to eat without me."

He walked over to Hope, held out his hand, and said, "Hello, I thought I should come over and introduce myself properly."

She smiled warmly and shook his hand. "I'm glad to be working with you, Mr. Bond. So far the trip is a beaut, don't you think? I'm sorry, I'm afraid I don't know much about your background."

"We've been here only a day," Bond said. "The law of inevitable rubbish will descend upon us before we know it. It always happens."

"You're not going into this with a bad attitude, are you, Mr. Bond?" she asked flirtatiously.

"Not at all. As you said, we all have to keep our wits about us. Would you care to accompany me to dinner?"

She shook her head. "I'm already promised to Roland. Some other time, maybe, all right?" She smiled, gave a little wave, then turned and walked away.

Chandra, who had observed the scene, was highly amused.

"Chandra, if your smile gets any bigger, your face will split in two," Bond said.

"I think she's the wrong girl for you, Commander Bond. *Khanu paryo*," he said, meaning that it was time to eat.

Bond replied with what little Nepalese he had learned in the past few days. *"Khanu Hos."*

Contrary to popular belief, cuisine in Nepal was quite varied. In Bond's opinion, Nepalese food in and of itself tended to be rather bland and uninteresting. There was only so much *dhal bhat* one could eat, and he was going to have plenty of that over the next weeks. In Kathmandu, at least, one could get a variety of international cuisines, and the Chimney in the hotel specialized in some of the finest Russian food he had ever tasted. Founded by Boris Lissanevitch, it is perhaps the oldest western restaurant in Nepal. It took its name from the huge copper chimney and open brick fireplace that occupy the center. It was the perfect place for an intimate dinner with live classical guitar music.

Bond sat with Chandra and Paul Baack. For starters, Bond had Ukrainian borscht made from a famous, "original" Boris Lissanevitch recipe. As a main course Bond chose yogurt-marinated chicken, which was lightly spiced and served skewered with buttered rice pilaf. With it he had aubergine and sun-dried tomato Charlotte with solferino potatoes and a black-eyed-pea stew.

"This is very good," Baack said, pouncing on an oven-roasted tenderloin with an onion relish and port wine *jus*. "Why can't we just stay at this hotel for the next six weeks?"

Chandra had smoked beckti, a Bengal fish. "Yes, it is good, but the Sherpa food is better," he said, grinning.

"Ha!" Baack laughed. "Are you mad?"

Chandra said, "I'm not mad, but I can be very crazy sometimes."

The Dutchman laughed again. "What's your story, Mr. Bond? Why are you on this trip?"

"I was ordered by the men in suits over

in Whitehall. They want me to make sure everything is shipshape."

"If you don't mind my asking, why do you need a Gurkha to accompany you?"

Bond and Chandra looked at each other. Chandra answered, "Commander Bond is my good friend. We always look after each other."

"Actually," Bond said, "the Foreign Office thought it would be helpful for us all to have someone here who knows the territory. Chandra has been on Kangchenjunga before."

"Really?" Baack asked. He was genuinely interested.

"Only halfway," Chandra said. "This time I'll do better. At least to the Great Scree Terrace."

"Tell me about the equipment our people gave you," Bond said.

"Ah! Very nice stuff, I can tell you," Baack said. "Of course, I helped design the satellite linkup. We have an extremely light laptop computer with enough power to last three months. It's equipped with the linkup, and that will be kept at Base Camp. With the use of cellular phones, every team member can stay in contact with each other and the outside world. We will all use the same channel, although the phones are capable of several private channels. We can even hook up to the Internet from wherever we are. I can send a fax from eight thousand meters if I want."

"Speaking of faxes, I need to send something to London. You have something handy?" Bond asked.

"Certainly. It's right here," he said, indicating a portable computer case at his side. "Would you like to do it now?"

Bond opened his own file folder containing information on the expedition and team members. He found the recently added photo of Otto Schrenk, scribbled a message on a Post-It note, stuck it to the bottom of the photo, then handed it to Baack. The Dutchman opened the case, turned on the computer, noted the phone number that Bond had written, then fed the photo into the machine.

"That should do it," he said, handing it back to Bond. "I'm in constant contact with London, Mr. Bond, so anytime you want to talk to the Foreign Office, just say so."

"Thanks. Let me know when you get a reply. And call me James."

He had a good feeling about Baack, and was pleased that he was on the team and looked forward to getting to know him better.

Roland Marquis and Hope Kendall entered the room. She had gone to the trouble to change clothes before coming in to dinner. Instead of the trousers she was wearing at the meeting, she now had on an attractive red evening gown. Marquis had put on a sleek dinner jacket but was still wearing the civilian clothes underneath.

She laughed as she walked by Bond's table. "I figured that this was my last chance to be a lady before six weeks of hell."

"Doesn't she look marvelous?" Marquis asked.

The three men muttered appreciative comments, then the couple sat at a table isolated from the others.

After a few glances in their direction, Bond decided that the two of them were indeed having some kind of love affair.

Although there was no rational reason for it, this notion gave Bond a twinge of jealousy.

SIXTEEN

The Trek Begins

The rest of the stay in Kathmandu was unremarkable, and local police never connected the deaths of Zakir Bedi and the Nepalese assassin, who might or might not have been Union, to the group of mountaineers staying at the Yak and Yeti. The remaining days were spent exercising and gathering supplies for the trek across eastern Nepal.

One of the more interesting events for Bond occurred the morning after the team meeting. Every member of the expedition had to submit to a physical examination performed by Dr. Hope Kendall. Bond reported to her in one of the hotel suites at the appointed time and found her to be cool, clinical, and objective, as a physician should be. At the same time, though, she seemed overly intrigued by his body and took her time feeling his muscles, testing reflexes, and looking into orifices. In fact, she was somewhat rough with him, pinching him here, jabbing him there. Perhaps, Bond thought, she was merely a very physical person.

"You sure have a lot of scars," she said, examining the faint mementos of Bond's illustrious career that adorned various parts of his naked body. "You're in the Foreign Office?"

"That's right."

"How does someone in the Foreign Office get so many scars?"

"I do a number of outdoor activities for sport. Sometimes you get injured," he said.

"Hmm, and I think you're lying," she said. "You're some kind of policeman, aren't you? Sorry, you don't have to answer that." He didn't. She turned to her table and put on a rubber glove. "Okay, Mr. Bond, let's see how your prostate feels."

She wasn't very gentle with that exam, either.

The expedition members flew in two Twin Otters to the Suketar airstrip near a small village called Taplejung in east Nepal. The stretch of dirt runway, located on a high ridge at 2,000 meters, is at a significantly higher altitude than Kathmandu, at 1,300 meters. The plan was to stay in crude lodges that had been erected in the village specifically for trekkers, then take a steep drop down to the Tamur Khola valley the following day. It was a more direct route to go down and north through the valley rather than east, over the alternate route to Khunjari.

The view was spectacular, and this was only the first day. The Himalayas could be seen from Kathmandu, but there they were so far in the distance that one felt they couldn't possibly be part of the same country. Here, however, it seemed as if the mountains were just over the next hill. The white-covered peaks spread over the northern and eastern sky, some disappearing into white clouds.

Their immediate surroundings were rich with the colors of spring. The hills were terraced so that farming could be accomplished on a steep surface. Bond thought it was a marvel that anyone could live their lives cultivating this difficult land. Yet, nearly everyone in Nepal did, and they did it well.

The wind was brisker here and Bond could immediately feel the thinness of the air, even at this relatively low altitude. He glanced at his Avocet Vertech Alpin watch that Q Branch had given him. It showed altitude, time, barometric pressure, and cumulative vertical ascent rates. It was three o'clock in the afternoon, but it felt later. The change in altitude made it seem as if he had already spent an entire day exerting himself: One of the Americans, Bill Scott, complained of a headache shortly after arriving. Hope Kendall examined him and told him to get plenty of sleep that night.

"I want everyone to go to bed immediately after dinner," Marquis ordered as they gathered at the small building that served as an air terminal. "We're to have dinner with the respective families who are putting us up. Remember — eat with your right hand, don't even gesture with the left, and leave your shoes at the door. Don't enter a Hindu kitchen unless invited. Let your hosts direct you to a seat. Don't touch any food unless you intend to eat it. Utensils or food is *jutho,* or impure, once it has touched your lips or tongue. Everyone eats from their own plate and drinks from their own glass. These people know that all food must be cooked, but just in case, don't eat anything that has to be washed or that isn't cooked immediately before it's served. Remember to offer a good hearty belch at the end of the meal, for that's a sign of contentment in this country."

Bond and Chandra helped the others

unload the equipment. Bond carried most of his gear in a Lowe Alpine Attack 50 backpack, which was designed primarily as a functional, lightweight summit pack. A lot of the tools for climbing would be carried by the Sherpas until it was time to use them.

Perhaps the best known and most widely respected of all Nepal's ethnic groups, the Sherpas resemble Tibetans more than other Nepalese. Hundreds of years of living in east Nepal have suitably adapted them to living and working in the mountains. Ever since mountaineers discovered them to be excellent companions and workers, the Sherpas came into a hitherto unforeseen popularity and prosperity. For an expedition the size of Bond's, nearly sixty porters would need to be hired.

Chandra, Bond, Paul Baack, and the French climber, Philippe Léaud, had been assigned to a family that consisted of a toothless, smiling old couple. Bond noticed that Marquis and Hope Kendall went into a lodge together. Nepalese were generally intolerant of openly displayed affection or sexuality, and he wondered how they would get around that.

Chandra, reading his mind, said, "Marquis claimed that he and Dr. Kendall were man and wife."

Léaud made a vulgar comment in French that went over the Gurkha's head, but he got the drift when the others laughed.

Sunset came and dinner was served on a low table inside the lodge. The food was a traditional *dhal bhat*, a lentil soup over rice. A few vegetables, or *sabji*, were served with cumin, garlic, and ginger. Hot tea accompanied the meal. By the time they had finished, Bond and Chandra were ready to turn in, the altitude and food having had a soporific effect on them. Bond unrolled his Marmot Col sleeping bag, which wasn't as warm as the more popular Cwm, but was lighter and more versatile at altitude. The wooden floor was hard, but at least there was the luxury of having a roof over their heads.

"Good night, Commander Bond," Chandra said as he slipped into his own bag. "Don't let the *kichkinni* get you."

"What?"

"The *kichkinni*. That's the spirit of a woman who died in childbirth and reappears as a beautiful and insatiable young woman intent on seduction."

"Sounds quite pleasant to me," Bond quipped.

"Ah, but her unlucky lover withers away as she saps his vital energies. The only way you can tell if she is a *kichkinni* is if you happen to notice that her feet are turned backward!"

"Just her feet?" Bond asked, struggling to get comfortable in the confines of the bedroll.

Chandra laughed loudly. It never ceased to amaze Bond that the Gurkha was always in a good humor. He enjoyed talking, sometimes to Bond's chagrin, but he had already become an entertaining and intelligent companion. He had started to tell stories of his life in the foothills of Lamjung and Annapurna Himal, a region that the Gurungs have farmed and covered with a network of trails paved with precisely cut and fitted stone blocks.

"In the higher regions of our homeland, Gurungs retain Buddhist traditions," Chandra said. "In the lower ones, they've converted to Hinduism."

"What are you?" Bond asked.

"A little of both," Chandra said. "Once you're born a Hindu, that never changes. The Buddhist religion fits neatly around Hinduism. You will find that in Nepal, many people say they are of both religions."

Baack began to snore loudly, keeping the other three men up for a while. Chandra continued to talk until finally Léaud said politely, "*Oui, oui, monsieur,* please, I need to sleep now. We have another bedtime story tomorrow night, okay?"

Chandra said, "Sure. *Shuba ratri.*"

"Huh?"

"That means 'good night.' "

"Oh. *Shuba ratri.*"

"*Shuba ratri,* Commander Bond," Chandra said, but there was silence. "Commander Bond?"

Bond was already fast asleep.

Mornings are always the most beautiful part of the day in Nepal. A magical mist accumulates in the valleys and lingers until the sun comes up and evaporates the moisture. The land is clear by midmorning, but the sight of the fog-laden land put Bond in a reflective mood. He was truly in a land quite apart from England, exotic and mystical. The idea of one day going back to the dull office by the Thames seemed impossible.

Bond and Chandra were up early with the lady of the house, whose duty it was to take care of the family's religious obligations, which meant that first there was worship of household deities followed by a visit to the neighborhood temple with a tray of small offerings. Bond accompanied Chandra to the temple and watched him perform *puja*, an offering meant to please divine senses by scattering flower blossoms and red *tika* powder on images of gods and ringing bells to alert them to his presence. The Gurkha paid special attention to the idol of Ganesh, the portly deity with the head of an elephant. Ganesh is known as the creator and remover of obstacles and brings luck to those who pay special attention to him. Therefore, it was important to pray to him at the onset of any undertaking, otherwise he might convey misfortune and malevolence on travelers.

The Sherpa porters left with the trekking equipment very early in order to set up a campsite in Phurumba by the time the rest of the group arrived there for lunch.

"They're always so cheerful," Bond commented to Chandra.

"I would be too if my pay for the expedition would support my family and sometimes my entire village for a year or more," the Gurkha replied.

Breakfast was served in the lodge at eight o'clock, and it consisted surprisingly of scrambled eggs. They weren't cooked to

Bond's specifications, but they were nevertheless welcome and he felt rested and ready to begin the mostly-downhill four-hour trek to Phurumba, the first stop on the way to the Base Camp. It would be a long, difficult day. Normally trekkers would stop overnight at Phurumba, but Marquis planned to continue to Chirwa, another four-hour trek . . . uphill.

It wasn't necessary to wear the heavy warm clothes yet. While it was cool at this altitude, the exertion of trekking could work up a sweat, especially when carrying fifty pounds or more on one's back. Bond wore a Patagonia Puffball lightweight and windproof shirt, dark denims, thick Smartwool socks, and a pair of Merrell M2 high-top boots. He would save the One Sport boots that Boothroyd had given him for the snow and ice. Water was boiled before leaving the village, and every member of the team got a full canteen and was told to conserve it. They wouldn't get more until they reached Chirwa.

The trekkers set out by nine o'clock, descending the peak into the misty valley. Dr. Kendall and Marquis walked together at the head of the group. Bond and Chandra trailed along near the back.

The views were exhilarating. They were

in magnificent hills colored in brown and green, and the vast Himalayas were just beyond them. They passed farmers working with water buffalo. The men were dressed in vests and loincloths, while some women were wearing the graceful Indian sari, a five-meter length of cloth draped over a tight, short-sleeved blouse called a *choli*. The saris were always brightly colored and they fluttered like banners. Nepali women delighted in decoration, layering themselves with jewelry in carnival colors. Their long, black hair was usually braided with red cotton tassels, or they twisted it into a neat bun with a flower set in it. The essential *tika* mark made on the forehead with red *sindhur* powder was part of the daily *puja*.

"In a mystic sense," Chandra explained, "the *tika* represents the third eye of spiritual insight. For women it's a cosmetic essential."

They reached Phurumba, a drop in altitude to 922 meters, right on schedule at one o'clock. The Sherpas had lunch ready, which again consisted of *dhal bhat*. Rumor had it that there would be chicken for dinner.

After two hours' rest, the team pushed on toward Chirwa, which was a significantly more difficult walk, as the altitude would have increased to 1,270 meters by the time they arrived. Because they had already trekked a fair distance that morning, it took them nearly six hours instead of the allotted four to reach their destination.

Again, the scenery was beautiful. At one point Bond noticed a temple built high on a hill, with a single dirt road winding up to it. An old man standing at the foot of the road with a stick for a cane smiled and beckoned them forward, asking for a handout. One of the Americans gave him a few rupees.

"Right," Marquis said as they approached Chirwa. The village looked similar to Taplejung but was smaller. "Congratulations on a good day's trekking. I know we're all tired. I'm certainly feeling the effects of the altitude change. Let's get another good night's sleep and will our bodies to acclimatize quickly! The Sherpas will have dinner ready in an hour. There are not enough lodges to go around, I'm afraid. Some of us will have to pitch tents. There is room for ten people in the lodges. We can draw straws for them, if you'd like, unless someone wants to volunteer to stay in their tents."

"We don't mind," Bond said. He looked

at Chandra for approval. The Gurkha shrugged.

"I'll stay in a tent," Hope Kendall said.

"Uhm, you don't have to do that," Marquis said.

"Why not? Just because I'm a woman? Stop giving me special attention, Roland. Pretty soon we'll all be in tents for a long time. It doesn't matter to me, really."

Bond could see that it was Marquis who didn't particularly want to sleep in a tent that night. Was she attempting to distance herself from him?

"Fine," Marquis said. "We'll do that, then."

"I'd rather stay in my own tent tonight, if you don't mind," she said. It was loud enough for the entire group to hear. Marquis was noticeably embarrassed. Something unpleasant must have occurred between them during the previous night.

Marquis made light of the comment, but Bond knew he was cross that she had said something like that in front of everyone. Marquis ended up staying in a lodge.

Bond and Chandra started to erect a two-man Bibler Torre tent, which was sturdy and could withstand high winds and keep the icy chill out when completely sealed. By the time they were done, a campfire had been lit and people gathered around it. The evening developed into a beautiful mild spring night. There were thousands of stars, and the silhouettes of the peaks against them produced a sky-scape that Bond had seldom seen.

Dinner was an Indian-style chicken curry that the cook, Girmi, had made less spicy than usual to accommodate the western tastes. Bond was becoming accustomed to the art of eating with his right hand. The Nepalese were experts at flicking a bite of food into the mouth with their thumb. One of the Americans brought a bottle of inexpensive red wine out of his knapsack, saying that he was saving it for Base Camp but knew that drinking alcohol at higher altitudes was not wise. There was just enough for everyone to have a little in a paper cup. Philippe Léaud produced a harmonica and began to play plaintive melodies. One by one people began to wander away from the campfire and settle in for the night.

Bond walked a short distance into the darkness to answer a call of nature. On the way back, he noticed Hope Kendall's tent, which she had put up a good hundred feet away from the others. An oil lamp was burning inside, and he could see the outline of her figure against the canvas. As he walked past, roughly fifteen feet away from it, he could see that the tent flap was open. The doctor was squatting on the mat in the middle of the tent. She was still dressed in pants, but she had removed her sweater, exposing a white T-shirt. He paused a moment, anticipating a wave.

She didn't see him. Instead, she took hold of the bottom of the T-shirt and pulled it off over her head. She was naked underneath. Her breasts were larger than was readily apparent when she was fully dressed, and the nipples were erect and extended. The areolas were also red and large, almost as if blush had been applied to them. The sight of her sitting there topless was very erotic.

Then she looked up and noticed him standing there. Rather than covering herself with a start, she simply looked at him knowingly and didn't say a word. Without averting her eyes from his, she reached out and unsnapped the flap of the tent, letting it fall to cover the opening.

What the hell was that all about? Bond wondered. Was she Marquis's girlfriend or not? It was almost as if she didn't mind that he got a good look at her and was daring him to do something.

He walked back toward the rest of the camp, pondering the mysteries of the opposite sex, when he noticed Paul Baack working at a portable table. He sat on a collapsible stool, and his large frame looked comical on top of it. He was busily typing on the laptop, which was connected to a Microcom-M Global Satellite Telephone.

"How are things back in civilization?" Bond asked.

"Ah, hello," Baack said. "This is a wonderful device. It's the world's smallest and lightest Inmarsat M satellite telephone. I just got a fix on a satellite and made a call to my girlfriend."

"Where is she?"

"She lives in Utrecht. Ingrid. Nice German girl. I'm glad you came by. I just received a message for you."

Baack punched a few more keys and brought up an e-mail written in code. "I can't understand a word of it, but you might be able to."

Bond leaned over to look at the monitor. It was in a standard SIS code that used word associations to get its message across. Bond frowned as he read it, then said, "Thanks. You can delete it."

Baack shrugged and said, "I hope it's not bad news."

"It's good and bad," Bond said. "Good night."

"Good night, Mr. Bond."

He walked back to his own tent, where Chandra had just boiled some water with a Bibler hanging stove. It hung from the tent roof to keep the floor clear, minimizing spillage.

"Want some tea?" he asked. "It's special herbs from Nepal. Help you sleep."

"I normally despise tea, but I'll have some," Bond said. "I just got a message from London."

"Oh?"

"No word on Otto Schrenk. SIS confirms that he is known to be a serious mountaineer, but they're still doing a background check. More interesting is that Dr. Steven Harding is dead. His body was found washed up on the shore at Gibraltar. His throat was cut. There was a note in his pocket that said, 'Your traitor has ceased to be useful. We hereby return him to you.' It was signed 'The Union.'"

Chandra gave a low whistle. "Then they are on to us, I expect."

"Have you observed anything unusual so far?"

He shook his head. "Only that Group Captain Marquis and Dr. Kendall aren't sleeping together tonight!" He chuckled.

Bond avoided that subject and said, "I have a sneaking suspicion that someone from the Union is here."

"I feel that, too. If not among us, then they are nearby. Perhaps with the Chinese or the Russian expedition?"

Bond removed his boots and put on Patagonia Activist Fleece sleeveless bibs, perfect sleepwear for chilly high altitudes.

"It's possible. Let's just be on our guard. Maybe you and I will take a side trip and take a look at the Chinese group."

"Okay, commander."

"Chandra?"

"Yes?"

"You can call me James."

"Fine, James."

Fatigue must have hit the Gurkha harder than on the previous night, for he was asleep within ten minutes. Bond, however, was wide awake. Sometimes it is difficult to sleep at high altitudes; insomnia is a common malady among mountaineers. Bond often experienced it himself, and he knew it would get worse as they kept ascending. Insomnia, however, wasn't what was keeping him awake tonight.

His mind was racing with thoughts of Steven Harding, the Union, the dangerous mission they were undertaking . . . and Hope Kendall's magnificent breasts.

SEVENTEEN

Eliminating the Competition

The team were in relatively good spirits when they awoke and prepared for the second day of trekking. The day's goal was to reach Ghaiya Bai, which was at an altitude of 2,050 meters — not much of an increase, but it was a good six hours' hike to get there. The Sherpas left early, as usual, and Bond and Chandra enjoyed a light breakfast of yogurt, known throughout the subcontinent as curd. The buffalo milk curd of Nepal was surprisingly good, Bond thought, but he also imagined that sending overweight people on a trek across Nepal for a month would be an excellent way to diet.

The team met in the center of Chirwa at eight-thirty. The sky was overcast, causing a drop in temperature. Everyone was dressed in more layers — sweaters, jackets — some were even wearing their parkas. Chandra preferred to dress in combat equipment marching order, which basically consisted of a bergen, or rucksack, topped by what he called a "grab bag." This contained essential bits of kit that he might need in a hurry, such as a radio, small gas stove, articles of warmer clothing, and a waterproof jacket. Ever present was the Gurkha staple, the outstanding *khukri* knife. It was carried at his waist in a shiny black leather sheath. Two smaller knives, the sharp *karta* and the blunt *jhi,* were also part of the *khukri* package, and these were used to light fires and peel fruit. The larger knife, which was eighteen inches long, was made of tempered steel with a handle of buffalo horn.

"The boomerang-like shape symbolizes the Hindu trilogy of Rama, Vishnu, and Shiva," Chandra explained when Bond asked him about it. He pointed to a little nick in the blade near the handle. "You know what this is for? It's to catch your enemy's blood as it runs down the blade and keep it from reaching your hand!"

Hope Kendall barely glanced at Bond. It was as if the voyeuristic episode of the previous evening never happened. As the team set off, she began by striding beside Roland Marquis, but after an hour she had dropped back and was walking and talking with one of the Americans. Marquis seemed to be most friendly with Carl Glass, who occasionally looked at Bond as if the "Foreign Office representative" were an outsider and didn't belong on the expedition. Bond expected a certain lack of acceptance from the other climbers, but Glass in particular looked down his nose at him.

Otto Schrenk always walked alone and rarely said much to anyone. Bond attempted to engage him in conversation, but the man was tight-lipped.

"How did they find you on such short notice?" he asked.

"In eight-thousand-meter climbing, one's reputation is known," Schrenk said, as if that explained everything.

A sudden downpour made the second hour into the trek less than pleasant. Everyone scrambled to put on rain parkas, but they kept moving.

Paul Baack caught up to Bond and said, "Hey, Mr. Englishman, where's your umbrella?" He laughed loudly.

"I left it at home with my bowler hat," Bond replied.

The rain stopped in thirty minutes, but it left the ground wet and muddy. Marquis gave the order to halt for fifteen minutes to air out the wet parkas. Magically, the sun appeared from behind the clouds and the rest of the day promised to be beautiful.

Bond sat on a rock near Hope Kendall. She was brushing her hair, which glistened in the new sunlight.

"I don't know about you," she said off-handedly, "but I'll be ready for a full aftermatch function when we're through today, providing I don't bust my boiler getting to camp."

"Oh, you like to drink?" Bond asked, referring to her kiwi jargon.

"I'm a doctor, I'm not supposed to drink," she said. "But I enjoy a pint or two. When I was in college it would make me chunder all the time, but not anymore."

"How long have you known Marquis?"

"Roland? Uhm . . . six years? I was on an expedition to Everest with him. We met again when he climbed Mount Cook in New Zealand. What about you?"

"Oh, we're old rivals from Eton. It was a long time ago."

"I *thought* there was something between you two," she said. She began to apply sunblock to her face and other exposed skin areas. "You have to admit that he's a good head sherang. He always goes for the doctor in everything he does. He's a hard case."

"Does that appeal to you?" he asked.

She shrugged. "I like men who are boots and all."

"I beg your pardon?"

"Sorry, I meant that I like men who give it everything they've got. You haven't been to New Zealand much, have you?"

"I'm afraid not. Once or twice."

"Where did you go?" She finished brushing her hair and began to reorganize her pack.

"Auckland, mostly."

"Ah, well, that's where I live and work," she said. "It's the big smoke of New Zealand, isn't it? I was born in Taupo. It's a fairly well-to-do place. I got out of there as soon as I could. I didn't like the snobbery."

Bond had thought that she might have come from money. She had an aristocratic air about her that bordered on being snooty. Somehow, though, she had risen above the stereotype and seemed to be a genuinely friendly person. Perhaps it was the medical profession that had changed her.

"I lived for a while on the west coast of the south island, where everyone is basically pretty weird," she said. "People say it's a lot like California there. I spent some time around Mount Cook — that's where I learned to climb."

"What made you become a doctor?"

"That's a long story. I was pretty wild when I was young. Hell, I'm still young. When I was *younger*, I should say. All I wanted to do was live in the outdoors, go camping, climb mountains, that sort of thing. And, uhm, there were men." She shook her head, whistled, and smiled. "I had a huge men problem. I thought there was something wrong with me! I couldn't get enough . . . hell, I don't know why I'm telling you this, I hardly know you!"

Bond laughed. "We're spending the next few weeks together, so I wouldn't worry about that. As a matter of fact, I sometimes I think I have the same problem. With women, of course."

"Well, I had it with women, too," she said under her breath and rolling her eyes. "I didn't think there could be such a thing as sex addiction, but I had it bad. When I was treated for it, I became interested in psychology, and that in turn led to medicine. I hadn't gone to college yet, so I did a complete turnaround. The wild child became a serious student. I moved to Auckland to study to be a doctor, and now I can name every part of your body and spell it, too. I turned the interest in sex into a specialization in sexology for a while — you know, sexual dysfunction and all that — but then I became more attracted to general practice. I suppose you could say I find the human body a very interesting machine. I'm fascinated by it, the way a bloke knows how to take apart a sports car and put it back together. I like to test the body's limits."

That explained the rather rough physical examination he experienced the other day.

"And how's that addiction now?" he asked.

She stood up and put the pack on her back. "Like any vice, as long as it's in moderation, it can't be too bad." She winked at him and walked away.

She was a "hard case" herself, Bond thought. He knew that he shouldn't bother attempting to figure her out, but he found that he was very attracted to her. Hope obviously exhibited a great deal of energy and intelligence, but she also possessed a distinct and unsubtle animal magnetism that was inviting.

They reached the picnic site set up by the Sherpas at approximately one o'clock. There was still another two hours or more to go before they reached the day's stop.

Lunch was *tama,* a Nepali soup made from dried bamboo shoots. Bond found it less than satisfying, but it would have to do.

As they rested for a half hour, Bond wandered over to Paul Baack and asked, "Any new messages from London?"

"Nothing," he said. "I'll let you know. I check the e-mail three times a day. I did receive a note from our liaison in Kathmandu. He says the Chinese are only a mile to the southwest of us and are gaining ground. If we stay on the same schedule, we'll still beat them to the mountain. But if they happen to double their efforts and attempt to pass us . . ."

"Noted," Bond said.

The team prepared to leave the site as the Sherpas packed up. The three Americans were standing on a ledge looking at a glorious view of a terraced hill that farmers were plowing. When they turned to join the others, Bill Scott, one of the Americans, tripped over a stone and fell. He cried out in pain and held on to his foot. Hope Kendall rushed to him.

"Now what?" Marquis muttered. He wandered over to the huddle and listened to what the doctor had to say.

Bond and Chandra joined them. Hope had unlashed Scott's boot and was examining his ankle. It was already swelling badly.

"It's broken," she said finally.

"Aw, hell," Scott said. "What will that mean?"

"You can't continue on," she said. "I mean, you could try, but you're going to be in a lot of pain. Once we reach Base Camp you'll certainly be in no condition to climb the mountain. I really think you should go back."

"Go back? Where?"

"To Taplejung," Marquis said. "You'll have to wait for us there."

"For a month?" Scott was angry and humiliated. "Aww, man . . ."

"One of the Sherpas will take you back. You'll just have to stay put there until we return, unless you can get a flight back to Kathmandu. That's possible, I suppose."

Hope did her best to wrap the ankle so that he could hobble. One of the Sherpas found a tree branch that could be used as a crutch.

"It's going to take you a long time, so you had better get going," Marquis said. "Bad luck, old man."

"Yeah." Scott said his good-byes to the rest of the team and his fellow Americans, then he and Chettan, one of the Sherpas, began the long trek back.

When they were out of earshot, Hope addressed everyone. "I was afraid that would happen. He had been complaining of headaches. He had a mild case of AMS and wasn't totally with it. It just goes to show you that accidents can happen quickly and unexpectedly."

"Can AMS really strike at this altitude?" the young American known as "the kid" asked.

"It varies with the individual," she replied. "We're really not very high yet, but that doesn't matter. Some people experience symptoms of AMS just driving a car up to a higher elevation than the one they're used to. Others have difficulty riding an elevator to the top of a skyscraper. Everyone is different. That's why you've got to be aware of the symptoms."

"Fine, fine," Marquis said impatiently. "Well, we've lost one team member, let's not lose any others, all right? We had better push on."

They picked up their gear and continued on the faint path that must have been trampled by a few hundred people over the last fifty years.

The next hour was a tough one. The terrain changed, and although the altitude increase was minimal, the ground was rockier and more difficult to walk on. One of the Sherpas said that a rock fall from the neighboring "hill" had caused the problem.

They eventually got to a smoother path, and Bond caught up with Roland Marquis, who was dressed in khakis and a wool flannel shirt that was embroidered with RAF insignia.

"Hello, Bond," he said, steadily marching as if he were on a treadmill. Keeping up with him meant not lagging for an instant. "Come to see how it feels to be leader for a while?"

"No, I came forward to see what that horrible smell was coming from the front of the team," Bond said with a straight face.

"Very funny. I suppose you think you can do better, eh?"

"Not at all, Roland. Can't you take a joke? I think you're doing a splendid job. I mean it."

"By Jove, Bond, it almost sounds as if you really do. Well, thanks. It's not easy, this. You know as well as I that the schedule is damn near impossible," Marquis said quietly. It was the first time Bond had ever heard him say anything without his macho facade.

"I can't believe that fool American tripped and broke his bloody ankle," he continued. "Somehow, when a member of my team gets hurt, I feel responsible."

"That's only natural," Bond said.

"But what happened was stupid. I should have looked at his credentials more carefully."

"Roland, I'm concerned about the new man, Schrenk," Bond said. "There wasn't time for SIS to completely clear him. What do you know about him?"

"Nothing, except that he doesn't say a bloody word to anyone. I wondered when you were going to mention him to me. I had no choice but to bring him on, Bond. He was the only one. Now with Scott gone, we'll really need the extra manpower. Besides, it was SIS's job to check him out, not mine. I reviewed only his mountaineering credentials, which were excellent, so don't complain to me."

They walked on in silence. Both men were breathing at the same rate, moving with the same speed, and thinking identical things about each other.

"I do love climbing," Marquis said after a while. "If I didn't love it so much, I certainly wouldn't be the leader. But it takes someone with experience to be leader, I suppose. Have you ever led an expedition, Bond?"

"No."

"No, of course you haven't. You don't make the sport a habit, do you."

"Not like you, Roland. I go climbing only once every three or four years."

"That's too long a gap. What if a golfer played only once every three or four years? He wouldn't be a very good golfer."

"It's a bit different."

"I'm just making a point, that's all," Marquis said.

"What is it?"

"That climbing isn't a sport for you. You're an amateur. You're a *good* amateur, don't get me wrong, but you're still an amateur."

"You haven't seen me in action yet, Roland."

"True, I suppose I should wait until we're at seven thousand meters before I make that assessment."

"Everything has to be a contest with you, doesn't it, Roland?" Bond said rhetorically.

Marquis laughed aloud. "Admit it, Bond, you've always been a little jealous of me. I beat you too many times on the wrestling mat back when we were boys."

"Once more, I seem to remember it the

other way around."

"There you go again distorting history," Marquis said.

"I wouldn't think of it." It took everything to keep Bond from losing his sense of humor. They walked for ten minutes in silence again.

Finally, Marquis asked, "So, Bond, what do you think of our good doctor?"

"She seems capable," Bond said tactfully.

Marquis laughed. "Oh, she's a fine doctor. I meant, what do you think of her as a *woman?*"

Again, Bond said, "She seems capable."

Marquis snorted. "I think she's simply amazing."

Bond normally didn't like to discuss other people's relationships. He was curious, though, to see what Marquis might have to say about her. He was the type of man who enjoyed boasting and had a loose tongue when it came to sexual exploits. The trouble was that his kind of man also tended to exaggerate.

"I know what you're thinking, Bond," Marquis said. "You're wondering what kind of relationship I have with her. We're not lovers, if that's what you think. We were once, a few years ago. We tried to rekindle it at the beginning of this little venture, but it didn't work out. We're just friends now."

"Are you saying she's fair game?" Bond asked.

Marquis stopped dramatically in his tracks. Bond almost stumbled, then halted and looked at Marquis, who had a glint in his eye that was full of menace.

"She's *absolutely* fair game, if you can manage it," he said. There was, however, an implicit warning in the voice.

At that moment Hope walked up and stood between them. Her long, golden tresses blew in the wind and around the pack on her back. Even with no makeup and none of the normal day-to-day personal conveniences enjoyed by western women, she was wholesomely attractive.

"I expected to find you two arm-wrestling up here," she said. "Roland, you look like you're ready to hit your friend, here. Did he say something mean?"

"It's nothing, my dear," Marquis said. "Bond and I go way back, that's all."

"So I've heard. You two had better behave. The smell of testosterone over here is overpowering. I don't want to have to patch up either of you after you've beaten each other into a pulp."

"We're not fighting," Marquis said.

"Not even over me?" she asked facetiously, but Bond thought she was more earnest than she let on.

Marquis turned to her and said, "Yes, Hope, my dear, that's *precisely* what we're doing. We're fighting over *you*."

She didn't rise to his anger at all. She turned up her nose flirtatiously and said, "Well, in that case, may the best man win." With that, she moved back toward the others, who had all interpreted Marquis's stopping as a signal for them to halt and rest.

"What are you doing sitting on your arses?" he shouted at them. "We've had our rest already! Get up! There's still about an hour to go before we reach camp."

Irritably, he turned and began trekking forward. Bond let him lead on and waited until Chandra caught up with him. Hope passed him, glancing at him out of the corner of her eye but not saying a word.

Bond thought that she was the biggest tease in the Eastern Hemisphere. Normally he disdained women of that ilk, but with her, the come-on was more of a challenge. He was beginning to understand her better. By her own admission, this was an intelligent woman who liked to get physical. She was unable to separate her rough, clinical manner as a medical practitioner from the rather coarse nature of her individual sexuality. Just as she liked to see what made human beings tick, she was stimulated by the primal rituals between males and females. She enjoyed the mating game in its purest sense. Perhaps this explained her love for the outdoors and for adventure. Bond was convinced that she probably had a healthy percentage of testosterone in her own body. He wondered what she might be like in bed. . . .

Bond continued up the path with Chandra and Paul Baack. The camp was a welcome sight when they finally reached it at four o'clock in the afternoon.

The overnight stay in Ghaiya Bai was uneventful, and the team had settled into a daily routine that would vary little until they reached the Base Camp. The goal for the day was to reach Kyapra, at 2,700 meters. The following day the team would ascend to a relatively major village called Ghunsa, located at 3,440 meters. Normally, a few days would be spent there acclimatizing, but that wasn't in Marquis's plan.

Bond stayed with Chandra most of the morning, purposefully avoiding any contact with either Roland Marquis or Hope Kendall. He had enough to worry about without getting into a match of wills with one or the other. Instead, he concentrated on the day's goal and tried to enjoy the scenery. They were seeing fewer and fewer signs of civilization as they ascended above 2,500 meters.

At lunchtime Paul Baack approached Bond and said, "The Chinese are less than a mile that way." He pointed toward the southwest. The big man handed him a pair of binoculars. Bond stood on a rock and looked through them.

He could see a group of at least ten men moving slowly across the side of a hill toward a site where many Sherpas had set up their own lunch stop.

Marquis climbed on the rock and asked, "What do you see?"

"We have company," Bond said. He handed the binoculars to Marquis so that he could look, then asked, "I think Chandra and I should leave you here and do a little reconnaissance. We'll meet you in Ghunsa tomorrow afternoon."

"What, you'll do a bivouac tonight?"

"That's right," Bond said, "we'll go

without a tent. We both have bivouac sacks. We each have copies of the trekking route. We'll be fine. We'll catch up with you tomorrow."

"I don't like the idea of you wandering off, Bond," Marquis said.

"Sorry, Roland," Bond said. "We're going." He jumped down from the rock and went to explain the plan to Chandra.

Roland Marquis frowned to himself. He needed Bond in one piece, at least until they found Skin 17.

Bond and Chandra slipped away from the others and made their way as surreptitiously as possible toward the Chinese expedition. They got within one hundred meters of them, close enough to make an assessment of their group.

"There are eleven of them," Chandra said, looking through binoculars. "And a lot of porters." He scanned each man carefully and noted, "At least three of the men are carrying rifles. Why would anyone want a rifle on an expedition up Kangchenjunga?"

"Unless they were planning to do someone some harm when they get there," Bond suggested. "Come on, they're moving."

Chandra moved stealthily, and Bond followed. The Gurkha was a superior mountaineer. He also knew tricks and techniques to move around the hills unseen. Bond gladly turned over the leadership of their side venture to him.

Shortly before sundown the Chinese set up camp not far from Kyapra. They pitched tents and were settling down for the night. Bond and Chandra took up a position above them, nestled in an array of rock formations surrounded by a few trees.

"We'll wait until dark, when they're asleep," Bond said. "Then we'll see what there is to see."

Chandra grinned. "I haven't had this much fun since Bosnia."

"Bosnia was fun?"

"Yes, sir! Any kind of action is better than sitting in England twiddling our thumbs. I've been to Zaire. The Gulf War was interesting. I had never been in that part of the world. I'm still waiting for the chance to use my *khukri* the way my ancestors did."

"You mean that you haven't killed anyone with it yet?"

"That's right," Chandra said. "I've chopped plenty of fruits and vegetables with it, but no enemy necks. Someday I make a good tossed salad with heads, and I don't mean lettuce, eh, James?"

"You Gurkhas have a morbid sense of humor, did anyone ever tell you that?"

"All the time."

"Chandra, if you're part Buddhist, how is it that you could kill if you had to?"

"That's a good question, James," the Gurkha said. "Buddhists are not supposed to kill any living creature. However, I am a soldier and a Gurkha. We are here to preserve the dignity and freedom of man. I know it's a contradiction in terms, but the Gurkhas have been a contradiction in terms for nearly two hundred years!"

Nightfall finally came, and they waited until the last embers of the Chinese campfire died. Then, slowly and silently, they crept down the hill toward the site. Bond had observed the group carefully so that he could pinpoint which tents held humans and which ones only equipment and food supplies. The portable kitchen, similar to their own, was built near there. The Sherpas were sleeping in tents close to this area, and Bond knew that they would probably be lighter sleepers than the Chinese.

Using a penlight, Bond found sacks of rice and lentils. Another group of bags held tea. There was a sack of dried figs and other fruits. He whispered to Chandra, "They seem fairly ill equipped, wouldn't you say? I'm afraid we have to play a dirty trick on them and contaminate the food somehow. Then they'll have to turn back to resupply themselves, and by then they'll be too late to catch up. Got any ideas?"

Chandra whispered back, "That's easy!" He removed the *khukri* from its sheath, then neatly slit open the bag of rice. He did it so swiftly that it didn't make a sound. The rice poured out onto the ground. The next thing he did flabbergasted Bond. The Gurkha unzipped his fly and proceeded to urinate all over the spilled rice. He grinned at Bond the entire time.

"Hand me your knife," Bond said, stifling a laugh. Chandra handed it over, still relieving himself. Bond slit open the other bags of food and poured the contents onto the pile of freshly sprayed rice. He took a stick and mixed it all up. Chandra zipped up, then removed the two tiny knives from the *khukri* sheath. He squatted down and rubbed the two blades together on the burlap sacks. A spark flew, then another, and another. After four tries, the burlap caught fire.

"I think it's time we run now, James," Chandra said.

A gunshot startled them, and they turned to flee. They heard several men shouting in Chinese. The flames grew in intensity as they climbed away from the camp. More gunshots whizzed past them, but by that time they were in the dark. The marksmen were firing blindly. Some of them retrieved torches and cast the beams over the hill, but they were ineffective. Bond could hear at least three men scrambling up the rocks after them. After more gunshots, the entire camp was up, running about and shouting. The Sherpas were busy trying to put out the fire, which had engulfed all their supplies. Bond and Chandra climbed back into their niche in the cliff and watched the chaos below. The pursuers had given up and returned to the campsite to help salvage what they could.

It took them half an hour to extinguish the fire. Bond and Chandra had achieved their goal. The Chinese expedition was completely sabotaged. They could hear them arguing and shouting at one another. The Sherpas began to argue as well, and Chandra could pick up a little of what they were saying.

"The Sherpas are very upset that the

Chinese fired guns here. They say the gods will not be pleased and will bring misfortune on them. They refuse to go farther. They are now without any food. They are turning back in the morning."

The Chinese calmed down after an hour. Someone had apparently brought out a couple of bottles of alcohol, and that did the trick. Eventually, they crawled back into their tents, leaving just one man with a rifle on guard.

Bond opened his North Face bivouac sack and secured it behind a large stone, where there was just enough room for him to stretch out. Chandra found a hole where he could curl up in his own sack.

"*Shuba ratri,* James," Chandra said quietly.

When they awoke the next morning, the Chinese expedition had given up, packed, and left.

EIGHTEEN

Tensions Rise

When Bond and Chandra saw the village of Ghunsa perched on the side of a snow-covered peak, they breathed a sigh of relief. The ascent to 3,440 meters had taken its toll on them, and Bond found himself becoming winded quickly and having to stop and rest more often. Chandra, on the other hand, seemed to be unaffected by the altitude.

There were some yak herders living there, and Bond admired how people could live this high in the mountains and make ends meet. The villagers stopped and stared at the two of them, more curious about the man who was obviously a Churkha soldier than the Caucasian encroaching on their land.

They rounded a bend and saw a campsite some two hundred meters away.

"That must be us," Bond said. "I hope lunch is ready, I'm starving."

They climbed up a slick wet rock face to

a ledge. It wasn't necessary to use climbing tools yet, but they knew they would be employing the ice axes soon enough. The trek from Ghunsa to the Base Camp was substantially steeper. The next two days would be more strenuous.

Bond and Chandra turned to continue toward the camp, when a bullet whizzed past them and struck the snow. Both men instinctively dived to the ground. Two more shots hit the snow around them. Chandra rolled next to a rock for better cover. Bond crawled on his belly to a large tree stump that must have been hundreds of years old.

"Do you see him?" Bond whispered.

Chandra carefully raised his head and looked about. "I don't see anything."

Bond looked up and saw a whiff of smoke on a cliff face overlooking the village. He pointed. "He's up there. See?"

Chandra squinted and nodded. "What do we do?"

"I suppose we wait."

"Who could it be?"

"Obviously someone who knows we're here and doesn't want us to rejoin our group."

"The Chinese?"

Bond shook his head. "I don't think so.

There was no trace of them this morning. They went back the way they came."

Chandra took a good look at their surroundings and pointed to a ledge fifty meters away. "If we can make it to that ledge, we can climb down, go around the cliff here, and come up on the other side of the camp."

"Good thinking," Bond said. "Let's go together. It'll give the sniper too many targets to aim for. On three. One . . . two . . . three!"

The men leaped from their cover and scrambled toward the ledge. Two more bullets zipped into the snow at their feet. Chandra reached the edge first, squatted, put his hands on a sturdy rock, and hurled himself over the side. Bond did the same thing, although not as gracefully. Together they hung for a few seconds, then gained a foothold on the side of the rock face. Carefully, they inched down ten feet to level ground.

"That was an impressive move," Bond said, completely out of breath. He coughed, then collapsed into a sitting position.

"Are you all right?"

He coughed again. "Yeah, I've already got climber's cough. You know how it is.

I'm surprised I'm getting it so soon." He took slow deep breaths for a few minutes.

"Do you have a headache?" Chandra asked.

"No, thank God. It's not that bad. Come on, let's go."

"Are you sure?"

"Let's go, dammit!" Bond was annoyed with himself. He wanted to be as resilient as his partner, but there was no competing with a native Nepalese, especially a Gurkha.

They skirted around the cliff and found another place to ascend. They came up on the other side of the camp and wandered in, keeping an eye on the cliff where the sniper had been. There was no sign of any movement there now.

Roland Marquis was deep in conversation with Carl Glass when he saw them coming and waved. "We were about to give up!" he called. "We have to make it to Kambachan before sunset."

"Christ," Bond said. "How far is that?"

Marquis shrugged. "Four and a half hours. Why? You're up to it, aren't you, Bond?"

Bond coughed and nodded.

"Sounds as if a night in a bivouac didn't do you much good," Marquis said. "Bad luck." Bond noted that there was a certain degree of pleasure in the man's voice. "What did you find out about our Chinese friends?"

"They won't be bothering us anytime soon. Is there anyone from the team missing?" Bond asked.

"You mean right now?"

"Yes."

"Uhm, three or four people are in the village. They're supposed to be back" — he looked at his watch — "any minute now. The plan was to leave at twelve-thirty. It's twelve-fifteen."

"Who's gone?"

"Why?"

"Never mind, Roland, just tell me!" Bond snapped.

Marquis's eyes narrowed. "Careful, Bond. Don't forget who's leader here."

Bond grabbed the man's parka and pulled him forward. Chandra interceded, saying, "Hey, hey, stop it. Move back, commander."

Bond let go and stepped back. "Roland, you're the leader, but you also have orders from SIS to assist me. Now, who went into the village?"

Marquis relaxed a little, then said, "Dr. Kendall, Paul Baack, Otto Schrenk, and the American kid."

Schrenk, Bond thought. The sniper was Schrenk.

At that moment Baack and Hope were seen coming down the path toward the campsite. Baack was wearing a bright, distinctive yellow and green parka that he hadn't worn earlier. Bond sat down on a collapsible stool and coughed some more. Hope approached him and said, "Hey, you already got the cough."

"Thank you, doctor," Bond said. "I appreciate the diagnosis. Where have you two been?"

Hope looked at Marquis and Baack. "You feeling all right, James?"

Chandra said, "We've had a rough night and day, that's all."

Baack said, "I was bartering with one of those yak herders for a gourd." He held it up. "It's supposed to taste like pumpkin. The good doctor appeared just in time. The old man must have had a thing for Caucasian women, for he went down in price when he saw she was with me."

Hope held up a necklace. "And I traded five packs of chewing gum for this. Not bad, eh? It's probably worthless, but it's pretty."

"Hey!" a voice called. They all turned to

see Otto Schrenk running slowly toward them. He, too, was out of breath and had to stop every few steps. Finally, he got to the site and collapsed onto a tarp. He began to hack and it was several seconds before he got his wind back. Finally, he said, "The kid . . . he's dead . . . he's been shot."

"What?" Marquis and Hope said simultaneously.

"Where?" Bond asked.

Schrenk pointed to the cliff where the sniper had been. "Just below that cliff, there. Come, I'll show you."

As they walked toward the site, Bond wondered where Schrenk might have hidden his gun. It had to have been a rifle. Where in his gear could he have stashed it? Did he abandon it on the cliff?

"The kid," whose name was David Black, was sprawled on the path where snow had given way to mud. Blood was seeping onto the ground where he lay.

Hope Kendall got on her knees to examine him. "Help me turn him," she said.

"Shouldn't we leave the body alone?" Baack asked.

"What, do you think the police are going to come and seal off the area?" Marquis said.

"Actually, there is a Nepalese police post in Ghunsa. They will be coming to check our permits before long," Baack replied.

Bond helped her turn Black over. The bullet had entered the center of his chest.

"This was done at point-blank range," Bond observed. Hope nodded in concurrence.

His eyes met Chandra's. They both knew what had happened. David Black had most likely stumbled upon or had heard the sniper fire. He was eliminated because he had seen the sniper.

The trek to Kambachan was called off and the team settled to spend the night at Ghunsa. Marquis was sullen and frustrated with the turn of events. Bond and Chandra took care of removing the body from the site and also spent some time on the cliff looking for evidence. Chandra found a 7.62mm shell and showed it to Bond.

"This is from a semi-automatic. A sniper rifle. A Dragunov, maybe?" Bond surmised.

"I fired an L1 A1 rifle once. It used ammunition like this." The L1 A1 was the British version of the Belgian FN FAL, one of the most widely used modern self-loading rifles. It was gas operated and held a twenty-round magazine.

"Chandra, I think you might be right."

"It has to be one of our team. No one living in Ghunsa would have this rifle," Chandra said. "Should we search Schrenk's belongings?"

"We might have to. Come on, let's make our report."

The team was bewildered and shocked that David Black had been murdered. When Bond announced that the killer was possibly one of their own, several of them protested.

"Are you out of your mind?" a climber named Delpy asked. "Why would any of us want to do such a thing?"

"Is there something about this expedition you're not telling us?" asked Doug McKee, the sole remaining American on the team.

"Calm down," Marquis said. "We're on a salvage mission, and that's all there is to it."

"Who would want to shoot at us, then?" Philippe Léaud asked.

"The Russians," Paul Baack answered. They all looked at him. "I just got word that their team will reach Base Camp tomorrow. Maybe they think there's something up there at that plane."

Everyone looked at Marquis. "Is there?" Hope asked.

"Just bodies," he said. "British and American ones."

Bond considered the possibility that the Russians might be involved. Could their team be Union members? They had been known to deal with the Russian Mafia. What if that entire expedition was made up of Union criminals?

"Are we in some kind of danger?" Tom Barlow asked. "I mean, danger from human beings, not danger from the elements."

"Of course not," Marquis said, attempting to reassure them. "I think what happened to Mr. Black was some kind of freak accident."

"How can being shot at point-blank range be a freak accident?" Baack asked. "I have a bad feeling about this."

"Me, too," another said.

"And me," one more ventured.

"Fine!" Marquis shouted. "Then you can all turn back. Look, you were hired to perform a mission and you're being paid bloody good money for it! Now, tomorrow morning, I'm going on to Kambachan, and then I'm going to push to Lhonak so that I will be at Base Camp the day after tomorrow. I'll be happy to lead whoever wants to join me!"

Hope cleared her throat. "From here to Lhonak is an increase in altitude of a little over a thousand meters. That's going to be difficult."

"We all knew this would be difficult," Marquis said. "You all knew the risks. If anyone wants to turn back, he's welcome. I for one am going on. Who's going with me?"

No one said anything until Bond raised his hand. "The way I see it, there's altitude sickness, HACE, HAPE, avalanches, frostbite, snow blindness, and dozens of other catastrophes that could happen. What's a little gunfire aimed in our direction?"

A few people snickered. Chandra spoke up then. "In the Gurkha forces, we have a saying in Gurkhali: *Kaphar hunu banda, marnu raamro.* It's our motto. It means 'It's better to die than be a coward.' I shall go with you and Commander Bond."

"Me, too," Hope Kendall said. "Besides, I have a feeling you'll need a good doctor up there."

Paul Baack shrugged. "Hell, I've come this far. Why not?"

The others ultimately agreed. Only Otto Schrenk was silent. They all looked at him, waiting for an answer. Finally, he said, "I'm in."

Keeping the murder from the Ghunsa police proved to be easier than they expected. Hope Kendall submitted a death certificate claiming that David Black had received a "puncture wound" when he fell on some equipment. Luckily, the police were accustomed to dealing with accident-prone westerners and allowed the team to take care of the matter without their interference. Permits were checked and the team were cleared to move on.

The Liaison Officer volunteered to take David Black's body to Kathmandu and attend to the appropriate bureaucracy involved. After he left with the corpse on a wagon, the Sherpas performed a token prayer service for the dead climber.

As night fell, the entire team went to their tents in silence. They attempted to put the events of the day behind them, but there was no escaping the feeling that impending disaster was just around the corner.

The trek grew more difficult after the overnight stop in Lhonak. Everyone on the team was feeling poorly. The ascent was overly ambitious, and even Roland Marquis was coughing and breathing heavily when they finally reached Base Camp, six days after leaving Kathmandu.

It was located on the north side of the great mountain at 5,140 meters. Remnants of past expeditions were still there — broken tents, rubbish, *puja* shrines, and, most conspicuous, a few gravestones that had been placed to honor those who had perished on Kangchenjunga.

The peak itself was massive, extending up into the clouds. It was a spectacular behemoth of rock, ice, and snow. Winds dangerously whipped around it. Billows of what appeared to be white "smoke" occasionally exploded off the upper regions. This was really snow and ice being thrown about by the high winds. From the base of the mountain, this phenomenon was beautiful to look at; but to be up there *in* it would be extremely hazardous. There, it would be a terrible blizzard. It was no wonder, Bond thought, that the Nepalese believed the gods lived at the top. The sight was so overpowering that his first instinct was to bow to it, proclaim himself unworthy to be in its vicinity, and then turn around and go home. The facts were well known to him — the mountain is eight miles in length and five in width, and its main summit is at 8,598 meters, or 28,208 feet, making it the third-highest peak in the world. Although Everest receives most of the attention in the Himalayas, Kangchenjunga is considered more difficult and "mightier." Many people have attempted to summit the Kanch from the north side. It wasn't until 1979 that three men made it to the top via the "north ridge," bypassing the lower glacial shelves. The Japanese were the first to summit via the north face in 1980.

"All in all," Marquis said as they approached the Base Camp, "there have been over twenty-five expeditions up this mountain, using seventeen possible routes. I've never tried the Kanch. I've always wanted to."

"We're not here to summit," Bond reminded him.

"If we get our job done and there's time, I'm bloody well going to do it," Marquis said with finality in his voice. "And you can't stop me, Bond."

"Some of the Sherpas might."

"Besides, I'd like to see Hope get to the top. Not many women have done it."

Dr. Kendall overheard this and said, "Unh-unh. As much as I'd like to, Mr. Bond is right. We're not here to set world records."

Marquis looked at them both with disgust and walked away from them.

In three hours the camp was set up and operational. Ang Tshering organized it quickly and efficiently. A tent was erected for Girmi to store the food supplies and cooking equipment. Paul Baack was in charge of expedition HQ, which consisted of all his various communications devices, cots, lamps, and other supplies. A portable satellite dish was constructed just outside the HQ tent, and it wasn't long before he was in communication with the outside world.

Nearly everyone was wheezing and coughing. As the altitude change was now quite serious, people retired to their tents immediately after dinner. Most of them weren't very hungry and had to force themselves to eat something.

The temperature was another factor that affected the team. At the Base Camp it was below freezing, and the windchill made it even worse. At subzero temperatures, Bond would wear a Marmot 8000 Meter down parka and trousers. Equipment and clothing weight is always something to consider, and Bond had chosen the parka because it weighed around one kilogram. His hands were kept covered by OR

Promodular gloves, which were very strong, supple, and warm. Even inside the Marmot sleeping bag, he was constantly aware of the chill.

The next morning Bond felt better and found that others did, too. He was eager to get up the side of the mountain, but he knew that a week had to be spent at the Base Camp so that the body could properly acclimatize. He joined the others for the traditional *puja* ceremony in which the Sherpas and Chandra built a small shrine out of rocks and hung prayer scarves on it. Prayers were said, as it was believed that they had to ask permission to climb the mountain. They made offerings, and a live chicken that Girmi had brought along in a wooden cage was sacrificed for just this purpose. Supposedly, this would appease the gods at the top, and the climbers would be looked upon favorably.

"It is important not to take the climb lightly," Chandra told everyone. "Always respect the mountain. The mountain is far more powerful than you will ever be. The gods don't like men to be overconfident. They despise anyone who thinks he can get the better of the mountain. Misfortune will most certainly fall upon anyone who believes they can 'trick' the mountain."

Everyone listened attentively, but Bond noticed Marquis holding back a snicker. He whispered to Bond, "You don't believe that mumbo jumbo, do you, Bond?"

"It's not a question of belief, Roland, it's a question of respect."

Marquis shook his head. "You always liked playing by the rules, didn't you. . . ."

Afterward, Marquis addressed the group. "Right. I hope you all had a good night's sleep. I know I didn't. But as our bodies acclimatize, the sleeping will improve, isn't that right, doctor?"

Hope said, "Well, for most people it should. Sleeping is automatically impaired at high altitudes. That's why it's important to take frequent rests. I should also remind you to drink lots of fluids."

"Now," Marquis continued, "all this week we'll spend the time doing just that. However, beginning the day after tomorrow, some of us will commence short excursions up the face. Each day we'll climb a little higher and return to Base Camp the same day. I'll be watching you all to see how you do, and on that basis I'll select those climbers who will accompany me in the Lead Team." The Lead Team was the group that had the most difficult job. They had to install the hardware that helped other climbers get up the mountain — ropes, anchors, ice screws, pitons, carabiners, runners, and the like.

After the meeting the team broke up for "free time," which Bond considered a joke, as there was absolutely nothing to do. He had brought two paperback books to read — an old thriller by John le Carré and a new nonfiction book about criminal profiling, written by a former FBI agent. Several of the men had brought playing cards and portable chess and checkers sets, and Paul Baack even had a television that picked up a few channels by satellite.

Base Camp life was long and dull in Bond's opinion, and he found himself becoming restless and agitated by the third day. Marquis didn't pick him to go on the first climb, but he did select Otto Schrenk. Bond thought he would use the opportunity to take a look inside Schrenk's tent.

He got Chandra to stand watch as he slipped inside. Typically, Schrenk had insisted on pitching his own tent and bunking alone. There were the usual accoutrements necessary for survival — a hanging Bibler stove, climbing gear, sleeping bag, clothing — but nothing that remotely resembled anything like a sniper rifle. The only weapon he found was an antique but beautifully preserved dress dagger that the Nazis wore as an item of uniform. They were special to each branch of the service, and this one was naval. It was not hidden but was lying in plain sight with a pile of other tools. A Union weapon perhaps?

Bond crept out of the tent and shook his head at Chandra. Perhaps they could find a way to search everyone's tent before the actual ascent began.

Two days later Bond was attempting to nap in his tent after lunch. Gunshots woke him, so he leaped out of the sleeping bag and slipped on his boots. He ran outside, where it had begun to snow.

The shots were coming from behind the mess. Three or four people were standing around, watching something. Bond pushed through and saw that Roland Marquis had set up targets of bottles and tin cans and was practicing his aim with a Browning Hi-Power handgun. The Sherpas were quite agitated with this behavior, and Bond understood why. The gunfire would displease the gods.

"Roland, what the hell are you doing?" Bond snapped.

"What does it look like, Bond? I'm keeping my trigger finger up to snuff."

"You're upsetting the Sherpas. Stop it, now."

Marquis turned and looked at Bond. "I don't give a damn what the Sherpas think. I'm the leader here, and if I feel like target practice, by God, I'm going to do it. Care to join me?"

"Hell, no. Put the gun away."

Marquis shrugged and laid the pistol on a rock. He picked up an ice ax that was at his side. "All right, how about a little game of ice ax throwing? Come on, Bond, aren't you bored, too? We'll throw ice axes at the targets. The Sherpas won't mind that."

Bond shook his head. He didn't want to get into this kind of brawl with Marquis. More team members had heard the noise and had by then ventured to the area. Hope Kendall was among them.

"Come on, Bond, it's all in fun. Don't tell me that our Foreign Office rep is afraid of being beaten?" Marquis said it loud enough for everyone to hear.

"You're acting like a schoolboy, Roland."

Without warning, Marquis flicked the ice ax at Bond. It struck the ground an inch away from his right foot. The tool perfectly embedded in the snow with the handle sticking straight up.

Whether it was the effects of the high altitude, the relentless boredom, or his lack of sleep, he didn't know; but this angered Bond to such an extent that he reached down and removed the ice ax, saying, "All right, Roland. Let's do it."

"Now you're talking, Bond!" Marquis laughed aloud and looked around for another ice ax. He got one from Carl Glass and then said, "Carl, go and set up those bottles and cans again, would you? What shall our stakes be? I'm sure you didn't bring much money with you, so we can't have a replay of our Stoke Poges match."

"This was your idea, Roland, you name it."

Marquis grinned and looked around at the crowd. He spotted the doctor looking at him with wide eyes.

"Very well. The winner gets to sleep with Dr. Kendall tonight."

"What?" she blurted out. "What the hell are you —"

Bond held up his hand. "Come on, Roland, that was out of line, and you know it."

Marquis gave her a little bow. "I'm sorry, my dear. Just a little joke."

"Screw you, Roland," she said, then walked away.

Marquis shook his head and said,

"Tsk-tsk, the fairer sex. I suppose they can't be saints and sluts at the same time."

It took all of Bond's willpower to keep from slugging him. He knew, though, that it wouldn't be good for morale to do so in front of the team. The man was behaving as badly as Bond had ever seen him.

"Well, never mind. We won't play for anything except the satisfaction of being the best. Is that all right?" Marquis asked.

"Fine."

"Shall I start?"

Bond gave a slight, mocking bow. "By all means."

Marquis sneered at him, then turned to face the targets. There were five bottles and five cans set on various objects — portable tables, rocks, canvas bags. . . .

Marquis raised the ice ax and tossed it. It knocked the first bottle cleanly off its base.

He smiled and said, "Your turn, Bond."

Bond took a position, tossed the ice ax from hand to hand to get a feel for its weight, then flicked it forward. The second bottle shattered.

"Oh, nice one, Bond! Do we get extra points for breaking the target? I think not."

Carl Glass retrieved the ice axes and handed them back to the players. The other members of the team were enthralled by the display of antagonism between the two men. Even Hope returned out of curiosity.

Marquis took a stance, raised the ice ax, and threw it. The tool whizzed past the third bottle, missing it by two inches.

"Oh, bloody hell," he said.

Bond took his place, raised his own ax, then tossed it. He knocked the third bottle into the snow.

The axes were retrieved again, and Marquis took his place for a third try. He flung the ice ax and missed the fourth bottle by a hair.

"God*dammit!*" he shouted. He was losing his temper. In fact, Bond thought, he was acting quite irrationally. Could he have AMS?

Bond knocked down the fourth bottle, which only angered Marquis more. Luckily for him, Marquis succeeded in demolishing the fifth bottle.

By the time they were into the tin cans, Bond was ahead by one hit. There were only two targets left. Bond had hit every object he had thrown at except for one, which had allowed Marquis to catch up a little.

Marquis took aim, threw the ax, and

knocked off the can. One to go.

Bond stood his ground, aimed, and threw. The pick missed the can. There was an audible gasp from the spectators.

"Oh, bad luck, Bond," Marquis said, cocky as hell. He took the retrieved ice ax and aimed carefully. He raised his arm slowly, then threw the ice ax hard. Instead of hitting the can, it struck the rock it was sitting on. The force of the blow, however, was enough to dislodge the can, causing it to fall into the snow.

"Ha! It's a draw!" Marquis shouted.

"I don't think so, Roland," Bond said. "You didn't hit the can. You hit the rock."

"The bloody thing got knocked off, though."

This time Carl Glass intervened. "Well, since I'm the unofficial referee here, I have to side with Mr. Bond on that one, Roland. You didn't hit the can."

"Who the hell asked you?" he shouted at Glass.

"Let Bond have another go," someone in the crowd said.

"Yes, that should clinch it."

Marquis was fuming. "Very well. Bond, if you hit it, fine, you win. But if you miss, I win."

"You'd still be tied," Glass reminded him.

"Shut up!" Marquis snapped. "Whose side are you on, anyway?"

"Fine, Roland," Bond said. "If I miss, you win." Bond took the ice ax, concentrated on the tin can that had been reset by Glass, then threw the tool. It spun around, hit a nearby rock, bounced off it, and struck the can. The spectators applauded and shouted.

"Whoa, fancy move!"

"Well done!"

Marquis glowered at Bond. "You cheated."

"How? It was your bloody game. There were no rules."

He stuck his finger into Bond's chest and said, "I never liked you, Bond. Not back at school, not when we were in the service, and not now. Someday you and I will really have it out."

Bond stood there, silently taking it. He couldn't jeopardize the mission by getting into a fight with Marquis now. They had to get to the plane, and Marquis was the only one who could adequately lead them up the mountain.

It was Hope who defused the situation. "Roland, I want you to go to bed. You're exhibiting AMS symptoms."

"No, I'm not."

"One of the first symptoms is denial that you have them."

"I agree with Dr. Kendall," Bond said. He attempted to control his anger and speak calmly. "Look, this was just a game. We'll do it again sometime if it will make you feel better. But the doctor is right. You're not thinking straight."

Marquis looked around him and saw that the entire team was staring at him. He began to protest, then backed down. "Fine," he said. He seemed to relax a little. "But you wait. I'm going to prove to you all that there's no one else who can summit this mountain faster than me."

"We're not summiting the mountain, Roland," Hope reminded him.

"Oh, believe me, I will," he said. "I haven't come all this way just to pick over a bunch of dead bodies in a plane wreck. I don't give a shit about your 'secret mission,' Bond."

That did it. Bond grabbed him by the parka. He whispered through his teeth, "Listen to me, *Marquis,* you had better start behaving. Might I remind you of your duty and of M's instructions? I will not hesitate to exercise my own authority to have you replaced. I can do it, too."

Hope Kendall was the only one who

heard him. She said, "Come on, Roland. Let's go to the medical tent. I want to take a look at you. Let's check your blood pressure." She gently pulled him away from Bond. Marquis glared at his adversary but allowed her to take him away.

NINETEEN

Kangch at Last

A week passed and Roland Marquis picked a small team to prepare the temporary camps up the north face of Kangchenjunga. The plan was to ascend the mountain over two weeks, with several days spent acclimatizing at the halfway mark. Camp Five would be set up at the crash site on the Great Scree Terrace.

Bond expected Marquis not to pick him, and when Marquis announced that the Lead Team would consist of himself, Philippe Léaud, Carl Glass, Tom Barlow, Otto Schrenk, Doug McKee, and two Sherpas, Bond protested.

"Let me and Chandra go with you," he insisted.

"Sorry, Bond, only professional climbers are allowed to be in the Lead Team. It's the rule."

"Bollocks, Roland. You know damned well I can do it. So can Chandra."

Marquis thought for a moment. He was

quite aware that Bond was properly acclimatized simply from observing his ability and stamina during the trek from Taplejung.

"All right, Bond," he said patronizingly. "I suppose we can use you."

Climbers usually work in pairs so that one can belay the other and take turns making pitches, so Marquis could not exclude Chandra.

Bond put on Boothroyd's One Sport boots and made a thorough inspection of his equipment. His various ice tools — axes, ice screws — were made by Black Diamond, among the finest available. His snow pickets, the stakes used as anchoring devices, were MSR Coyotes. He had chosen the Deadman model simply because he liked the name. He examined the points on his Grivel 2F crampons to satisfy himself that they were sharp enough. Crampons are necessary for ice climbing, allowing the climber to gain a solid foothold on hard ice and snow. They were hinged so that they would bend naturally. He used the Scottish method of strapping them to his boots — a strap with a ring in the middle is permanently connected to the two front posts of the crampon; a strap then runs from one side post through the ring to the other side post, with a rear strap wrapping around the ankle from the two back posts. He knew it was a rather old-fashioned way of doing it, but it was how his father had taught him when Bond first started climbing at the age of five. Like everyone else, he carried Edelweiss 9mm Stratos ropes, made with polyamide braid in fifty-meter sections, and fixing ropes, which are different and made of 7mm Kevlar cord in one-hundred-meter sections.

Marquis and Léaud set off in the lead, followed by Barlow and Glass, then Bond and Chandra. The two Sherpas, Holung and Chettan, who had come back to the Base Camp after leaving the injured Bill Scott in Taplejung, were next, and Schrenk and McKee brought up the rear.

To get to Camp One at 5,500 meters, the team had to walk up a moraine and across a low-angle rock and ice glacier. They had made such a trip at least once during practice runs the previous week, so they were familiar with the path. Unfortunately, the wind was now blowing hard and the temperature had dropped significantly.

The first part of the ascent was relatively easy. The French had developed a widely used technique for ice climbing called "flat-footing," which requires the climber to keep his feet as flat against the ice as possible at all times to keep all crampon points on the ice. The Germans developed a technique known as "front-pointing," in which the climber kicks the front crampon points hard into the ice and then steps directly up on them. In both techniques, climbers must progress by moving their weight from one point of balance to another, supporting themselves as much as possible on their legs, and planning several moves in advance. Bond liked to call it "climbing with one's eyes." Climbers learn to rely on surface features, seeking out buckets and protrusions for handholds, footholds, and ice-tool placements.

Technical expertise was needed once they reached the upper glacier. One man climbed while his partner belayed. The belay had to be connected to an anchor, the point of secure attachment to the rock or ice. The belayer paid out or took in rope as the climber ascended, ready to use one of the various methods of applying friction in case the climber fell. Marquis took the lead, belayed from below, and moved up the rock face to the next desirable spot to set up a new belay. The last climber would take apart the belay and climb up, belayed from above. The distance between belays is known as a pitch. The climbers leapfrogged their way up so that the one who went first led all the odd-numbered pitches, and followed second on all even-numbered ones. The leader attached hardware — called "protection" — to the rock or ice on the way up.

All along the way the team pitched flags and ropes, marking the route so that the others would have less difficulty ascending. It was a strenuous four hours, but Bond felt great to be climbing again. It reminded him of his youth in the Austrian Tyrol, when he first fell in love with the sport. The cold air that burned his lungs was a painful yet exhilarating sensation.

As he and Chandra pitched their tent at Camp One, though, he got the disconcerting feeling that he was in grave danger. He felt that the Union could raise their ugly head at any time.

At dawn Bond and Chandra were awoken by the Sherpas, who brought them hot tea. The tea was welcome, but he would have given a year's salary just to have a plate of his housekeeper May's scrambled eggs. He also would have killed to have a cigarette, but this was truly a situation when having a cigarette would have killed him.

He rose stiffly from the sleeping bag, coughed and hacked for several minutes, then sipped the tea. Chandra sat up, said "Good morning" but was otherwise atypically speechless. The climb was getting to them both. Bond had slept fitfully, with very vivid, disturbing dreams, which was quite normal at high altitude. What was worrying was that the conditions would worsen as they got higher. That day they were ascending to 6,000 meters. It wouldn't be long before they would require oxygen.

The team met at Marquis's tent, which would remain as Camp One HQ.

"Right," Marquis said, breathing heavily. "Today's climb is another five hundred meters up the ice glacier above us. It's a relatively easy jaunt. First we have to climb through that small, low-angle icefall to get to the main glacier. We'll set up Camp Two there."

"There are some short ice steps we'll have to fix rope on," Philippe Léaud said. "How big are they, Roland?"

"Ten to twenty meters. No problem. How does everyone feel?"

They all mumbled, "Fine."

"Let's go, then."

The team kept the same formation as the previous day, with Marquis and Léaud leading. The ropes were attached easily enough, and they trudged up the slope in silence. As the air grew thinner, their strength diminished with each step. It took twice as long to travel a few feet as it would have at sea level.

They got to Camp Two midafternoon, totally exhausted. Tom Barlow fell to his knees, gasping for breath.

"Chettan, take a look at him," Marquis told the Sherpa. "Make sure he's all right. The rest of you, set up the tents. The sooner we get this done, the sooner we can collapse."

Barlow regained his wind after a few minutes. So far no one except Marquis had shown any signs of AMS. They erected the tents and huddled in two of them to eat. Bond found himself in a tent with Chandra, Marquis, and Léaud. Marquis brought out his cell phone and punched the memory dial.

"Camp Two to Base, Camp Two to Base," he said.

"Hello? Roland?" It was Paul Baack.

"Paul, we're here. We're at Camp Two."

"Congratulations!"

"How are things down there?"

"Fine. We're all restless, but we just watched *Gone With the Wind* on television. Uncut. No commercials. That passed the time."

"Frankly, my dear, I don't give a damn," Marquis said, laughing at his own joke.

"Hope wants to know how everyone is feeling," Baack said.

"Tell her we're fine. Tom had a few moments of breathlessness, but he's all right now. Tomorrow we'll push on to Camp Three and wait for you to join us. In the meantime, can we order some Chinese takeaway?"

"Sorry, we're all out of Chinese food. You don't want Chinese food tonight. Why don't you order a pizza?"

"That sounds fine, too," Marquis said, laughing. "Over and out."

He put away the phone as they began to eat Alpine Aire freeze-dried rations, which were types of casseroles made of vegetables and/or meat. Sealed tightly in waterproof plastic bags, the rations were lightweight and easily boiled to produce a high-calorie meal with no dishes to clean.

"Hey, come out here!" a voice called outside.

"Who's that?" Marquis asked.

"Sounds like McKee," Bond said. He stuck his head out the tent flap. Doug McKee was standing a few feet away, pointing at something.

"Come look at this," he said. The others were gathered around a dark object in the snow.

Bond and his group climbed out and stomped through the ice and snow to see what the fuss was about.

"I wonder how long he's been here," McKee said, pointing to the thing frozen in the ice.

It was a man's skeleton, fully dressed in climbing gear.

Bond's dreams that night were filled with unholy terrors. He thought that an avalanche had buried him at one point and that he was suffocating and freezing. As he dug frantically in the snow with his bare, frostbitten hands, he came upon the frozen skeletons of an entire expedition. The skulls were laughing at him. One addressed him in Roland Marquis's voice: "Oh, bad luck! You never were the best, Bond. But you tried to be, didn't you? Now look at you!"

He awoke with a start. Chandra was shaking him. "James, there's a fire. Wake up!"

"What?" Bond snapped out of it, groggy and disoriented. The first thing he noticed was the biting, cold air attacking his lungs. He coughed hard and wheezed for a few seconds.

"One of the tents is on fire!"

Bond leaped out of the sleeping bag, slipped on his boots, and followed Chandra outside. The sun was just rising, casting an eerie orange glow over the ice around them.

Three men were stomping on a tent that was ablaze. Bond had to think a moment to remember whose tent it was.

"Schrenk?"

"He got out. He's over there." Chandra pointed. Otto Schrenk was one of the men putting out the fire. They were using snow shovels and blankets to snuff it out. Bond and Chandra jumped in to help, and within minutes it was extinguished.

"How did this happen?" Marquis asked, stumbling up to the scene. His voice was hoarse.

"The goddamn stove in my tent," Schrenk said. "I was trying to boil water, and the tent caught fire. Look, it's all ruined."

"What gear did you lose?"

"I'm not sure yet. My extra clothes, I

know." Schrenk began to rummage through the blackened fabrics and pulled out some tools that were still intact. "There are these, thank God."

"He can borrow some of my clothes until we reach Camp Three," Philippe Léaud said. "You're my size, Otto?"

"I think so, thanks."

The team settled down for breakfast and attempted to get their wits about them. No one was thinking particularly straight. They gathered by Marquis's tent as he pulled out a map of the route.

"Today we come to our first big obstacle. After we cross the glacier, we come to the so-called ice building. Now, we have a couple of options. The normal route is to climb six hundred meters on a steep ice slope to the left of the seracs of the ice building. We would then traverse right across the first snow plateau to make Camp Three at sixty-six hundred meters. Now, this is very steep ice climbing, which we will fix rope on. I know that an American team who did this claimed it wasn't that difficult, just extremely tiring. The other possibility is to do what the Japanese did and climb directly through the ice building. This would be easier going technically, but it could be dangerous. This ice building is really the key to the north face — how to get around it. A serac collapse in the area killed a Sherpa in 1930. It's pretty scary, I must say, and different teams chose different strategies for getting around it."

"What do you recommend?" McKee asked.

"I say we should try the Warth method from 1983 and climb the icewall to the left of the ice building. Above that we would go right across the glacier back to the north face."

"You're the boss," Léaud said.

"Now, when Schrenk — where is Schrenk?" Marquis asked, looking around. Only then did everyone realize he was the one member of the team missing.

"Maybe he's putting his gear back together?" McKee suggested.

They looked around and found Schrenk walking toward them with his gear packed and ready to go.

"Sorry," he said. "Did I miss anything?"

"It's all right," Marquis said. "Just follow us. Let's go, everyone! I want to start climbing in ten minutes!"

Bond and Chandra rushed back to the tent and packed quickly. Bond slipped on his crampons and joined the party outside.

The wind had died down, the sun had risen, and it was a relatively beautiful day considering the fact that they were on the side of the third tallest mountain in the world. They were already higher than many of the peaks around them. This was what Bond truly loved about mountain climbing. It was a vigorous, dangerous sport that, when one achieved the goal, gave one a sense of accomplishing the impossible. Here one really was the king of the world.

The "ice building" is a beautiful but frightening formation that is virtually a tunnel of ice. It could have been used as a shortcut up to the plateau, but, as Marquis said, the possibility of icefalls is very high.

Instead, Marquis led them up the ice slope to the left, which was at a steep angle ranging from forty-five degrees to seventy. Slowly and carefully, they worked their way up a gully that proved to be quite strenuous an operation.

They were nearly halfway up the gully when it was Bond's turn to make the next pitch. Chandra belayed while Bond used the ropes already set in place by Marquis and Léaud, who were a hundred meters above them.

Just when the angle was at its steepest,

Bond's crampons suddenly slipped off his boots. He lost his footing and began to plummet. He slid backward on the ice and attempted to stop himself with his ice ax, but he was unable to obtain a secure hold with it. Chandra jumped into action and held the belay rope tightly.

Bond fell thirty meters and was jerked to a halt by the rope. His back felt as if it had snapped in two. He yelled in pain as he dropped his ice ax.

"Hold on, James!" Chandra called.

Bond swung limply on the rope. The others became aware of what happened and stopped climbing.

"What happened?" Marquis called from above.

"James?" Chandra called. "Are you conscious?"

Bond lifted his hand and waved.

"Can you swing yourself to the wall and get a foothold?"

"I'll try," Bond called. He began to swerve and kick, gaining enough momentum to rock himself back and forth on the rope. Finally, he hit the wall of ice but couldn't find a handhold. He kicked away once again, attempting to maneuver himself toward an anchor that had been set a few feet to his right. After two more tries he grabbed hold of it and slowly worked his way down the rope to the ledge where Chandra was.

"What happened? Are you all right?" Chandra asked.

"Yes. Gave me a hell of a fright, though. Bloody crampons. They slipped right off my boots!"

"How could that happen?"

"Where are they? Did you see them fall?"

"I think so. Over there somewhere." They moved carefully along the ledge and found one of them. The other had fallen into oblivion.

Bond picked it up and examined it. The ring that the straps went through was bent and had a two-millimeter gap in it. Bond removed his goggles for a moment to look at it closely.

"This ring was filed," he said. "Look, it has serrated edges there. Someone tampered with it!"

"When was the last time you looked at them?"

"Well, last night, I suppose. But they were in my tent all night. Who could have . . . ?"

He thought a minute. "Schrenk. He was missing at the team meeting over breakfast.

He could have had time to slip into our tent and do the damage."

Chandra nodded. "It's possible. Maybe that fire was something he set on purpose to cause a diversion."

At that moment the two Sherpas caught up with them. Schrenk and McKee were not far behind at the rear. When they appeared on the ledge, Bond cheerfully addressed them.

"My crampons slipped off. Anyone have a spare pair?"

McKee said, "I do. I'm not sure if they'll fit you. What happened?"

"I don't know. They came undone somehow." Bond looked directly at Schrenk, who averted his eyes.

McKee pulled off his backpack and dug into it. He found the two extra crampons, which were wrapped in cloth to protect the other gear from the sharp spikes. Bond tried them on. They were a little small but would do the job.

"Thanks. I'll make sure the others bring up more when they meet us at Camp Three."

"What the hell is going on down there?" Marquis called. He was quite some distance away.

Chandra waved the okay sign and they

began to climb again.

Four hours later they reached the plateau, 6,600 meters above sea level. Everyone was coughing and attempting to take slow, deep breaths.

"What about oxygen?" McKee asked Marquis.

"We don't need oxygen until we're higher up. If you need it now, you're going to use it all up. How many canisters did you bring?"

"Three, but the Sherpas have the team's entire supply."

Marquis nodded. "But we have to conserve it. We'll need the oxygen at Camp Five, where the plane is. We don't know how long we'll be there. Try to make do without it, okay?"

McKee coughed and nodded.

Marquis looked at Bond. "What the hell happened to you down there?"

"Nothing," Bond said. He thought it best not to alarm anyone about the tampering. "The crampons slipped off. I must not have fastened them very well. My fault."

"Don't let it happen again, Bond. As much as I can't stand you, I'd hate to lose you."

"Thanks, Roland, that's comforting."

Marquis walked away toward his tent. Bond and Chandra looked over at Otto Schrenk, who was helping Doug McKee erect a tent for the two of them.

Was it Schrenk? Or could it have been someone else?

At least they were safely at Camp Three, where they would spend the next week acclimatizing. The rest of the group would be joining them over the next few days.

Bond knew, though, that someone on the team definitely wanted him out of the picture.

TWENTY

Higher and Higher

The others from the Base Camp began to arrive in groups the following day. Paul Baack was one of the first, carrying the lightweight laptop satellite phone with his own equipment. Hope Kendall had partnered him, and insisted on examining the Lead Team — but not until she had had a night's sleep. Bond thought she didn't look well, but then he remembered how he had felt on reaching Camp Three.

The next day Bond visited the doctor in her tent. They sat cross-legged opposite from each other as she examined him. Bond thought she seemed much better, but he could see that the climb was taking its toll. She wore no makeup, of course, had dark circles under her eyes, and looked thinner.

"How are you feeling, James?" she asked, listening to his breathing with a stethoscope.

"I'm fine now. When I first got to Camp

391

Three, I felt like hell."

"I know what you mean," she replied. "I haven't been sleeping well."

"You should heed your own advice and get plenty of rest, then."

"This is my job," she said. "Cough, please."

He did. It was a horrid, dry croup.

"That cough's a beaut. Does your throat hurt?" she asked.

"Yes."

"I'm going to give you some lozenges. You need to drink more water. Are you drinking water?"

"Yes." He coughed again.

"Then drink more." She reached into her bag and gave him a packet of vitamin C and eucalyptus lozenges. "Otherwise, you're fit as a buck rat."

"I'll take that as a compliment."

She smiled, but then rubbed her forehead and shut her eyes tightly. "Damn," she said. "I can't shake this headache."

"You need to take it easy," he said. He put a hand on the back of her neck and massaged it. That brought the smile back.

"Mmm, that's nice," she said. "Would you just do that for the next twenty-four hours?"

"Seriously," he said, "are you all right?"

"Yeah, I think so," she answered but wasn't very convincing. "Go on, now. Send in your cuzzy."

"My what?"

"Your cuzzy, your cousin, your brother, your mate . . ." she explained. "It's Maori talk. Chandra. Send him in. Please."

Bond let it go and crawled out of the tent.

It was about three hours later when he noticed Marquis rushing to Hope's tent. Paul Baack was standing outside it, looking as if he were lost and didn't know what to do. Bond approached him and asked, "Is something wrong?"

"Yes," Baack said. "Dr. Kendall is sick."

Bond stuck his head in the tent. Marquis was kneeling by Hope, who was lying on her sleeping bag. Carl Glass was with them.

"We have it under control, Bond, you can leave," Marquis said rudely.

"It's all right, he can stay," Hope mumbled. "God, just let me die now."

"She's got acute altitude sickness," Glass told Bond.

"My head feels like it's going to explode," she said. "Goddammit, this has never happened to me before!"

She coughed loudly and gasped when

she attempted to breathe deeply.

"My dear Hope," Marquis said, "you yourself said it could strike anyone at any time. You're no exception. Now, please, let me take you down to Camp Two. You need to descend as quickly as possible. I can carry you on —"

"Shut up, Roland!" she snapped. "I'm not going anywhere. This will pass. Stop fussing over me. I hate it!"

"I'm only trying to —"

"Please just leave me *alone!* Get out of here!" she screamed.

Marquis stiffened, embarrassed and angry. He moved away and, without a word, glared at Bond and left the tent.

"What should we do?" Glass asked her.

"I'm sorry. He's right, dammit," she said. "I need to go to Camp Two but I just don't have the strength. For three days I haven't slept, haven't eaten, haven't peed . . . I'm constipated as hell. . . ." She was on the verge of tears, but she didn't have the energy for it.

"Wait, I'll get the Gamow Bag," Bond said.

He left the tent as she mumbled, "Why the hell didn't I think of that?"

Bond retrieved Major Boothroyd's modified device from the Sherpas and brought it back to the tent. She climbed into it and sealed it up after thanking Bond and telling everyone to let her be for a few hours. Since the bag had its own generator to pump air into it, it was inflated within minutes.

A Gamow Bag artificially reproduces the pressure of a lower altitude. It temporarily cures symptoms of AMS, but the victim normally has to descend anyway to recover fully.

Bond looked up through his goggles and saw that the sun was still high in the sky, so there was possibly time for her to get down before nightfall, as descending wouldn't be as time-consuming as the trip up. He then found Paul Baack and asked to use the satellite linkup. The Dutchman gave him the privacy of his tent.

Alone, Bond phoned London. After several rings the voice-messaging service kicked in.

"You have reached Helena Marksbury. I'm sorry that I am away from my desk . . ."

It was almost a surreal experience. Here he was, halfway around the world, on the side of a fierce mountain and isolated from civilization, yet he was able to hear the voice of a lover, albeit a former one.

"I'm halfway up Kangch," he said after the beep. "Camp Three. Where are you? I'll switch over to Bill. It was nice to hear your voice."

He quickly pressed the code sequence that transferred him to Bill Tanner's office. Christ, Bond thought. He was thankful that she hadn't picked up after all. It would have been awkward. He hoped that she was not still upset about their relationship.

There were a few pips, and Tanner picked up. "James?"

"Hello, Bill. I'm calling from sixty-six hundred meters. Nothing on Schrenk?"

"No, but we received some interesting intelligence from our new man in India. His name is Banerjee. He's Zakir Bedi's replacement."

"What's that?"

"They intercepted Union communications to Kathmandu. The man who tried to kill you there was indeed employed by the Union. An accomplice was snatched, a go-between apparently, and he confessed that the Union have infiltrated your expedition. It's someone in your party, James."

"I've suspected that all along. Thanks for confirming it."

"Any idea who it might be?"

"I've been thinking it's Schrenk."

"If we find anything that ties him to the Union, I'll certainly get a coded message to you. We also learned that the Russian expedition is being financed by certain military authorities in Moscow who have files in our offices a mile long. They have strong ties to the Russian Mafia. There can be only one reason they're up there."

"Thanks for the tip. I had better go. I don't want the Ministry of Defence complaining about the phone bill."

"There's one other thing, James."

Bond detected hesitation in his voice.

"What's that?"

"Helena is missing. She's been gone for two days and hasn't phoned in. As you know, our security procedures are such that when someone in her position doesn't call in, we —"

"I know," Bond said, "you send someone to her flat. And?"

"She wasn't there, either. The flat had been ransacked."

Oh, no. Bond squeezed his eyes tightly shut.

"James," Tanner said. "We concluded our investigation into the leak at MI6."

Bond said it before the Chief of Staff could. "It's her."

Tanner's silence confirmed it.

"She's probably in trouble if she's mixed up with the Union," Bond said.

"James," Tanner said gently. "She's probably dead. But we'll keep looking. Try not to worry about it. Concentrate on the job at hand."

Right. Bond gripped the phone tightly and said, "Keep me informed."

"Watch your back, James."

Bond rang off and stepped outside the tent. Paul Baack was standing there, shivering.

"All done?" he asked.

"Yes, thanks. Better get inside and get warm."

"I will. You might tell the same thing to our illustrious leader over there." Baack gestured toward Marquis's tent, then went inside his own.

Bond found Marquis throwing his ice ax at a solid boulder of ice. He seemed to be in a trance. He threw the ax, walked over and retrieved it, returned to his position, and threw it again. And again.

Bond felt like joining him but decided not to bother.

Three hours later Hope Kendall emerged from the Gamow Bag and announced that she was going down to Camp

Two for a couple of days. Bond offered to accompany her, but she said it wasn't necessary. Marquis knew better than to volunteer, but he insisted that a Sherpa go with her.

Two days later Bond was in his own tent, having just completed reading the criminal profiling book, when Paul Baack stuck his head inside.

"I must show you something, James," he said. Bond got up and followed the Dutchman back to his tent. There was a blurry photograph displayed on the monitor of his laptop.

"It's a satellite photo," he said. "It's the north face of the mountain as seen from space, but magnified many times. Look, this is our camp here." As he pointed to objects on the screen, Bond began to comprehend what he was looking at.

"Over here is something that wasn't there yesterday." He pointed to another mass of dark objects, slightly east of them. "Those are the Russians."

"We knew they were close, but what is that, a thousand meters?" Bond asked.

"Less. Maybe eight hundred. They set up their equivalent of Camp Three there. To get there you would have to climb up and over the *Bergschrund,* see?" He pointed to a deep slit that delineated a glacier's upper terminus. It was a phenomenon that formed as the body of ice slid away from the steeper wall immediately above, leaving a gap between glacier and rock.

Bond nodded. "We have to cross that to get to Camp Four," he said.

"But then, to get to the Russians, you have to go down this way here. That's quite a hike, at least an eight-hour journey. I don't think we have to worry about them making a sneak attack on our camp."

They're probably waiting for *us* to make the next move, Bond thought.

"Thanks," Bond said. "Keep an eye on them. If they show signs of activity, let me know."

"Will do." Bond started to leave, but Baack stopped him. "James?"

"Yes?"

"What was Roland talking about the other day when he said you were on a secret mission? I mean, I *know* you're on a secret mission. I have known all along. They wouldn't have given me all this *stuff.* Ministry of Defence . . . a Gurkha assistant . . . I mean, what's going on? I have a right to know, I think."

Bond sighed and clapped the big man on

the shoulder. "Sorry, it's classified, but I appreciate your hard work. Let's just say I have to find something on that plane and bring it back to England."

Baack nodded and said, "Well, you can count on me to help however I can."

"Thanks. You're doing a great job already," Bond said, then he left the tent.

The news about Helena still hung heavy on his heart. He had done his best to put it aside, but there was no denying that he was worried. What he needed was a different sort of distraction.

On the way back to his quarters, he saw Hope Kendall.

"Well, hello. When did you get back?"

"An hour ago," she said. She pointed to her new tent. "I'm over there."

"You sound much better."

"I feel a *lot* better," she said. "I guess I needed the extra two days at Camp Two before coming up here. This time the ascent didn't bother me at all. I did it in less than four hours."

"I'm glad you're back," Bond said.

"Hey, and thanks for that Gamow Bag. It saved my life."

"Don't mention it. Can I buy you dinner? I know a great little Nepalese takeaway in the neighborhood."

She laughed. "You never give up, do you?"

Not now, Bond thought.

Roland Marquis finally deemed the Lead Team adequately acclimatized to ascend to Camp Four. Marquis, Glass, Léaud, and Barlow had all made practice runs and reported that it would take two, maybe three days, one pitch at a time, to get to Camp Four.

The first day went relatively well. On the second day they had to cross thirty-degree snow slopes that ended at the rock wall over the *Bergschrund*. The Sherpas had hauled an aluminum ladder that could extend across the crevasse. Roland Marquis, belayed by more than one person, carefully crossed the ladder and fastened anchors on the opposite side. He looked back at the others, then saw something in the *Bergschrund*.

"There's a person down there," he called, pointing. One by one they all crossed the ladder and were in a position to see. It was indeed a corpse, a woman, with a blanket wrapped loosely around her. Bond thought that she looked well preserved.

"She has to be one of the plane survivors," Bond said. "Look, she's hardly dressed for climbing."

Both Marquis and Bond thought it best to attempt to retrieve the body. Using an elaborate system of belays and anchors, the Sherpas climbed clown into the *Bergschrund* and tied a rope around the woman's shoulders and upper arms. They gave the signal and she was brought up to the ledge.

She was wearing blue jeans, tennis shoes, a sweatshirt, and the blanket. The woman had been a tourist in a comfortably pressurized plane. She had obviously survived the crash and had attempted to climb down the mountain. Now she was frozen stiff.

Bond broke the ice surrounding the blanket and pried it away from her body. He searched her pockets and found an American passport.

"Cheryl Kay Mitchell, from Washington, D.C.," Bond read. "She's the American senator's wife."

It was also apparent that her skull was cracked and the head and shoulders were horribly misshapen. Her clothes were torn in some places, and there were cuts and bruises on exposed patches of skin.

"Poor woman," Léaud said softly.

"She fell," Marquis surmised. "From a

great height, too. Her body must have bounced and bounced and slid all the way down here from the crash site. There is absolutely *no way* she could have survived this far. Look at the way her body has frozen. I would bet that she has a million broken bones."

"If she didn't fall immediately, then I suspect she died within an hour or two after leaving the plane and *then* the body slid off the edge up there somewhere," Bond said. "She was probably desperate to do something and knew she wouldn't survive inside the plane. . . ."

"We'll take her back to Camp Three tonight. Let's leave her here for now. There's nothing else for us to do but press on."

The discovery cast a pall over the group, but they continued over the rock band in silence. It was the most technically difficult climbing they had done so far.

Camp Four was finally reached, and the next day the group began the assault to the final stop — the Great Scree Terrace at 7,900 meters. They had to climb 250 meters of a rock band via a snow gully and 100 meters of rock wall to reach an upper snowfield at around 7,500 meters. Tom Barlow and Doug McKee began using oxygen, something the Sherpas liked to call "English Air."

On the thirty-first day of their journey, with five days left in the month of May, the Lead Team finally made it. The Great Scree Terrace was a bizarre, sparkling-white, gently sloping plateau that seemed to be out of place at such a high altitude. The remainder of the mountain, only 686 meters of it, towered over the plateau like a malevolent sentinel.

The Sherpas began to set up Camp Five while Bond, Marquis, and Chandra examined the wreckage spread out before them. One broken wing was half buried in snow and ice. Forty meters beyond that were pieces of the tail. Sixty meters farther was the fuselage, remarkably intact. The other wing must have been completely buried or blown off the plateau. The cabin door was wide open. Any footprints that might have led from the plane had long been covered.

"I have to go in there first, Roland," Bond said.

Marquis said, "Be my guest."

"Come on, Chandra," Bond said as he trudged through the knee-deep snow toward the aircraft.

TWENTY-ONE

The Missing Body

Bond turned on a flashlight and stepped into the cold, dark cabin. Light filtering in from windows had a ghostly, incandescent quality that was unnerving even to him. Ice and snow had built up through holes in the fuselage, so it appeared that the passenger seats had been built in snowdrifts. An eerie whistling sound echoed throughout the cabin.

Nearly all the seats contained a body each.

Bond shined the light at the cockpit. The pilot and copilot were slumped forward in their seats, frozen in a macabre still-frame of death. Another man was lying in the aisle between the cockpit and cabin. He didn't appear to be dressed like the crew.

"Help me pull this one up," he said to Chandra.

Together they tugged on the hard, stiff body and turned it so that they could get a good look at the man's face. Ice had formed a grotesque transparent mask across half of it. There was a bullet hole in his neck.

Bond recognized him from Station I's mug shots. "This is one of the hijackers."

Chandra nodded. "I remember."

"Come on, let's look back there." Bond stepped over the body and moved back into the small main cabin. He counted the corpses.

"The plane has twelve seats for passengers. The crew consisted of the pilot, copilot, and an attendant." He indicated a woman sitting in a single seat facing the other passengers. "Here she is. There were ten tourists booked on the flight, which would have left two empty seats, right? I count nine bodies."

"The woman we found near Camp Four would make ten," Chandra said.

"But Lee Ming and the three hijackers would have made fourteen. One hijacker is accounted for, making eleven. That means there should be eleven bodies in here. Where are the other three?"

"Wait, here's someone not sitting in a chair," Chandra said, shining his light in the back of the cabin. It was another man, dressed similarly to the hijacker they found in the cockpit.

"It's one of them," Bond said, examining him. "All right, that means there are two missing. Let's see if Lee Ming is one of these people."

They each took a side of the plane and shined their flashlights on the faces one by one. The dead were all Caucasian men and women of varying ages. At least three had their eyes open, fixed in a frosty expression of fear.

"He's not here!" Bond said through his teeth. "Damn!"

"Hold on, James," Chandra said. "If that woman survived and got out, maybe Lee did, too. And the other hijacker. They couldn't have got far. They must be in the vicinity."

"Unless they dropped off the face of the mountain like that woman did. They could be *anywhere!*"

Chandra knew Bond could be right. "What do we do?"

"Nothing to do except search the area. Let's look at the ground outside again. Maybe there are some faint traces of foot-prints or something."

They came out of the plane and found Marquis and Glass waiting patiently. Paul Baack was standing anxiously nearby, and Otto Schrenk was not far behind him.

"Well?" Marquis asked Bond.

"He's not in there," Bond said quietly. "We're going to have to search the surrounding area. Chandra and I will do that. You go on with the salvage operation."

"Not in there? Are you sure?" Marquis looked as if he might panic.

"Quite sure."

"Oh, for Christ's sake!" Marquis said. He threw the ski pole he was holding against the side of the aircraft. "That's just great."

"Why are you so concerned, Roland?" Bond asked. "You did your job. You got me up here."

"I just . . . I just wanted you to succeed in your mission, that's all. I want Skin 17 back in the UK as much as you do."

For a brief moment Bond thought that Marquis might be the Union operative. Could that be possible? Usually Bond's instincts were sharp, but at such a high altitude all his senses and reflexes were numbed. He suspected everybody and anybody.

"We're going to see what we can find," Bond said, and walked away.

Marquis composed himself and turned to the others. "Right, let's help set up camp."

★ ★ ★

By the second day Camp Five was completed and the rest of the party had made it up to the site. The salvage operation began, with the first stage being the removal of the corpses from the plane and hauling them down to Camp Four, one at a time. The plan was to start a convoy, assembly-line fashion, with some workers stationed at each of the four lower camps. The *sirdar* arranged for a yak herd to pick up the bodies at the Base Camp and take them back to Taplejung for a flight to Kathmandu. It was an expensive, time-consuming, dangerous, and absurd thing to do, Bond thought. The families and governments paying for this needless operation should have left the remains on the mountain. It would have been a different story had they been alive. But to go to all this trouble for the dead? At least it made a somewhat feasible cover story. Bond was thankful that he had a different job, although it was one he was afraid he wouldn't be able to complete.

After three days Bond and Chandra had found no traces of Lee Ming or the other hijacker.

The physical changes one experiences at 7,900 meters are remarkable. Bond felt that every move he made was in slow motion. It was quite like being underwater in a JIM diving suit. He was packed in solid warm clothing, every inch of skin covered, with an oxygen canister on his back and a hose running to his mouth. He was concerned that the team might not have brought enough oxygen to last for the next few days. Even with oxygen, the team still found that they were able to perform only a few seconds of work before having to stop and catch their breath.

Bond sent a message to London via Baack's laptop that Lee's body wasn't in the plane. Tanner came back with M's instructions to keep looking until Marquis's job was finished. If Lee wasn't found by then, there was nothing to do but come home. Bond read between the lines of the coded message and saw her disappointment. He hated to let her down.

There was no news about Helena.

Tired and frustrated, Bond left the tent and found his companion.

"Dammit, Chandra," Bond said. "If you stumbled out of that plane onto this plateau, where would you go?"

"I'd try to find my way down . . . over there," he said, pointing to a gradual slope on the south side.

"That's the first place we looked, remember?"

"Maybe we should look again. There were crevasses down that way that we didn't examine. Maybe they fell in one."

"You could be right. The ice seemed very unstable when we were there the other day. Freezing to death in a crevasse isn't very appealing," Bond said.

"It is not the way in which one dies that is important," Chandra said. "It is the reason. Let's look again."

Bond knew he was right. "We also haven't looked over there on the east side of the plateau. Let's try there first. I want to find that bloody body and go home. All right?"

They had begun to trudge through the snow, when they heard Marquis calling.

"Damn," Bond said. "Come on, let's see what he wants now."

They turned around and went back to the camp HQ, where everyone had gathered. Marquis had already begun talking.

"— with the extra men we hired for the lower camps. The yaks are in place at Base Camp now, and we shouldn't have too much more to do. Oh, there you are, Bond. I was just saying that our time here is being cut short and we're trying to determine how much more we can do before we have to get out of here."

"Why? What's wrong?"

"Storms coming," Baack said. "I got the weather report a few minutes ago. Two successive storms are on their way and will reach the upper altitudes of the mountain by tonight."

"Bad storms?"

"Severe. Monsoons. One today and one tomorrow."

"Right," said Marquis, "and they can be quite deadly up here. We either have to take shelter for several hours or get down."

"I can't go yet," Bond said. "I haven't come all this way just to turn around. Our tents are built to withstand a storm. I'll risk waiting the two storms out."

"I figured you would say that. However, I must offer the option to everyone on the team of going down now. Some of you can make it all the way to Camp Three before the storm hits, or at the very least Camp Four. The next day you can descend to Base Camp. Just remember that you'd have to come all the way back up so we can finish the job."

"How much is left?" Léaud asked.

"We've estimated it to be at least two more days, not counting the rest of today.

That would completely clean out the plane. At the rate we're going, we can send down only three bodies a day. There are six left."

"What about you?" McKee asked.

"I'm staying," Marquis said.

"So am I," Hope Kendall said.

"No, you're not," he said.

"Look, I don't —"

"I don't want to argue with —"

"I'm *staying!*" she said forcefully.

Marquis glared at her. "Very well. Who else wants to stay? It would be less wear and tear on you, I think. We'll just have to hunker down in our tents when the storms hit. But I can't guarantee we'll live through them."

When all was said and done, everyone decided to leave except for the core group, which consisted of Marquis, Bond, Chandra, Hope, Baack, Léaud, Glass, Barlow, Schrenk, and three Sherpas. Those who elected to descend promised to be back in two days. Some of them were going to stay put at Camp Three rather than go all the way down.

One thing was certain, Bond thought. The Union man had to be one of those who had elected to stay.

An hour after the others left, the wind began to pick up.

★ ★ ★

Bond was looking on the far east side of the plateau for any traces of the missing men, when his cell phone rang. Digging it out of the parka pocket with the gloves was clumsy, but he managed to get it open.

"James, I think I found them!" It was Chandra.

"Where are you?"

"Where I said they would be. In a crevasse. Come down and look."

The plateau was large enough that it would take him an hour of strenuous walking to cross it. "All right, I'm on my way. Mark your position and meet me at the top in an hour."

It was midafternoon when Bond got to the slope that Chandra had pointed to earlier. The Gurkha was waiting for him, bundled up like a polar bear. The wind was stronger now, and dark clouds were forming in the sky. They hadn't much time left.

Chandra led him a hundred meters over one crevasse to a second one that had a natural ice bridge at one end. Fifty feet down, wedged in tightly, were two bodies.

"Chandra, I could kiss you, but I don't think I can find your face," Bond said. "We're going to need some help getting them out of there."

Bond got on the phone to Marquis and Léaud, who arrived on the scene just as the snow started falling. With the wind-chill, the temperature dropped to eighty degrees below freezing. Bond pointed out the bodies to them, and Marquis said, "You had better wait until tomorrow, after the first storm passes. Paul said we should have ten to twelve hours of clear weather between the two storms."

"I'm going down now," Bond said. "We have at least an hour. Help Chandra belay me."

"You're mad, Bond, but all right. I'm as curious as you are at this point."

It took Bond forty-five minutes to get down to the bodies. They had set up a Z-pulley system, which offers a three-to-one mechanical advantage through the use of two pulleys. The result was an ingenious method of hauling heavy objects safely on what could possibly be unstable ice.

Bond had his back flat against one wall of the crevasse, and his feet pushing against the opposite one. He inched down to one of the bodies and used the ice ax to free it enough to turn it over. It was the corpse of the third hijacker. The other body was five feet below. Chandra gave him more slack as he inched down into an even tighter squeeze. When he got to the body, Bond had to work for another twenty minutes chopping ice away from around the head and shoulders so that he could pull it up.

"The wind is getting stronger, Bond," Marquis said over the phone. "You had better come up."

"I'm almost finished," Bond said. "Five minutes."

Finally, he tore away the frozen blanket covering the man's face. It was Lee Ming.

"All right, I got him," Bond said into the phone. "I'm going to fasten the harness around him." Since Lee was dead, Bond didn't have to worry about fashioning a comfortable harness. He wrapped the rope around the man's shoulders and arms and tied a Prusik knot.

The storm hit with frightening strength just as Lee's body was near the top of the crevasse. Marquis, Chandra, and Léaud were pulling as hard as they could, but the wind proved to be a formidable opponent. Getting Bond up was much easier, as he could help by using his crampons to "walk" up the side of the crevasse as they pulled.

"We have to get into the tents as quickly as possible!" Marquis shouted. He could barely be heard over the howling wind.

They threw Lee's body onto a plastic sled, then all four men fought their way to the camp. They were in a full-scale blizzard now, and they could barely see where they were going. Bond directed them to his tent, where they laid down the corpse on a sleeping bag. Hope Kendall had provided Bond with some sharp instruments and tools, although she didn't know what he needed them for.

"I'll stay in here," he told them. "You all go back to your tents, and hurry. Chandra, keep the phone handy."

Marquis nodded and the others left the tent. Bond closed the flap, but the noise outside was so loud that he could barely hear himself think. He didn't particularly relish the thought of spending the night with the corpse, but he didn't want to take the chance that the Union operative might get to the body if he left it alone.

The cadaver was frozen solid. Bond lit the Bibler stove, which generated a little heat. He took the standard-issue chemical hot packs, normally used when activated to treat frostbite, and placed them on Lee's chest. He lit them, melting away the ice that held the man's clothes in a solid straitjacket.

In ten minutes Bond was able to cut away Lee's shirt and expose his chest. The skin was cold and hard. He carefully examined the area above Lee's breast and found the pocket of skin where the pacemaker had been inserted. It was still intact. Now all he had to do was wait awhile for the skin to thaw.

The storm raged outside. To pass the time, Bond took a snow shovel, opened the tent, and spent fifteen minutes clearing the entrance. It was quite common for climbers to find themselves buried inside their tents by huge snowdrifts after a big storm. Anyone caught inside without their shovel might never get out.

Bond came back into the tent and examined Lee's skin. It was now a bit like rubber, not totally fleshy, but soft enough to cut.

He took a scalpel from Hope's tools and began to carefully cut a square out of the man's chest. It was tough, almost like cutting leather. Once the square was outlined, he used scissors to grasp a corner and pull it up, revealing bluish pink inner flesh and a gold-plated pacemaker.

Bond breathed a sigh of relief. He removed his oxygen mask so that he could get a better look. He snapped the leads with the clippers, then, with his bare fingers, wrenched it out of the now-pliant, liquidless flesh.

He had it! It was in his hand! Bond clutched the device triumphantly, ready to pick up the phone and call Chandra. He dialed his number and started to speak, when he felt a sudden sharp, heavy blow on the back of his head. The tent spun chaotically as everything went black.

Bond fell forward on top of Lee's mutilated cadaver, dead to the world.

TWENTY-TWO

Love and Death at 7,900 Meters

Otto Schrenk had watched Bond's projected shadow from the outside of the tent, waiting until it was in the ideal position. Not wanting to kill him yet, Schrenk used a stone to knock Bond unconscious. He then tore open the flap, crawled in, and squatted over the two bodies. He rolled Bond off Lee, pried open the clenched fist, took the pacemaker, and reached for his mobile phone.

"You there?" he spoke into it.

"Yes," came a voice from the other end. The storm made the connection tentative.

"Where are you?"

"I'm at our agreed rendezvous. Where else would I be in this storm? Do you have it?"

"I have it."

"Good. Make sure Bond doesn't wake up."

"*Ja.*" Schrenk rang off, put the phone away, and drew the Nazi dress dagger from

421

the inside of his parka. He grabbed Bond's black hair and pulled his head back, exposing his neck. Schrenk placed the blade against Bond's neck and was about to slit his throat, when a bullet shot through the tent.

Schrenk's blood and brain matter splattered over Bond's body as the German slumped over to the side.

Roland Marquis crawled into the tent, lowered his Browning 9mm, then wrenched the pacemaker from Schrenk's hand. He put it in his pocket, then aimed the gun at Bond's head.

The phone that Bond had dropped suddenly spurted to life with a burst of static. "James? Are you there?" Marquis thought it sounded like Chandra's voice, but it was difficult to tell because of the noise. "If you can hear me, I'm on my way!" the voice said.

Damn, Marquis thought. He quickly put away the gun, covered his head, and left the tent.

Chandra, fighting his way through the blizzard, pushed forward toward Bond's tent. He never should have left him alone. It was a good thing he had been watching with his Common Weapon Sight, which greatly intensified images. He had seen a figure enter the tent, followed by another.

He plowed ahead, barely able to see even through his goggles. There was a dark shape ahead, and it was moving toward him. It was a person. Chandra moved closer until they were face-to-face. He recognized Roland Marquis.

Chandra started to speak but saw that Marquis was pointing a pistol at him. He reacted quickly, turning away just as the weapon flashed. The bullet caught Chandra in the shoulder and spun him around. He fell to the snow and lay still. Marquis looked around to make sure he wasn't seen, but everyone was safely in tents. The gunshot was muffled by the intense sound of the wind.

Chandra felt the cold snow on his face and opened his eyes. He could just see Marquis's silhouette turn and walk away from the campsite. The Gurkha managed to pull himself off the ground. His quick defensive move and the thick layers of clothing had luckily helped to deflect the bullet so that it hadn't entered his chest. Nevertheless, he was in an immense amount of pain. Chandra breathed deeply from his respirator, savoring the oxygen contained in the canister on his back, then began to follow Marquis.

★ ★ ★

"Wake up, damn you!"

The slaps came hard and fast on his face. Bond's vision was blurred and his head was pounding. Someone was crouched over him, and the voice was decidedly feminine.

"James? Wake *up!*"

He groaned, felt a rush of nausea, then rolled to his side and stopped himself from vomiting. After a moment he turned on his back and looked up at Hope Kendall, who began to wipe his face and forehead with a cloth.

"Are you all right?" she asked. "You were out cold. You have a nasty bump on the back of your head. Answer me!"

Bond nodded. "I think I'm okay."

"Can you sit up?"

He did so, slowly. His hand went to his head and felt a lump there.

"I was afraid you were dead. Everyone else is!" she said. He realized there was pure terror in her voice.

"What did you say?" She was terribly upset and in tears.

"Everyone — Philippe, Tom Barlow, Paul Baack, the *sirdar* — well, I can't find *everyone*, but there are six people dead up here. James, they've been *murdered!* Their throats were cut! And look at him —" She pointed at the body of Otto Schrenk. "He's been shot in the head!"

The news brought Bond out of the fog. The years of experience and living on the edge had long ago honed his ability to shake away pain and discomfort and focus on the matter at hand.

"Who's missing?" he asked.

"Roland, Carl Glass . . . I'm not sure who else, I'm not thinking straight," she said.

"What about Chandra?"

"I haven't seen him, either."

The storm was still raging outside. Bond peered outside the tent. It was night, and there was absolutely no visibility. He turned back and surveyed the scene in the tent. Lee's body lay where he had left it. Schrenk was crumpled up next to him. The Nazi dagger was lying by his side. There was a bullet hole in the tent.

"I think I know what happened," he said. "Schrenk. He hit me with something from outside the tent. He got the pacemaker."

"The what?"

"Something I need," he said. "He got it but was shot by someone else. Whoever shot him took the pacemaker."

"What pacemaker? What are you talking about?" she asked.

He pointed to Lee's body. She lifted the bit of clothing covering his chest and recoiled.

"Christ," she said. "Someone dug a pacemaker out of this guy?"

"Yes, I did. That was my whole purpose for being on this expedition. You might as well know. Some classified military information was hidden inside it. I have to return it to England. Come on, let's make some more room in here. Help me get rid of these bodies."

He began to drag Schrenk's corpse toward the opening. She got hold of the legs and helped push the cadaver out into the snow. They did the same with Lee, making the tent comfortable enough for two people.

"We're going to have to wait until morning," Bond said. "The storm is too severe to go out. At least we can stretch out now."

"I don't understand," she said. "What was in this pacemaker?"

"Military secrets. The entire reason this expedition was put together was for me to retrieve them."

"You mean — this whole thing, I mean, this 'salvage operation' — was just a cover story?"

He nodded.

She sat back and folded her arms. "You son of a bitch," she said. "Why the hell am I here? I'm lucky I'm not dead, too! You mean to tell me that you risked the lives of all these climbers and Sherpas just so your government could get hold of these so-called secrets? Are you out of your mind?"

"Look, Hope," he said. "I'm a civil servant. I do what I'm told. I've always thought it was a crazy, almost suicidal mission. Sometimes I'm ordered to do some very unpleasant things. Often there are other lives at stake. I'm sorry you got involved."

She was flabbergasted and, Bond thought, possibly in shock. She sat there, shivering, despite the layers of clothing she had on.

"Now tell me about the dead people," he said. "Start at the beginning."

She took some breaths from her oxygen canister, coughed, then began the story.

"After you and the others brought back the body of that guy from the plane, Roland told us all to get into our tents, use a tank of oxygen and try to sleep through the storm. So that's what I did, except I didn't go to my own tent. I went to the supply tent, where I had set up medical HQ. I got into the bedroll there, mainly because it was warmer in there with all that stuff than my own tent. I think I got about two hours of sleep, but I woke up restless. I decided to go out and grope my way to Roland's tent. I found it empty."

"Who was he sharing the tent with?"

"Carl Glass. He was gone."

"Go on."

"I then went over to Philippe and Tom's tent, and that's where I found them. They were both dead, their throats cut. I don't know, I guess I panicked. I went to the next tent, the Sherpas', and found them dead, too. Same thing, throats cut. All of them. Paul Baack was lying in his tent covered by that parka of his . . . blood all over the place. Then I came here and found you. I thought you'd been killed, too, until I examined you. You have a slight nick on your neck, there's dried blood there. Then I noticed the bump on your head."

"It's a good thing you weren't in your own tent," Bond said. "You might be dead now, too. Have you tried reaching anyone by phone?"

"Yes, and it's impossible to make a connection in this storm. All I get is static on all channels."

Bond considered the story. Had Schrenk committed the murders? He examined the Nazi dagger and saw that there was dried blood on it. Schrenk had most likely been in the act of slitting his throat when he was shot, but by whom? Could it have been Marquis? Was Marquis working against all of them? If so, which of them was Union? And if one was Union, whom was the other working for?

He then noticed his own mobile phone lying in the corner of the tent, still switched on. He picked it up, made sure it was working, and dialed Chandra's number. A message appeared on the digital display that read "No Connection."

"I told you that you'll never get anything in this weather," Hope said.

"I had to try," Bond said. He put it away and closed his eyes. His head was throbbing.

"How important is that thing you're after?" she asked.

"Important enough for it to be essential to keep it from the wrong hands. It contains technology that could upset the balance of power."

"War stuff," she said.

"I suppose." There was silence for several long moments.

"Have you ever killed anyone?" she asked softly.

The absurdity of the question caught Bond off guard, but he was too weary and cold to laugh. Instead, he simply nodded.

"I should have known," she said. "I did know, instinctually, I guess. It's why I found you attractive."

"You're attracted to killers?"

"That's not what I meant. Is there any water in that thermos?" She pointed to one in an open sack. Bond shook it, heard a splashing sound, and handed it to her. She took a long drink, then said, "Remember I told you that I like to see how far a human being can go? Killing is related to that. I've always wondered how someone can kill another human being. You see, in my career, I try to save lives. We all lose patients, of course, but I vividly remember a particular one. It was a Maori woman, a mother who died during childbirth. She was brought into the emergency room at the hospital where I worked. She had an ectopic pregnancy. I did everything I could to save her. The baby lived, but she died. I always blamed myself for her death."

Bond put his hand on her leg and said, "It wasn't your fault. Surely you know that?"

"Of course, but still . . . Actually, once I knew that she wasn't going to live, I used her to satisfy something in myself. I was so goddamned *curious* about her condition.

I wanted to *see* it. Remember I told you that I look at the human body as a machine? I wanted to see if I could fix it. What I tried didn't work. She would have died anyway, but I think I might have helped her along. And to tell you the truth, I was horrified and saddened, but at the same time excited by the thought that I had that power. Do you understand what I'm saying?"

She took a breath of oxygen from the respirator hanging over her shoulder. She coughed a couple of times, then continued talking. Bond thought she might be exhibiting shell-shock symptoms.

"When I think of us up here where God never intended humans to be, the concept of life and death becomes such a trivial thing. Any one of us could die quickly and suddenly. Some of us already have. In the grand scheme of things, we're just like bugs. Are we ants that wandered too far from home? I mean, here we are, stuck in this tent, sitting under God's microscope — a male and female of the species. What kind of experiment is waiting for us? What kind of test?"

She looked at him and laughed, but it quickly turned into coughing. She grabbed the respirator again and took some deep breaths of oxygen. Then she said, "I'm babbling. Don't pay any attention to me. Hey, you know, it's medically advisable that one snuggle with a partner to keep warm at high altitude. Would you like to do that?"

Bond moved closer to her, and she clutched him tightly.

"Wait," he whispered. He loosened her grip, then pulled out the bivouac sack with the built-in electric heaters. He unzipped and held it open. She laughed again and slipped her legs inside. He got in with her and zipped it closed.

They held each other for what seemed like an hour as the wind howled outside. Their bodies gradually warmed, and soon their hands were exploring each other. Her face, ashen and dirty, never looked more beautiful. Bond ran his hand through her blond hair and brought her head closer to his. Their mouths met in a passionate kiss, then they broke away, breathless. They read each other's thoughts, then kissed again . . . and again. She unzipped his parka and slipped her hands inside so that she could feel his chest through his shirt. He did the same, running his fingers slowly and sensually around her firm breasts. They kissed some more, then he felt her hand exploring between his legs, encouraging his arousal.

They were breathing heavily, fighting for air. Bond managed to say, "We're going to asphyxiate if we continue this way. Wait, I have another toy. Just a second . . ."

He reached for his bag and removed the dual respirator that Major Boothroyd had given him, then attached it to his oxygen canister.

"Oh, my God," she said when she figured out what he was doing. He slipped the respirator on her face and attached the other to his own. Then he slipped his hands underneath her sweater and shirt and felt her nipples harden beneath the bra she was wearing. She moaned slightly, then moved in to kiss him, forgetting that they were both wearing respirators. They bumped and she laughed.

He expertly removed her bra and pulled it out from under her clothes. Then he began to work on her trousers, slowly inching them off, while her hands were busy with his clothes. It was awkward and clumsy, but in ten minutes they had undressed each other inside the bivouac sack.

It was a first for Bond . . . sex at 7,900 meters.

They used up the precious air in the canister quite quickly, but it was worth it.

TWENTY-THREE

Blood, Sweat, and Death

Chandra did his best to follow Roland Marquis across the plateau. The wind was so fierce that it was an effort to place one foot in front of the other. Marquis's footprints were covered within minutes of his making them, so Chandra had to force himself to keep moving or he would lose the trail. Using an ice ax as a walking stick, Chandra pulled himself forward one step at a time until he came to a rock face. Anchors and a rope had been affixed there, and there was no other possible route. Marquis had gone farther up.

Chandra found climbing the rock face surprisingly easier than walking against the wind. Here, the wind pushed him snugly against the wall. It took him nearly an hour, but he finally made it to the top, where a blast of wet snow and ice hit him in the face. He nearly lost his grip and fell, but he hung on for dear life and willed one leg to swing up and over the lip. Chandra slammed his ice ax into the rock and ice, using it as a lever to pull himself up. He lay there, totally exhausted, dangerously exposed to the vicious elements. He said a silent prayer to Shiva and breathed through his oxygen respirator for several minutes, trying to regain some strength.

After an eternity, he knew he had to move or he would freeze to death. He rolled over and crawled away from the ledge, searching for some kind of shelter.

Through the blinding snow he saw a tent set up some forty meters away. That was where Marquis had holed up, Chandra thought. He wouldn't be going anywhere until the storm let up, so the Gurkha figured he must find a bivouac for the night.

There was a *Bergschrund* to his left. His father had taught him how to enlarge a crack in the ice big enough to crawl into. It was his only hope. Mustering every ounce of strength, Chandra got to his feet and slowly moved forward.

He raised the ice ax and let it fall over and over as chunks of ice flew about him. It was tremendously hard work, and he had to stop every minute or so to take deep breaths of oxygen. His legs were beginning to feel numb, but he kept chopping.

Eventually, it was done. He had made a

hole that he could crawl inside and assume the fetal position. He did so, closed his eyes, and was immediately asleep.

He awoke with a start. The storm had stopped, and the light of the new day was beginning to spread over the mountain. Chandra was stiff and cold, but alive.

Then he noticed his left hand. Somehow he had lost his glove during the climb or while he was digging the hole. His hand was completely frostbitten. The fingers were dark blue and the rest of the hand was purple. He tried to flex his fingers, but they were paralyzed. The skin was insensitive to touch.

He crawled out of the hole and stood. The rest of him appeared to be in one piece. With his good hand he slowly ripped off his backpack, opened it, and dug around for anything he could wrap around his hand. There was a prayer scarf that his father had given him when he was a boy, so he used that. It didn't help much. He knew it was entirely possible he would lose the hand when they got back to civilization.

Never mind! he told himself. Get on with the job! He repeated the Gurkhali motto to himself, over and over: It is better to die than be a coward . . . it is better to die than be a coward. It served as a mantra of sorts. He found a bar of chocolate in his pack and ate it for energy, then put the pack on again and tromped forward toward Marquis's tent.

Chandra flattened himself on the snow when he got around the glacier. Roland Marquis and Carl Glass were together, packing the tent. He decided to stay back and see where they went rather than confront them.

Soon they were off, moving toward the north ridge of the great mountain. What were they going to do? Summit? Were they mad?

Chandra followed them over the ridge, which was one route to the summit taken by many explorers over the years. But Marquis and Glass didn't continue the ascent. They went over and down to a level plane, where four tents had been set up.

The Russians.

Chandra held back, got out his CWS and peered through it, watching Marquis's every move.

Roland Marquis and Carl Glass had spent a rough night in the single tent. Marquis was anxious about the coming negotiations with the Russians, not sure if he wanted to go through with the deal he had arranged. In the early hours of the morning he had decided what he was going to do and made a plan with Glass.

They trekked to the Russian encampment, where they were greeted by two men with AK-47s. The sentries ushered them into a tent, where the leader, a man named Igor Mislov, was waiting.

He looked a lot like Joseph Stalin, with a thick black mustache and bushy eyebrows.

"Mr. Marquis!" he hailed in English. "Have some hot tea?"

"Thank you, Igor," Marquis said. "It's nice to meet face-to-face after all this time, eh?"

"Indeed, indeed." Mislov looked curiously at Glass.

"Oh, this is my associate, Carl Glass," Marquis said. "Igor Mislov."

The men shook hands and sat down.

One of the guards served the tea, and it warmed Marquis considerably. Finally, he said, "Right, I have the specification for Skin 17. It is worth . . . billions."

"Well, let's see it!" the Russian said.

"It's in the form of a microdot. The goddamned Union have been trying to get their hands on it, and they almost did. I got it first, and I even kept it from the

Double-O agent who was on our team!"

"Ha!" Mislov roared. "Double-O agent? I didn't know they still existed! When the KGB disbanded, I thought there was no more use for those guys."

"One would think so," Marquis agreed, humoring the man. "But I'm afraid SIS keeps them around to keep tabs on the Russian Mafia, too."

Mislov dismissed the label with a wave of his hand. "Don't call us that, it's an idiotic name. We're businessmen, that's all. Russian Mafia — phooey! The Mafia lives in Sicily. We live in Moscow. That's a long way from Sicily!" He laughed boisterously.

"Whatever you say, Igor," Marquis said. "Now let's talk business. I've come a long fucking way to get here. You picked one hell of a rendezvous spot."

Mislov shrugged. "I know how valuable Skin 17 is. I knew the Union were after it, too. We found out one of our team was working for them. He . . . uhm, met with an unfortunate accident. They are everywhere these days, those goddamned Union. I've done business with them, but they have no loyalty to customers. Hey, I saved you the trouble of having to carry Skin 17 all the way down the mountain.

Who knows what might have happened to you? This is a dangerous place. That was some storm last night, huh?"

"There's another one in about eight hours," Marquis said. "We'd like to get going before it hits. Now — we had agreed upon a starting price of one billion dollars. We both know it's worth more than that. What are you prepared to offer now?"

"Two billion American dollars. We can pay you fifty thousand dollars in uncut diamonds right now. The rest you'll get in Kathmandu after we get out of here."

"Are you mad?" Marquis asked. He had been afraid of this.

"Am I mad? What do you mean?"

"You think I'd let this go for only fifty thousand in diamonds?"

"Are *you* mad?" the Russian asked. Suddenly there was a heavy tension in the air. "You don't think we would carry two billion dollars in cash up Kangchenjunga, do you? It was difficult enough carrying these goddamned diamonds."

"Where are they?"

Mislov nodded at one of the two guards, who produced an ordinary water thermos. He unscrewed it and showed the contents to Marquis. It was full of off-color stones. Marquis recognized them as uncut diamonds. He nodded, and the guard replaced the lid.

"I'm afraid it won't be enough," Marquis said carefully. "Perhaps the Union will pay more."

"Mr. Marquis, we, too, came a long way for this. You will sell us the specification, or things will get unpleasant."

Marquis turned to Glass and gave him a well-rehearsed signal. "I don't know, Igor, but it seems that since we last talked, the demand for Skin 17 has skyrocketed. The Union want it, my country wants it back, the Chinese want it . . . I understand there's a few Belgians that want it . . ."

Glass heard the code word "Belgians," pulled a Glock out of his pocket with lightning speed, and shot the two guards neatly and efficiently. Marquis drew his own Browning and held it to Mislov's head. Glass picked up one of the AK-47s and aimed it at the tent flap. Two more men rushed in but saw that their leader was in danger.

"Tell them to drop their guns," Marquis said. Mislov spoke to them in Russian, and they did as they were told. Marquis then nodded to Glass, who calmly blasted them with the automatic weapon.

"Now, Igor," Marquis said. "You're all

alone. How much is the *Russian Mafia* willing to pay me now?"

Mislov swallowed hard, then stammered, "Two . . . two billion now, and two more when we reach Kathmandu."

"You have it?"

"In diamonds, yes."

"Where?"

Mislov gestured to a bag. Glass looked inside and found several more water thermoses. They were each filled with uncut stones.

"Why the hell didn't you offer us these diamonds before?"

Mislov shrugged and laughed nervously. "I'm a businessman. I was going to tell my superiors that we paid you the diamonds, but, of course, I would have kept the rest."

"I see. Well, thank you, Igor. I accept your offer," Marquis said, then pulled the trigger. The side of the Russian's head exploded as the bullet slammed through it.

They were alone in the camp now. After a moment of silence Glass said, "Christ, Roland, we're rich." He began to stuff half of the thermoses into his pack. Marquis took the remainder and put them in his own.

"Come on, let's go."

They left the tent and started to move

up the slope toward the north ridge. As they passed an icewall, Chandra Gurung jumped from a perch and tackled Carl Glass. Glass dropped the AK-47, and it slid on the ice toward the edge of a cliff and into space.

Both men got to their feet. Chandra slugged Glass hard in the face with his good fist, knocking him into Marquis, who was in the process of drawing the Browning. He, too, lost his grip on the gun, and it sailed into the air and lodged in a snowdrift behind Chandra. The Gurkha backed off and stood between the two men and the drift.

They were dangerously close to the precipice.

"You are both under arrest," Chandra said. "You must accompany me back to Camp Five."

Marquis laughed. Glass, not sure how to react, laughed with him.

"Oh, really!" Marquis said. "*You* are going to arrest *us!* I tell you what. How about we pay you twenty rupees to porter our bags for us?"

"Give me the pacemaker," Chandra said. "And I will let you both live."

"Carl, throw this stinking Gurung off the mountain."

Glass, a sizable and very strong man, rushed Chandra. The Gurkha, however, was far better trained and much faster.

"Ayo Gurkhali!" Chandra shouted as he drew the *khukri* from the sheath at his side.

With one swift movement Chandra swung the *khukri* evenly and neatly. All it took was one stroke. Carl Glass's head separated from his shoulders, spun around in the air, and sailed off the edge of the cliff. The body stood there a moment, trembling, blood gushing from the gruesome wound at the top.

This so unnerved Marquis that he turned to flee. Chandra knocked Glass's body over the cliff and ran in pursuit.

A slick rock face stood in Marquis's path, but that didn't stop him. Using an ice ax in one hand, he began to ascend, finding footholds and handholds where he could. There was no time to use hardware — this was climbing using brute strength and skill.

Chandra stood at the bottom of the wall and looked up at the figure who was already thirty feet ahead of him. He didn't know if he could do it. His left hand was useless. How could he climb with only one good hand? Should he let the traitor go?

The mantra reemerged in the Gurkha's

head: It is better to die than be a coward.

With determination Chandra swung his ice ax at the rock, lodged it in tightly, and pulled himself up. His boots found edges in the rock to hold his weight as he hugged the wall. He pulled out the ax, almost losing his balance in doing so, but swung it back into the rock just as quickly. It was slow going, but he managed to ascend a few feet with every try. Marquis, on the other hand, was rapidly approaching the top of the ridge.

Chandra had climbed twenty feet when the air in the respirator noticeably changed. The oxygen canister was empty! He winced, spat the respirator out of his mouth, took a lungful of cold, biting air, and kept going.

He looked up at his prey and saw that Marquis was sitting on the ridge, watching him. The man had something shiny and metallic in his hand. Marquis let it go, and the tool fell straight for Chandra. It was a carabiner, and it struck the Gurkha on the shoulder. The surprise almost caused Chandra to let go of the ice ax.

He had to get down. He couldn't climb farther or he would surely die.

Marquis extracted an ice screw from his pack, held it in the air, and dropped it.

The object struck Chandra on the head. He clung to the handle of the ax, hugging the wall, praying that his feet wouldn't slip. He was breathing in gasps, and never knew that pain could be so severe.

A few seconds later, another ice screw struck him on the forehead, successfully disorienting him enough for him to lose his balance.

One foot slipped. He struggled to hold on to the ax handle, but it was wet and slippery now. He reached with his dead left hand, but this proved to be the fatal handicap. The other boot lost its footing as his hand slipped away from the ax. He fell backward into thin air and bounced off the edge of the cliff.

Instead of screaming, the Gurkha was aware of the words running through his head as he plummeted to the vast lower depths.

It is better to die than be a coward ... it is better to die than ...

Roland Marquis cursed the fact that Carl Glass had been carrying half of the diamonds. He didn't know how much he had in his own pack, but it wouldn't be enough to buy his way out of England and into a foreign country where he could hide behind a false identity and live out the rest of his life in splendor. That had been the plan, such as it was.

If only the Union hadn't interfered. Nevertheless, this was still *his* show, and he wasn't going to let anyone wreck it — not them, not the Russians, not the damned Gurkha, and certainly not James Bond.

He could still find a buyer for Skin 17. Perhaps, he thought, perhaps he could sell it to the Union! They wanted it badly enough. Their incompetent minion, Schrenk, had been unsuccessful in getting it. Perhaps they would pay *him* a handsome fee. After all, they had employed him before to help steal it in the first place. It was only a matter of finding the right person to talk to. He hadn't known who Steven Harding's contact was. When Harding had approached him several months before with the Union's pitifully low offer, he could see that the doctor was a greedy bastard and could be turned. He had talked Harding into going along with the Union's orders, but instead of delivering the specification to them, Harding and he would "lose" it, sell it to the Russian Mafia, and make even more money together. Harding had been afraid of the Union, but Marquis was able to ease his fears. They had worked together. They had stolen the formula and were successful in diverting it from the Union. Now he had it and could name his price.

Would the Union seek revenge on him? Would they refuse to deal with him? He thought not. They wanted it too badly. They were probably the most likely buyers. The Chinese would offer too little. He didn't know who was behind the Belgian team, but he didn't care. They were probably being funded by a European consortium of some kind.

The trick would be contacting the Union before *they* found *him*. He wasn't sure how he would do it, but he had plenty of connections. He would go back to Camp Five, keep the pacemaker under wraps, and try to avoid Bond at all costs, if he was still alive.

He looked up at the sky. Dark clouds were beginning to form again. The storm was probably three or four hours away. He had to make it back to camp before then. It wasn't very far. The trouble was, he was exhausted and had a splitting headache. Marquis checked his oxygen canister and saw that it was nearly empty. That must be the cause of the headache, he thought. He found his last canister and attached the respirator to it. The new air felt good. That was another reason to risk going back to Camp Five. He needed more oxygen. He took another five minutes to eat two granola bars and drink some water from his canteen, then he set off toward the camp. Now if he could only avoid running into 007.

James Bond and Hope Kendall had spent the morning looking around the camp for any signs of the missing people. The storm had completely covered any tracks, so they thought it best to stay put and see if anyone came back. They had decided that they would perform crevasse burials for the dead, stay put through the coming storm by sharing the bivouac sack again, and begin their descent the following day. Bond hated to give up, but there was nothing else to do. Attempting to search the upper reaches of Kangchenjunga for people who might be lost or buried was foolhardy. To hell with Skin 17, he thought. If it had been created once, it could be created again. Britain had plenty of intelligent physicists. If Marquis had indeed stolen the specification and had found a way down the mountain, then so be it. If it fell into the wrong hands, it was beyond Bond's control at this point.

He was past caring.

Hope pulled Barlow's and Léaud's bodies out of their tent so that they could be buried. Bond went into Paul Baack's tent, looked at the bright yellow and green parka covering the body, and sighed. It was too bad. He had liked the Dutchman. Before pulling him out, though, Bond decided to get a message to London on Baack's satellite phone.

Reception was surprisingly good. He got Tanner, who put him through to M herself. She agreed with Bond's plan to descend the following day if the missing climbers failed to show up. As for Roland Marquis, an all-points warrant was issued for his arrest. If he dared to show his face at any western airport, he would be nabbed.

"Don't worry, Double-O Seven," M said. "I've explained to the Minister what has happened. He was furious, but he'll get over it. You did your best."

"I'm afraid I didn't, ma'am," Bond said. "I feel as if I let you down. I'm also very concerned about Sergeant Gurung. If he died up here, I would —"

"If he died up there," she interrupted, "he died for Britain. That was his job. He knew the risks. Now put it behind you.

That's an order, Double-O Seven."

"Yes, ma'am. Uhm, any news on Miss Marksbury?"

"Nothing. Not a trace of her. Now, finish your own job and get home safely."

He rang off and sat there a moment. Had he tried hard enough? Had he pushed himself to the limit? Had he gone the distance? And what about Helena? Had there been a clue of her betrayal — some sign that he may have missed? Bond suddenly experienced a crushing feeling of guilt and anger. What could he have done better?

He stood and prepared to drag Baack's body out of the tent but then decided to let it go. He would do it later. At that moment he felt like taking a good look at the Himalayan range and cursing the gods.

He emerged from the tent and called for Hope. There was no answer.

He walked back to his own tent, calling her name.

"Over here!" she yelled. She was busy digging out the snow from the front of the plane fuselage. Bond joined her, took another shovel, and began to help.

"We should have buried the plane passengers in the first place instead of trying to haul them down the mountain," he said. "How many are still in the plane?"

"I don't know, five or six," she said. They would have to make do with giving the victims crevasse burials, which meant that they would simply haul the bodies to the nearest crevasse and throw them in. This avoided having to dig in the ice and snow, which was a major expenditure of energy.

They worked hard for several minutes, then stopped to take a break. They sat on rocks, breathed oxygen, and drank from their water bottles.

"I'm hungry," she said. "How about I boil up some freeze-dried?"

"Why, I haven't had a dish like that in such a long time. By all means!"

She laughed and started to get up, but he surprised her by standing quickly, shoving her out of the way, drawing the P99 from his outer holster, and firing into the distance. She screamed.

"Stop right there!" Bond shouted, holding the gun level. Hope turned to look and was shocked by what she saw.

Roland Marquis was fifty feet away, his hands raised.

TWENTY-FOUR

A Better Way to Die

Marquis stood his ground, not moving. Bond walked toward him, the Walther still in hand. Hope stood spellbound, watching the two of them.

"Put the gun away, Bond," Marquis said. "I'm not the bad guy."

"How do I know that's true?" Bond asked.

"I saved your miserable life, you fool. It was Carl Glass and Otto Schrenk. They were working together. They tried to kill you and take the pacemaker."

"What happened to the pacemaker? Where have you been?"

"I saw Schrenk and Glass enter your tent. It was a good thing I was watching with a CWS. I didn't like the look of it, so I went over to the tent but stood outside. I heard a gunshot and rushed in. They had already hit you on the head, and Glass had just shot Schrenk. I don't know why Glass turned on Schrenk. I suppose he got greedy. Anyway, I surprised him, and Glass panicked. He knocked me down running out of the tent. I chased him over the north ridge."

The story was plausible but something wasn't right. "Go on."

"Not much else to tell except that Glass fell. I never did catch up with him. He was near a precipice and lost his footing. He saw that I was behind him and he got careless. The weather was bloody horrific. I was mad to go after him, but I thought you would appreciate it if *someone* did."

"So the pacemaker . . . ?"

"It went down with Glass. It's gone forever. Can I put down my hands now?"

"I'd feel better if you empty your pockets and throw down any weapons you might be carrying," Bond said.

"I assure you that I've lost my Browning. I tried to shoot Glass, but I dropped the bloody thing. Couldn't find it."

Bond approached him and patted the pockets on his parka. He looked through the goggles into Marquis's eyes, attempting to judge whether or not something there would betray him. All Bond saw, though, was the familiar hatred eminating from his old school rival.

"All right, Roland, but don't try any

sudden moves. I've got an itchy trigger finger."

Marquis lowered his hands. He looked around and said, "Where's everyone else?"

"They're dead," Hope said, walking up to them with an ice ax in hand. "Everyone is accounted for now that you're back and you've confirmed why Glass is missing. Except for Chandra."

Bond said, "We don't know where he is. Do you?"

Marquis shook his head. "No. I haven't seen him since we brought up Lee Ming's body. Everyone else is dead? The Sherpas, too?"

"Yes," Hope said. "They were all murdered in their tents. We think Schrenk did it."

"So you're burying people? That's what you're doing now?"

"Yeah," Hope said. "We were going to stay here tonight, sit through the storm, and go home tomorrow."

"Well, then," Marquis said. "I'll help you. I'd like to go home, too. I daresay we'd be safer traveling together, don't you think?"

"You're no longer our leader, though," Bond said. "I take no more orders from you, Roland."

"Fine, Bond. If it makes you feel victorious or something, then you be the leader."

Bond didn't comment. He lowered the gun and said, "We had better hurry and finish the job with these corpses. The storm is coming." He put away the Walther but was still wary. There was something about Marquis's story he didn't like.

They walked back to the hole that Hope had begun to dig. She asked, "Have you had food? Do you need something before we get to work?"

"That would be very nice," Marquis said. "Some hot tea would be quite welcome indeed, Hope."

Bond stopped her and said, "Wait. Roland, did you happen to run into the Russians?"

Marquis replied, "As a matter of fact, yes. Just saw their campsite, is all. It was over on the other side of the ridge. We steered clear of it."

Bond's eyes narrowed. "*We?*"

Marquis flinched. He knew he had said the wrong thing. Without a moment's hesitation he lashed out at Hope, grabbed her ice ax, and swung it at Bond. The point buried itself in Bond's right shoulder. He cried out in pain as Hope screamed. Marquis pulled the ax out, turned, and ran the way he had come. Bond fell to his knees and clutched his arm. Blood was pouring out of the wound. Hope squatted beside him and tried to examine the injury.

Bond watched Marquis running, or, rather, trudging through the snow toward the rock face. The bastard had done it. He had betrayed his country and the security of the western world. Bond couldn't let him get away with it. Not Roland Marquis. Not the only son of a bitch at Eton who believed he beat Bond at wrestling. All this time Marquis had been in denial that in reality, Bond had gotten the better of him back then. Everyone watching had known that Bond had been the victor. The bloody instructor gave the match to Marquis and the bastard never let Bond forget it.

"Stay here," Bond said to Hope. He struggled to his feet.

"You can't go after him, you're hurt!" she cried.

"Stay *here!*" Bond said firmly, then set off after Marquis.

Neither man was wearing a backpack. Bond had his weapon and an ice ax, but no oxygen canisters. Chasing Marquis at this altitude was complete madness, but he was determined to catch the bastard. Bond hoped that Marquis was telling the truth when he said he hadn't eaten. Perhaps he would be more fatigued than Bond and that would slow him down.

Even so, Bond was under extreme physical stress. He was already breathing so rapidly that he was afraid he might hyperventilate. The wound in his arm didn't help.

Marquis scaled the wall like a lizard. It was uncanny the way the man could climb. Bond conceded to himself that his rival was indeed the superior mountaineer, but it was time to push himself further than his body could go.

Bond found handholds in the rock wall and attempted to follow along Marquis's route. He felt as if he were moving in slow motion again. He was gasping for air, and every move he made was torture.

Thirty minutes later Marquis was over the wall. Bond was not far behind, but he was ascending at a snail's pace. When he got to the top, he collapsed onto his back as his lungs screamed for oxygen. He felt dizzy and disoriented. If he stood up, he would surely fall.

If only he had brought an oxygen canister! He had been about to put one on his back when Marquis had hit him with the ax. He should have heeded Hope's admonitions to stay put. This was madness indeed!

The sky was darkening above him. He felt cold, wet drops on his face, reminding him to cover his skin with the muffler. The wind was picking up again and the snow began to fall in earnest.

His lungs were on fire. Could he make it back down the wall without falling?

Wait! How could he have forgotten? He reached into the side pocket of his parka, praying that Major Boothroyd's little tube was there. Bond grabbed it and brought it to his mouth.

The emergency air breather was a godsend. The oxygen was cold and dry, but it sent bursts of energy into Bond's veins. He took several deep breaths, willing the clouds of confusion from his mind. He would have to conserve the air, though, and use it only when necessary. After a few minutes he put it away, got to his feet, and continued the chase.

They were climbing a snow gully of mixed rock and ice that cut through a rock wall to reach the West Ridge, which was a hundred meters from the summit. Marquis was climbing without oxygen at all, something that many professional mountaineers dared to do. Bond had never attempted an

8,000-meter peak without oxygen, but he had known men who had. They were usually like Marquis, cocky and egotistical, believing that they were invincible against the might of the mountain. Perhaps this time, Bond thought, the gods would not look favorably on Marquis. Perhaps his arrogance would be his downfall.

As he climbed higher, Bond lost sight of Marquis. He stopped and looked around frantically, wondering what had happened to the man. Had the falling snow somehow obscured his escape?

Suddenly Marquis leaped from a ledge, jumping on Bond and knocking him to the rock. He raised the ice ax and attempted to smash it into Bond's head. Bond grabbed Marquis's arm and held it tightly, forcing it back in a life-or-death arm wrestle. Marquis, too, was wheezing loudly, fighting for air. Bond shoved with all his might, rolling the man off him. Without giving him time to counter, Bond jumped on his opponent and hit him twice in the face. The thin air inhibited the blows' effectiveness, for the degree of force behind the punches was nowhere near what Bond perceived it to be.

Marquis slammed the side of the ice ax against Bond's head, stunning him. Bond fell over and was momentarily helpless. His vision blurred and he began to gasp for breath again. He expected the point of the ice ax to come crashing down into his chest, but it never did.

He forced himself to shake away the stars and stand up. His vision returned, but his head was pounding. Marquis had run. He was climbing farther up the mountain — toward the summit. Bond took a few more breaths from the emergency breather, then continued the ascent.

The snow fell faster as the wind blew harder.

Marquis, doing his best to move in rhythm, felt like hell. He was totally exhausted from the climbing he had already done that day. He was hungry and thirsty, and his headache had increased by the minute. It was so excruciating that he wanted to scream. He was certain that he had developed High Altitude Cerebral Edema. The symptoms were quite evident. If he didn't descend soon, he might have a stroke.

He *had* to get over the top, he thought. His only hope was to go up and over the summit and descend Kangchenjunga into Sikkim. He could easily lose himself there if he could get away from Bond. That's what he would do, then!

Roland Marquis might have recognized the symptoms of HACE, but he didn't realize how delusional he was. He had completely forgotten that he was without supplies, a tent, a sleeping bag, or any other necessities for spending a night on the mountain, much less surviving a monsoon and attempting to descend to the bottom. He didn't think about the fact that it would take three or four days, or more, to get to the Sikkim-side Base Camp. He was convinced that he was going to reach the top of Kangch and escape.

He made it to the West Ridge. All he had to do now was scramble a hundred meters to the summit, then he would be across the border and over. Marquis thought he was running, but in reality he was taking two steps every ten seconds. To him, everything around him was a blur. He had to concentrate on the goal . . . the top of the third highest mountain in the world.

Why did it seem like he was on a treadmill? It felt as if he were not moving any nearer to the summit. He had to push harder. Run, dammit! he told himself.

I *will* conquer this mountain! he screamed in his head.

"To *hell* with you, Kangchenjunga!" he

yelled, but he was so breathless that it came out as a whisper.

The Nepalese believe that the gods see and hear everything, and what happened next might have been attributed to this faith. Through the heavy snow Marquis thought he could see the markers, prayer flags, and spikes that other climbers had left on the summit. It was within reach! He crawled forward on hands and knees, and then suddenly went blind. It was an unexpected, horrible sensation. This was followed by a searing pain moving through his skull. He thought his head was going to explode.

Marquis screamed and fell to his knees.

Hope had warned them about retinal hemorrhage. It had struck him hard in both eyes. Simultaneously, he experienced severe symptoms of HACE. He writhed on the ground and beat his head, trying to knock the pain away. It was no use.

He continued to crawl foward, feeling his way to the summit.

Breathe . . . breathe . . . !

His lungs couldn't take it. His heart was pounding in his chest.

Just a little farther . . .

He reached out his hand and felt a flagpole. He had made it — 8,598 meters!

Marquis collapsed and lay still, trying to breathe the thin, precious air.

He could rest here, he told himself. He deserved a reward for making it to the summit. He could afford the rest he needed. Whoever was following him would surely never make it. It was *he* who was king of the world now. He was Roland Marquis! He was . . . invincible!

Then James Bond caught up with him. He, too, fell beside Marquis in exhaustion, fighting for air. He removed the emergency breather from his pocket and inhaled. The Himalayan range spread out before him in all directions. It was as if he were in an airplane but without the plane.

"Who's there?" Marquis gasped.

"It's your old friend from Eton," Bond managed to say between breaths. He put away the breather.

Marquis was confused. Who?

"Oh . . . right," he said. "Bond. I almost forgot who I was running from," he whispered. "We're at the top, aren't we?"

"Yes."

"How . . . how are you?"

"I'm alive," Bond coughed. "You . . . you don't look so good, Roland."

"No," he agreed. "I probably don't. I can't see a damned thing. Bad . . . bad luck. You have any air?"

"Yes."

"You wouldn't want to give me some, would you?" Marquis pleaded, but with dignity. "For old time's sake?"

"Where's the pacemaker?" Bond asked coldly.

Marquis coughed and choked. The spasm lasted for nearly a minute. Finally, the officer caught his breath and said, "See what happens when I try to laugh?"

"It's an honest offer, Roland," Bond said. "Oxygen for the pacemaker."

"You bastard."

There was silence. The storm was getting worse. The wind was screaming, and Bond could feel the subzero temperatures penetrating his parka. They had to get out of there.

"Come on, Roland, I haven't got all day."

Roland reached into a pocket. Bond caught his hand. "It's all right, Bond," Marquis said. "There's no gun there."

Marquis brought out the gold object and held it in his palm. Bond took it, verified that it was indeed Lee's pacemaker, and put it in a pouch. He then removed the emergency breather and placed the mouthpiece to Marquis's lips. Marquis choked on the air but was soon breathing steadily.

"How much was the Union paying you?" Bond asked.

Marquis tried to laugh but coughed again. He said, "I'm not Union, Bond. I never was. It was Steven Harding, not me." He began to tell the story slowly, between breaths. "The Union got to him and paid him something to steal Skin 17. . . . He came to me and offered me an insulting fifteen thousand pounds to help him. . . . I, of course, would remain a silent partner because of my high profile in the RAF, but I was the ideal person to bring in on the job because of my proximity to the Skin 17 project. . . . Even though the money was ridiculous, I thought about the scheme's potential. I talked him into double-crossing the Union and helping *me* sell it to the Russian Mafia. . . . You see, I've done business with them before. . . . I convinced Harding that he would make a lot more money. . . . Besides, better the Russian Mafia get it than the Chinese, which is whom the Union wanted to sell it to. . . . We were just eliminating the middlemen and their commission!"

"Then the business with the pacemaker, and Lee Ming . . . ?"

"That was the Union's plan all along. . . . When you interfered in Belgium, the Union changed the scheme. . . . They decided to reroute Lee's journey to China through Nepal and Tibet. . . . Since I had connections in Nepal, I came up with the plot to hire hijackers, kidnap Lee from his hotel, and whisk him away to an airfield in Sikkim. . . . There he would have been picked up by my people and hidden. . . . Harding made most of the arrangements. . . . After selling the formula, Harding and I were going to split the money, but he was careless. . . . I knew the Union would eliminate him and then the fortune would be all mine. . . . Unfortunately, the damned tourist plane crashed on this . . . fucking mountain . . . it was carrying a goddamned MP and an American senator. . . . I knew that the Skin 17 microdot was somewhere on Lee Ming's body, but exactly where was one piece of information that was withheld from me. You knew where it was. . . . I needed you to find it for me. And now . . . here we are."

He returned the emergency breather to Bond.

"You had better get going," Marquis said. "That storm is getting worse."

"You're coming with me," Bond said.

Marquis shook his head. "I don't want to be court-martialed. I couldn't face it. I don't want to die in prison. No, this is a much better way to die. Leave me here. Let me die at the top of the world."

"What happened to Chandra?" Bond asked.

"He did his best to stop me. He fell. He didn't die a coward, that's certain. Unlike me. I'm sorry, Bond."

Bond became aware of another person climbing toward them. At first he thought it might be a supernatural being — a yeti or a ghost. But it was only Hope Kendall. She was carrying a backpack and had oxygen. She dropped the respirator from her mouth and yelled, "Christ, what the hell are you two *doing* here? We have to get *down!*"

"Hope . . ." Marquis said. "Congratulations . . ."

"What?"

"Congratulations," he gasped. "You can count on one hand the number of women who have summited Kangchenjunga."

That news surprised her. She involuntarily laughed, then dropped to her knees beside Bond.

"Well, I'll be damned," she said. "I was in, boots and all, and didn't even think about that. I just wanted to catch up with you two."

"Both of you," Marquis said. "Go. Leave me. I'm staying here."

Bond pulled on Hope's arm. "Come on."

"What?"

"We're leaving him."

"We can't leave him!" She struggled against Bond. "Let's give him oxygen. We can get him down the —"

But Marquis gasped, choked a moment, and went limp. Hope examined him, reached for his wrist, and felt for a pulse. She put her head to his chest.

Bond gently tugged on her arm again. "The storm is getting bad," he said.

She finally raised herself, nodded, and got to her feet. She helped Bond stand, but his legs were very weak. She reached into her pack and brought out an extra oxygen canister. "Here, put this on," she said.

The new air helped tremendously, and they began the torturous descent back to Camp Five. Bond paused to look at the figure of Roland Marquis, lying amid the prayer flags and country markers. He might have been a great man, Bond thought, but his pride got him in trouble.

The gods disapproved of it. He had not shown the mountain the proper respect. As he had betrayed his country, he had betrayed his pact with the deities who controlled the elements in this cold hell, high above the living earth.

"Come on," Hope urged.

She helped him as he stumbled along, trying to keep his balance on the West Ridge. He hadn't realized how wrecked he was until he started moving. The wind was intense and was getting worse by the minute. If they stopped at all, they would perish.

The storm hit full force when they were a hundred and fifty meters from camp. Hope could see the Great Scree Terrace below them. All they had to do was climb down the rock wall.

Bond took one look and knew that he couldn't do it. Like Marquis, he was ready to give up and die.

"Get up, damn you!" Hope cried. "You're not wimping out on me now! You're coming down with *me*."

Bond attempted to wave her away.

"Breathe, dammit! Breathe the oxygen!" she yelled.

Bond took some breaths, but he could barely find the strength to inhale.

"Fine, I'll have to do it the hard way," she said.

Working as quickly as she could, Hope removed anchors, rope, a harness, and a pulley from her bag. She got the harness around Bond, who was barely conscious. She drove the anchors into the rock with her ice ax, fixed the pulley and threaded the rope through it. She then attached the rope to the harness and pushed Bond over the wall.

She slowly lowered him, belaying his body as he bounced like a marionette against the side of the rock. When he reached the bottom, he crumpled as if he had no skeleton.

Hope then began her descent, holding on to the bits of rock and ice, praying that the wind wouldn't blow her off. It was more difficult than she had thought it would be, but she kept going without looking down.

After what seemed like an eternity, her boots touched the plateau. She fell against a snowdrift and rested for a minute, then pulled Bond to his knees.

"Get up, you bastard," she yelled at him. "We're almost there!"

Bond mumbled something. He was completely out of it. He could barely stand and lean in to her. She helped him along, acting as a crutch.

"Right foot . . . left foot . . ." she called, telling his brain what to do, for it had ceased to function. Nevertheless, he understood her commands, moved his feet forward, and marched with her.

"That's right," she said. "You're doing great! Right foot . . . left foot . . . !"

They continued in this manner until they reached the tents. She opened the flap, pushed Bond inside, then crawled in after him.

This time, the Q Branch bivouac sack saved their lives.

TWENTY-FIVE

Human Machines

"Are you awake?" she asked him.

They were both inside the bivouac sack. Bond moved slowly and groaned. He had slept the sleep of the dead.

Sunlight oozed through the top of the tent. Hope didn't know how long they had been asleep, but it was obviously the next day. She put on her boots and opened the tent to inspect the damage. The entrance was completely blocked by snow and ice. She took a snow shovel and began to dig her way out.

Bond heard the scraping and sat up. "What year is it?" he asked. His voice was hoarse.

"It's the year they'll put on our tombstones if we don't dig ourselves out of here and get moving, what do you say?" She continued to scrape. "How do you feel?"

"Terrible. How did I get here? The last thing I remember was leaving the summit." He then noticed a large bandage wrapped around the wound that Marquis had made with the ice ax.

"Your fairy godmother took care of you," she said. She stopped and put down the shovel. "I suppose I should boil some water before exhausting myself."

The few hours of sleep had worked miracles. Bond recovered quickly. His shoulder was extremely sore, but he could manage. He pulled his down jacket over him and together they cleared the entrance to the tent. While Hope continued to drag bodies out of the fuselage, Bond dug his way into Paul Baack's tent to use the satellite phone. He wanted to make another call to London before they made the descent to Camp Four. He also wanted to alert Ang Tshering at the Base Camp that they were on the way.

As soon as he entered, Bond felt a burst of adrenaline.

The satellite phone was not sitting on Baack's portable table. Someone had been in the tent before the storm had hit.

The body was still there, covered by the brightly colored parka. If he remembered the tent's contents correctly, there was a pack missing, but the rest of the Dutchman's belongings seemed to be intact.

On an impulse Bond stooped over Baack's pack, which had been stored in the corner of the tent with other things. He dug in the clothing and found pieces of a rifle: a stock, barrel, telescopic sight — and 7.62mm cartridges. It was a gas-operated sniper rifle much like a Belgian FN FAL.

A chill slithered down Bond's back. It couldn't be! This was the weapon used to shoot at Bond and Chandra during the trek. The gun that killed young David Black. The sniper had been Paul Baack!

He turned to the body on the tent floor. Bond took hold of the parka and yanked it off the corpse.

It wasn't Baack at all. It was a Sherpa, one of the new men who had come up from the Base Camp to help haul. His throat had been cut, like all the others.

Bond leaped to his feet and ran outside.

"Hope?" he called. She wasn't out by the plane. Bond tromped as fast as he could through the deep snow. He could now clearly see another set of footprints other than Hope's around the fuselage.

Paul Baack was standing in the open hatch, holding a Hechler and Koch VP70 to Hope's head.

"Hello, James," he said. "Raise your hands. Now. Where I can see them."

Bond did so. Carefully, his gun still trained on Hope, Baack ordered, "Dr. Kendall, please take Mr. Bond's pistol out of that little pouch on the side of his parka. Pick it up with your thumb and index finger, please."

She did as she was told and held it gingerly.

"Throw it over there," Baack commanded. Bond watched as his Walther sailed several feet away, landed with a plop, and sank into a soft snowdrift. Baack pulled her next to him again and repositioned his gun to her head.

"I heard you were still at Camp Five," Baack continued, "so I thought I'd pay you a visit. It's a pity that Otto didn't kill you and our good doctor like he was supposed to."

"Let her go, Baack."

"No, James, I have to finish the job that Otto botched up. He was working for me, you see. I hired him. In the eyes of my superiors, if he fails, then I fail. I have to make sure they don't see me as a failure. It could damage my reputation. That damned Roland Marquis. I didn't count on *him* being a free agent in this mess. He screwed up my plan."

"So that's it," Bond said. "I didn't count

on *two* Union operatives infiltrating the team. Schrenk was the muscleman and you were the brains, right?"

"If you say so," Baack said. "I'll take that as a compliment."

Bond's eyes narrowed. "And you had constant contact with London. You knew my every move. You hired the hit man in Kathmandu and had me followed."

"He was a disgraceful amateur. I apologize for that," Baack said.

"You knew where we were going to be and when. Where were you hiding all this time?"

"I went down to Camp Four to wait for Otto, but he never showed. As you say, I overheard your conversation with London that you were still alive. That's the problem with mobile phones. They're very easy to eavesdrop on. I waited for you and Hope to descend, but you insisted on staying here through those dreadful storms. So I came up here to surprise you this morning."

Bond was furious. "Did you recruit my personal assistant? Do you know what's happened to her?"

Baack laughed. "Miss Marksbury? I had a part in recruiting her, yes. As for her whereabouts, do you think I'll tell you?

Forget it. If she's not dead already, she will be soon. Now give me the pacemaker."

"It's gone," Bond lied. "Roland had it. It went down the mountain with him."

Baack studied Bond's face. Finally he said, "That's very disappointing. And too bad for you. Now let's march to the edge of the plateau over there. You two are going on a thrill ride that beats anything they have at Disneyland."

"Why don't you just shoot us?" Bond asked. "Or cut our throats? Isn't that the Union's preferred method of disposal?"

"Oh, this will be much more fun," Baack said with a smile. "I want to hear that wonderful scream that fades out when someone falls, like you hear in the movies. You know, *Aaaaaaaiiiiiiiiieeeeeee!*" He laughed at his sound effect, then wiped away the smile. "Now, move."

Bond turned and walked through the deep snow toward the edge. Baack shoved Hope out of the plane but kept hold of her. "Follow him," he said.

When they got to the cliff, Baack said, "It's high time to kill, James. You first."

"You're making a big mistake, Paul," Bond said. "How are you going to get down the mountain by yourself?"

"I'm an experienced mountaineer. I'll be

fine. You'll get there before me, though. You're going headfirst."

Bond turned to face him. Baack was still holding the gun to Hope's head.

"You're going to have to push me," he said.

"Either you jump off the edge, or you get to see me blow a hole in her head. Which is it?"

Bond looked at Hope and peered through the goggles. He could see a flicker of understanding in her eyes. Bond blinked twice.

Hope raised her right boot and kicked Baack hard in the shin. The sharp points of the crampon dug through his clothing and into his skin.

Baack screamed. Hope pushed the gun away and dropped to her knees. At the same time, Bond lunged for the big man. They fell together and rolled. The VP70 arced through the air and made a deep hole in the snow.

Bond hit Baack hard in the face, cracking the goggles. Baack roared like a bear, grabbed Bond's hood, and pulled it off. The cold air felt like needles on Bond's skin and head. Baack's large hand fixed on Bond's face, his fingers digging into the skin and pushing him back.

There was genuine strength behind Baack's size. Bond fell backward, giving his opponent time to regain his balance and stand. He kicked Bond hard in the chest, the crampons ripping the fabric like tiger claws. The boot came down again, but Bond grabbed Baack's ankle and twisted it sharply. Baack yelled again and lost his balance. He toppled over, dangerously close to the edge of the cliff.

Bond wasted no time counterattacking. He leaped on top of the big man and attempted to roll him over. Baack lodged his shoulder against a rock to brace himself, but it was very slippery from ice. As he started to slip over it, he took hold of Bond's parka and said, "You're coming with me!"

Hope jumped into action and held Bond's legs. "I've got you!"

Bond kept pushing and hitting the man, forcing him closer to the dropoff. Finally, Baack's waist went over, pulling his legs with it. Now he was hanging on to Bond's shoulders for dear life. His weight was dragging them both over the cliff. Hope dug her crampons into the ground, trying her best to keep Bond from sliding forward.

Bond was face-to-face with Baack. Now

there was terror in the man's eyes, but he wasn't about to plead for mercy.

"Going down, James?" he said through clenched teeth. "First floor. . . lingerie?"

Bond dug his fingers into Baack's hands, trying to wrench them away from his parka.

"Christ!" Hope said, gasping for air. "I can't . . . hold . . . much . . . longer!"

Bond felt his torso slipping forward. Except for his head, shoulders, and arms, Baack's entire body was now over the edge.

"The Union . . . will . . . crush . . . you," he spat out between gasps.

A blast of cold wind reminded Bond that his hood was off, and that sensation prompted Bond's next action. He slammed his forehead into Baack's, inflicting the hardest possible head-butt he could give. Baack's eyes rolled up into his head as his hands loosened their grip. Bond broke free, sending the man off the cliff and into space.

"Aaaaaiiiiiieeeee . . . !"

Bond inched back onto the ledge and held Hope in his arms as the scream faded into thin air.

"Just like in the movies . . ." he said.

It took them three days to get to the

Base Camp, where Ang Tshering met them with open arms. Since he had heard nothing by mobile phone, he was convinced they were dead. He had resolved to wait a few more days before leading the surviving team members back to Taplejung.

That night they built shrines to the men who had died on the mountain. Bond spent two hours scratching Chandra's name on a stone, then drove a piton in above it and attached a white prayer scarf through the eye. When Hope made a stone for Roland Marquis, he made no objections.

They began the long trek back to civilization the next morning. Bond had regained much of his strength after descending the mountain, and the rest at Base Camp worked wonders. Bond and Hope were inseparable, ignoring the disapproving looks of the Sherpas. The Nepalese, shaking their heads, would never understand the decadent ways of the west.

The couple made the seven-day journey a memorable one, if not by day, then certainly by night. They made love for hours every evening after dinner, knowing full well that they might never see each other again after they left Nepal.

One night, as they lay naked in the sleeping bag at the Gunsa campsite, Bond lit his first cigarette in weeks, coughed loudly, then said, "You realize that we've been to the brink of disaster and lived to tell the tale."

"What has it taught you?" she asked. "Other than that you really should give up smoking."

"No way," he said, taking another drag. "Actually, I've been thinking about our earlier conversation concerning limitations. Despite what my government thinks, I'm just a man. You don't realize how mortal you really are until you're fighting for your life at eight thousand meters."

"In my opinion," she said, "you're the finest specimen of a man I've ever seen. Speaking as a medical doctor, of course."

He smiled. "Hope, you saved my life up there. More than once. I'll be forever grateful."

"Don't mention it. I've learned a lot as well."

"Such as?"

She sighed. "I don't think I have something to prove anymore. Hey, I summited the third tallest mountain in the world, right? I now know that the capabilities of the human machine are far greater than I could ever have imagined. I need not concern myself with limitations anymore, because there are no such things."

"Doesn't one's mind have a lot to do with it as well?" he asked. "Without the will, the body doesn't have much of a chance."

"Quite right," she said. She reached between his legs and held him. "Speaking of will, *will* you please make love to me again?"

She didn't have to ask him twice.

They said good-bye at the Kathmandu airport. She was flying to Bangkok, then on to Auckland. He was traveling in the opposite direction, to London by way of Delhi.

As her flight was called over the intercom, she said, "Take care of yourself, James. Keep in touch."

"I'm not very good at that," Bond admitted. "But we can try."

Hope placed a hand over his face and let her fingers run smoothly over the faint scar on his cheek. She gazed into his clear blue eyes, then pushed the comma of black hair off his forehead. She leaned up and kissed the cruel mouth she had come to know so well. Without another word she turned away, picked up her bag, and walked toward the gate.

Bond watched her as a wave of melancholy washed over him. It was a familiar friend, a bittersweet companion for his wretchedly solitary life.

Hope handed her ticket to the flight attendant, then went through the door to board her plane.

She never looked back.

TWENTY-SIX

The Cold Stone Heart

M looked hard at Bill Tanner and said, "I don't care how little time you've had. I want your new proposal for security procedures on my desk in the morning!"

"Yes, ma'am," Tanner said. He stood, glanced at Bond, and left the office. M turned to Bond, took a breath to redirect her thoughts, then said, "Needless to say, the Minister is very happy with your work on this case. Skin 17 was returned to the DERA and they have some new people working on it. I must admit I had my doubts about this one, Double-O Seven, but you pulled through. Well done."

Bond sat stiffly across from his chief with a frown on his face. He wasn't used to such praise. It disturbed him. There also seemed to be an edge to her voice that wasn't quite right.

"I'm supposed to extend an invitation to you," she continued. "The Minister asked that you come to a dinner tonight. Black tie. Ministry of Defence dining room. Seven-thirty. You're to receive a commendation, Double-O Seven."

Bond didn't think he had heard right. "Ma'am?"

"A medal. You're going to get a medal." She looked at him, waiting for some kind of response.

"Ma'am, I've never accepted commendations in the past, not even a knighthood. Your predecessor knew that. I thought you did, too."

"The Minister thought you might reconsider this time," she said.

"I'm sorry, ma'am, but please give the Minister my thanks and my apologies. I have an engagement."

M knew he was lying. She was silent for a moment, then said, "It's just as well. I must admit I didn't approve of you receiving it, either."

Bond now knew what was coming.

"Double-O Seven," she said. "I have to turn down your request for two months' leave. I want you around London in case the Union retaliate. Although you did a fine job in Nepal, I'm extremely unhappy with what has occurred with Miss Marksbury."

"I understand, ma'am."

"No, you don't," she said. She leaned closer to him and narrowed her cold blue eyes. "Your relationship with that girl nearly cost you your life. It caused a massive security breach in our organization. Didn't you ever learn that you cannot be romantically involved with colleagues at SIS? *Especially* your bloody personal assistant! What the hell was the matter with you?"

"I'm sorry, ma'am."

"Yes, well, of course you are. Now she's probably lying at the bottom of the Thames and the Union have a good idea of how we work. This better not happen again, Double-O Seven, do you follow me?"

"Yes, ma'am."

"That's all. Take a week, then we'll talk about how we can go after this Union."

"Yes, ma'am. Thank you," he said, then got up and left the room.

Barbara Mawdsley sighed and shook her head. She should have taken disciplinary action and had his head on a platter.

But that was something she could never do to her best agent.

Bond sat in the sitting room of his flat off the King's Road, a double bourbon in hand and a cigarette hanging from his mouth. He had sent May away so that he could be alone with his demons. Sometimes they were the only things that could comfort him.

The white phone rang. He was tempted to let it go, but he inexplicably detected an urgency in the pips that forced him to pick up the receiver.

"Yes?"

"James! Thank God, you're there!"

It was Helena Marksbury.

Bond sat up abruptly, completely alert. "Christ, Helena, where are you?"

"I'm . . . I'm in a hotel in Brighton. I came here a few days ago. I've been hiding. I assume you know —"

"Yes, Helena. I know."

"Oh, God, James . . . James . . ." She started to cry.

"Helena," he said, attempting to control his rising anger that he knew would be inappropriate. "Tell me what happened. From the beginning."

She sobbed uncontrollably. "Oh, James, I'm so sorry, I'm so sorry. . . ."

He waited a few moments for her to get it out of her system. He was unable to detect that any of it might be pretense; her sorrow was genuine.

"It's best if you tell me everything, Helena," he said.

She gained control of herself and slowly began the story. "They got in touch with me the night we had that fight, after your golf game at Stoke Poges."

"The Union?"

"Yes."

"Go on."

"They must have been watching my flat. They waited until you left, then two men came to the door. At first I wouldn't let them in, but they convinced me they were from SIS. But they really weren't."

"Who were they? What did they look like?"

"One was English. The other was Dutch or Belgian, I think. They told me that they were from the Union. They showed me . . . oh, God, James . . . they showed me photographs . . ."

"Of?"

"My sister. In America. Her two children. Photographs of her dropping them off at school. The men threatened their lives if I didn't cooperate with them."

"What did they say?"

"Only that my nephew and niece would meet with a horrible accident, and that my sister would suffer terrible torture."

"What did they want from you?"

He knew that she was trembling. Her voice shook as she answered him. "They said they wanted to know everything you were going to do with regard to Skin 17. I had to report to them where you would be and when. I had to tell them what the Ministry of Defence were planning at all times. I had to answer any questions they asked."

"For how long?"

"As long as they deemed necessary, they said. Oh, James . . . I didn't want to do it. It was extortion, you see that, don't you?"

"Of course I do," he said. "But I'm not sure how the Ministry of Defence will see it. You could be in a lot of trouble, Helena. How would you contact them?"

"I wouldn't. They contacted me."

"At the office?"

"They had my private number, somehow. They would call and demand to know everything. I tried to put a trace on the calls, but it was never any good. They had some kind of block on the line. They warned me not to alert anyone about them or my sister and her children would die."

"And you believed them?"

"Of course I believed them! I had no choice but to believe them!"

"They could have been bluffing."

"I thought about that, but there were the photos. They seemed to know exactly what my sister was doing at any given time. Oh, James, I've been a nervous wreck. I've been horrible to you. You could have been . . . killed! It would have been my fault!" She broke down again.

Now he knew that her treatment of him those days before he left on assignment had nothing to do with their relationship. He had selfishly thought that she was upset about *him*, when, in fact, she was in torment over what she was being forced to do.

He might have taken her in his arms, but his heart was quickly cooling toward her. Betrayal was something that never sat well with him.

"I'm in danger," she said quietly.

"I should think so."

"A blue van is parked outside on the street. It's been there for two days. A man has been watching the hotel. They know I'm in here."

"Is he there now?"

There was a pause as she peered out the window. "The van is, but it doesn't look like anyone is inside now."

"Listen to me, Helena," he said. "Tell me where you are. I'm coming to fetch you. You have to turn yourself in. It's the only way out of this mess. It's the only way to protect you."

"I don't want to go to prison," she choked.

"Better that than lose your life. We'll make sure that the FBI in the States is contacted so that they can get your sister and her family to a safe place."

"Oh, James, will you help me? Please?"

"I'll do what I can, Helena. I must warn you, though, that there will be a question of treason. Only the courts can answer that one, I'm afraid."

He heard her crying again. The poor girl was in agony.

"Helena, you have to surrender. It's the only way. I'll take you straight to head-quarters."

After a few seconds of silence she said, "All right." She gave him the address.

"Don't do anything stupid," he said. "I'll be there as soon as I can."

He hung up the phone and rushed out of the flat. He drove the Aston Martin reck-lessly across the river and down to the popular seaside resort, where there are lit-erally hundreds of small hotels. He quickly found the street she had mentioned in the less fashionable part of Brighton some five minutes' walk from the seafront.

He parked in front of the building and looked around. The blue van was nowhere in sight. He got out and went inside the building. Ignoring the elderly woman at the reception desk, Bond rushed through the small lobby as a feeling of dread poured over him.

He took the stairs two at a time to the second floor, drew the Walther, and peered carefully around the landing. The hallway was clear. He quietly moved to the correct room and listened at the door. A radio inside was broadcasting the second movement of Beethoven's Seventh Symphony. Bond raised his hand to knock but realized it was slightly ajar. He slowly pushed it open, his gun ready.

Helena Marksbury was lying in the middle of the floor in a pool of blood.

Bond entered and shut the door behind him. He quickly checked the bedroom to make sure he was alone with the corpse, then kneeled down beside her.

The Union had gotten to her first. Her throat was completely severed.

He took a moment to collect his thoughts, then picked up the phone and dialed the emergency number at headquarters. After ordering a cleanup crew, he sat down in a chair and stared at the body of the beautiful girl he had once made passionate love to.

The music filled the room as the orchestra on the radio reached an emotionally charged climax.

He was sorry for her, but he no longer felt any affection for the girl who had been a wonderful part of his life for some time. Just as he had always shut his heart to other women who had betrayed him in the past, Bond forced Helena out of his life then and there.

As he took out a cigarette and lit it, Bond wondered what was colder — the cruel realm of espionage that had victimized and ultimately destroyed Helena Marksbury, the icy summit of Kangchenjunga, or his own hardened heart.

About the Author

Raymond Benson is the author of *The James Bond Bedside Companion*, which was nominated for an Edgar Allan Poe Award for Best Biographical/Critical Work and is considered by 007 fans to be the definitive work on the world of James Bond. He is the author also of the James Bond adventures *Zero Minus Ten* and *The Facts of Death* and the James Bond movie novelization *Tomorrow Never Dies*, based on the screenplay by Bruce Feirstein. Mr. Benson is a director of the Ian Fleming Foundation and served as vice-president of the American James Bond 007 Fan Club for several years. He is married, has one son, and lives in the Chicago area.